**Mr. Alson Claus**
3552 S. Bay Dr.
Sedro Woolley, WA 98284

# DUST

# Martha Grimes

# DUST

A Richard Jury Mystery

DOUBLEDAY LARGE PRINT HOME LIBRARY EDITION

Viking

VIKING
Published by the Penguin Group
Penguin Group (USA) Inc., 375 Hudson Street,
New York, New York 10014, U.S.A.
Penguin Group (Canada), 90 Eglinton Avenue East,
Suite 700,
Toronto, Ontario, Canada M4P 2Y3
(a division of Pearson Penguin Canada Inc.)
Penguin Books Ltd, 80 Strand, London WC2R 0RL,
England
Penguin Ireland, 25 St. Stephen's Green, Dublin 2, Ireland
(a division of Penguin Books Ltd)
Penguin Books Australia Ltd, 250 Camberwell Road,
Camberwell,
Victoria 3124, Australia
(a division of Pearson Australia Group Pty Ltd)
Penguin Books India Pvt Ltd, 11 Community Centre,
Panchsheel Park,
New Delhi—110 017, India
Penguin Group (NZ), Cnr Airborne and Rosedale Roads,
Albany,
Auckland 1310, New Zealand
(a division of Pearson New Zealand Ltd)
Penguin Books (South Africa) (Pty) Ltd, 24 Sturdee
Avenue,
Rosebank, Johannesburg 2196, South Africa

Penguin Books Ltd, Registered Offices:
80 Strand, London WC2R 0RL, England

First published in 2007 by Viking Penguin,
a member of Penguin Group (USA) Inc.

ISBN 978-0-7394-7774-8

Printed in the United States of America

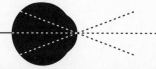

This Large Print Book carries the
Seal of Approval of N.A.V.H.

*Dust in the air suspended
Marks the place where a
story ended.
Dust inbreathed was a
house—
The wall, the wainscot and
the mouse.*

T. S. Eliot, *Four Quartets*

*This is just love. It's nothing like the storm.*

Clive James, "After the Storm"

# THE FIGURE IN THE CARPET

# ONE

Benny Keegan whistled his way down the hall of the Zetter's fifth floor, his small dog Sparky obediently at his heels. Benny hoisted the tray on one hand, as he'd watched Gilbert do. The French press slid a few inches and the cups rattled a bit, so he lowered it and held it with both hands. He needed practice.

Not that the hotel would ever hire him as a waiter; they'd said a sixteen-year-old would need a lot of "seasoning" to acquire that job. The ones who had interviewed him laughed at the word "seasoning"—*food, get it?* Benny got it and in his head went one better. He was only thirteen: *I lied, get it?*

Thirteen, but what he lacked in height and experience he made up for in depth—in his glance, his sober expression, his seeming seriousness, and his experience of the world.

And they'd gone on: "As you'll be in the kitchen, mostly on the washing up, and the late shift too . . ."

Now here he was, with his unhired dog, pinch-hitting for old Gilbert Snow, bringing coffee on a tray.

He knocked at the door. No reply. Knocked again. What was the drill? Old Gilbert hadn't gone into the finer points, given the guest had ordered coffee separately from his dinner; given that, this guest should be here. He knocked again. He had Gilbert's key card. ("Keep that safe now, young Benny. No one needs to know; I'll only be gone for a bit. Got to get meself topped up." His laugh was phlegmy as he pulled on his coat.)

But the door had given in to the last knock, had opened a quarter inch, and now Benny pushed it delicately, again announced himself. "Room service." No one answered. He hoped he hadn't got the wrong room. He and Sparky were all the way into the dimly lit space and looking around. Right or wrong, it was posh—really modern, or modish. Not three-hundred-quid-a-night posh, but he wouldn't mind stopping here for a night—sheets on the bed white as glare ice, towels you could pitch a tent with, wood polished to gleaming. Very nice.

A long ledge against the left wall that could be used as a desk or a table held the dinner service that Gilbert had delivered an hour or so ago. Heavy cutlery, good china. Remains of a hamburger, chipped potatoes, little pots of mustard and ketchup and pickle, their contents slathered around on chips and a half-eaten burger. Where was this person? Maybe gone down to the entrance to speak to the desk clerk or something. Not to the restaurant, hardly, if he'd gotten room service. The sliding door was open to the balcony—patios the hotel called them— and Sparky had gone out there to nose about. All the rooftop studios had them, and this one was really big. He might be out there, enjoying the April night.

Sparky started up barking, so Benny, still with his tray, stepped out onto the patio. There were a couple of metal chairs out here, and a table. Plants, big ones in big pots. That was when he saw him with Sparky sitting beside. The man was lying face-up or face skewed in an uncomfortable position near the table.

Benny held fast to the tray, the French press shivering, the little cups clicking. The tray felt glued to his hands. He took some deep breaths, trying to start his thinking going again. He kept on clutching the tray and staring down at what he could see of the man's face. Young, kind of. Probably a nob; that was a really good jacket he was wearing. But it wasn't so good now, not with that wide blood stain across it.

He finally managed to set down the tray. He pushed the dog aside and bent down to get a better look, only, to see more he'd have to turn the body over and police didn't like that, he knew. He had to call the hotel manager or someone, but not yet. After all the agro he'd gotten down in the kitchen, he wanted to be in charge for once, just a few minutes to be in charge of the situation.

He looked at the man, thought him young. He was certain he was dead; he'd seen dead and it looked altogether different than a coma or passed-out. (He'd seen plenty of passed-outs under Waterloo Bridge.) Dead was a look of departure, of left, of the last good-bye, of gone. Still, he should check the signs—vital signs they called it. Like an artery in the neck? That was the best place. He knelt down and put his fingers on the spot where the neck met the shoulder. Nothing, no little throb or anything.

He heard his own heart hammering away.

The man was dead, no question. Benny stood and looked carefully around the patio for a sign of something, not sure what. But that's what detectives did. They looked.

Your eyes might alight on something amiss or out of place like that. Hands on his hips, Benny slowly rotated his head, looking carefully around. But the balcony was swept absolutely clean.

Benny whistled for Sparky to follow and went back into the room. He noticed again that the nob's supper was half eaten. Did that mean the shooter had interrupted him in the eating of it? Or had he not been all that hungry? Burger, potatoes with a couple lines of ketchup over them, house salad. So what this bloke had told Gilbert when he'd brought the dinner was he wanted coffee later for two.

Two. Well there you have it, plain as the nose on your face: man hears a knock, goes to the door, says hi, and his mate comes in. Maybe the dead bloke sits down to finish his meal and—Benny raised his hands, left gripping right and fired his imaginary pistol. *Pow!*

Sparky had his nose tucked in a corner by the telly. Benny bet he could pick up stuff your police K-9s left behind in the dust. He was smart.

Taking care, using the white napkin from the tray as a glove, he went through the man's pockets—knowing he wasn't sup-posed to touch anything, but bloody hell, he wanted to find some identification. There was a wallet in the hip pocket, which he drew out and opened carefully. There he was.

Benny took out his own tiny address book. It had once belonged to a big soft doll in the Moonraker bookshop, where he worked afternoons. The doll was called Traveling Girl and was all tricked out in coat and hat, and with a suitcase and this address book. When the owner said she might as well give the doll to Oxfam, as obviously nobody wanted it, Benny had asked for the address book. He didn't want the doll. Well, actually, he wouldn't've minded having it, but how would he look, a big lad such as he, carting a doll with a suitcase around?

He had listed two numbers in the address book. (He knew them by heart, but he still liked referring to his address book.) One was the Moonraker. He found the other one and went to the phone and dialed.

Richard Jury was sitting mostly dressed in his Islington flat in a very contented mood, listening to the shower in his bathroom spilling down over arguably the most beautiful shoulders in the Greater London area.

At the same time he hoped that the feet clattering down the stairs from the third-floor flat were not aimed at his door.

Do not stop here, Carole-anne. Do not knock. Do not come in and ask, "If you're on the sofa, who's in the shower?" Unlike the majority of prayers sent up, this one was answered. The noisy clodhoppers continued on to the front door, which opened and closed. . . .

(Thank you, God . . .)

. . . then thought better of it and started back.

(. . . for nothing. Yes, thanks for setting me up and then *pow!* Right in the kisser.)

*Tap tap tap,* heels on the floor.

*Rap rap rap,* hand on door.

Jury cupped his hands around his mouth: "I'm taking a shower! Come back later!"

Silence, then the feet moving off. Jury settled back into his former state of dazed contentment and picked up his tea.

Front door again. Different steps. Softer, slipperlike: *flap flap flap.* They stopped at his door.

This would be the tenant in the basement flat who rarely came to his door. Mrs. Wasserman. There was a gentle rapping of old knuckles.

This time Jury got up hurriedly and made tracks back to his kitchen to give his voice more distance to travel. "I'm in the bathroom!" In the bathroom, the water drummed down.

Muffled words came from the hallway. He crept back to the sofa and heard the slipper tread move away, the building's front door open and close.

He sighed heavily and picked up his mug of tea.

A scrabbling sound on the stairs alerted him. The scrabble stopped at his door. Then silence. Then a brief thumping.

My God! Had he no private life? Was he the poster boy for Interruptions, Inc.? Was he the standard-bearer for "You-Have-No-Secrets-from-Us, Ltd.?" Was his personal hell going to be a hallway down which an eternity of footsteps come and go belonging to people he could not see?

Oh, the bloody hell with it! He got up and flung open his door. "Come in, come in, never mind your coming is unbelievably poorly timed! That's my girl in the shower, smartening herself up. When she comes out you can ask her lots of questions about who she is and what she's doing here in my shower. Our love life's an open book. Come in. Come in. Can I get you something? Beans on toast? A quart of gin?" Jury stood aside and swept his arm from door sill to living room in a welcoming way.

The dog walked in.

The dog plopped itself down and yawned.

"What? Bored already? Oh, I'm sorry we didn't bring a doggy bag from the restaurant with that leftover caviar. Would you like me to rustle up a crème brûlée? Cadbury bar? Bone?"

Jury reached under a foot rest and pulled out a heavily chewed rawhide number and slid it over to the dog.

"Who're you talking to?"

Jury hadn't realized the shower had stopped until he heard her voice.

"Stone. The dog from upstairs."

Phyllis's wet head popped out of the door. He could see the top line of a towel wrapped around her chest. She ducked back in. "I'll be out in a minute."

"Take your time. We've got all of Islington coming through." But he said it to himself, for the bathroom door had closed.

So he talked to Stone for a while. Nothing earthshaking, just pleasantries, as they both settled comfortably back.

The phone rang. Of course! It was only half past ten; what was keeping people?

It was Benny Keegan on the other end.

Jury was astonished. "Benny! How are

you? Where are you? What's going on?" It was understood Benny could call him anytime, day or night. The boy never had before this.

"I'm at the Zetter; it's this posh place in Clerk'nwell. Clerk'nwell Road it's on. See, I got me this job here where I help in the kitchen some nights." Benny lowered his voice. "Tonight they're low on staff, on room service, and they asked me to take up a tray to this guest."

Jury smiled. The last time he had checked, Benny Keegan was thirteen. The hotel must have rescinded the child labor laws. But this was hardly the time to bring up age. "Go on."

"I take this what you call a French press— too many nobs in this place for my tastes— on me tray up to the fif' floor. I knock and the door kind of opens. Still I knock and keep knocking but nobody comes. So I goes in and nobody's in the room and I goes out to the balcony. See, rooms on this floor all have them. Then I see him. He's dead, in't he?" That last part was more or less squeaked out.

Jury sat forward suddenly. "Benny, are you okay?"

"Me? I'm okay, Mr. Jury. But I can't say the same for this fella in Room 523. That's where I am right now."

"You haven't called anyone?"

Benny sighed. "Yeah, I have. You, Mr. Jury. You tol' me if there was ever any trouble—"

"You're absolutely right. I'm glad you did. Now—"

Benny lowered his voice as if the dead were all ears. "Now, here's the thing. I told 'em, the guy that hired me, I was sixteen. Small for my age, see. But I guess the hotel din't much care as long as I was just hauling trash. But me findin' dead people, well, it'd probably tell against me, you know, bein' under the legal age."

"Give me the address, Benny."

"It's in EC 1. 86–88 Clerk'nwell Road."

Jury wrote it down, tore off the sheet of paper, said, "Look. Right now, you'll have to notify the hotel. Why don't you tell the cook, whoever sent you up there, what you found. Let him be the one to tell management and let them be the ones to call in police. It'd probably be Islington police there. It would leave you right out of it. Temporarily." Very temporarily. "So do that, will you?"

"Sure. If you say so. Bloke's name's Maples. Says here on his license."

"What?"

"The dead guy. His name's Billy Maples."

Jury stuck the pen back in his pocket. "Benny, you shouldn't touch anything."

An exasperated sigh came from the other end of the phone. "A' course, I know that. I got at the wallet with a napkin for a glove. I could lift it outta this punter's pocket."

"Get the management up there, Benny."

"But me, I'm first on the scene, Mr. Jury. They'll be askin' me all kindsa questions."

"Not to worry. I'll be there inside of twenty minutes."

"What about a doctor, then?"

"I'm bringing one. Stay put." He hung up.

Jury rapped on the bathroom door. "Phyllis?" He smiled. Even the air in the bathroom would be mistily covering her shoulders.

The door opened an inch and then another. She was still wrapped in the big towel.

"Dr. Nancy. We're needed."

Phyllis Nancy said, "Is this going to be another episode of *The Avengers*? Do I wear my Emma Peel wet suit? Or the backless black?"

The "backless black" was the silk confection she had worn that very night when they'd gone to dinner in the West End. The dress completely covered her front, but left her naked in back from her neck to her waist.

Jury had commented on the physics of the dress.

"It isn't," Phyllis had said, while peeling the dress downward, "exactly the uniform of a Scotland Yard pathologist."

The black dress slid to the floor.

Now, as she opened the door wider, he hitched his fingers in the towel where it was folded over to tie. This too he watched fall.

"Get dressed. Billy Maples needs us."

"Who's Billy Maples?"

Jury started to slide his arms around her, thought of Benny alone with a corpse, and resisted. "Our next case."

# Two

The Zetter, advertising itself as a "restaurant with rooms," stood in the Clerkenwell Road. It had the spare, angular lines of an old warehouse, the spareness become sleekness and the angularity become minimalist. These things could be accounted for when simply renamed.

Jury wondered if the Zetter bespoke a trend. Probably, given the upswing of high-end restaurants in London over the last years. Unthinkable, twenty years ago, that London would have a kitchen, or a hotel, naming its restaurant as its primary attraction.

They couldn't park in Clerkenwell Road,

which even at this hour saw heavy traffic, so Jury pulled into a slot at St. James's Green.

Phyllis had no coat, but claimed her black cashmere shawl could protect her from intemperate weather: hurricanes, cyclones, tidal waves. For a while now, rain had been falling hard and steadily, so they crossed the road at a run, and came upon an alley-like walkway called Jerusalem Passage. They took the cover gratefully.

Coming from the other end was a figure in dark clothes, perhaps running from the rain, but continuing to run through the passage, head down, bumping into Phyllis.

"Hey!" said Jury.

Over his shoulder, the man threw back an apology. Jury would have stopped him then and there, had it not been for the dark clothes, the white collar that advertised his vocation. Running from an angry God? wondered Jury. Phyllis laughed and they went on.

As they stood at the hotel's front desk, Jury saw that the death had had precious little effect on the restaurant, which, even at nearly eleven o'clock, appeared to be doing brisk business.

He produced his ID for the good-looking

desk clerk, who, in a true, new voguish-hotel-with-murder calm, plucked up a house phone, spoke quietly, and then said, "You're to go right up. It's on the fifth floor, 523." She smiled and nodded at Jury and gave Phyllis, in her brief black dress, a questioning look before Phyllis produced her own ID.

They walked into a room where the forensic team was already in the process of capturing whatever evidence it could. A youngish woman, a maid, perhaps, was being questioned by whoever was in charge. Her English was poor and she was having a hard time of it. Jury thought the detective's back looked familiar. Then he turned.

"Ron Chilten!" said Jury.

Ron smiled his sphinxlike smile, hinting at a richness of disclosure that Jury knew was never coming, largely because there wasn't anything to disclose. It was Chilten's forte. "Richard, for God's sake." He simulated deep puzzlement. "I stand here and search my brain and can't remember sending up an SOS."

"Stop. You know you need me. What are you doing out of Fulham?"

"You make it sound like Dartmoor. Maybe it was." Ron was too easygoing for full-blown rancor. Anyway, he had no need for rancor. It was all about the turf, the patch. Islington police would get on quite well without the rest of the Met horning in. "I ask again, what brought you here?"

"Your star witness." Jury nodded toward Benny Keegan, who was talking to an older man, both of them anxiously watching and waiting. "I know Benny well, and I don't think he's on intimate terms with Islington police."

They had stepped from the room out onto a patio, a huge wooden deck bigger than the room itself. At one end were a table, two chairs, and a body. And Dr. Nancy.

"Who's this?" He looked down at Phyllis.

Phyllis was already kneeling beside the body, giving it a quick examination. She looked up. "Dr. Phyllis Nancy. Superintendent Jury asked me to come along."

"We've got a doctor," said DS Chilten, in a tone more uncertain than annoyed. The victim wouldn't be needing one. He was lying on his back, shot in the chest, blood pooled at his side.

Phyllis looked at him. "Of course. I just

happened to be there and came along. Busman's holiday." She snapped on latex gloves she'd borrowed from one of the technicians and turned back to the body. She had a manner that was so short on attitude it was all but impossible to view her as a threat. "I'd like to turn him over?"

With a slight frown, Chilten nodded.

She did this in a single neat movement. It wasn't weight, it was leverage. It occurred to Jury that most things were. It was a thought, anyway. "We'll be off in a minute; it's your case, Ron."

Chilten snapped his fingers at one of the crime scene operatives for a plastic bag, dropped something into it, and handed it to the technician. Then, in a considering sort of way, he folded first one, then another, stick of gum into his mouth and slowly chewed, as if that's what the nights were made for. "Not exactly."

Jury raised his eyebrows. "Not exactly what?"

"My case."

"It's Islington's."

"Yeah, I mean it's Lu's."

Since he didn't add to that pronouncement, Jury figured he was in for a night of

Chilten's little manufactured mysteries, smoke and mirrors mise-en-scènes. "Who the hell's Lou?"

Now Chilten raised his brows. "Aguilar? You don't know DI Aguilar?"

"Should I? Don't make me dig all the way to China for the information."

But Chilten was prepared to let Jury dig. He looked at the tray—the two trays—delivered that night by room service. Chilten turned to the waiters, Benny and the old man whose name was Gilbert Snow. "Now, is this tray of food what you brought up?" He was looking at Snow.

"That's it, except it's been half-et."

Chilten nodded. "You didn't take anything from it, did you, Young Benny?"

"What?" Benny looked aghast that he'd be asked such a question. "I'd know better'n to take somethin' from a crime scene, wouldn't I?"

"You didn't *know* it was a crime scene, Young Benny. Did you?" Chilten's tone was the condescending one grown-ups use with children, the "How-could-you-know-anything-that-mattered?" tone, you being only thirteen or ten, or six or eight. *No wonder kids clammed up,* thought Jury.

Benny said, "If it wasn't a crime scene, well, he was pretty dead, wasn't he?"

A crime scene technician stuck his head around the doorjamb of the bathroom. " 'Scuse me, sir, but there's a dog in the shower."

Chilten frowned. "The victim had a *dog*? Why in hell hasn't it barked or something? Why would he be—? Perhaps the villain wanted to get him out of the way."

"Looks that way."

Chilten took long strides toward the bathroom.

"Sparky?" asked Jury.

Benny cringed, nodded. "See, Sparky always waits for me in the alley. I was over an hour late because of this coffee delivery, and it was raining somethin' awful. So I thought, well, no harm in him comin' with me on this one delivery, so I got him into the lift and we come up here."

Phyllis Nancy said, "Is this the Sparky who saved Superintendent Jury's life?"

Benny's chest puffed out a little. "Thass right." He was happy to have Sparky's role remembered.

Chilten was back, the crime scene fellow following with the dog.

Sparky, a small white terrier, was quiet until he saw Jury, whereupon he started barking and wriggling.

Chilten asked, "Was this mutt here when you brought the coffee?"

Benny looked at Jury, saw by his expression he'd just as well tell the truth. "Actually, Sparky's my dog."

"Your dog. *Your* dog? Did he carry the tray, or what?"

The technician chortled. Chilten looked at him. He stopped. Chilten went on: "What's the story on this dog, Young Benny?"

Jury watched Benny cringe at being addressed in this manner. But he replied, "Like I said, I just had him along with me. We were to go home right after."

"I'm sure the management likes your dog running round a crime scene—"

"We din't know it was a crime scene, did we?"

Jury turned away. Benny was cutting a bit too close to DS Chilten's bone, wasn't he?

"Funny." Chilten looked down at Sparky. "All we need, isn't it? A dead body and a dog."

As far as Jury was concerned, there

couldn't be enough dogs in the world for him: Arnold. Stone. Sparky. Mungo.

Benny said, "When I saw this dead man, well, I put Sparky in the bathroom there as I was afraid he might knock up against some bit of evidence."

Skillfull, thought Jury. He put his hand on Benny's shoulder. They all seemed to have forgotten that finding a dead body might be traumatic for a kid.

Chilten looked over at the door to the room. A man had just been admitted. "Mr. Lewis?"

"That's right. I'm pinch-hitting for the manager, the manager not being here this evening. You wanted to know about the, ah, victim? His name is Maples, Billy Maples." Mr. Lewis looked grim. He could have done without this murder's happening on his watch. "All I can tell you is that he checked in this afternoon, about two o'clock. I did a quick computer search before I came up here. Well, I knew something bad had happened, didn't I?"

Chilten nodded. "Go on."

"Mr. Maples had listed his home address as Chelsea. Here. I wrote it and the phone number down for you." Lewis held out a small piece of paper taken from a Zetter message pad. There was one like it by the telephone. He looked from Chilten to Jury, uncertain as to which one was in charge.

Jury inclined his head toward Chilten.

Chilten took the note. "One thing, Mr. Lewis. These rooms on this floor—you call them studios, right? They're pricey, aren't they?"

Lewis shrugged. "Yes, I expect they are. Superior studio is what this one's called. Then there's the deluxe, which is a little more. But they have some of the best views over London. Well, as you can see." He swept his arm toward the patio. They stepped onto it and took in the Zetter's view.

A view with a corpse, thought Jury. But it was still quite wonderful, the spire of St. Paul's in one direction, the spire of the post office building in another. London at night and from this height was a knockout. He smiled at it, at London.

"I didn't take the booking, but I can find out exactly what transpired."

"If you would. I expect he could afford it, if that suit he's wearing is any indication." Chilten looked down at the body as if he'd call it back to life, just so he could ask about the suit. "I saw one like it in a window in upper Sloane Street. Get me any information you can, including telephone records. Outgoing, incoming calls. We haven't spotted a mobile yet, though it's hard to believe he hadn't one, a sport like this."

Jury smiled at the description. How long had it been since he'd heard "sport" used in that way.

Chilten nodded toward the assistant manager. "That's all for now. Thank you."

Mr. Lewis took his leave.

Phyllis rose, peeled off the gloves, shivered in the night air. "I'd say that's about right, something over an hour. Two hours would be stretching it. Well, but we know the time frame, right?

"The dinner comes up around nine o'clock according to this Gilbert—"

"Snow, sir. Nine o'clock, right."

"And the coffee comes up around ten o'clock."

Ron nodded and flicked through his notebook.

How many pages could he possibly have accumulated if he'd only been here fifteen minutes before Jury?

"Okay. The waiter, Snow, brings up dinner at nine. Young Benny brings up the coffee—" Notes consulted again. "At ten or ten-ten. He's not absolutely sure, but knows that's close enough—"

"Excuse me, sir."

Benny was standing at Jury's elbow, together with the old waiter.

"Gil here says you're missing somethin' significant." Benny brought that out as a dozen different syllables, probably to make sure Chilten and Jury understood the significance. "Tell 'em, Gil."

The waiter, Gilbert Snow, looked to be in his sixties. He had sad eyes and a slightly sallow complexion, and although by no means corpulent, seemed to have had his share of Zetter dinners.

"It's this, like: the young gentleman orders his dinner be brought up, which is what I did. He then said he wanted coffee, but to be brought up around ten. He wanted coffee for two people, for *two.* He was very particular about that."

Jury said, "He was expecting someone, then."

Benny nodded. So did Gil. "I mean, well, that's what you'd think, right?"

Jury wondered why Snow hadn't brought the coffee up himself, but didn't ask it. Save it for later. Unless Chilten asked. He didn't. Maybe he already had. Gilbert Snow seemed all too aware that except for the expected guest, he might have been the last person to see the victim alive, and who wants that on his platter?

"Let's say time of death was one and a half hours ago. That includes the time it took us to get here, of course."

"Phyllis?" Jury looked at her. "Give or take how much?"

"I can't say precisely. The time looks pretty fixed to me. You don't often have a witness at both ends of a death—" Her frown deepened. "I can be a little more exact when—I mean when whoever does the autopsy—when that's done. But I don't see what you're driving at."

"Remember your Sherlock Holmes, Jury," said Chilten.

"He's never far from my mind. What?"

"The simplest theory is preferable. Is usually right."

"That's not Holmes. That's Occam's razor."

Phyllis stepped on Jury's foot and gave

him a look. Then she said to them, "I'm leaving. I think I should give Benny a ride, don't you?"

"Take the car." Jury dug in his pocket for the keys.

She shook her head. "I'll get us a cab. I'll call down to the desk."

"I think Benny'd better wait for the guv'ner," said Ron.

Jury sighed. "Where in hell is this Detective Inspector Aguilar? He's taking his own sweet time—"

"Right behind you."

# THREE

Jury had been standing with his back to the door. Quickly he turned and saw that, obviously, Chilten's "Lou" wasn't male. Detective Inspector Aguilar was a woman.

There would be no argument about that. DI Aguilar had walked in and sucked all the oxygen out of the air. Tall, willowy, black hair, nearly black eyes, a faint golden glow to her skin. Aguilar: could be Latino, could be Spanish, South American, even Indian. The Lu could be Louise, Lucille, Louella, hell, she could be Lucretia Borgia, for all he cared. She looked like she'd just come off a Paris runway with that shape, those cheekbones, and that hauteur, rather than out of an Islington police station. He wondered if her appearance always had this effect on her team. They stood, as if breathless and waiting. Except for Ron Chilten, whom Jury had never known to get breathless about anything.

Rather than ask who he was, in a gesture of utter disdain, DI Aguilar raised her eyebrows.

He almost laughed. "Richard Jury."

This did not satisfy the eyebrows, which stayed up.

"Superintendent, New Scotland Yard CID."

Still not satisfied, but she did use words. "And how do you come to be at our crime scene, Superintendent?"

Chilten—who was enjoying the little contretemps enormously, as Jury had known he would—offered: "The kid, Benny Keegan, called him. Benny found the body."

She nodded. "Who've we got here?"

One of the crime scene technicians handed her a wallet. "His name's Billy Maples."

She looked through it, at the driver's license, the credit cards, whatever bits and bobs were stuffed in it, then took out the license and handed the wallet to Ron.

DI Aguilar then turned to Benny, who,

with Sparky, had been hovering by Phyllis. "You're Benny," she said.

"Yes, sir—uh—mu'm."

"And you?" She was addressing Sparky.

"His name's Sparky." Phyllis said this. "And I'm Doctor Phyllis Nancy. Pathologist."

*Get over it.* That's what Jury heard Phyllis saying.

"And has the dog given up anything useful?"

Benny's eyes narrowed. "On'y his dinner. We been here for a goodish hour, y'know." Then he repeated what he'd told Jury and Ron Chilten.

Lu Aguilar thanked him quite simply. "You can go, Benny, but I may want to talk to you later. And I'll expect you to keep mum about all this."

Jury could imagine how mum Benny would keep once he got back to his friends and cohorts beneath Waterloo Bridge. "Mum" would take a dive straight into the Thames.

But the boy nodded obediently.

Phyllis said, "Come on, Benny; I'll give you a ride home. You and Sparky." She turned to Aguilar. Although Phyllis's tone was frosty, her hair seemed to be on fire.

"You'll have your own pathologist. I've told DS Chilten my findings."

He'd seen her hair spark before. He'd never seen it go up in flames. Her smile could have followed. Phyllis did not wait to be excused. She said to Jury, "I'll see you tomorrow, I expect."

"I expect so." He felt quietly uncomfortable about his private life leaking into his public one. Then felt immediately remorseful for the thought. If there was anyone who respected privacy and knew the need to keep one's work separate, it was Phyllis.

They left with Sparky.

Ron filled DI Aguilar in on what had been discovered up to that point.

"So where was the dinner companion?"

"Coffee companion, more, who might have been the murderer."

He nodded toward Snow, who was sitting on a side chair. "That's the waiter, Gilbert Snow, the one that brought up the dinner. Then Benny Keegan brings up coffee at ten-ten." Chilten looked at his notes.

"Call him over," she said, nodding toward the waiter.

Ron did.

She could, reflected Jury, have walked over to Snow.

The old waiter repeated to DI Aguilar the same story he had told Jury. Then he asked her if he could leave.

"Been a long day, I'm not up to this kind of thing." He pounded his chest softly. "Dodgy heart, like."

She smiled at him, nodded. He left.

Ron was talking. "I guess what I'm wondering is, if Maples was murdered between dinner and coffee, where was the shooter when Benny came along? I mean, could he still have been here?"

"If they're all telling the truth," said DI Aguilar, before turning to exchange words with the two crime scene technicians who had yet to leave. "Anything?"

"Things, yes, but nothing to nail down, m'um. We're through here. I mean except for Connie. He's in the bathroom putting the drain back together."

Aguilar nodded and watched them go. They moved quietly, as if to keep from disturbing the air around her, as if it too might be needed for future examination. Then she turned back to Jury and Chilten.

Chilten frowned. "By they, you mean—?"

"The two room service waiters and the desk clerk," said Aguilar.

Chilten flipped through his notes and it seemed to take forever.

"Okay. Snow brings up the food at nine, he said." Ron stopped to indicate the remnants of the supper. "Hamburger, chips, whatever that salad is."

"House salad," said Aguilar. She'd picked up the room service menu, which she now opened and pointed to.

Jury smiled. Perhaps it was Aguilar's moment of domesticity that made him smile.

Chilten went on: "Say Gilbert Snow left about nine, Maples had about fifteen minutes of eating, maybe more, when whoever he was to meet gets here. Presumably our shooter. Then Benny shows up at ten and finds the body. Desk clerk puts Maples coming in around eight-thirty. There's confirmation between the two of them. I don't think they could be lying."

"The chef would have to be lying too," Jury said. "Or whoever prepared this food. It's only a burger but I still think it was carefully arranged, with all of those little china pots of condiments." Mustard, relish, and ketchup had been laid on with a heavy hand.

Aguilar smiled. Or smirked. "Why's that? It could have been anyone. Snow himself. It's only a burger and chips."

Jury shook his head.

Aguilar nodded. "Check with the kitchen, Ron. The restaurant here is supposed to be really hot, so the superintendent is probably right about the painstaking presentation. And bag this stuff."

"The meal? Why?" asked Ron.

"Why not? You never know." She turned to Jury.

"You're afraid that Benny might have walked in on the killer? That he might still have been here?"

"Possibly."

She said, "But the boy wouldn't have stood around, surely. When he saw the body he ran out."

"No. He called me. From here. Benny's not exactly the type of lad to run." Jury looked around the room. "The killer might have thought Benny had seen something, if he was still here, and that's a big if. Our shooter might have forgotten something— but this is useless speculation."

"That's it, m'um," said the technician who must've been Connie, coming out of the bathroom.

Chilten nodded. "If you don't need me, I'm off." He stuck a cigarette in his mouth, not lighting it. "You need a lift?"

"No, thanks, Ron," said Jury. "I think I'll walk for a while. Helps me think."

"I'll take him," said Aguilar, looking at neither of them and dismissing Jury's comment about walking. The ones remaining now were the two who were about to move the body into a body bag.

Ron Chilten gave Jury a brief salute and left the room, together with Connie. Conrad, probably.

What Aguilar was doing was having a long look at the food on the table. With a ballpoint pen she raised the uneaten half of the hamburger, let it drop. She looked at the potatoes, poked the salad. "I'll bet that mayonnaise is homemade."

The scene-of-crime fellows were still waiting for a signal to proceed, but she was still taken up with the food. "I'm surprised he got a burger and chips. I'm surprised he *could* get it, to tell the truth. Looking at what's on the menu." She shook her head. "Everything's half eaten."

"I noticed."

She nodded and gave him a long, considering look.

But he knew it was a thought, not him, she was considering. "Doesn't that strike you as strange?"

"No. He was interrupted."

"But—" She frowned, made a foray again with the pen. Then she shrugged, and they moved out onto the patio. She looked down at the body and the two technicians looked inquiringly at her. She nodded. They zipped up the bag, moved it to a stretcher, and bore it away.

"Billy," she said as if tasting the name for the first time. "That's how he signed the card downstairs. Not William or Bill." She was poking the ballpoint in a large ashtray that held coins, matches, and a room card. She slipped the pen through a matchbook cover and raised it. "Dust. It's that club over the road there." She tilted her head and made as if to look out over the dark balcony. "He'd been there, according to the desk clerk."

"Tonight?"

She nodded. "After a gallery show he went to and before he came back here for his late supper."

Ah. Here was another reason to hate her: that she'd been more efficient than he himself. The first reason was her beauty.

Lu Aguilar started to walk around the room, trailing her long fingers over the backs of the chairs, inspecting the old books the hotel provided, looking at paintings, less like a detective seeking evidence than a woman sizing up a property to see if it pleased her. Then she was back to stand beside him. "He met someone here, or was to, who might not necessarily have been his killer."

Jury shook his head. "I'd think that's exactly whom he met: someone he'd mistakenly thought to be his friend. He'd ordered coffee for two. What makes you think there was a third party?"

She didn't answer that; instead she raised the pen on which the matchbook swung like a little gate in a wind.

"Let's go."

"There?"

"Dust. Come on."

# Four

He knew better than to try to buy her a drink. Probably a stickler for procedure. If she'd been there with the authority to do it, she'd have tossed him out on his arse after that Hester Street business.

"Whiskey, rocks." She ordered this up from the Adonis of a barman. She turned to Jury, raised her eyebrows. "You?"

So much for the stickler. "The same. No ice. You like *ice* in it? I thought that was largely an American perversion."

"I do. Where have you been? Ice is in."

He put his fingers in a bowl of mixed nuts and palmed a few into his mouth. The barman slid two chunky glasses toward them. When Aguilar went for the bag slung across her chair, Jury put his hand on her arm and shook his head.

"Let me." He pulled out his wallet. The barman named a sum that would renovate the Tower and Jury slapped down a bill.

She raised her glass. "Just like a real date. Thanks."

Of course the tone was sardonic, but he still smiled.

She drew Billy Maples's driver's license from her coat pocket. "Have you seen him in here?"

The barman glanced at it, shook his head. "Don't think so."

"Have you been here all evening?"

He nodded. "Came on at six o'clock."

As far as Jury was concerned, the barman was the type who routinely lied to the police. Just second nature. "What's your name?"

"Matt."

It would be. Jury took the license and shoved it up to his face. "He comes here a lot. Suppose we look again."

Matt glanced from Jury to Aguilar and

back. "You the police?" When Jury nodded, Matt went on. "What's he done? What do you want him for."

"Nothing," said Aguilar. "He's dead."

Matt's quick eyes went back from Aguilar to Jury as if he knew what dead meant in this case. "He was murdered?"

"Why do you think that?"

Now he regained some of his former insouciance. "Come on, you're police. You wouldn't be doing this for some bloke who went into cardiac arrest."

"The Zetter, across the road, I'm sure you know it, says he had been in here earlier. So who else was working here? I mean besides you and the general rave-ups?" She inclined her head toward the group—guitars, drums, keyboard—making something that wasn't exactly music.

"You could try Ty Haigh. He's one of the guys at the bar out there, where you came in. He might know him." Matt looked down at the license, still lying on the bar.

Aguilar rolled off her bar stool.

Straight-faced, Jury asked, "You want to dance?"

That earned him a look he wouldn't soon

forget. He spread his hands. "You're the one who said it was a date."

"Yeah, that's Billy Maples," said Ty Haigh, whose muscular arms were on display in a sleeveless vest, "and he's a friend. I've known him for a year or so." He was working on a champagne bottle, loosening the wire from around the cork. "Why?" He smiled broadly, which made his face even handsomer.

Jury wondered if looks were one of the top criteria for working here.

Ty added, "He's not in trouble, is he?"

Aguilar pocketed the license and said, "No. He's out of trouble now."

"Meaning?" Ty had stopped smiling.

Jury hated that swift change in a look, always did, and cut it short. "I'm sorry. He's dead."

"Christ." Ty breathed this out.

"You knew him well?" asked Jury.

Ty nodded vaguely and then seemed to want to take it back, that or he really wasn't sure about how well he knew Billy Maples. He said, "I'm an artist. This job buys canvas and paint, not much else. The gallery, the one near Smithfield Market, it's called Melville Gallery. They had the showing today; they've shown my work. That's how I met him, Billy. He donates a lot of money to it; he's—he was—a very generous fellow. You could always count on Billy. God." He propped his elbows on the bar, leaned his head into his hands. "I can't believe it." Jury thought he might be going to cry, but he looked up at them, dry-eyed.

"He had money, then?" said Aguilar.

Ty nodded. "Family money, I gathered. He certainly seemed to. Didn't work or anything."

Aguilar had her notebook out and a pen uncapped. A fountain pen. Jury hadn't seen one in years.

She said, "Where do they live, his family?"

"In . . . Kent? No, East Sussex, I think. Somewhere in East Sussex, not far from the coast."

"What do you know about them, except that they're rich?"

"Next to nothing. He never talked about them, didn't much like them is what I thought. Except his grandfather, who he seemed really fond of. And I think there was a grandmother he liked. Not a couple, I mean one on his father's side, one on his mother's."

"Do they live in Sussex?"

"No. London. The grandfather lives in Chelsea, I think. So did Billy. Near Sloane Square. He didn't really talk much about himself. We talked about art, mostly." Ty laughed and then abruptly stopped, apparently thinking it the wrong time for laughter. "He didn't know all that much, though."

"He had a flat in Sloane Street is our information."

"Right." Ty looked off across the room, oddly silent in this part of the club. "The war."

"What?" said Jury.

"The Second World War. Billy was fascinated by that period. He was always going off to the War Museum, that place in Lambeth? It had something to do with his grandad—the war did, I mean. He was some kind of code expert?"

Jury stared at him. "Wait. The grandfather: he wouldn't be Sir Oswald Maples, would he?"

Ty thought. "I don't remember Billy ever saying. He just referred to him as grandad.

Said he had an important job during the war, breaking codes, or something."

"Who is this?" DI Aguilar asked Jury.

"Sir Oswald Maples played a significant part in codes and ciphers. He was at Bletchley."

Ty looked blank. "What's that?"

*Were we ever really this young?* wondered Jury.

Aguilar said, "They were code breakers, weren't they? Top secret stuff. Bletchley Park was where they gathered."

Jury nodded.

"And you know him? This Oswald Maples?"

Again, Jury nodded.

"Good," said Aguilar. To Ty she said, "We'll probably want to talk to you again. Give me a number."

He did, together with a Clerkenwell address. "The place is getting too rich for my blood," he added.

She capped her pen, stowed it and the notebook in her bag. Smiled. "Move to Wandsworth. That'll thin your blood out."

Ty laughed and again abruptly stopped.

Aguilar and Jury headed out the door.

"Car's over there," she said. "In St. John."

They walked along Clerkenwell Road.

Clerkenwell was becoming more trendy with each passing day, more upscale, more of a draw to the young professionals. It was just on the boundary of the City, where he had of late been spending a lot of his time. It was also one part of Islington, where he spent less time, though Islington was home.

"We'll need to see his flat tomorrow."

"Maples's? We? I was under the impression I was intruding."

"You are. But it turns out you know everyone. What choice do I have?"

Was she trying not to smile? Jury said, "God, but it's a bitch, isn't it, to have to ask Scotland Yard CID for help?"

"I didn't say I needed help; I said you know everyone. It saves time if you do the interviewing of the grandfather."

She had stopped by a gray Fiat, a car that Jury had always thought a joke. "You live in Islington, correct?"

He was mildly surprised. "Yes, but how did you know?"

"I know a lot about you. Have you forgotten? You were splashed all over the news not long ago. Get in."

They took St. John Street to Islington

High Street and Upper Street, made a few right turns and came to his street.

"Right here."

She pulled up, braked, and before Jury could say thanks or good night, she was out of the car.

He watched her walk around to the pavement, stand for a moment looking in at him. When he didn't get out, she threw out her arms in a fine gesture of impatience.

Jury got out of the car, puzzled. "What?"

"You've got the keys." She turned and walked up the front steps.

When he stopped being stunned, or pretending to himself he was, he followed and unlocked the front door.

"Which floor?"

"The next."

"Thank God. I'm too tired to climb more than one flight."

Jury smiled as they walked up that flight. He had the impression she'd have climbed to the top floor, if need be.

He unlocked his door, stood back, and held out an arm to usher her in. He told himself he still didn't know exactly what she was doing here or what she wanted.

Except to drop her coat on his old faded

sofa and say, "Thanks, yes, I will have that drink."

He stood there as if he were the visitor and she the tenant of his flat and looked at her for a long moment.

She didn't move her eyes from his face. Indeed, she seemed to be charting it as if it might reveal a destination. "You can get me a drink. And in the circumstances, you can call me Lu."

"God, thanks. But I don't have any ice, Lu."

"Hell. Now we'll have to make up something else to do." She took a step toward him, her dark eyes never leaving his face.

Why this pretense of surprise? He was not surprised; he'd just been shoving it aside. From the moment she'd walked into that first room, he'd known in some dimly lit part of his head that this was going to happen.

He pulled her to him and their lips dissolved into a kiss. It was long, infinite, the horizon gone. There should have been another word for kiss. Had he pulled her down to her knees, to the rug, or she him? Did he shove her down on the floor, or she him? They were rolling over, pushing at clothes, trying to unwrap each other, trapped in some cocoon, trying to pull apart to do it, but only tangling more.

Then he did pull her up and into the bedroom and down onto the bed.

They separated, finally. They lay there hardly breathing, as if the breath had been knocked out of them.

Eventually, he said, "How are we going to be able to work together?"

"We aren't. You're off the case."

"No, I'm not. You need me."

"Yes. But this way." She slid on top of him and it was like slipping into the sea.

Held together again they rolled across and off the bed, he hitting his head on the nightstand and not noticing, she twisting her foot in something, blanket or rug—not noticing—and then pulling themselves by some act of levitation up and onto the bed. It was turmoil, like grabbing at air and finding flesh.

"This," she said, "is too frightening. I thought we were finished."

"We'll never be finished." He reached for her, but she pulled away.

"I'm leaving. Right now. I'll find the door."

She gathered up her clothes, a delicate

trail of them, laid out almost by design—
bra, panties, skirt, sweater, coat—dressed
as she went and went out the door.

He heard it close.

He lay there, unable to move. Had he
been the one who'd had to leave, he didn't
know if he could. What was it? It wasn't
love, it was something else. He thought of
those hurricanes that battered the coast of
Florida every summer.

This wasn't the purple light of a summer
night in Spain. It was a hurricane.

# FIVE

Forensic had already been over it, but Jury wanted to see Billy Maples's flat for himself. There were other things besides forensic evidence that might go a step toward understanding Billy's life.

It was in a building with few flats and a caged lift; it was handsome and undoubtedly pricey. In this area, Chelsea, Knightsbridge, Belgravia, you'd be looking at half a million quid, he bet. It had not one but two en suite bedrooms, one with a small sitting room, the other with a connecting den or study.

"I'll take this side," said Ron. "You go there."

Jury smiled. Under the aegis of DI Aguilar, Ron was in charge here.

The study was generous in size, book-shelves across one wall and the overflow caught in neat stacks on the floor in front of the lower shelf.

The books weren't there to fill out the decor, either. Jury pulled out and examined several; they were much thumbed and marked. Billy Maples liked to read. It was the sort of room that anyone who liked to read longed for: deep cushioned chairs, including one of dark supple leather with a matching footrest. A floor lamp, a glass-topped side table.

From what Jury could tell, Billy favored the nineteenth century, a lot of it Ameri-can—Melville, Hawthorne, and a surprising number of novels by Henry James.

One shelf was taken up with books about the Second World War, reflecting his interest in Sir Oswald's life, ostensibly. Assuming Oswald Maples was his grandfather.

There were two paintings, both showing the tortured influence of someone like Francis Bacon. The dull, boxed-in form of a man one could hardly distinguish from the thick woods around him. For torture, Jury preferred Munch.

There was a desk, not large, with a leather swivel chair. He went round to the front and started pulling out drawers. He sat down and looked at a small silver-framed photograph of Billy and another man. They looked as if they'd been skiing or involved in some other winter sport. A lot of snow, a mountain.

Ron came in carrying some letters. "Fellow that Maples lived with." He waved the envelopes and sat down.

Jury waited. Ron did not expand upon his information. Jury said, "I'm with you so far. What about him?"

"Well"—Ron looked down at the letters— "I'd say he's German."

"And does he have a name? German or otherwise?" Blood from a stone.

"Kurt Brunner. At least that's the name on these." He looked down at the envelopes. "Berlin. Kurt Brunner. Maples's 'partner,' as they say?"

Jury turned the photo around so that Ron could see it. "Maybe, maybe not. This chap's a lot older than Billy Maples."

Ron shrugged. "When's that ever made a

difference? Father figure, maybe? That can get seriously sexual."

"Sometimes a father figure is only a father figure." Karl Brunner, though, didn't really look the type. He was older, but in very good shape and with a handsome face.

"Could be."

"What about the weapon, the gun?"

"We haven't found it. Probably a .38, possibly a Luger. German?" Ron squiggled his eyebrows up and down.

Jury leaned back in the swivel chair, turned it right and left, left and right, kept doing it as he thought. "Why did Billy Maples take a room at the Zetter, which is—how far from here?"

Ron scratched the back of his neck. It looked inflamed. "Could take you over a half hour in rush hour. This gallery is near Smithfield Market and that's not far from the Zetter. Half hour, maybe, no more."

"So why did he stay at the Zetter?"

"Because he had the three hundred quid to do it. He had money, all right, a trust fund. Maybe he stayed at the Zetter because he wanted to be near the club? Dust?"

"He was in it. Why would he have to be near it? He was meeting someone, and if

so, we could conjecture that it was someone he didn't want to meet in his own flat."

Ron shook his head. "I wouldn't draw that
conclusion. He wants to do all this: go to
gallery, to Dust, to meeting someone at the
hotel—so he picks a place right there. The
Zetter. The best solution," he said, showing
some teeth, "is the easier one."

Jury snorted. "Back at me, right? Maybe
it's as you say." Jury rose. "I've got to go,
Ron. I've got to tell his grandfather before
the *Telegraph* does. Let me know if you
come up with anything here."

# Six

Jury stood in front of the mews house off Cadogan Square with his finger on the bell, hoping he was wrong though fairly certain he wasn't. This was not owing to his powers of deduction but to a very simple notion: how many men named Maples who had "worked on codes" and done it at Bletchley Park could there be?

Just one.

This time Jury hoped for the house-keeper, anything to delay telling Oswald Maples this sad news. Right now, Jury sincerely wished Lu Aguilar *had* taken him off the case; if he and Aguilar had a grain of sense between them, he *would* be off the case, he wouldn't be within twenty miles of the Islington police. Emotional involvement with the detective in charge—is that what he was calling it this morning? How could anything so violently physical be talked away as "emotional involvement"?

Then he thought of Phyllis and his throat went dry.

"Superintendent!"

Smiling, Sir Oswald Maples had answered the door himself this time, walking with the help of a single cane. Most of the time he needed two. If that's what accounted for the smile, probably a good day.

It was about to turn bad.

"Is something wrong, Mr. Jury?"

*Yes,* Jury wanted to say, *I am fucking up my life and your grandson was murdered last night.* "Sir Oswald," he said as he tried to work some sense into the day. He knew he looked grim and the grimness was all for himself, he was ashamed to say. "I need to talk to you." A peculiar way of putting it.

"Of course. Come in, come in." With a little difficulty, Oswald Maples moved aside to allow Jury to pass into the tiny foyer. "It

can't be all that bad, Superintendent."
Oswald gave a short laugh.

Jury opened his mouth to make some
rejoinder and didn't. They went into the living room. Jury sat down and Oswald sat
across from him on a blue sofa. Beneath
their feet was a handsome Turkish carpet,
swimming with muted blues, reds, and
greens.

Jury said, "There was a young man murdered last night in Clerkenwell. I think—we
think—he may have been related to you,
may be your grandson." He let that rest for
a moment.

Maples had picked up his cane, holding it
in front of him, both hands on the knob at
the top. He sat forward and bent his head
over his hands. He was silent.

"His name was Billy Maples."

In the deep silence that sometimes
attends bad news, Sir Oswald waited, as if
another piece of news might cancel out
what he'd just heard. None was forthcoming. "Make us a drink, man." He leaned
heavily on his cane, his head bent, studying
the carpet.

Jury splashed some brandy into a balloon
glass and handed it to him. "I'm sorry; I'm

truly sorry." He felt hopelessly inadequate. He sat down opposite Oswald on a chair covered in the same blue as the sofa.

Maples said nothing for a few moments, just sat looking at the brandy in his glass and finally drank it in one go. Then he placed the glass on the antique side table carefully, as if it, and not he, needed the care. He cleared his throat. "All right, tell me."

Jury did. Every detail.

Oswald sat back. "I'll spare you a few questions, Superintendent. First, I can't think of anyone at all who could possibly want to do this to Billy, but then, I didn't know his friends—or his enemies, though I can't imagine Billy's having enemies. But I do, did, know Billy. He had a quixotic nature and he was very intense, given to moods. He had trouble with his parents because of that, since they're not."

Jury smiled slightly.

"You know what I mean; you yourself are intense. Don't give me that look, of course you are. So you know what it's like to deal with superficial people. I'm only saying they didn't understand Billy. And nor did I. But I understood him *better.* The thing is he was quite unpredictable. Like his mum." Oswald smiled. The smile looked hurt.

"Your daughter?"

"No, no. My son, Roderick's, first wife, Mary. She died." The smile vanished. "I was very fond of her. So was Billy. He was a child when she died. She set up a trust fund for him; that's what he lives on. Mary's own mother, Billy's maternal grandmother, also lives in London, but I seldom see her." He held up the cane in explanation. "Her name is Rose Ames, and she does occasionally come to see me. A very nice woman. My own wife has been dead for seven years. So has Rose's husband, his other grandfather. Been dead, I mean." He stopped. He went on. "Roderick—my son—is a good enough man, but rather stuffy. And his second wife, Olivia, is quite a bit younger, forty, I think. She's beautiful in the way porcelain is beautiful, but she does drain one. I think she tried to drain Billy. Not Roderick, though. He seems impervious to emotional abuse. Perhaps he was abused as a child; perhaps those around him were cold, especially his father. I don't know."

Jury knew Sir Oswald was tired and that he should go, but he didn't follow what the man had just said. "His father? I don't understand. I thought Roderick was *your* son."

"Adopted. After the war. He was mine. Have you talked to him and Olivia? Have you talked to Kurt Brunner? That's your man, Superintendent. He and Billy were very close. He's still in Rye, I think."

"Rye?"

"Yes, that's where they've been living for the last eight or nine months. Lamb House. I mean there and his Chelsea flat."

"But that's National Trust property. That's the home of Henry James."

"I know. Billy took over the tenancy. Billy was extremely fond of James's writing, and I expect he thought it would be a lark. He'd read somewhere that the Trust was looking for someone. So he applied. He would have met their fussy high standards." He looked at the floor, drew his cane around the elaborate design at his feet. "But then Billy would have met anyone's standards, I think."

For some reason this was the most sorrowful thing Oswald Maples had said. Jury offered, "Detectives from Islington are going to see your son and his wife today. In East Sussex. But Kurt Brunner—"

"Billy's assistant, or secretary, or plain friend. Talk to him. It's not your case?" There was disappointment in his tone.

"I'm officially helping out. I intend to help a lot." He smiled.

"Thank you for sending yourself here, Superintendent. I appreciate it."

"Not at all." Jury rose. "I'll be going, but I'll probably want to talk to you later on. No, don't get up. I'll see myself out."

Oswald Maples looked grateful, whether because he wouldn't have to hoist himself off the sofa or because Jury would be back, he didn't know.

"Do you read James?" he mused, not looking for an answer, but sitting there, tracing the rug's complicated red and blue pattern with the tip of his cane. "There's a story of his called 'The Figure in the Carpet.' It's about a writer who has this bittersweet awareness that no critic who has written about his books has ever understood the most important thing in them, his 'little trick,' which he describes as being a figure in a Persian carpet. It blends in so well that it becomes invisible although it's perfectly distinct, if you can see it." Sir Oswald looked up at Jury. "I hope you don't have that problem, Superintendent, with Billy's murder. You must come up against it all the time, that transparent figure, the one that you want so much to see and yet can only see through." Oswald smiled bleakly. "You'll have to forgive me this little lecture. It's just that I do hope you catch him."

Jury looked down at him, and nodded, and left.

For what could he say? What could anyone?

# SEVEN

"You're coming down with something," said Wiggins the next morning as he waited for the kettle to boil.

"No," said Jury, who felt he was coming down with everything, settling into his office chair. "I didn't sleep much last night."

"Looks as if you didn't sleep much this *year.* Your eyes look like something on the ocean floor. You need a cuppa. Be ready in a minute. Oh, the guv'nor wants to see you." Wiggins was concentrating now on peeling what looked like bits of bark off what looked like a root. *Or,* thought Jury, *it could be a branch from the rare jingoborah tree.*

*Don't ask,* Jury told himself. He had to bite his tongue.

The kettle was on the boil and Wiggins pulled out the hot plate plug, poured water into two mugs whose tea bags tumbled upward to the top. Aside from the mugs and the root, the surface of Sergeant Wiggins's desk was as uncluttered and clear as an ice floe.

"Fiona rang at eight-thirty. Says he wants to see you the minute you come in," Wiggins added, as he waited for the tea bags to leach color into the water.

"That minute, alas, is lost to us forever."

Wiggins chortled.

"And did he give us a clue as to why he was so anxious to see me?"

"No."

Eight-thirty. Jury was surprised DCS Racer was even in the office. Unless he'd been sleeping rough after a rave and couldn't make it home. Talking to Racer was no way to start off a day. Jury picked up the phone and rang Fiona Clingmore, Racer's secretary of many years (and who still looked just as she had looked when she first came here). "I'm here," he said. "You can inform your boss the games can begin."

"Took your time, din't you?" she said and hung up.

"I expect," said Wiggins, "it's about the Harry Johnson debacle." He spooned sugar into one of the mugs, what looked like a never-ending stream of it.

"Debacle? I'd hardly call it that. Anyway, it wasn't my case. That's Surrey police. Detective Inspector Dryer. We are not reaching back into the mists of time on this; it only happened a little over two weeks ago."

"I'd say if it wasn't for you, those two kids might be dead."

"Wrong. Wrong. Mungo saved them." Jury unhitched his jacket from the back of his chair and got up.

"Mungo's a dog."

He grabbed his mug of tea. "Don't I know it."

"The assistant commissioner wants to know why you're ignoring his order to lay off Harry Johnson," said Racer, the guv'nor and chief superintendent.

"I don't know what you're talking about. Did Harry make a complaint?"

Racer said nothing, probably because he didn't know. Jury asked, "Why doesn't the AC tell Detective Inspector Dryer to lay off? It's Surrey police's case, not mine."

"Exactly, Jury. Not yours."

Jury drank his tea and kept his face empty, an expression he never had any trouble with in here, where emptiness was the dish *du jour.*

Racer went on ignoring Tom Dryer's role in the Surrey case. "There's not a shred of evidence that says Harry Johnson is guilty of abducting those children."

Jury said nothing, just watched the cat Cyril, who had materialized out of one of his nowheres and was now down on the carpet behind Racer, stalking between bookcase and drinks cupboard. Cyril had learned how to open the drinks cupboard. As far as Jury knew Cyril wasn't after a drink.

"And now," said Racer with relish, "I hear you're moonlighting again."

Jury feigned surprise. "Moonlighting?"

"You're investigating a murder that properly belongs to the Islington police."

"I was there because a boy I know discovered the body."

"He should have called Isling—"

"Do you think that every British citizen knows the structure of the Metropolitan Police?" He sat forward to say this; now he sat back and sighed. "I told him to call the hotel management and have them in turn call the station."

"So what were you doing there?"

"I told you. This lad, Benny Keegan, is twelve—well, now thirteen—years old. He knows me. He was scared." The first two statements were certainly true. But he wondered about the third as he watched Cyril study the bottom doors of the cabinet. Now a paw reached out and worked its way between the doors and pulled slightly. As Cyril pushed inside, the bottles rattled a bit. Racer didn't seem to hear it. He was too busy lecturing Jury. The paw reached out again, this time from the inside, and pulled the door inward. Not closed, but nearly.

"Well, get your skates on, Jury, and get this damned Clerkenwell hotel thing sorted." He mused. "I've heard of it."

Jury asked innocently, "Clerkenwell?"

"*No!* The Zetter. Very good restaurant. I got a call from"—Racer looked down at a yellow pad on which he'd made notes (well, a note, as there seemed to be one line of writing)—"an Inspector Algar—"

"Aguilar."

"Yes. Who said they'd like you to assist them, especially as you know this lad. Get this Harry Johnson thing wound up, for God's sakes."

"It's not my case."

Racer smacked his hand down on the table so hard that even the whiskey bottles shivered like wind chimes. "If you say it once more, I'll have you *working* for Surrey."

"It's Tom Dryer's patch. The body was found in Surrey—"

"It might be Dryer's patch, but you're the one getting all the publicity! It wasn't enough your getting that press in the Hester Street thing, now you've got the rags on our back about this Belgravia house, also involving kiddies, I might add, and nothing gets up the public's nose like kiddies being molested."

"They weren't molested. Abducted, but not molested."

"It makes no difference, people get wrathful about children being mistreated."

Jury leaned forward again. "Look. I've said it again and again to the *Daily*

*Excrescence on Lies and Bad Taste,* I didn't save those children. The dog did."

Racer ran his locked fingers over his bald pate. "Oh God, that goddamned dog again! That's just so much sentimental rubbish. Of course the damned dog didn't rescue them. So then you get credit for not taking credit. You should have been a goddamned politician; by now you'd be PM!"

"If you're going to torture yourself with the vagaries of the *Daily Express,* you need a drink. Is that all?" Jury got up.

"Oh go on, get out of here."

On his way out of the office, he left the door open. He smiled at Fiona and stood there for a moment. He heard Racer get up. Three seconds later there was a monstrous *ya-owwwlll!* which could have been Racer or Cyril or both.

"What fun," he said to Fiona, as Cyril rushed through the door.

It struck him as he walked back to his office that Cyril's way was his way: stretched out and low to the ground. *Oh, for God's sakes*, he reconsidered. *Cyril could run rings around you any day.*

————

Wiggins looked up from some paperwork when Jury walked in.

"Some" paperwork hardly described it. Jury looked at a desk awash in it: papers, folder, envelopes, memos, directives, printed matter about the Metropolitan Police. Wiggins might have been the Met's publicist.

"Wiggins, twenty minutes ago there wasn't a scrap anywhere near your desk. It was like a no-fly zone for paper. Where in hell did this lot come from?"

"Oh, this? Messenger. You know, comes round at eleven every day. But don't worry, I'll have this sorted in a jiff."

In awe, Jury watched Wiggins's fingers, moving faster than a Vegas card dealer's, toss, flip, pitch, and flick the desk's contents into waste basket, drawer, and file.

"Amazing. You missed your calling; you should've been a dip."

Wiggins stretched his upper lip, Humphrey Bogart style. "Thanks, sweetheart. Oh, Dr. Nancy called. Says you'll want to see her. And DS Chilten called. It's on your desk."

Jury looked at the messages: Ron, Phyllis.

*"Aguilar wants you."*
That was one way of putting it.
"I'll be in the morgue," Jury said.
That was another way.

# EIGHT

She was gowned in green—green coverall,
green apron—leaning over a middle-aged,
corpulent corpse. Her gloves glistened with
blood.

She looked up. "Richard! You look like
hell; you look like him." She pointed to the
body beneath her hands, chest cavity open
for all to see. Quickly, Phyllis smiled.

Maybe that's how she hoped he'd look.
Tentatively, Jury returned the smile. He said
nothing.

Phyllis moved to another stainless steel
slab, stripped off her gloves, raised the
sheet on the body of Billy Maples. "You
came about Billy."

*I came about you.* Oh, he was in fine fettle, he was! "What have you got?" That sounded cold. Was this how he was to traverse the ground between them now? Adopting attitudes that she would most likely never believe?

He saw her watching him, and although but a few seconds elapsed between them, it felt like an hour.

She said his name, "Billy." It was as if she had to snag his attention. "He died from the first bullet that entered the chest; it caused lung collapse from broken ribs, tore the esophagus, and exited; the second inflicted more internal damage: liver, bone, vertebrae. But it's the first that killed him. No surprises here."

"I'm off this case, Phyllis." He had decided this the moment he saw her, and would reverse that decision when he saw Aguilar. And it was a stupid thing to say. What was that supposed to do? Cause her to pardon him? But he didn't know if she knew there was anything to pardon him *for.* Oh, she probably knew, just not the extent of it. He shut his eyes. He opened them again.

Her arms folded, her head cocked to one side, she looked disbelieving of what he'd just said, which she'd misunderstood. "The damned *idiots.* There did look like a lot of fulminating jealousies and thwarted egos in that hotel room." She waved her hand over the cold body. "And do they want my Billy back?"

The way she said that, Jury felt tears crowding at the corners of his eyes.

"No. Billy's yours."

"That DI—what's her name?"

Jury cleared his throat, wondering how the name would come out. "Aguilar. Islington police. The one in charge."

Phyllis nodded, her freshly gloved hand now wandering along Billy's chest, examining what had already been thoroughly examined. "I've worked this job for fifteen years and still can't believe the possessiveness and preening. You're all like a bunch of jaded film stars." She gave him a wicked smile. "Well, not all of you. Oh, hell." She stripped off the second pair of gloves and dropped them in the same metal container as the first pair. "Lunch?"


Danny Wu was the most self-contained man Jury had ever met. Nothing rattled or ruffled him, including a body on his doorstep. To Jury, Danny wasn't a suspect, not because he wouldn't shoot a man down in the middle of Soho, but because Danny was obsessively neat and wouldn't have tolerated a mess on the sidewalk outside Ruiyi. However, who had done the murder, Danny might well know, but if it was something that related to him, he'd take care of it himself. It would turn out to have nothing at all to do with the Triad (as Racer suspected) or any gang. What Racer didn't realize was that Danny was very much his own man; he belonged to nothing except the restaurateurs' association.

Here he came now in one of his Stegna suits, dark gray wool and silk, a tie that Van Gogh might have painted (had he been into haberdashery) with its swirl of brilliant colors. Lavender shirt that he got away with, although few men could have.

"Ah! Detectives and doctor!" He bowed toward Phyllis, turned back to Jury. "Can you wipe out crime in London if you're in here noshing all the time? Not that I'm not delighted to see you." He snapped his fingers and one of the little, ageless ladies who served here shuffled over bearing a clay pot and little clay cups that she set before them with a smile.

"Aren't you any closer to collaring my killer?" said Danny with a smile brilliant enough for a toothpaste ad. He meant the murder of the man who had fallen in an untidy heap directly on his doorsill.

When Jury didn't answer and Wiggins didn't look up from the menu, Danny went on. "No? Surely you're not still deluding yourselves that I did it?"

"You're right; we're not, Danny. You don't kill people in Soho. You do that over in Limehouse."

"Really? Who do you have in mind? Or is it the entire Docklands population? I understand the suits who live in those swanky condos in Butler's Wharf are actually living over opium dens."

Said Wiggins with a snigger: "No, they probably live in the opium dens. I'm having the crispy fish."

"You always have the crispy fish," said Jury.

Wiggins looked happy, bathed in the ocher light and muted sounds of Ruiyi. It always surprised Jury that a room this crowded could be so low-key. There was the inevitable queue at the door, heads cranking this way and that, looking for tables where the diners were nearly finished. "Maybe he got tired," said Wiggins, still on the subject of the Ruiyi corpse, "of waiting for a table."

Phyllis laughed and read the menu.

"May I suggest today's special? Shrimp in garlic sauce."

"I'm having the crispy fish," said Wiggins again.

"You said."

"Or," Danny continued, "the Peking duck with apricots."

"I'll have the shrimp," said Phyllis as she poured herself a morsel of tea.

"Duck," said Jury. He went on: "The thing is, Danny, I'm also pretty certain you knew our victim and even, maybe, who shot him."

"He was a Caucasian," said Danny, adjusting his lavender shirt sleeve.

"Are you saying you don't know any Caucasians?"

"Only you Scotland Yard lot."

"Yes. Sure." Jury drank the tea that Phyllis had poured him. The cup was thimble-sized.

Danny smiled and went off to put in their

order, stopping at several tables along his way.

They were all eating the glazed banana dessert when the unwelcome ring of his mobile phone made Jury cringe. "Hell." He whipped it from his pocket. "Yes?"

It was Detective Inspector Aguilar.

"I'm at Dust." She hung up.

Jury frowned and slapped the phone shut.

"Trouble?" asked Phyllis.

"Sir, if you don't mind my saying," said Wiggins, "you really ought to change that ring over from 'Three Blind Mice.' "

Phyllis said, "Oh, I don't know. I think it suits him," and went back to cracking the thin shell of glaze with her teeth as she smiled at him.

Jury glared.

# NINE

Dust in daylight was much the same as Dust at dark. Same customers, it appeared, though fewer, which didn't make it less noisy; simply more cavernous, more of an echo chamber. As he made his way to the bar, Jury felt as though he had to wave away each sound, as if they covered him like cobwebs.

She was at the bar, and Jury sat down. "You're here why?"

Aguilar lit a cigarette with a wafer-thin lighter that looked as if it should be in the silver vaults. She must have been getting by on more than her police pay. It was none of his business.

"It was a gift," she said, blowing smoke in a razor thin stream.

Jury was sick of mind readers.

"From whom?"

"Aren't we testy today?" she said.

"And tomorrow we'll be even testier."

"An uncle," she said, answering his question about the lighter. "Rodrigo. He lives in Buenos Aires. Filthy rich."

"You're from Argentina?"

"Brazil."

"Care to go into it?"

"No." She blew a smoke ring.

"No details about your difficult childhood, your drug-hampered youth?"

She turned to look at him. "You don't need details."

"Right." Jury ordered a pint of Foster's from the current barman. "Why are you here?"

"Instead of Brazil?" She looked at him full face, eyebrows making their point. "How easily you forget. This is a murder investigation and you're helping me. I'm talking to Ty."

"I'm off—" He had meant to say it and couldn't. He hated her. No, he hated himself. He hated the both of them. Neither. It was nobody's fault. It was simply a collision that shouldn't have occurred, but had.

"Didn't we finish with him?" *Or with us?*

The barman slid a Foster's to him and gave him a thumbs-up and Jury wasn't sure what the gesture implied. That he'd found this woman?

"No, we didn't finish. The guy's gay as a maypole."

"So what? That doesn't mean Billy Maples was."

She turned her dark liquid eyes on him and Jury felt he was swimming into them. "You're so naive."

*Naive? Christ.* "I don't know that I like you."

"I don't know that I care."

Ty reappeared with two magnums of champagne from some depth or other of Dust.

Aguilar glanced around. "I thought this was the cellar."

Part of Ty's mouth smiled; neither of his eyes did. "You getting any leads about Billy?" He was asking Jury. He'd apparently had enough of Lu.

But she answered anyway, "That's why we're here, Ty. I told you."

Ty's forehead crinkled like old parchment. "I told you all I know. Look: I want to help—"

"Then stop dicking around." She gave him a quick false smile.

His caramel-colored skin looked soaked in ashes. "What are you talking about?"

Again, he addressed Jury, and again Aguilar answered.

"Ty, Ty, Ty. We know all about it." Her sigh, smooth and false, was like the smile. She pulled a tiny leather notebook from her carryall. Rather, Jury had thought it was a notebook. But on the front in Italian was the word *"Indirizzi."* She hadn't taken any notes in it; it was an address book. He had to admit he was fascinated watching her sift through it, little page after little page, stopping to run her long finger down a blank page. "I count eight people we talked to, including Billy's latest woman, who know you and knew Billy. So come on Ty, chapter and verse. I'll buy you a drink."

He didn't capitulate to the drink, but he did to her tenacity; her heady presence could be smothering. Jury ought to know.

"Listen." Ty leaned over the bar, close in, his voice low. "I'm not a fag; neither was he—"

Aguilar, so close to Ty he must have felt breath on his face, said, "I don't care if you took it up your arse, in your ear, or down your throat. All I want to know is what happened to Billy Maples. That's all."

His voice went up a few decibels: "Well, so do I, dammit."

Jury thought he heard tears in Ty's voice now.

"Then tell the damned truth!"

She should have left it at that, should have let him set the pace. But she didn't. "Was it you who had a date with him at the Zetter? You were supposed to join him for coffee and other things."

"*No.* Okay, okay, we did have something going—well, that's not a hundred percent true; let's say I *thought* we had something going; then he broke it off."

"When? When did he tell you he was through?"

What was she doing? She was alienating him. No. She was trying to piss him off, make him thoughtless so he might give up in anger what he wouldn't under a milder form of questioning. Jury's kind. Jury didn't believe in bullying suspects; he thought what you get, what information you pull from an unwilling witness was unreliable. Some would do or say anything to get you off their backs.

Ty said, "He didn't exactly say that."

"He was here last night. He left to keep a date with someone at the Zetter where he'd booked a room. You say it wasn't you. But he told you, didn't he, that he was meeting somebody at the Zetter?"

"He told me nothing. All he said was that he'd booked a room there; said he was tired. I thought it was bloody funny for him to be doing that considering all he had to do was fall into a cab and go back to Chelsea."

"You were suspicious, is that it? So you went to the Zetter later and sussed it out, is that it? We know you weren't here after nine-thirty."

Ty looked blank.

Jury said, "Inspector Aguilar."

Not at all happy about being interrupted, she turned the intense heat of her gaze from Ty to Jury. "What?"

Jury motioned his head toward the door.

Less out of curiosity than of having nothing else to say to Ty, she got off the stool and drained the last of her drink. "I'll talk to you later."

Ty started wiping down the bar.

Lu Aguilar looked at Jury, looked away.

"We appreciate your help," said Jury. "Good night."


"I don't have my car."

"I have mine." They were dodging a lorry, a Mini Cooper, and a Morris battling it out in the Clerkenwell Road. "It's over the road in St. James's Green. Through the passage-way."

They passed the Zetter and were making their way through the dark of Jerusalem Passage, when Jury said, "You can be damned tough, Lu." He laughed. "I'm glad I'm not one of your bloody suspects." But the laughter dissolved as soon as it started. He felt a rising anger and got angrier yet because she made him feel that way. "I don't know why you thought you needed me here."

Lu stopped suddenly, turned to face him and pushed him against the wall. "You don't? Really?" Her mouth was near his but not on it. The words came out in hot little puffs. "You're pretty dim then; how did you make it to superintendent?"

"I can always make my way back down the chain." He said this against her lips, not quite, but almost there. A breeze stirred the few leaves at their feet, the few cast-off bits of paper, and her hair, long and loose, floated up like a veil.

"We need to discuss this, you know. At your place or mine? I told you he was lying."

"No, you said he was full of shit." This was whispered with his mouth so close to hers they seemed to be breathing together, air lacking oxygen if they'd breathed apart. He felt the same thing he'd felt when she'd walked into Billy's room at the Zetter.

"Your place or mine?" she whispered.

"Mine," said Jury, his hand on the back of her hair, cutting out the sliver of light, the whispering, the air. Again, he felt he was smothering.

Naked, sheet pulled up to her chin, she smoked a cigarette and watched him through the scrim of smoke. "You going somewhere?"

He had pulled on pants, vest, shirt, was sitting on the edge of the bed, starting to button the shirt. "I've got this case, see, that occasionally demands some of my atten—"

Lu slapped his hand away from the buttons, grabbed onto the collar and pulled his face down to hers. "At least, don't button it." She kissed him.

"Is this love, then? What?"

"Love? Is that what you want?"

He smiled and brought his face down to hers again. He was close enough to brush his lips across her cheek. He said, "I want . . ." then across the bridge of her nose, and over the other cheek, at the same time running his hand down her arm and then up to her hand. "This!" He snatched the cigarette and stuck it in his mouth.

She swung the pillow around and hit him, laughing. "So that's all I am to you! A source for all of your sinful addictions."

"Pretty much, yeah." Cigarette still in his mouth, he rose, buttoned up his shirt. "Get up. I'm going upstairs to check on Stone."

"Stone?"

"A dog. His owner's in Europe somewhere. He's a musician. Has a group, plays guitar. Be back in a minute." He leaned down, kissed her, left.

---

She was gone when he returned, leaving no trace of herself behind. Clothes on the floor, shoulder bag and shoes, her damned cigarettes had all been gathered up and gone with her. Not a trace, not a clue, that is, except the general wreckage of the flat.

Jury had to smile. The living room looked as if it had been tossed by Vice. He padded into the kitchen, filled the kettle, and set it down smartly on the burner, as if the violence that had risen in his blood after the last twenty-four—no, not that even—would now be forced onto anything that happened to cross his path.

He opened the cupboard, pulled out a mug, and slammed the unprovoking cupboard door shut. He leaned his forehead against it. Then he turned his back, head in hands. *Are you fucking insane?*

For one wild second he feared the cupboard door would answer. All of the inanimate things around him seemed to be pulsing, attuned to the same current. It was as if there were a crying-to-be-used leftover violence or rage. Was this supposed to be the legacy of love? But it wasn't love. Love, he feared, wasn't big enough to hold it.

They couldn't keep this up.

He couldn't resist it.

A knock at the door yanked him away from the wall. He hoped it wasn't anyone he knew; he might just land a punch on a jaw. Quickly, he finished buttoning his shirt, and on the way to the door set the coffee table upright again, but hadn't time to upturn the chair and end table. They weren't in the line of vision from his door so that was all right. He opened it.

"Mr. Jury." She was wringing her hands.

It was Mrs. Wasserman, the tenant of the basement flat.

"Did you hear it?"

He arranged his face in simple greeting. "Hello, Mrs. Wasserman. Hear what?"

Anxiously, she whispered, as if "it" might hear her and knock her down. "The awful noise last night." As Jury stood his ground in the doorway, blocking her view, she looked upward, as though she were seeing through the second- and-third floor flats. "Could Carole-anne have had friends over?" "Friends" to be counted of course as one particular friend, but not by her. "A party, perhaps? It was so wild I'd think you would have heard it."

Jury looked at the ceiling where, in the flat above them, the dog Stone's nails *click clicked* as he paced. "Stone?"

"A dog making that racket? Now you're just teasing. What worries me is an intruder—"

Jury held up his hand, palm out. He'd got it. "Stan's back." Why did that statement sound so ridiculous? He cleared his throat. "That's what you heard."

"But I haven't seen him." Her voice wavered, wanting it to be Stan, but still afraid it was an intruder. "One person making such noise?" Slowly, she shook her head.

"He had his group with him. Haven't you heard them overhead before? They're a weird jazz bunch."

Worry bit into her brow, making tiny crevices. "That's *music,* Mr. Jury. This wasn't music."

"Music? Sometimes I think when they get going they make sounds like falling furniture." Jury laughed. *Ha Ha Ha.*

"I'll have to speak to Carole-anne."

She wasn't giving up on the Carole-anne

and her friends idea. He had to get her off that tack. If she told Carole-anne about the noise, Carole-anne would suss it out in five seconds and be livid. *Livid*. She hated the idea of Jury's looking at other women. Livid and heartbroken, she wouldn't speak to him ever again for the rest of their natural lives together.

"Listen, Mrs. Wasserman, don't say anything to Carole-anne. Let me take care of that. I'm a detective, after all. I have ways of getting information." He winked. Her answering smile was small and weak. "But I'm sure it's not an intruder. Probably Stan came back and he and Stone had a tussle on the floor. You know how much he loves that dog." In the circumstances, that hadn't come out very well.

But Mrs. Wasserman seemed appeased. "Well . . . you're probably right, Mr. Jury. But if you see him, tell him to stop by and say hello."

"I will."

"Sorry to bother you." She turned toward the stairs.

"No bother at all, Mrs. Wasserman."

Jury turned and shut the door, congratulating himself on the way he'd handled that, including his brilliant solution, and went whistling back to the kitchen and the kettle.

On his way he looked around the living room at the overturned chair and small side table, the newspapers and magazines that had spilled from the upset coffee table and lay strewn across the rug, the rug itself scudded into little waves, pillows, books— and why were the desk drawers pulled out of their sockets?

*Are you fucking insane?*

# TEN

In St. James's Church, a woman was arranging flowers, pink peonies and blue hydrangeas, in a large vase near the altar. He walked down the nave to where she stood, holding a peony as if debating where to put it. "Very pretty," he said, not knowing why he was commenting and startling her in the bargain.

"Oh!"

"Sorry, I was looking for whoever's in charge. Actually, I don't know this priest, but—" He described the man who had bumped into him last night. "Fairly young, a little shorter than I, maybe six feet. In his thirties, perhaps?"

She laughed. "Oh, no. I think what you'd be wanting isn't St. James's. It's Our Most Holy Redeemer. But I don't know the name of the priest there. I think the present one might be there just temporarily. Anyway, you want to go to Exmouth Market."

"I'm not sure where that is."

"You just go back out to Clerkenwell Close, you'll pass Northampton Road, then round to Exmouth Market. It's a lively place. You can't miss it."

Jury thanked her and left.


Exmouth Market was a sudden eruption of restaurants and coffeehouses and cafés that probably hadn't been there yesterday. Another trendy little area.

The Church of Our Most Holy Redeemer was located in among these bristling little businesses. It was surprising in its architecture, more in the Italian Renaissance style. Or so he guessed from its gabled front, reminiscent of a basilica's. At least he thought so, knowing little about architecture, especially church architecture.

Inside, it was even more Italianate. Above him was a lovely vaulted ceiling that featured in one of the many cards and pictures Marshall Trueblood had brought back from Florence. It would be no use asking Melrose Plant; all he brought back were gloves. His only interest appeared to be the glove store. Jury kept his eyes trained upward. Who was the famous, very famous, dome builder?

"Brunelleschi," said a mind reader at his elbow.

Jury whipped around and looked into the face of the man who had passed him in Jerusalem Passage. He had seen him only in half light and for only a couple of seconds, but he was the man who had run into Phyllis the night before.

"Oh. Brunelleschi's dome; now I remember."

"This church is modeled on Santo Spirito. Florence. Have you been there?"

Jury smiled. "No. Friends have."

The priest looked up. "It's a copy. Or rather I should say it's based on that ceiling."

"Is Holy Redeemer your church, then?"

"Mine? Oh, no. I'm more or less pinch-hitting for a few months."

He seemed quite young. But Jury thought that might simply be the agelessness of faith or, possibly, art. Of where they stood, both looking up at the Brunelleschi-inspired ceiling. Jury found himself suddenly very tired. The deep restfulness of the church seemed to enrobe him. The air seemed to be thinning.

"I haven't seen you in here before," said the priest. "You're visiting? Traveling?"

Jury smiled at that. "I wish I were. No, I live in Islington."

"I'm Father Martin. I get the impression you're here for something other than our ceiling."

"You don't remember me, do you?"

The priest cocked his head. "No. We've met?"

Jury realized he hadn't produced his ID and fished it out. "Sorry. I'm from New Scotland Yard."

Father Martin looked astonished, as if he wondered what old crime had caught up with him.

"We haven't really met. You bumped into us last night near the Zetter. That narrow passage—?"

"Of course. I think you were with someone . . . a woman. I'm sorry. But then I don't expect you came here for an apology."

"Right. You probably know there's been a man murdered at the Zetter. That sort of news travels fast."

Father Martin's expression underwent a series of changes, none of them happy, yet none of them as unhappy as the man last night had worn. "Yes, I did hear about it."

"His name is—was—Billy Maples. Do you know anything about him?"

The priest studied Jury's face closely enough to make him uncomfortable. *Probably sees right through me,* Jury thought.

"I'm not sure, Superintendent. Let me think about it a bit."

*He knew him,* thought Jury, but he wasn't going to press him.

"Of course. I'll be back. Thank you, Father. In the meantime if you hear anything at all that might be relevant, get in touch right away, will you?" Jury handed him a card.

"Yes, of course," said the priest, looking at it. "I will."


"You'll find him in the kitchen," said the clerk or concierge, he couldn't be sure which, in answer to Jury's request to see Gilbert Snow.

Jury said, "I'd rather not go looking for him in the kitchen; I'd much prefer he come out here. Or perhaps"—Jury looked toward the dining room—"in there?"

She tossed her long hair back from her face, called the kitchen, said to Jury that Gilbert Snow would be right out. She nodded toward an area behind Jury. "Why don't you wait in the bar? It's quite comfortable." She motioned toward an area raised a little above the lobby.

Jury sat down on a well-cushioned couch, thought about getting some water. There was a sort of window that joined the bar and the dining room. He could see waiters and waitresses going about the tables.

Gilbert Snow was prompt in coming. Jury stood up and shook his hand, then asked him to sit down.

Jury said, "You've been working here for a while, have you?"

"Yes, sir. Been here since it opened. That weren't long ago. It's quite new. I was one o' the first to be taken on."

"Before that, had you been in hotel work?"

"Oh no, sir, no. I was one o' them worked the barges from the Isle o' Dogs down to Gravesend. Then, all this buildin' started up, with all them warehouses turned into flats, or lofts, I believe that's what they call 'em. Bit fancy. I mean, the Isle o' Dogs, it's but a bedroom community now. Clerkenwell, you remember what Clerkenwell was? It's not been but a few years; it's not decades we're talkin' about, no sir, just a matter of a few years." Gilbert leaned closer, elbow on the little table, as if about to impart confidences. "Soon it'll be Spitalfields that'll go the way of Covent Garden. I mean London was goin' along fine in its old ways then people decide they got to have their lofts and garages and water views." He flapped his hand in dismissal of Thames views. "I used to like us, I did. I liked how we could do with less. Not like America. Can you imagine an American doin' without her dishwasher? She'd be sunk."

Jury said, "There's a lot of America that does make do with less, a lot less. We don't hear about it, though. The old coal-mining towns stripped bare. The Appalachians, parts of the Midwest. You know what I think is wrong with America?"

"No, sir, I don't."

"It's just too big. It's too bloody big."

Gilbert nodded. "I think you just might be right, there, I do indeed. It's so big not even half of it knows what's going on in the other half."

Jury nodded and said, "To go back to Mr. Maples. Had you ever seen him before?"

"Once when he was a guest here before."

"So you recognized him?"

Gilbert frowned. "He was out on the patio when I brought the supper up and he came into the room to sign the check and add on to the gratuity. Very generous person."

"So you're sure it was Maples."

"Well, yes, of course. It'd be pretty crazy to think someone else comes in and shoots him then orders dinner and pretends to be him and then just leaves? That'd be a peculiar thing to do."

Jury smiled. "You'd be surprised what these villains can get up to."

Gilbert shook his head. "Well, that's your job then, sir. I wouldn't fancy it myself."

Jury smiled. "Yes, that's my job, unfortunately."

# ELEVEN

Waterloo Bridge lay under a dense fog when Jury parked his car on the Victoria Embankment an hour later. It was one of those pea soupers people liked to talk about, back when they called London the Smoke.

The area beneath the bridge was used as a sort of encampment and shelter for a dozen or so of the ill-fated men and women who, during the day, begged for their supper or investigated dustbins.

They all knew one another from camping here over a long period of time. They were by way of being mates, a family almost. Seldom were they all here at any one time during the night; usually it was only four or six of them.

Jury thought it was remarkable the way the police turned a blind eye to these lodging arrangements, but they did, as long as the group was gone—and their chattels with them—during the day. At night, they were left alone, out of sight, out of mind.

Benny Keegan was one of them.

"Wot? You've come again?" said Mags, then sang, "Lookin' better than anyone has a right to—"

Jury laughed. It would've sounded like that Dolly Parton favorite had there been any possibility of mistaking Mags for Dolly. Mags sat in a huddle of shawls and scarves, looking up at Jury.

She went on: "That's like t'ree times in the last mumph you been here. Things must be tough if they let you lot off to cruise under the bridges. What's a matter? You ain't meetin' yer quota so you gotta come here and shake down us law-abidin' citizens?"

"Don't be so hard on the Filth, Mags. It's them that let you doss down here. Where's Benny?"

Serious now, she lowered her voice. "That was tur'ble, wot happened. And our Benny bein' t'one to find the body!"

Jury had picked up a magazine from one of the piles around her. That was how she'd gotten her nickname. "So where is he?"

"Prob'ly along there—" She raised an arm and pointed down the length of the Embankment.

A fire was going strong in an oil drum, blazing up in the hollow-cheekboned face of a tall man in a long dark coat whom they called the sergeant. He had put himself in charge of keeping the place drug free, though not, of course, drink free, which would be expecting entirely too much. He liked his nip now and then. He had also taken on the responsibility of seeing that the others cleared out during the day.

"You can 'ave that one." She nodded at the ancient copy of *Playboy.* "Look like you could use it, you not 'avin' anything like a love life."

"I've got you, Mags."

"You got that centerfold is wot you got."

"Better than nothing."

"Better'n somfing, ya mean. Just look at the size of 'er!"

"Mr. Jury!" he heard Benny call, followed by a bark. Sparky.

"Hullo, Benny. I need to talk to you. 'lo, Sparky." Jury knelt to give Sparky a good head rub. The rougher, the better Sparky liked it.

The three went over to sit on the stone steps that led from the Embankment down to the river.

Benny asked with some anxiety, "Do I have to go down the nick and talk to some yob?"

"Just this yob at the moment."

Sparky sat at their feet, looking from one to the other, reminding Jury of Harry Johnson's dog, Mungo. How is it that he knew what were probably the three smartest dogs in London—Sparky, Mungo, and Stone? How often did he think of getting one for himself?

"I'm just wondering if you've remembered anything else about the crime scene." Jury imagined Benny would like it thus referred to.

"I been thinkin' on it and can't come up with nothing, Mr. Jury. There must've been somebody else there."

"And it was somebody he knew."

Benny nodded and leaned back on his elbows. "But Gil, now, he didn't see anybody else when he took up the dinner, or he'd've said."

"This mystery person mightn't have arrived yet, or if he was there, he—"

"Or she, don't forget."

"You're right. Or *she* could have gone out on the patio."

"That's where Gil said Billy Maples was when he took up the dinner. Supposing it could of been somebody else—the killer? And maybe he was still there?"

"I don't see how he could have been. You were in the room and out on the patio yourself. He couldn't have been in the bathroom, either, as you put Sparky in there."

Benny hadn't, as one of the room service staff might have, given a yell and run for it. Benny had instead shown quite a bit of self-command, in addition to curiosity, and had examined the body and the room. He only hoped the boy hadn't shown more interest in it than was good for him.

"Have you noticed anybody hanging about, Benny?"

"Hangin' about? No. What'd'ya mean?"

"Nothing, really."

Benny pulled a battered chew toy from his pocket and offered it to Sparky, who looked at it and let it lie. It was as if Sparky knew there were graver issues at hand and he wasn't to be diverted by anything as trivial as a toy. Sparky even took a step backward to put a distance between himself and the worn twist of rope.

Jury looked at him and said, "You want to quit your Southwark gig and work for the Yard?"

Even in the dark, Jury could sense the blush.

"Ah, go on, Mr. Jury."

# TWELVE

As Jury remembered it, the garden was walled and very quiet. Very private.

He sat by a window on the 9:18 train to Rye, watching a line of oasthouses as the train trundled through the Kent countryside. He was thinking about Lamb House.

Across from him sat a boy of ten or eleven, reading something difficult, to judge from the deep frown. Jury could not see the title of the book, a textbook, perhaps, as it had no dust jacket. Why were all textbooks so lacking in verve and color? The boy looked up from the book and the frown disappeared, replaced by a smile, as if he recognized that this man sitting across from him had once had to deal with lusterless books, too.

He reminded Jury of someone. A face not unhandsome, clear pale eyes and skin. Chestnut brown hair. Himself. They had lived here, in Kent or Sussex, after his mum had died. He had come to live with his uncle and aunt and that single cousin, his old childhood nemesis who had died so recently. Sarah had died in March.

The train pulled into the station. Both he and the boy rose and left.

Rye sat along that line of coast that supported Brighton and Hastings to the west and Dover to the east. Rye had been part of the Confederation of the Cinque Ports, but was no more. Instead of the water eroding the land, it had pulled back from it, leaving an expanse of sand and mud and shale. The town itself was known to be one of the most charming of English villages: cobblestones, tight little houses, the famous Mermaid Street and tavern that had been the haunt of pirates.

Lamb House sat at the end of one of these narrow cobbled streets, a modest brick establishment that gave no clue as to the beautiful garden behind it, nor of one of the writers who had lived here.

A plump and pleasant woman answered the door and admitted him. Housekeeper, probably. She showed him into a sitting room and excused herself, saying that Mr. Brunner was on the phone and would be along in a minute or two.

When she'd left, Jury wandered into the dining room, where windows gave out onto the garden he remembered. He turned back to the book—no, journal—on the dining room table, opened to a page so the James pilgrim could read it. Jury did so. What astonished him in this writing was the lack of corrections; James wrote with the same exacting use of language, the same tone, the same nuance as in his finished books. Only here and there was a word or phrase excised and replaced by another. What might have served as a first draft for James, a lesser writer would be happy to call the final copy.

The man who walked in as he was reading was tall and light haired and good-looking with a square jaw and a slender nose.

Although he was probably in his fifties, he looked a decade younger.

Jury extended his hand. "Richard Jury. We spoke on the telephone?"

"Kurt Brunner. You're here about Billy." The voice seemed to pitch into a different register, as if they were on a ship blasted by a wave.

"I'm sorry, Mr. Brunner."

He recovered himself and led Jury back to the sitting room. It was quite attractive in its unlived-in way. But Lamb House was, after all, a little museum of sorts, or at least its ground floor was. The tenant would be responsible for keeping it spotless and prepared for visitors for a good part of the year. The sign outside had given Wednesdays and Saturdays as the public days.

And this room, certainly, was meticulously cared for: the books on those shelves lovingly dusted, the brilliants of that candlestick holder on the mantel carefully polished. The crystal was touched by the darting, uncertain sunlight that came and went as the two of them sat there in what seemed more than silence, a hush.

"I'm sorry about Billy Maples. And I'm sorry you're being bothered again by police.

I was asked to help out on the case since I knew one of the witnesses and also a family member." Jury paused. "You were with Billy for several years, I understand."

"I was, yes." Brunner looked away, looked off toward the window through which light came and went swiftly. "For about five years. In London and also here."

There was no question about the effect of Billy Maples's death on Kurt Brunner. The man looked and sounded desolate. But he kept it up. There was little left of a German accent and none of the idiom; perhaps he'd consciously tried to drill them out of his speech.

"You weren't at the family estate then?"

Brunner shook his head. "Billy didn't care for the house."

"Yet he had grown up there. It was his childhood home."

"Yes, but he didn't get on very well with his family. He didn't like the place. I think perhaps it was why he'd have such mood swings." He frowned slightly.

Jury thought about this. "But you can't really say?"

Brunner shook his head.

Jury said, "What were your duties? I

mean, in what capacity did you work for him?"

"He wanted, for lack of better term, an administrative assistant; he needed someone to keep things sorted."

" 'Things'?"

"He had many interests. Sometimes they'd conflict. I'm speaking on a very simple level here—I mean conflicts of time or meetings."

Jury thought about this, then said, "From what I've heard, your employer was very generous. Where did that come from?"

Kurt Brunner's eyebrows rose, puzzled. "I'm not sure what you mean, Superintendent."

"I'm not quite sure either. He made hefty contributions to this gallery in Clerkenwell, and gave a good deal of money to artists. And then there's this"—Jury looked up at the ceiling—"this literary landscape. Not just any writer, but Henry James, no less." Jury frowned, thinking. "I haven't read much, but there's something about his writing that's so . . . hermetic. If that makes any sense."

"James had a very active social life.

Traveled widely. Was a worldly man. He wasn't a recluse, if that's what you mean."

"So I've heard, but . . . can't you do all that and still remain, well, *sealed*?"

Brunner's expression became serious. "You think Billy lived that sort of life?"

"I don't know; I'm merely tossing it out." Jury thought of Father Martin and Our Most Holy Redeemer Church. "Was he of a religious bent? Perhaps he'd been saved."

Kurt Brunner just looked at him. "From what?"

"I wouldn't know, would I?" Jury smiled. "I expect from his formerly wastrel ways." Jury thought somehow he might have offended Kurt Brunner. He wanted to revive Brunner's earlier mood and brought the subject down to a more literal level. "You handled his finances and kept his calendar and were his friend?"

"I like to think so, I mean, that I was his friend."

"You must have given his murder a lot of thought."

Brunner nodded. "I certainly have. And I've no idea why it happened."

"Did he have enemies?"

"Enemies." Brunner frowned, as if the

word had little connection with his dead friend. "None I knew of."

Jury leaned his head in the palm of his hand, elbow braced on the arm of his chair. Prepared to be patient. "You must have tried to sort it out—what caused someone to shoot Billy Maples."

Kurt Brunner leaned toward Jury. "As I said before, yes. Yes, I have. I've thought of little else, Superintendent."

"I'm sure. But this is what I mean. You must have thought of certain possibilities— people, places, situations—before discarding them. I expect that's what I'm looking for: the discards."

"That would be irresponsible of me, wouldn't it? Merely to toss out names like bread to a swan?"

Jury grinned. "First time I've been likened to a swan. Let's call it more free association than accusation or irresponsibility on your part. I'm merely trying to put together a picture of your employer, what he was really like. Who better to come to than you?"

"But look: I'm betraying no confidences."

Jury sighed. Still, he was happy to hear there were things to betray.

Brunner grew thoughtful but said nothing.

Neither did Jury. He sat, patient as a hawk. He had all day, all evening, if it came to it. While he waited he thought about Henry James. That notebook, the pages with so few alterations. To get it so right the first time around. What genius always to have access to such elegant language, such perfect prose. It was genius enough that he wound up with it in the book's final form. But to begin with it, to dictate it! No wonder they called him the Master.

As if coming in on his wavelength, Brunner said, "Have you read many of James's novels?" He had moved toward one of the bookcases.

Jury shook his head. "Three, I think."

"This one makes use of the vampire theme." Brunner held up a slender volume.

Jury couldn't help it—he laughed. "Henry James writing about vampires?"

Brunner fixed him with a quirky smile. "It depends on how you interpret them." He sat down again.

"Vampires."

Brunner nodded, the slightly deprecating smile in place.

Jury understood the smile: living here as he did, Brunner might feel he had access to the mind of Henry James. But Jury wanted access to the mind of Billy Maples. Perhaps Brunner meant to suggest that the one was the other. "Vampires. I find that really hard to believe."

Brunner hitched his chair a bit closer. He was a man of great intensity, realized Jury. "*The Sacred Fount* isn't one of his most popular novels, perhaps because it's rather obscure."

"All of James is 'obscure' from my point of view. But then I've not read that much."

"Oh, but *The Sacred Fount* is even more so." Kurt Brunner smiled and reached for a silver cigarette box, took a cigarette from it, offered the box to Jury, who shook his head. Brunner went on: "I don't ordinarily smoke in here. Could we go into the garden?"

They rose and passed out through the French doors into the walled garden. It was just as Jury remembered it. How strange, he thought, that something as inconsequential as another man's garden would stick with him for so long.

Brunner lit his cigarette. Jury watched the match—its strike, its small bloom of flame, its progress to the tip of the cigarette. It was rather excruciating. He coughed.

"Sorry. Does the smoke bother you?"

"No, no. You were talking about this vampire business."

"Yes. In the book an older wife has drained her younger husband of his youth, or a large measure of it. One of the partners flourishes as the other one sickens."

"And that's the vampire theme?"

"That's the vampire theme."

Jury shook his head, smiled. "I have a hard time imagining James writing about it."

"He wrote *The Turn of the Screw,* remember."

"Yes. That's one of the ones I read. How does this pertain to Billy Maples?"

"His stepmother, Olivia. They didn't get on. That's putting it mildly. They had terrible arguments. He hated going there. He'd always swear, never again. But Olivia claimed to need him, to miss him and would set about manipulating him to come back. He would go for a few days. It would take him a day to recover. 'I don't know what it is,' he'd say. 'She grows more brilliant, even younger, when I'm there, but me, I'm completely done in, feel ten years older. Fagged.' Well, it's as if one of them had to pay the price for the other."

"Utterly ghoulish." Jury thought how banal that remark was. "Are you suggesting that his stepmother is in some way responsible for Billy's death?"

Kurt Brunner shrugged. "You're forgetting what it is you asked for: any person that came to mind on my way to 'I have no idea who did it.' You were looking for the discards is how you put it."

Jury shook his head. "This woman doesn't sound as if she can be so easily discarded."

Brunner nodded. "I agree. But I'd have no idea at all as to how she might have been involved. I don't know how to answer your question."

"A detective named Chilten has spoken to the parents. He'll want to know where they were two nights ago."

"Well, you see, 'they' probably don't come into it much. Billy's father, from what I can gather, is fond of his son, but not very able to show it.

"And you? Where were you?"

"In London, at the flat in Sloane Street. I'd just come back from Berlin. So, no, I don't have an alibi." Brunner smiled uncertainly.

"Do you own a gun?"

Brunner shook his head. "They asked me that, too, the detectives from, where? Islington police station? Indeed they asked me a lot of things."

Jury opened his mouth to speak when the phone rang. Brunner excused himself, put out his cigarette. Wanting to spend more time in the house, Jury followed him inside.

While Brunner was engaged with the call, Jury moved about the sitting room, grateful for the silence. Not that he'd minded the talk, or Brunner's voice, for none of that had disturbed it. Their voices had intruded upon the mood of the house about as much as a layer of dust. There was no dust, of course. The place had to be kept up. For some peculiar reason, Jury would have liked to turn a book spine toward him and blow dust from its surface. He did not know why he felt this; perhaps it had to do with letting things lie.

He picked up a book of short stories, looked at the contents page and found the story Oswald Maples had mentioned: "The Figure in the Carpet."

He held on to it as he looked over the shelves of books and wondered if they had been Billy Maples's or the property of the National Trust. Probably the Trust's.

For some reason, he was reminded of his dead cousin and how she had given him a version of his childhood that he remembered completely differently. He had been five or six—or so he thought—when his mother had been killed in the air raid.

"No, you were only a baby, and, no, you weren't there when it happened," she'd said.

It had been highly charged, that apparently mistaken memory of his dead mother in the ruins of their house, and unless his cousin had been lying ("she would, you know," her husband, Brendan, had said, with a laugh), he had got it all wrong. But the feelings of desolation and devastation, that he had got right.

Kurt Brunner returned with the information that it had been the National Trust who'd called. "They need a tenant; they want me to stay on for two or three weeks until the couple who are to take up the tenancy, who were in line for it, can make their plans and get themselves sorted."

"Well, at least it means you won't have to reorganize your own for a while."

"Oh, *I* don't want it!"

"The tenancy? But I should think you wouldn't want to be cut free straightaway," said Jury, surprised.

"That's just what I do want. To be cut free. It's no work, really. If there were a salary attached, I'd call it a sinecure." He smiled. "And there are not that many visitors."

"It doesn't attract the masses, does it?"

"More than you'd think, but fewer than James deserves." Brunner smiled. "It's too isolated for anyone other than those who absolutely want to see it."

Idly, Jury turned the thin pages of the book of short stories he held. "It would be treated with a kind of, well, reverence, I'd think."

Brunner folded his arms across his chest. "Yes, we all pretty much hold our breath here."

Jury smiled. It was a good way of putting it. He thought of the undisturbed dust and his wish to blow it away.

"So, they look to me to find someone else; it's as if I'd betrayed them by turning down their offer. Almost as if Billy had betrayed them by getting himself killed."

"What will you do, then?"

"Go back to London. Stay in the flat. I think I need a large dose of London life at this point. Rye can be claustrophobic." He took out a card and made a note. "Here's the address and telephone in case you need to get in touch with me."

"Thank you." He didn't bother telling Kurt Brunner that police had already been to the flat. Glancing at the book in his hands, Jury said, "I don't imagine one is permitted to borrow books? I'd like to read one or two of these."

"Oh, take it, by all means. It's actually mine."

"Thanks. I'll get it back to you. When do you leave?"

"In two or three days, I expect."

"So Billy's housekeeper—she'll need to find other work?"

"Mrs. Jessup? She's the cook. If the new tenant is willing to employ her, then she'd stay." With an unconvincing try at jocularity, Brunner said, "I don't expect you know anyone who enjoys a crabbed and hermitlike life? Some James fanatic or other?"

Jury slipped the card into his wallet. "I certainly know someone who leads a crabbed life. As far as Henry James is concerned, I believe he holds contests."

"Contests?" Brunner was puzzled.

"Something like that." Jury held out his hand. "Good-bye, Mr. Brunner, and thanks very much."

He walked to the station in the rain, wondering if other writers' houses left one feeling this way. He felt drenched, not by the rain, which was light and fitful, but by Henry James, as the train sailed through Kent and passed another line of oasthouses.

He spent the journey reading "The Figure in the Carpet." It made him wonder about Billy Maples, but he couldn't work out why it did. It was that feeling that had overtaken him in Lamb House. Perhaps it was Billy's protean nature that prompted this feeling. Generous to a fault, apparently. A Londoner, and young, and yet he settles in a small village and takes on the tenancy of Lamb House, the tenancy of which includes the maintenance of the house and short tours for visitors.

Jury pulled out his small notebook and

some coins when he saw the tea trolley rolling up the aisle. He handed over a five-pound note for a cup of tea and a Cadbury biscuit and told the attendant to keep the change. After the server had given Jury profuse thanks, the trolley rolled on.

What had been the attraction of Lamb House? To saddle one's self with the job of conducting visitors through its rooms surely bespeaks a commitment to books—and to this man's books.

Why had Billy gone to the hotel in Clerkenwell? Why had he gone to Our Most Holy Redeemer? Why to Dust?

Dust.

The movement of the train lulled him into a doze. He dreamed about blood snaking down the aisle of his car, and the friendly tea-trolley attendant morphing into Dracula.

# THIRTEEN

"Did he tell you anything helpful?" asked Ron Chilten on the phone when Jury told him about that day's trip to Rye.

"He did. Have the parents identified Billy Maples's body yet?"

"The father did. He took it hard. I didn't want to ask him a lot of questions right then, so I drove to Sussex and put the questions there. Mum's actually stepmum, a looker, but a bit of an iceberg. All I got out of them was they couldn't imagine Billy being involved with anyone who'd do him this harm."

Jury turned at the sound of a thud against

his door. "Hold on while I get the door, Ron—"

It was Stone, Stan Keeler's dog. Jury looked up the staircase and called to Carole-anne. No Carole-anne. He wondered how Stone had gotten out of Keeler's flat.

Stone, possibly the calmest and most self-contained dog Jury had ever known— except for Harry Johnson's Mungo—walked in and quietly settled himself by Jury's chair. Jury plucked a fake bone from under the sofa table and tossed it to Stone, who caught it in his teeth. "Good move," said Jury.

"Why? What'd I—"

"Not you, Ron. I was going to say that Billy Maples wasn't your stereotypical play-boy. Not with his taking up the tenancy of Lamb House."

"Yeah, that's pretty much the picture I got from Malcolm."

Jury waited. No enlightenment. "Who is Malcolm?"

"Oh, I didn't say? He's a nephew of Roderick's. He's a little villain, Malcolm is. He's the kind that ties firecrackers to a dog's tail."

"He's a kid?"

"Well, yes. You think Roderick was doing it?"

"Roderick?"

"You know, the father."

"So is your best source of information a kid?"

"Not really. His specialty is climbing brick walls. Like the one behind the house. Don't ask me. He's probably ten but he says he's twelve. He lies a lot."

"Just what we need in an informant."

"Hell, there's your Benny Keegan. He's thirteen but you seem to think he's a font of information."

Jury thought of *The Sacred Fount.* He wondered about this vampire theme. "Benny doesn't tie stuff to his dog's tail. Benny's very grown-up. Does this Malcolm live with the Maples family full time?"

"Yeah. If he could, he'd have Roderick tied to a chair while he built a fire under it. Last I saw of Malcolm he was in the garden rappelling a brick wall with Waldo at the other end of the rope. Kind of hanging there."

"Waldo?"

"That's the one. At the end of the rope."

"Ron, who is Waldo?"

"The dog. The cook finally came out and put a stop to it. I'll say this, though. Malcolm knows something, but he's not giving it up." Ron heaved a tired sigh. "I'm not a bloody inch closer to solving this."

"It happened only two nights ago, Ron."

"You know as well as I do, it's the first twenty-four that are crucial. There's no will, incidentally. Lu talked to the solicitor the family's been using for years."

"That's too bad. He died intestate."

"Yeah, a mess, but it pretty much removes money as a motive, except maybe the parents, and they seem to have plenty as it is. Have you talked to young Benny since?"

"Yes, last night."

"You know where he lives? I couldn't pry it out of him. I was getting ready to have him up on obstruction of justice."

Jury laughed. "Yes, I know where he lives. No, I'm not telling."

# FOURTEEN

"No," said Melrose Plant.

"Oh, come on. It's right up your street. You're titled and bored."

"Actually, I'm neither. I sent my title to the moon—as you well know—and how can I be bored with you there hatching plots that only a nutter would involve himself in?"

"Well, you do involve yourself. You went along with Niels Bohr. Like, what are you doing right this minute?"

"Like, I'm reading."

Jury heard on his end of the phone a rather artificial crackling of paper. "What?"

There was a brief silence. *"Hermit News."*

Jury stopped doodling dogs. "I beg your pardon?"

*"Hermit News."*

Jury waited. It was like talking to Chilten. "Do you think you could fill me in on that?"

"On what?"

"I'm going to leap through this receiver and kill you."

Melrose sighed. "It's Mr. Blodgett's small newspaper. I got him a subscription."

Jury waited. Nothing. "You're probably lying since I can no more believe there's a *Hermit News* anymore than I could *Love Nest in the CID.* But just to give you the benefit of the doubt, I'm asking, why would hermits want a newspaper? I mean, doesn't that somehow go against the very *essence* of hermithood? I mean, if they're reading newspapers why not just go for *The Times*?"

There was a brief (and refreshing) silence as Melrose yawned. "Because it doesn't have this hermit news in it."

"Did you know Henry James had a vampire theme?"

"Had a vampire?"

"Not *had* a vampire, a vampire *theme.* Haven't you read *The Sacred Fount*?"

"No."

"Well, read it before you go there."

"I'm not going there. Here's an interesting little column on the rise of goat farming around Northampton."

"I've never seen a goat in Northampton."

"Not in. I said around."

"In or around, I've never seen one."

"You most certainly have."

Jury was doodling on a pad he kept by the phone in his flat for apparently that purpose, as he never wrote anything on it. "Oh, you mean your goat."

"Well, don't sound so dismissive. He's a *goat* after all."

"Astound."

"No, his name's Aghast. The horse is Aggrieved."

Jury drew horns on the goat he'd just made. "God, I hope you don't get a bunch of chickens. I'd be hearing names like Annoyed, Announced, Anesthetized—"

"Oh, please. Who'd ever name a chicken Anesthetized?"

"I'm talking to him." Jury frowned. "Let's get back to Lamb House. You'd have your own cook"—probably a lie—"and butler, too." A definite lie.

"I've already got my own cook and butler. And hermit, don't forget. I bet there's no hermit there."

Jury balled up the notepaper and aimed it toward the wastebasket. "You can be your own hermit. Lamb House strikes me as a bit of a hermitage."

"Good, then I can install Mr. Blodgett."

"Mr. Blodgett. He'd make a great installation at the Tate Modern." Mr. Blodgett was the elderly man Melrose had taken on as hermit. He was disheveled and wild-looking, although in truth a mild and sweet-dispositioned man. His main purpose was to keep Melrose's aunt away from Ardry End. His success in this quarter had been spotty. But that was no surprise.

"Anyway," said Melrose. "What's the point?"

"Of what?"

"My God! You can't even keep your mind on your own idea!"

"Oh, yes. The point is you'd find things out." Jury was doodling a hermit.

"What things?"

"I don't know, do I? That's why I want you there."

A huge sigh. "This is the Met? The Old Bill? The rozzers?"

"The Filth."

"The Filth. Wot's protectin' us from crime and chaos? No wonder you're the darling of Internal Affairs. You can be as vague as fog."

"Oh, they don't mind me anymore. Anyway, I'll have to be pushing off one of these years. Mandatory retirement, you know. I've never understood that rule. Cutting us off when we're at peak performance."

Melrose feigned uproarious laughter.

"So that means you'll do it." Jury stuck a pole in his hermit's hand and hung up.

# FIFTEEN

Church doors always seemed to thud instead of simply closing. Jury rarely heard the thud, as he so rarely visited churches. When he did, he preferred a country church, usually empty and giving the impression of sanctuary. Churches were no more sanctuaries than pubs or train stations. They were simply quieter.

He had walked around the row of pews on the left side and was standing looking into the little lady chapel, with its statue of Mary. These chapels always seemed even quieter than the rest of the church. He wondered if silence gathered in some places: a wood in deep winter; a dock where a boat moored in still water; an abandoned farm-house.

The world at large was against silence, which made it all the more restful and the more necessary when one came upon it. He stood looking at Mary and thinking of the priest. Father Martin, he bet, had been with someone he shouldn't have, or in some place he shouldn't have been. But that this had anything to do with the murder was doubtful. There was no reason to connect the two, except via the most tenuous con-nection with Billy Maples. Nothing.

He could not say how long he'd been standing there, looking at the figure of Mary, when the voice behind him made him flinch.

"Superintendent."

Jury turned, smiled at Father Martin, who did indeed look good. But Jury supposed if he himself put on those black clothes and bright white collar, he'd look good, too. Spirituality clung to those clothes. Why did he doubt what the man had—or hadn't—told him?

"Father Martin," said Jury. Turning away from the chapel, he felt the emptiness, felt the sheer, unstoppable fall from some dizzy-ing height.

"Shall we sit down for a moment?" Father Martin took one of the little chairs in the chapel and motioned for Jury to do the same. "How is your investigation going?"

"Not speedily. I can say that."

"But it only happened—what? Two days ago," said the priest.

"In that amount of time, God had nearly half the world up and running."

Father Martin laughed. It rang out in an astonishing way; the acoustics here must have been hellishly good. He'd like to hear the choir.

"So," said Jury, "all that tells me is I'm not God."

"But he doesn't have your forensic people, either."

"He doesn't need them."

Father Martin smiled and asked, "How can I help?"

"If you remember, you said you'd think for a bit about Billy Maples. Did you?"

Right now, the priest looked like one of those handsome, pale lads one sees walking with others in the grounds of a prep or public school, on their way to morning prayers or evening chapel, talking or even larking about. Right now, in the flicker of candlelight, this boy's face was full of shadows.

Father Martin sat back. "I saw him two or three times. The first was during an evening service. The next time was for confession. This was the reason I told you I needed to think about it, you see."

Jury didn't. "You mean in the confessional?"

The priest nodded. "He came into the church. When I came through from the sacristy he was sitting in one of the pews up front. He came up to me and asked if I'd hear his confession. It wasn't the hour for confession, but he seemed distraught, so I agreed, of course."

Jury waited. "And you're going to say you cannot divulge the contents."

A slight smile. "I expect so."

"Despite his having been murdered."

Father Martin looked at the floor. "Even so, I can't see what possible connection there could be between that and what he said in confession."

Surely, the man was not that stupid or disingenuous. "You're not supposed to see it, Father. I am. I get paid to see it." *Even if I don't know what "it" is.* He thought again of

Oswald's talking about James's figure in the carpet. "And that still doesn't explain why you didn't tell me this yesterday, when we first spoke."

"I'm sorry. I didn't tell you because—"

He was thinking again. Witnesses who told the truth didn't have to think about it, normally.

"Because, since I knew I wouldn't be telling you what he—what Billy—said in the confessional, I didn't see how it would help you at all to know"—the priest shrugged—"that he'd said it in the confessional."

"You know perfectly well it could make a difference, Father. A man is murdered in a hotel not far from here, a man who felt a need to confess. Dot, dot, dot. Now try and connect those dots, will you? Murder, dot; confession, dot dot; murder related to what was confessed, dot dot dot."

"I'm sorry. But if I told you nothing was said during that confession that would have anything to do with your investigation?"

"I'd say you don't know what you're talking about."

Father Martin was silent.

"Tell me about his state of mind."

"Unhappy, certainly."

"I was told Billy had dramatic mood swings, perhaps what we used to call manic depression."

"It's possible. I would of course see him in the depressive side of that. People don't generally want our help if they're manic." He gave Jury a weak smile.

"No. But you might be oversimplifying there." There were too damned many ways of looking at a problem to see an answer clearly.

"How do you mean?"

"A person torn between faith and doubt, say, wouldn't necessarily be unhappy."

The priest shook his head. "I think that would be the greatest unhappiness of all."

Jury felt the man so self-satisfied he wanted to shout: *Shut it, will you?* These clerics with their preordained solutions. Instead he said, "If you're considering the biggest question of all, happiness doesn't even come into it, does it?"

"It sounds as if you've given the matter some thought."

"No, I've given it no thought at all. Thanks for your time. I've got to be going."

Jury rose and was halfway up the aisle

when he turned and asked, "What about the third time?"

Father Martin looked puzzled. "The third time?"

"You said you'd seen him two or three times. When was the third?"

The priest frowned, thinking. "Oh, that would have been another time he came to church. Morning matins, I think."

"He wasn't a Catholic."

"For some, that doesn't keep them away."

# SIXTEEN

All of this having been said about Lamb
House—and contrary to his refusal to go—
Melrose immediately began to ready himself, if not in the sense of packing up the
Bentley, then of trying on, like traveling
clothes, various attitudes. The mere mention of Henry James did this to him, especially after that Henry James contest they
had all begun in the Jack and Hammer, having been inspired by that ridiculous con
man who'd turned up calling himself
Lambert Strether.

And if there was ever a Lady Watermouth,
she sat now opposite him on the sofa, stuffing in currant scones buttered, jammed,

and double creamed. Nothing was left to the imagination on his aunt's plate.

Melrose put aside his *Hermit News,* wondering where Mr. Blodgett had gotten to. It was high time he showed up as unkempt hermit, wild-eyed and shock-headed and raised-fisted, to rattle her and send her running. Sometimes it worked, sometimes not. Mr. Blodgett was as nice an old soul as Melrose had ever met, and it was hard for him to play the madman, no matter how much he was paid, and he was paid plenty.

Agatha (Lady Watermouth née Ardry) certainly never stopped objecting to Mr. Blodgett. "Don't you think the joke has gone far enough, Melrose?"

"No joke can." He picked up his thimble of port and *Country Life,* eager to see what the young lady of the week was doing.

"Can what?"

He leveled a look at her. "What you just said: can go far enough."

She shook her head and rolled her eyes. "Riddles, riddles."

*Country Life* was a handsome magazine; it glimmered and shimmered with a promise that largely went unkept. The doll of the week was a Miss Gertrude Frobisher-

Stauton, and she was holding a pig. Well, why not? If the magazine ever wanted to do a series on British peers who had jettisoned their titles (himself, in other words, although he imagined there must be others), he would be happy to pose holding a goat. He didn't want to break the spell his imagination could toss over this picture like a veil, so he just made up the caption. The captions were pretty much always the same, giving age and rank and—in this case—what the pig meant. It would also likely state where this lovely girl was going to school, or where she would be spending her gap year—in Miss Frobisher-Stauton's case, Paris. How terribly adventurous of her! He flipped back to the beginning of the magazine and its endless shots of overpriced properties. Melrose had actually found here the house that he had let for a few weeks in Cornwall. That was a year or so ago.

He turned another page and thought about this poor Maples chap and wondered what he had been doing at Lamb House. One would of course wonder what Maples had been doing at the hotel in Clerkenwell Road, since he'd been murdered there, but why had Billy Maples opted for the tenancy of Lamb House?

Did he love Henry James? A lot of people liked Henry James, but that didn't mean they wanted to go to bed with him, in a manner of speaking. From the story sketched out by Jury, Lamb House seemed an unlikely venue for a man like Billy Maples.

"I don't know why you read that magazine, Melrose."

"Because it's got pictures in it. I'm checking out the housing market."

"Why?"

"To see how much I could get for Ardry End."

The sound of choking coming from the sofa caused him to look over the top of *Country Life,* in hopes that the choking might lead to something. No such luck. She was scanning the room, the Oriental rug, the doors, the sconces, the ceiling molding, like a valuer.

"Don't be silly. Why on earth would you even think about selling up?" She set about robbing a fairy cake of its pale pink fluting.

He hadn't been thinking of selling, but it was a tack to take: "Why not? It's too big for

me to be rattling around in all on my own."
He decided to throw out another delicious
prospect. "Of course, I could marry, have a
few children . . ."

Agatha stopped the fairy cake halfway to
her mouth and exclaimed, "What? And who
in heaven's name would you marry?"

He had returned to the photo of the honorable Gertrude Frobisher-Stauton. "I met a
lovely young lady the last time I was in
London at my club. Gertie Frobisher. We
talked at length. She was a bit young, perhaps, but that signifies nothing these days.
She loves farm animals. She'd be great with
Aghast." He went back to his magazine.

"That's absolutely ridiculous!"

"No, it's true. She has a penchant for
pigs."

"I'm not talking about that, I'm talking
about her marrying you!"

"Lots of women would marry me. I'm rich,
I have this estate." Here he swept his arm
round the room. "And my father was the
seventh earl of Caverness."

"And you are no longer the eighth earl, in
case you've forgotten." She simpered,
proud of the point she'd made.

Hmph! "Oh, most women don't give a

damn for a title anymore." He again regarded the Honorable Gertrude. They didn't? Since when? Even the pig looked as if it would not eschew a title.

"You're wrong there, I can tell you!"

Well, she should know, not being Lady Ardry at all, but having decided to call herself that after her husband (who was another "honorable") had died. He'd also been Melrose's uncle, who'd had the great misfortune of being in the wrong place at the wrong time.

"No, I'm not wrong at all. Gertie is quite all right with my not having a title. She has one of her own. It probably makes her feel a little superior."

"Well, really. You wouldn't want to marry a woman who felt she was better than you!"

"Why not? It would keep her from messing in my affairs, as she'd think her own were more important."

Another scone half was being marmaladed. "Is she from a good family?"

"A pig-farming one."

Agatha actually set her scone down on her small glass plate. "Pig? *Pig farmers!* Now I know you can't be serious!"

"I see nothing objectionable. She wants to bring along several of them. She's afraid she'd miss them."

"Surely, you're not acquiescing to this monstrous plan!"

Melrose was looking at the honorable G. F.-S., raking the paragraph under her picture for fresh ideas. What amazed him was that Agatha apparently thought Melrose had indeed proposed marriage, despite his telling her he had only just met Gertrude. "When she's finished her gap year. She intends to spend it in Zimbabwe, working as a volunteer with Médicins Sans Frontières."

"What on earth is that?"

"Doctors Without Borders. They got the Nobel Peace Prize, in case you didn't know."

"Are you saying she's a doctor?"

"No, of course not. Although she's thinking about veterinary medicine."

Then it struck Agatha, apparently, that Gertrude was still in school. "Gap year! Melrose, how old is this person?"

"Oh, twentyish." G. F.-S. was more eighteenish, according to the magazine.

"You're old enough to be her father!"

"Yes, but I'm not." He slapped the arms of his cozy chair and rose. "Well, I'm off!"

"The Jack and Hammer, I expect."

"For a farewell drink. Then, to Rye."

That stopped a rock cake in midair. Twice in a morning, a record! "What are you talking about? That's the coast of Sussex, for heaven's sakes."

"The last I heard. Don't get up. I'll see myself out."

# SEVENTEEN

Trueblood, looking out of the Jack and Hammer's bay window, said, "But this is perfect!" He looked at Melrose. "Take it as a sign!"

Melrose, occupying the window seat with Vivian, turned, as did Vivian. Joanna stood up to see. Diane Demorney didn't bother.

"Agatha and, would you believe it, our own Mr. Lambert Strether."

That got Diane's attention. "How marvelous! We can continue the Henry James experiment."

"Here they come," said Joanna. "Here they come."

The five of them arranged themselves for the encounter.

A gust of air wrapped them in its chilly embrace as the outside door was shoved open and the two appeared.

"Agatha!" exclaimed Melrose. "That was quick. I just left you at the house. And I do believe it's Mr. Strether."

"Yes, Mr. Strether," said Diane. "We wondered where you'd got to. You left in such a rush."

Trueblood and Melrose had risen to shake the impossibly named Lambert Strether's hand. Trueblood pulled a couple of chairs around from another table and insisted the two join them. Strether barked out an order to Dick Scroggs for a gin and tonic and a shooting sherry. Dick did not regard Lambert Strether—as did the other five—as a source of horseplay. Dick merely thought him an idiot.

"Now Strether, are you riding around on your horse, or mine, looking at property?" said Melrose.

Strether gave a bellicose laugh. "*Your* horse? Neither. But I have indeed viewed some property. If you recall, I was interested in the old pub on the hill."

"The Man with a Load of Mischief," said Vivian.

"And I believe it was you"—here he looked at Joanna—"who led me to believe you were buying it?"

Joanna had about as much interest in the pub as in a flea circus, but she nodded to him.

Strether smiled meanly. "Except the agent said there was no offer on the table."

Joanna wrote some words in her notebook with a flourish. "That agent. She's so absent-minded, it's absurd."

Said Strether, "It's a *he!*"

"See what I mean?" said Joanna.

At this, both Agatha and Strether knit their brows. The others acted as if the answer made sense.

Strether went on. "Anyway, you might be surprised to hear that the for sale sign has come down."

"I can't remember there was ever one up," said Melrose.

"Metaphorically speaking, then."

"Melrose remembers nothing of importance," said Agatha, taking the sherry from Dick's tray, after which Dick set down the gin and tonic.

"Actually," said Strether, pausing to drink. "I've inherited it." His smile put his tarnished teeth on vivid display.

"How do you like that?" Agatha said, as if she'd just trumped every ace in their deck. She was pleased as punch that Mr. Lambert Strether had thrown a spanner in the works, whatever the works and whatever the spanner. "So you see, the Mischief will be opening soon!"

Strether had the grace to appear humble. "Let's not count our chickens, Lady Ardry."

If one could call the objets d'art in Ardry End chickens, Agatha was always counting them, apparently convinced that, number one, she would inherit the lot and, number two, Melrose, some thirty years younger, would die first.

"I don't understand," said Trueblood, pretending to be vexed by all of this. "When you were here before—and it's only been a couple of weeks—you did not know about your good luck, or your inheritance."

"We-ll, I didn't know for a certainty, so I wasn't prepared to raise the point, especially after you"—he tilted his head in Joanna's direction—"said you were buying it."

Not rising to the bait, Joanna simply

turned a page of her marked-in-red manuscript.

Melrose said, "Now, the last owner was a man by the name of Matchett, Simon Matchett. Before that, it was a Mr. Lipseed, who owned it for some time before he got arrested. Before him we had a woman named Elerbee and her seven children. Now that's going a long way back." Indeed, it was so far back that Melrose hadn't the slightest idea where it would lead. The pub could have been owned by his goat, Aghast, for all he knew, in partnership with his hermit, Mr. Blodgett. "Hence I'm wondering, Mr. Strether, just who these ancestors of yours were."

Strether poured the rest of his gin down his throat and smiled. "A great-great-great-granduncle and -aunt, the White-Winterbothams."

"White-Winterbotham? The only time I've heard that name was in connection with a triple murder in Clapham. A grisly affair. Are these your people?"

"Of *course* not. It's an old, old family from Yorkshire. They've had their share of OBEs."

"We've had our share of DUIs but it hasn't

got us anywhere." Trueblood was severing the tip from one of his Montecristo cigars. Rarely did he smoke one.

Vivian said, "This is the first we've heard about anyone's having a connection to the pub. It's been well over a decade since it was occupied. That was when Mr. Matchett ran it. And since he had no wife, no children, no relations at all, he left The Man with a Load of Mischief to the village. Long Piddleton. Yes, we thought that extremely generous of him."

*No, he didn't and no, we didn't, certainly not after he made a pig's breakfast of everything on his way out of town,* thought Melrose.

There were wide eyes and slightly open mouths when Vivian produced this bit of high history, and from other than Mr. Strether.

"Well, Vivian," said Trueblood, fascinated by her inventiveness. "You're right. I'd forgotten that. Damned decent of him."

But Strether was not giving up so easily. "I'm sorry to disappoint you, Miss—"

"Rivington."

"Miss Rivington. But the White-Winterbothams passed it on to their progeny.

Perhaps this Matchett fellow was landlord, just renting it. He hadn't it within his power to dispose of it."

"You can prove all of this, Mr. Strether?" inquired Melrose.

Mr. Strether was looking over his shoulder, trying to corral Dick Scroggs for another gin. So Agatha answered for him. "Certainly he's got proof. The documents are with his lawyer in London."

Scroggs came with another gin, half of which Strether got down in one go. He sat and gave a bleary smile.

Diane, smoking in her languid way, said: "I think, Mr. Strether, you might find your claim to this pub less certain than you suppose. You are not, you know, the only claimant."

Both Lambert Strether and Agatha looked at her narrowly. Diane was a complete mystery to Agatha. An unpleasant one.

"If you're talking about this village's inheriting, as I've just said—"

"No, no," said Diane. "The claims are far more certain than that."

Now all of them were leaning slightly toward her, all with a curious gaze.

"Then what on earth are you talking about?"

"Well, good heavens, Agatha, are you so out of touch with Long Piddleton you don't *know*?" Diane's smile was crafty.

Agatha hesitated, "Well, yes, I do have my ear to the ground . . ."

*And the wall and the door and the keyhole,* thought Melrose, who was himself fascinated by what Diane had just said.

Lambert Strether looked at her, hoping probably for some cue. He returned his gaze to Diane. "Exactly what are you talking about?" He could not keep the anxious note out of his voice.

"About the many claims to the property? It's a bit mixed up. You know. Extremely difficult to sort: whose father was whose son or whose cousin was whose wife or whose aunt was whose grandmother. Well, you get the picture." Diane raised her glass as if toasting confusion. "And all of them, at least the ones we know about, all of them have the papers. Why do you think the old pub has been untenanted for fifteen years?"

Agatha shut her mouth and opened it again. "I don't know what on earth you're on about. I know nothing of this." To her companion she said, "Lambert, are we going?"

Lambert Strether looked disinclined to leave the present company. He clearly wanted to hear more.

"Come on, Lambert! They haven't a grain of sense among them."

Fully baffled by this turn in the talk, he mumbled a yes-yes and drank off his gin and tonic. "Let's go, then, shall we?"

They rose—neither of them leaving even a deposit on the table toward their drinks— and bundled themselves out the door.

"Now what in hell? White-Winterbotham?" said Melrose. "Well, he couldn't possibly have any legal right to the place, surely."

"Diane, I'm intrigued. You certainly put the wind up our local confidence man. What are you thinking of?"

"*Bleak House,* obviously. You know, the interminable legal battle over Jaundice and Jaundice."

"Jarndyce," said Melrose. "Jarndyce and Jarndyce. Are you telling us you read *Bleak House*?"

"Not the entire book, no, probably the only one who did was Dickens. But I did skim over the marvelous legal and court-room scenes; they reminded me of my divorces. As far as wrangling is concerned, Dickens is right on the money. Thank God there weren't estate agents tossed into the mix or he would've died with the book unfinished."

"It rattled our friend Strether, certainly," said Vivian.

"Rattling isn't enough," said Diane. "No." She sipped her drink and drew in on her cigarette. "No, Mr. Strether does not give up easily." Diane looked through the scrim of smoke with narrowed eyes.

They waited. She thought. Thinking was not an experience that came around every day for Diane. "We need a few strangers—or at least strangers to Mr. Strether—which shouldn't be too hard." Diane looked around the room, her eyes falling on Dick's char.

Undescended from Cinderella, Mrs. Withersby was taking her rest, sitting on one of the trestle benches on either side of the fire, which roared along like the last steam engine to leave Victoria. Mrs. Withersby spat into the fire. The fire spat back.

"Do you think she could round up a few of her nearest and dearest? She has relations, doesn't she?"

"By all accounts, yes."

"Would she do it for fifty quid, d'you think?"

"She'd do it for fifty pee, Diane. She'd do it for a fag."

"Let's call her over."

It was unusual that they'd have to, as Mrs. Withersby ordinarily found some excuse to hang around their window table to cadge cigarettes and gin.

"Shall I ask her if she wants to earn a bit of money?"

That was like asking a cactus if it would like to spend a while in the sun and sand.

"What've you got in mind, Diane?" Melrose was absolutely fascinated that Diane had anything at all in mind. Although, he reminded himself, she had worked out a brilliant scheme for getting rid of Vivian's old flame. Count Dracula had beat it back to Florence after Diane shot a few home truths at him. Perhaps getting rid of people was her forte? Perhaps she should get mobbed-up?

Diane must have been reading his mind.

"Melrose, you'll have to keep Agatha out of the way."

"Permanently?"

"Sorry," she said to him with a sly smile. "Just for this; just to get rid of Mr. Strether."

"How?"

"What I said before: Jaundice—"

"Jarndyce."

"Right." She sighed. "I wish Richard Jury were here. He added such panache to Mr. Strether's departure the first time."

They all agreed and sent up a collective sigh.

"But I suppose," Diane added, "he's got other things to do."

# EIGHTEEN

He had other things to do, yet they all seemed to take the form of Lu Aguilar. That voice: he had never paid much attention to its tone and timbre before because they'd been otherwise engaged. And the phone talk had never been more than a handful of words, until this morning, as she was speaking at length—or for her, at length. She was calling from the Zetter.

"Aren't you dressed yet?"

He had the phone in the curve of his shoulder, rather wishing it were her face. He was tying a shoelace. "It's eight a.m."

"Half the world's at work by now."

"That would be your half, I take it?"

"I'm in the dining room. I've just ordered breakfast. I said not to take the other place setting away."

"That would be for me, would it?"

She took the question as rhetorical. "I ordered granola."

Jury set down his half-drunk tea. "Not my dish. I'm full English breakfast to the hilt."

"We need to put our heads together."

"Is that what it's called these days?"

"Don't be bloody stupid. Come on."

*Click.*

Jury drank off his tea and pulled on his coat. He took the stairs beyond his door three at a time.


The Zetter's dining room had a fair number of customers and yet the tables were far enough apart that you weren't putting your spoon in another table's granola—an image Jury found faintly erotic. He smiled.

It was what Lu was eating, a mountainous bowl of granola, topped with rhubarb. She was wearing a stoplight red sweater, but her face still looked sleepy. He sat down before the other place setting and he watched her shove a spoonful of the cereal in a mouth he'd gotten to know well. "Rhubarb?"

"Can you imagine? If you don't like granola, believe me, this will change your mind." She spooned up a cluster of grains, nuts, and rhubarb and held it to his mouth.

The gesture was so intimate, he felt like booking a room. "You're right," he said as he chewed it. "It's good."

"Here comes your breakfast now."

"How did you know—"

Her look said *oh, please.*

The fresh-faced waitress put down Jury's plate: eggs, bacon, mushrooms, tomato.

He was hungrier than he'd thought. He plowed right in. The eggs were so perfectly cooked they were luminous.

"Tell me about Rye. You saw Kurt Brunner?"

Jury told her what they'd said.

"Do you like him for this shooting?"

"I don't know yet. If he was the one coming to see Billy, I'd find that odd."

"Why?"

"Brunner would hardly make an appointment to see him; he saw him every day."

She nodded, sat back. "Are you done?" She eyed his plate.

"Almost. More coffee?" He picked up the French press. She shook her head. He poured more for himself.

"I've been eating this granola for twenty minutes and the bowl's still full. I want to go up to the room."

"The crime scene. You want me to go? Us?" He tried to make the "us" bristle with implications, all unwise.

Aguilar rolled her eyes. "This is a murder investigation—"

Jury sniggered and polished off his last bit of egg.

"And we have *some* self-control, I'd hope."

"Maybe I do, but you don't."

She balled up her napkin and tossed it at him.

Upstairs, Jury kept his distance.

She was reviewing a probable sequence of events. "He comes in, tosses his key card down, picks up the phone to call room service. Maybe at some point, he uses the bathroom. He orders his supper." Aguilar sat in the chair at the long shelf where the tray had been, picked up the phone receiver, set it down. Then she rose and stood looking at Jury, but he didn't think she was seeing him. She looked bemused. "Why didn't he take off his jacket? You'd have done, wouldn't you?"

"Perhaps. Perhaps not. There might have been other things of greater immediacy."

"Such as?"

"Phone calls. He calls room service, he makes another call. Or calls."

"But that doesn't explain *after* the food comes. *Especially* before he ate something as messy as that hamburger. Mustard, ketchup drips, and you're eating with your hands, too. That Italian-designer jacket? Armani, was it? What was it? You'd take that off, surely."

"Maybe he did and then put it on again."

She thought about that. She went on: "He makes another phone call, and then goes out to the terrace." She trailed her little story out there.

He followed, stood near the table in the corner against the wall.

She was leaning on the balustrade, wind blowing her hair. "He stood out here. . . . He didn't smoke, did he?"

"Not if this ashtray is evidence." Jury

picked it up from the table, set it back, leaned against the wall. It was an open invitation.

She walked around the table, pressed him back.

"This is a crime scene, love," he said. The wind virtually blew the words across her face.

Close to his mouth, she said, "So's your flat."

"Told you."

"Told me what?"

"No self-control."

"Ha. I'm going to the station." She stepped back. "What about you?"

"The Melville Gallery. I've a thirst for art."

"Or something." She smiled and turned away.

# NINETEEN

The tall, very blond girl named Hilda Tripp who worked at the Melville Gallery said, "He was just so generous." She made a pass at her eyes with a sodden tissue. "Most artists, as you can appreciate, have a hard time making ends meet."

Jury said, "Billy Maples put up his own money to help some of your artists, is that right?"

She nodded as she pushed up the sleeves of her vivid lavender cashmere sweater. She was remarkably blond; her eyes remarkably empty, except of tears. It surprised Jury that a person with such little affect would be working in the heady environs of the Melville Gallery. Yet she had been for six years, stationed here to greet customers, so perhaps he was wrong about the emptiness of the eyes.

The owner was out, so Hilda would try, she said, to help about the Billy Maples case.

"We were devastated," said Hilda.

Jury nodded. "It was a blow, I expect. Do you know anyone who might have wanted to harm him?"

She shook her head in such a decisive manner that her pale hair swirled above her shoulders like wheat in the wind. "Not given the way he was."

"What way was that?"

"He was, you know, like an angel. I mean, the way West End theaters and Broadway plays have them."

"You mean a benefactor?"

"That's right. And he'd do it through the gallery, anonymously. He'd arrange with Linda—Linda Bevins, the owner—to give the money to whatever artist he wanted to have it. You know, an angel, as I said."

"I know. But after he'd done this more than once, the painters must have worked it

out that he was the 'angel.' " Jury smiled.
He liked the word in this context.

"Not really. Linda would say it was one or
another elderly art lover who wished to
remain anonymous. And it wasn't based on
which artist was the best. There were other
conditions."

"What were they? The criteria?"

"Of course they would have to have a lot
of talent, but they would, wouldn't they, if
they were showing here? Then there was
need. Some of these paintings sell for a
great deal more than others. For instance,
there's this one by Calvin Lipp." Here she
moved Jury to a large canvas on the west
wall suffused in natural light. "It sold for four
thousand pounds."

Jury's eyebrows shot up. Not only at the
amount but at what the four thousand had
bought. It was a generic scene, bucolic, of
sheep in a field with trees. No matter how
the painting had tried to disguise its ordinar-
iness with a blur of brush strokes, it was
simply representational and boring.

Hilda apparently thought so, too. She
whispered, although the few people in the
gallery were well out of earshot, "Calvin

thinks he's another Constable. Can you imagine?"

Jury laughed. "No, I can't. But the one who bought it apparently thought he was. So I take it that this Calvin Lipp would not be a front-runner for Mr. Maples's largesse?"

The hair swung again, decisively. "Definitely not."

"How often did he do this? Was it an annual contribution?"

"Oh, much more often than that. When he sees—saw—work that he was especially enthusiastic about."

"He came here frequently, then?"

She nodded. "He was at the reception for Getz Johns. It wasn't very well attended."

"That was the same night—"

Sadly, she smiled, and again dabbed at her eyes.

"What prompted this role of benefactor? He wasn't a painter himself, was he?"

"No. But he seemed so sympathetic to the whole process, to the whole notion of art. Well, I don't know. I don't know how to put it or what prompted him." She frowned slightly, as if in not knowing she had somehow failed. "Excuse me—"

A phone was ringing somewhere and she took herself off to answer it.

Jury looked around; there were only three people in the gallery besides himself and Hilda: a boy and girl holding hands, both with backpacks, both in jeans; a middle-aged man in an expensive overcoat with a dark green velvet collar, who had been standing for a long time before an ambrosial concoction of clouds as plump as marsh-mallows in a sky of liquid blue.

The whole thing, Jury thought, might just leap off the wall. He wondered why it hung here, it was so wrong—even he, hardly a judge of art, thought it bad—except, per-haps it wasn't. After all it was here and had captured the attention of a perfectly intelli-gent looking viewer. Jury wanted to ask him, to go over and pin him down about the painting's artistic merit.

But the experience set him thinking about Billy Maples and how Jury suspected peo-ple, including himself, had got him wrong. His attention drifted, like the marshmallow clouds themselves, to the painting. Getting Billy Maples wrong, or not telling the truth.

While he waited, he decided to join the gentleman in front of the cloud painting.

After a few moments, Jury said, "I guess I just don't see it."

The man in the overcoat glanced at him, not bothered by a stranger's interrupting his meditation on clouds. "Don't see what?"

"Well, you've been looking at this for a long time. Apparently you think it's rather good."

The observer's smile was thin-lipped but still warm and amused. "Not necessarily. But it's hanging here in this gallery, which rarely puts a foot wrong, so perhaps I've been studying it for the same reason you've been studying me. Trying to work out why they'd hang such a bloody awful painting. At least that's how I see it."

Jury had been expecting a rebuff or a lecture on contemporary art, not agreement. Certainly not agreement couched in the language he himself would use. Now they were both looking at it. The little card beside it announced the painting as *Nebulae.*

"The point is, I think," began Jury's new acquaintance, "to look for a good long time before deciding whether one likes something or not."

"To be fair, you mean?"

"Yes, but not to the painting, which still

looks to me like a child's painting; no, not
fair to art, but to yourself. I imagine we'd be
the losers if we'd pronounced an artist like,
say, Roy Lichtenstein—"

"The comic book painter?"

"Yes, had we said Roy Lichtenstein was a
comic book painter."

Jury laughed. The couple who'd been
transfixed by their own painting—one of
cows—had heard and looked around and
smiled, then turned back to the cows and
laughed, too, as if the antics of these other
two had freed them to do so. They moved
on to the next painting: similar cows, different configuration. They stood each with
hands clasped behind their backs as they
rolled slightly, back and forth, on their feet.
They laughed again.

Jury wondered what had happened to
Hilda. *Jesus, what sort of copper are you
that instead of lighting dynamite under a
witness, you're standing here bouncing on
your feet? What do you think this is, Jury? A
game?* Racer wasn't there to ask the question, so Jury asked it for him, and in just as
snarly a voice.

Then, as if wondering about Hilda had
conjured her up out of fog and ashes, she

came toward him. "I'm sorry; a friend was in a bit of a muddle." She shrugged her shoulders in place of any further explanation. She turned to lead Jury into another part of the gallery.

"It's been nice talking to you," said Jury to the art lover.

"I won't be long, George," she said to him.

George nodded. "No hurry."

As they moved away, Jury said, "I take it he's a return customer."

"One who's awfully particular."

Jury would have thought that art was something to be particular about.

"I wanted to tell you about someone you might wish to speak to. She's . . . she was a friend of Billy's. I don't know how close they were but I do know they chummed about together."

It had been a long time since he'd heard that expression, but it seemed to fit this dreamy place, with its cotton candy clouds and cows and the young couple who dressed and acted in every way alike.

"Though I don't think," Hilda continued, "well, they might have been lovers. It's a woman named Angela Riffley. She lives in the West End. Mayfair. I know she's home now; that was her I was speaking to on the telephone. Here." Hilda slipped a gallery card from the silver card holder on the table, turned it over, and wrote down the address. Then she handed it to Jury. "I think they might even have been engaged at one point, though, you know, she's a bit older."

"His fiancée? Have police talked to her?" Why hadn't this woman been mentioned?

"Yes. Police were just round to her house. That's why she called."

"Thanks for your help. I'll go to see her." Jury looked at the card. "Mayfair. And the phone number?"

"It's near Berkeley Square." Hilda gave him the number and he thanked her again.

On his way out of the Melville Gallery, he stopped by the cloud painting again and shook his head again.

No sale.

# THE TALENTED MRS. RIPLEY

# TWENTY

It must have been Jury's year for lovely women, although Angela Riffley's power was to be undercut by the manner she was intent on assuming, an ostentatious air of mystery.

She gestured for him to come in. "Just go on through, Superintendent. I'm right behind you."

For a few uncomfortable moments, he was sure she literally was.

"On through" turned out to be a resplendent study or library, where she left him to take a seat, saying, "I'm just organizing some coffee; I'll be back in a moment." She was dressed in something scandalously lightweight and translucent and she seemed to leave on wings.

It was a well-furnished room, the furnishings being largely antiques that might have whetted Trueblood's appetite. An inlaid gilt and mahogany library table against the far wall; the long case clock whose tone was so dulcet—it had just struck the half hour— it might have been apologizing for time passing; a carved oak *dressoir* near the marble fireplace in front of which sat a serpentine fire fender. Dark wood paneling stopped halfway up the walls, on which hung perhaps a dozen wild animal heads— several different kinds of big cats: tiger, cheetah, leopard—as well as a zebra, a mountain goat of some kind, and others that Jury couldn't even identify. There were numerous animal skins and Jury hoped the zebra-striped love seat he was sitting on wasn't one of them. Jury thought about Ernest Hemingway. Among these trophy heads hung a few dark brown and shriveled things that he wondered about. He was sitting some distance away from this wall and had no intention of drawing any closer.

Sitting around on tables and up on wall brackets was a heady collection of Lalique

and Polish crystal and a parian figure of the
Lady of the Lake. At least that's who he
assumed the beauty in the flowing gown to
be; she was holding an oar and standing in
the front of a boat. He picked it up, checked
under the base. Minton. He had frankly
never seen such swag. He picked up and
then put down an object that looked like a
miniature stump, dark and rough-hewn, a
piece of wood or thick vine one might have
to hack one's way through in an Amazonian
forest. What the hell was it doing on the coffee table? The table itself had a glass top
that seemed to be protecting some document filled with a dense and untranslatable
language. At this point, the Wiggins defense
was coming into play: he would refuse to
ask.

Angela Riffley was back with the coffee
tray, which Jury rose immediately to help
her with.

"You're welcome, you know, to something stronger."

He smiled. "Coffee's fine."

"Well, then *I'm* welcome to something
stronger." She poured his coffee, left him
with the sugar and cream and repaired to a

drinks table, where she added ice to a few fingers of Glenlivet.

"Ice in drinks seems to be the thing these days, but I don't see why."

Returning to her seat on the sofa she said, "Decadent, isn't it?"

"It's not decadent; it just melts, that's all. Miss Riffley, I'm here about Billy Maples."

"It's Mrs., actually, and I'm devastated by Billy's death."

Interesting that marital status came before devastation.

"I'm sorry. I had the impression you were single."

"Well, of course. But I haven't always been. That's my ex's little collection there on the wall." She plugged a cigarette into a jade holder and smiled. "Norman was quite the adventurer, and I, too, though on a smaller scale."

"There were safaris, I take it?"

She laughed; it was a little like the ice cubes plinking about in her drink. "There were safaris, yes."

His look went up to the zebra's head, which struck him as particularly poignant. "Why the zebra?"

"Why *any* of them? Souvenirs."

"Then you didn't go with your husband?"

"Of course I did. I wasn't about to be left out of that male enclave."

"I was thinking about Hemingway, looking at that wall." He tilted his head toward it as if there might be a dispute as to where the "souvenirs" hung.

"Ah, yes, Ernest. We knew him. At a distance, but we knew him. My family I mean, my father. I was a small child that summer in Paris, but I can still remember sitting at a table at Flore and Ernest at the one beside ours with a friend who was telling stories and making him laugh like crazy. It might have been Scott Fitzgerald, I don't know. And after that—"

Thus her conversation went among luminaries and those lit by them, from Provence to Alpine heights, to roaring waters, to some island in the Caspian Sea, to a savage tribe in Borneo that had Jury looking back at the wall and those misshapen brown objects.

She seemed to have done everything that was doable. Except, perhaps, murder—not that she couldn't do it, but had she? He wouldn't have been surprised. In all of this geography, she wasn't attempting to avoid

Clerkenwell, Jury was pretty certain. He was also pretty certain she would be up to the murder at the Zetter, or any place else. If she hadn't been the one to barter for those shrunken things on the wall, she was just the one to display them. If she wasn't a Kurtz, neither was she a Marlow who worried about the collapse, the crumbling of civilization. Mrs. Riffley would be worried only about where she might be seated in the rubble.

No, Angela Riffley's mise-en-scène was the mysterious and exotic and her conversation was all in the interest of keeping her companion's attention. If she felt interest in her was flagging, she would leap from one smooth rock to the next in very dangerous waters. She took, really, all sorts of chances, including the one that you wouldn't believe her. For one like Mrs. Riffley, whose life was all anecdote, that could result in disaster.

Had Billy Maples been serious about this woman? Very possibly. She was entertaining, seductive, obviously rich. There wouldn't have been a question about being after Billy's money.

"I understand Billy Maples was your fiancé."

"Lover is a better word."

"You weren't planning on marrying?"

"God, no. Why would we do that?"

"Too bourgeois?"

She smiled. "Too boring."

"But you broke it off."

"Yes, by mutual agreement."

"There were no hard feelings?"

"Not at all. Ah!" she inhaled deeply. "A motive: the woman scorned. Or perhaps the older woman left for a younger?"

"Did that happen?"

"No. I'm a suspect?"

"Of course." She'd like that. "Although we like to say witness."

"Say anything you like!"

"You went about together?"

She gave him a look. " 'About'? What else is a couple to do?" She said this with a chortle. "But I haven't seen him in weeks."

"Have you been to Dust? More club than pub, really. A bit of nightlife."

"No, I've never been, actually. Was that one of Billy's haunts? Dust. That reminds me of Byron. Billy liked poetry, you know. Byron described himself as 'half deity, half dust.' Billy liked to say, 'Drop the deity half and you have me.' "

Jury smiled. "Dust. That's how he saw himself?"

"I think he would have said that's how *all* of us must see ourselves. Byron claimed he was cursed, that is, he thought the Byron name was cursed."

"Did Billy think that of the Maples name?"

Angela gave a short laugh. "Not Billy. He wasn't really into self-dramatization. Although I will say he was awfully moody, rather mercurial."

"What caused this, do you know?"

She shook her head. "There never seemed to be, you know, an actual reason."

"These places—hotel, club, church—are quite close to one another. The barman in Dust remembered Billy. The priest at Holy Redeemer had seen him in church. Indeed, Billy had taken confession."

Her eyes widened. "Billy? *Confession?* That's ridiculous."

"Was Billy then so opposed to organized religion?"

"Not at all. He simply wasn't involved. Oh, it's a long story." She waved away the long story with a gesture of her cigarette holder, stubbed out the cigarette, and planted another in it.

"I'm good for long stories."

"I'm not."

She was, apparently, not going to add to this. "Had his behavior changed at all recently? Did he seem, well, distant?"

"Preoccupied. Yes, something did change. But I don't know what caused it. What was different was hard to pin down."

"But you felt it."

"Oh, I felt it, yes."

Jury thought for a moment. "You didn't go to the art gallery reception? No, you couldn't have done because you said you hadn't seen Billy in weeks."

"That's right."

"According to Hilda Tripp, this reception was for an artist named Getz Johns."

"John Getz, that's his name. He switched the name around so it would sound more interesting. Perhaps he was thinking of Jasper. Did you see his work? It's what you'd expect. Insufferable. Like him."

Jury laughed. "It certainly sounds so. Who's the man—Kurt Brunner—that Billy shared his flat with in Sloane Street?"

"Oh. Him." A slight shrug of the shoulders. "He was somebody Billy met when he was in Germany. Berlin, I think. As Billy put it, they just fell in together. So he took Kurt on as a kind of assistant. I don't know why he'd need one. But Billy was funny that way. He didn't have many friends, but the ones he had—like me—he was very intense about."

It was clear she didn't like Kurt Brunner, possibly because she was jealous of that particular intensity. She might regard these relationships as taking away from her own. "Why did he decide to take on Lamb House?"

She looked quizzical. "Lamb House?"

"The house in Rye. It once belonged to Henry James."

"Oh, that. I've never been there."

It almost sounded as if she thought her absence or presence in Billy's affairs was what validated them. That she'd never been to Rye to see him made Jury wonder just how "intense" Billy had been about her.

She said: "I do remember his talking about it. I told him he was ridiculous for thinking he'd like living in a little town like Rye, nothing to do, no museums, no Tate

Modern *or* Britain, no theaters. I told him he'd not last more than a day there. So I expect I was wrong as he was there for months." She reached for the coffeepot, set a hand against it. "Cold. But I could do some more."

"No, thank you. I've got to be getting on."

She went with him to the door. Sadly, she said, "I'm really going to miss him."

This at least Jury could accept as utterly sincere and true.

Even Jury was beginning to miss him.

# TWENTY-ONE

Melrose Plant set his mental clock back forty years and walked into Boring's and felt right on time and right at home.

There were many gentlemen's clubs in London but none quite like this one. There was White's, there was Boodle's. There was the Garrick Club, catering for those men who shared an interest in the theater.

Boring's, on the other hand, catered to nothing. The only reason to be in Boring's today was because one had been here yesterday. Its members shared no particular interest, interest being pretty much catch as catch can when one was talking over a glass of whiskey in front of one of the lazy fireplaces, resting places for logs that drifted their flames about instead of shooting them.

Looking around, one might think the members had a lot in common, or shared some common goal, but that was in appearance only, skin deep, or newspaper deep. It was as though there used to be a world here in which members and staff "hung fire" (as James's characters are always doing), just sitting around waiting for the end of the sentence. It was delightful.

His suitcase beside him, Melrose stood in the hall, marveling at Boring's managing to look exactly the same as before. True, "before" had been only a few weeks ago, but weeks or years made no difference in Boring's. Wasn't that the same fly that hung in the golden motes of light streaming through the front windows?

Melrose's light-drenched daydream was interrupted by a voice addressing him. "Lord Ardry! So nice to have you with us again!"

On the other side of the reception desk stood a small man with a face like a walnut who looked a hundred and probably was.

Probably born in Boring's and happy to remain.

"It's Wendell, isn't it?" said Melrose. Wendell hadn't been here the last two or three times; Melrose had naturally assumed he was dead.

"That's right. How've you been keeping, m'lord?"

"Fine, just fine." Melrose took a mint from a Lalique bowl. "What room am I to be in tonight?"

"We've put you in the Dolphin Room, Lord Ardry. I hope that will be to your satisfaction." The old porter came around from behind the desk and made to pick up Melrose's case.

"No, no, thank you, Wendell. I'll do it." He was afraid the little man might drop down in a heap if he carried as much as a whiskey glass.

The Dolphin Room looked to be exactly like the room he'd had before, which had another name—Whale or Great White Shark?—all equally irrelevant. He stood looking around and was then struck by a small epiphany: Boring's was in the realm of the Platonic idea; Boring's was the idea from which all other men's clubs were fashioned. The others were but shades. Boring's was the real thing!

This pleasant realization stayed with him as he did his mite of unpacking after which he went downstairs for a drink.

Thus at seven o'clock, Melrose was seated in the Members' Room, waiting for Jury, whiskey in hand and looking, he was sure, as if he'd never left, like the little group chatting over there, or the several more in various states of somnolence. And this was the lively hour, the sacred hour when drinks are taken and dinner is soon to be.

His pals, Major Champs and Colonel Neame, were not here. He enjoyed the hush. No raised voices, no raucous laughter, no mobile phones.

He opened *The Sacred Fount,* followed the account of a house party at Newmarch that was relayed by the unbelievably nosey narrator, and thought about this singular exchange of a life force that rendered the young partner old and the old one young. So it was for the Brissendens, and so it might be for others at Newmarch, were the narrator able to discover them.

What the deuce was Henry James up to with this vampire theme? Mulling this over, Melrose held his not-quite-empty glass up over the back of his wing chair as a sign for the porter to bring another and felt it immediately slipped from his hand—damn but these porters were quick!—and a voice saying thanks.

He whipped his head around and found Richard Jury downing the last of the whiskey. He returned the empty glass to Melrose. "I needed that."

"Well, get your own."

"I intend to. What are you reading?"

The young (the only young) ginger-haired porter was sloping by with his tray and took the order for two whiskies.

"*The Sacred Fount*. It's ponderous."

"It's Henry James, for God's sakes. What would you expect?"

"Well, I can't picture Henry James writing about vampires."

"It's not about them; it's the *theme*."

"How can it be a theme if there aren't any vampires trooping in from Transylvania?"

"That's Dracula," said Jury. "He is not the only vampire in town."

"So there are vampires in the story, just not Dracula."

Trying to be patient, Jury said, "No. There are no actual, real, living—well that could be better put—no actual vampires."

"So that's what's going on with the Brissendens? There's this couple named Brissenden. The narrator is startled to see that Mrs. Brissenden looks much, much younger than she did when last he saw her, and that Brissenden, who is actually over a decade younger than his wife, now looks twenty years older." Melrose, as enamored of this tale as if he himself had written it, leaned forward in his chair. "So you see, Mrs. Brissenden is drinking at the sacred fount of her husband's life force. She is not drinking blood, but life."

"What's for dinner tonight?"

Melrose fell backward. "You didn't hear one thing of what I just said."

"Yes, I did. I drank in every bloody word."

"Very funny. Hysterical. Let's eat."


They had their long-running contest over what Boring's would be serving for dinner.

This evening Jury had guessed sole and Melrose beef.

Young Higgins snapped the big snowy napkins into their laps and said, "Tonight, we've an excellent Dover sole."

Melrose swore softly. They ordered sole.

"I've worked it out, the reason you win," said Melrose when Young Higgins had taken himself off to get the soup. "Before you come into the Members' Room you nip round to the kitchen and see what's on for dinner."

"Don't be absurd. Do you really think I'm that childish? You're just sore because you lost again. What wine are we having?" Jury had opened the wine list. "Here's a nice Côtes du Rhône for a hundred quid the half. Can you afford that?"

Melrose snatched the leather holder from Jury's hand. He settled on a Chardonnay at thirty quid and said, "Can I afford it? Why am I always paying for dinner?"

"Because you're rich."

"Well, it's a point. What have you found out?" he asked as Young Higgins placed their soup before them.

"About what?"

"About what? About the reason we're

here. About Billy Maples, about murder, about Lamb House."

"Just a bit ago I talked with Billy's former lover. They split up. She's a woman named Angela Riffley." Jury laughed and shook his head.

"What's so funny."

"It's just that she's so . . . indefatigable. I mean, I doubt there's anything you can think of she hasn't done, or at least is extremely talented in giving the impression she's done."

"Heh, heh. The talented Mrs. Ripley."

Jury laughed. "Very good. That's her in a nutshell. Everyone says Billy Maples was moody. I get the impression it might be more than moodiness. He might have been manic-depressive. Now of course we use the euphemism bipolar disorder."

"You think that was Billy's problem?"

"I know I'd like to see some medical records. Or it's quite possible that he was never diagnosed." Jury felt cheered by the displacement of soup for sole. Was there anything finer than a Dover sole? With it were new potatoes, carrots, and brussels sprouts. "Hilda Tripp—"

"Who's she?" Melrose broke off part of a bread roll.

"As far as Hilda's concerned, Billy walked on water." Jury went over the conversation in the art gallery.

"What about this Brunner chap? Or Billy's grandfather? He should know him better than almost anyone, from what you've told me."

"Sir Oswald said he had mood swings. My mood right now, for instance, is really good because once more I won the dinner contest."

"I'm glad you weren't in on the Henry James contest. I'm looking forward, actually, to Lamb House. It will be quite pleasant to steep myself in the Jamesian atmosphere."

Jury wasn't sure he liked the sound of that. "Just remember what you're there for. Don't start in writing, or anything like that, for God's sakes."

"Writing who? You?"

"Not letters. A book. Before you've been in Lamb House twenty-four hours, you'll be fancying yourself a novelist."

"Don't be absurd. Although, you know, I could finish my detective novel."

Jury speared a new potato and groaned. "With that detecting couple? Nick and Nora?"

"Norma."

"Oh, well, that's a relief. I thought you were ripping off *The Thin Man*." Jury cast about for Young Higgins. "Where is he? I'd like some more sprouts."

"Veggies."

"That's a word that should be driven to the ground with a stake through its heart. One more American expression that managed to make the transatlantic trip when it should have drowned. Why do Americans have to be so damned cute?"

"I don't know. We could ask the Boston Strangler. What am I there for? In Lamb House, I mean."

"To look and listen. Not to write a novel."

"I'm looking and listening twenty-four hours a day?"

Jury nodded.

"What, I can't entertain myself by puttering around the garden and snapping beans for the cook?"

"No. The cook, incidentally, you should keep on, along with any other staff. It's Kurt Brunner, especially, I want you to listen to."

"Should I be wired?"

Jury looked up from his Dover sole at Melrose's simpering grin. He matched it with a grin of his own. "You already are."

*What was that supposed to mean?*

# TWENTY-TWO

It was a soft April day and his lamb's wool coat was too hot. Melrose removed it and was about to toss it over a chair when he remembered whose house this was. Or had been.

Was it to be like this with every curtain and rug, every ornament and ashtray? Ashtrays made him wonder if Lamb House was a smoke-free establishment. That was a detail he hadn't stopped to consider. He would probably be taking his smokes on the stoop or in the garden. He could only hope that wasn't part of the zone, too.

It was absurd for him to feel like an intruder, as if even displacing the air he moved through was an intrusion. Would he be able to sit in a chair, drink from a cup, eat with a fork? Well, it was he who had told the lady from the National Trust that, no, he didn't need to be met at the house; he could handle the move.

He was still holding his coat. He did not see a coat cupboard or a hook and he carefully draped the coat over a banister and began his tour of the house.

Well, he would get used to it. He would come to be more relaxed. He did not convince himself that this was entirely true.

In the dining room, he inspected the James notebook that had been put on display. What elegant handwriting! To say nothing about the play of language. Together, they made Melrose feel he should never write another word. Instead of words, he'd use smoke signals.

From there he went into what was probably a sitting room and was ranging over the bookcase when he heard a throat being cleared and turned around.

The woman—ah, he had forgotten the cook!—stood there, as round as a pudding, starched and clean to the point of purification, a relic of the old days.

"You're Mrs. Jessup?"

"Yes, sir. I am sorry, sir, that I didn't open the door for you. I was out in the garden."

"That's all right. I'm very pleased you're staying on, especially since my last cooking experience occurred that time I tried to boil the neighbor's cat. I was four."

Mrs. Jessup laughed. "You're making that up, sir, aren't you?"

"Don't be too sure. Have you come to ask if I want tea?"

"Indeed I have."

"Thank heavens. I certainly do."

"And would you want it in here, sir, or in the dining room?"

"Oh, this room will do nicely."

She took herself off.

Melrose thought he should take his case upstairs and unpack, but he didn't want to. He wanted to sit in this pleasant room and look at these books, most of which, not surprisingly, were by Henry James. He wondered if they were first editions. Would the Trust leave such valuable books around for tenants to filch or visitors to cart away? Probably not, probably just later copies. He took down one of them—*The Wings of the Dove*—looked at the copyright page and saw that this indeed appeared to be a first edition. He opened the book somewhere around the middle. Here were Kate Croy and Milly Theale. He tried to remember the story. Didn't Kate set her poor lover on rich Milly in the expectation that the doomed girl would leave her fortune to the man? What manipulation! What maneuvering!

What a perfect horror of a story. But there was always the element of violence in James's novels. The torture of Charlotte— who? He couldn't think of the last name: Stant?—in *The Golden Bowl*. The Ververs might just as well have tossed acid in her face as send her off to the States where she would never have the joy of London society or the Prince again. And the worst punishment of all was that everyone knew what was going on, except poor old Charlotte. And yet no one would speak of it. As with all of James, it was one thing to be gliding smoothly over the frozen lake's surface; but quite another when the hatchets were brought out to break the ice.

*The Portrait of a Lady.* The dreadful, dreaded Gilbert Osmond. Talk of torture! And of course there was *The Sacred Fount*. Melrose had never really thought about this side of James. Violence muffled by the most exquisite and civilized conversation.

He wondered about this all the while his tea was brought, poured, drunk.

Not that it had anything to do with the murder of Billy Maples.

A young man—worldly, rich, and hand-some—decides to take up residence in an ancient port town in what had once been the home of a famous writer. A house he could inhabit only by going through the venerable, no doubt exacting, National Trust. He himself had not been subjected to such scrutiny, since it was arranged by a Scotland Yard superintendent:

*"You mean,"* Melrose had said to Jury, *"they're taking me on such short notice and without digging up my past and so forth?"*

*"They can't afford to be picky."*

Melrose wasn't sure he'd liked the sound of that.

He looked around the room as if it might offer up some clue as to Billy's behavior.

Scones, raspberry jam, clotted cream. He looked at the tea tray that had been set before him and sighed. Putting a spoonful of jam on a scone, he could almost sympa-thize with his aunt's devotion to the afternoon ritual. Except Agatha did not partake of the silence that should surround it. As was this silence. Melrose sat back with a deep sense of contentment. Except for the long case clock ticking away and a small clatter coming from the kitchen, there was nothing to be heard. The rain had stopped; the sun shone wetly on the garden wall. A writer's house, pure and simple.

Had Billy fancied himself a writer, then? No. There had been no hint of that from the people Jury had talked to. Melrose couldn't imagine any writer keeping his mouth shut about his work for long. He would be passing around pages and even paragraphs to his friends while talking their ears off. Billy Maples would certainly have said something about it. It could of course have been a secret ambition, but to realize it he would surely have had to be deluding himself if he thought it would help to live in a dead writer's house.

He turned and looked at the books behind him, James's collected works, and felt fairly numbed by them. Characters tumbled through his mind, people so meticulously drawn that not a hair, not a pore, went unaccounted for.

The clock chimed and he realized he'd been holding the same scone in his hand for a quarter of an hour. Pleased to know he could master such a state of inertia, he thought he should move about a bit, as a man on a long railway journey decides to leave his seat and move up and down the aisle. He didn't get up.

He set his cup in the saucer, thinking them rather fine to be trotted out for anyone who happened to be a tenant here. He sat for another few minutes. He thought he should take his case up and unpack and rose, then sat back down. The chair was by now molded to his contours. Was he going to invest insensate objects with sense? That was more the Poe school of thought than the Henry James one.

Melrose reached behind him and pulled out a collection of James's stories, one that included "The Lesson of the Master." He remembered this story because he had found it rather menacing: a renowned writer advised the narrator, an up-and-coming one, never to marry, as the demands of marriage would weaken his writing arm considerably. He would begin to write for money, which is what the older writer had come to, seeming to blame his wife for much of this as she had encouraged the inclination to write slick books for which he was handsomely compensated.

But James had done something rather horrible here. At the end, after the successful writer's wife dies, he turns right around and marries the girl whom his young writer friend had sacrificed for the sake of his writing. Melrose wondered what the "lesson" actually was. Was it merely self-serving? He closed the book and thought about it. Then he closed his eyes.

"I beg your parden, sir . . ."

The cook was hovering over him. "I believe you must've fallen asleep. I'm sorry to bother you, but I must be chugging along now."

Melrose was stunned that he'd gone to sleep. He never slept in the afternoon. Not that he hadn't tried when Agatha was there. "Oh, Mrs. Jessup. I expect I just nodded off."

"The trip probably tired you."

The trip had been less than an hour and a half.

"Anyway," she said, "I've got to be somewhere at six-thirty, so I've left your dinner in the fridge and on the hob, all except the chop, which will be no trouble for you at all. It's marinating now. Then the veggies are all done, and you only need to pop them in the oven to heat up. Or the microwave . . ." She went on.

*Pull up a chair,* thought Melrose. In the time she was explaining what he was to do—and he could hardly keep a straight face, seeing himself with that marinated chop—the meal could have been cooked and eaten and the two of them could be telling each other their life stories over coffee and brandy.

"That's perfectly all right, Mrs. Jessup. I'll just poke about on my own. Dinner will be no problem." Especially since he meant to go to the Mermaid Tavern right up the street and order it.

"Well, then." And she turned to go.

"The gentleman who lived here before . . ." He watched her hand fall away from her coat.

"Mr. Maples, you mean. I still can't believe it."

"Sit down for a moment, would you?"

She sat and looked vacantly out of the window.

"I read about that in the paper," said Melrose. "One never knows whether newspapers give the whole story. Still, it did seem very peculiar."

"It was that, indeed. I'll never understand it."

He felt she said this as one who, for some reason, should. The topic had certainly stilled her, as if now she had no place to be at six-thirty. "He lived in London, did he?"

"In Chelsea, yes. Sloane Street."

"Seems a bit strange, doesn't it, a chap like that taking on a National Trust property."

"No stranger than you, sir." Then she seemed to realize this was impertinent and apologized.

He was a bit jolted by that response. But he smiled and said, "Not at all."

She blushed and hurried on. "I mean, you're to be here for such a short time, I was told."

"That's perfectly true." He smiled. "Favor for a friend."

"I appreciate you keeping me on, sir. It'll just give me some time to find another place before the permanent tenants move in."

"Perhaps they'll want you to stay, too."

"I don't think so, sir. People who take up

tenancy here, it's not usual for them to have staff."

They were getting wide of the mark and he inched the talk back to Billy Maples. "Did he strike you as"—what stupid question was this going to be, *as the type who'd get himself murdered?*—"as a person who was terrifically fond of Henry James's books?"

She thought about this. "I do know he liked reading these ones. Well, I've tried reading them, several times. I can't make any sense out of them, either."

Melrose liked the "either." It was as if the murder of Maples and the words of Henry James were of equal weight.

"Was he a very sociable person? Given this"—Melrose looked round the room, gestured to take it all in—"this house and this small town, I'd think he was somewhat reclusive."

"To tell the truth, sir, yes, he did like society. He sometimes went back to his London flat for a day or two here and there. As I see it, he was a bit spoiled. I think he was used to having things done for him. Maybe that was the reason for Mr. Brunner—that was his assistant, though I don't know what needed assisting—but Mr. Brunner was the one he spent his time with. You'd think a rich and handsome man such as he, Billy Maples, quite the London playboy, I shouldn't wonder, would have a string of lady friends after him but I never saw one."

She didn't go on, perhaps because what she was saying was so disapproving, so Melrose fell back upon the subject of James. "Could he have been writing something himself, say, a book about Henry James?"

"Oh, I shouldn't think so, sir. Never saw him writing anything but the odd letter. If he was doing such a big project as a book, I expect he'd've mentioned it."

The long case clock chimed the half hour.

"Oh, good heavens, it's gone half-six. I must go." She rose and so did Melrose, who helped her with her coat. "That was an excellent tea, Mrs. Jessup. Thank you."

" 'Twas nothing. Now for supper you just take that chop from the marinade and slip it in the oven for about thirty minutes. But you'll want to check it after twenty, as that oven's always been kind of dodgy."

He smiled. "It won't fool me."

She laughed merrily and went out.

Melrose wandered.

He wandered into the next room where hung a series of portraits of James at various periods in his life. They were all by John Singer Sargent and all wonderful, especially the last and justly famous. Sargent had caught the intellectual power of the man. Just looking at it, Melrose felt bathed in acuity, intelligence. James's quick bright eyes, his domed forehead. Melrose felt his own forehead to see if there was any resemblance. He guessed not.

He sat himself down in a Windsor chair and stared at it. *What is it that brought this young man here? Come on, you saw him every day. Was it something of a spiritual search, and if so, I wouldn't have thought you'd be chosen for that sort of pilgrimage.* Or maybe Melrose was dead wrong about that.

Melrose sighed deeply. He was tired of trying to work things out for himself. *You're restraining a laugh, Mr. J., aren't you?*

He sat in the chair, looked at James through narrowed eyes and chewed at the corner of his mouth. *Of course . . .*

A spiritual guide? James himself had joined the Anglican Church, but leaving out the church just for the sake of argument. *Why wouldn't you make a spiritual guide?*

Melrose sat for a few more minutes and then, fed up with feeling like a rhetorical question, he slapped the chair arms and rose and went to the stairs, where his coat lay over the bannister.

He looked at his suitcase and decided that he could unpack later; right now he wanted to walk the cobbled streets of Rye.

# TWENTY-THREE

It was a dreamy little town, stone streets no wider than lanes, shining now with rain and the ghostly light of dusk drawing in. The days were getting a little longer.

As long as he was here on the Sussex coast, he should do something touristy, take a walk back through history: Battle of Hastings and the whole 1066 thing. On second thought, he might overload his mind if he started with all that—it was already threatening to short-circuit on Henry James—and if there was anyone who could cause an electrical meltdown it was James.

He was walking up Mermaid Street to the tavern, looking at the life going on behind lit windows, a life blurred and indistinct seen through the leaded glass.

The Mermaid Tavern, now genteel and with its quite good restaurant, had once been a raucous, riotous pirate hangout. There was a famous gang—Hawkhurst? Hawksmoor? No, that was the architect. The gang had holed up in the Mermaid. The entire town, the entire coast around here had been the haunt of smugglers.

Melrose wondered if Henry James had been attracted by Rye's piratical past. Probably. Some of his finer characters were emotional looters, that was certain. Look at Gilbert Osmond, on the surface a refined and worldly collector of artifacts. And people, and souls. It was the refinement, the gentility, the perfect calculation and calibrated behavior that made what he was doing so dreadful.

In the past few days, Melrose had read a great deal of James. In his coat pocket now, accompanying him to dinner, was "The Aspern Papers." Talk about *loot*! Talk about spoilation! He hit his fist into his hand. It was so *perfect*!

"I beg your pardon?"

A voice at his elbow. Melrose must have bumped into this man.

"You were saying something?"

"Oh. I'm awfully sorry. One of those mental conversations."

"It was getting out of hand," came the smiling rejoinder.

Melrose laughed and felt sheepish and for some odd reason turned up his coat collar.

The Mermaid Tavern being full and with no prospect of a table for a half hour, Melrose chose another, far less renowned eatery. The surroundings here were comprised of a lot of dark wood, softly lit with the pleasant tinkle of cutlery tapping on china.

He was shown a table by a hostess of questionable provenance, as the accent seemed to hover somewhere between Ste. Germain-des-Prés and Bermondsey. She handed him a menu and flitted away. There were few other diners and a menu fueled largely by wishful thinking and a very big freezer. (Could they really have enough chefs back there to prepare lobster broiled, boiled, scampi, or thermidor; *pollo rostizado estilo Yucatán;* and the far more mundane *boeuf Burgundy*. This menu was a testament to optimism. He was surprised it didn't offer escalloped peacock and ragout of brindled ocelot.

He could hardly wait to see the wine list!

And here it was, handed him by the hostess, before she whisked the other place setting away.

The *carte de vin* lived up to the menu. There must have been a half dozen pages of offerings, running from the house plonk (cheap enough at five pounds for the half carafe) to a Vosne Romanée at a price that would purchase Sandringham.

Good lord! This was Rye! East Sussex! Not the Place Vendôme! Not the Ritz! It'd be hard to flog this list in Mayfair.

When the waitress came, a stout, Germanic-looking blonde, but with a beaming smile, he ordered the most elaborate dish on the menu, which he had to point to, since he couldn't pronounce it. All he knew was *poisson,* and its preparation looked as if it had been choreographed by Tommy Tune.

"Will you be having wine, sir?"

"Oh, absolutely! I'll have the Vosne Romanée."

As if she used this wine for mouthwash,

she didn't blink an eye, wheeled on her heel, and marched off, presumably to get it. Melrose only wished Henry James were here. What would he make of this setup?

The wish being father to the thought, Henry took the seat opposite and answered the question: *Well, it's all perfect for you, dear fellow, I, however, am a man of simpler tastes. A good boiled potato and chop are all I require. Remember, there's one in your oven.* With that he used a small tool to cut off the end of his cigar.

Melrose waited, humming. He wished Jury were here to place a bet. He wondered if the expressionless couple one table over would like to place one. They looked as if they'd never had a drink in their lives. Well, that's what life is like if you're a teetotaler.

Ah! Here she came with a bottle in tow.

Breezily, the waitress said, "Sorry, but we just served our last bottle of that wine. Our sommelier—"

(How he loved that!)

"—said as how you might enjoy this in its place." She turned the bottle so that he could peruse the label. "Not so pricey, nei-ther." She was delighted to give him this information.

It bore no resemblance to the Vosne (at least as he imagined that noble wine).

"This is a Beaujolais," he replied, in good humor. Surely, he could outwit this raw country girl!

She stood there with her bright face beaming. "Chef thought it would complement your dish, better'n that other one, anyway."

Across the table, Henry stuck his thumb in his waistcoat pocket and laughed.

"Perhaps it would complement it, but I prefer the insult of a Vosne Romanée." Melrose opened the wine list, which she had not collected, drummed his fingers on it and hit on the next least-likely bottle. "How about the Musigny? The Grand Cru?"

"I'll see, sir." She breezed off with her bottle of plonk and her self-assurance.

Melrose grew quite merry. He was in for an evening of deceit, evasion, and manipulation.

Henry had to comment, of course: *I'd be happy to wager ten guineas that she wins round two.* With this he drew out his worn leather billfold and slapped a note on the table.

Melrose was astounded at this profligacy.

*You don't seriously think this place is going to have the Musigny?*

*Oh, but they don't have to have it. That's the point, isn't it?* Henry smoked his cigar.

*In a moment, he's going to blow smoke rings,* thought Melrose.

He did.

She was back *tout de suite.*

"Oh, we *are* sorry, sir—"

*We.* Now it was a conspiracy!

"—but we didn't get our delivery of the Musigny."

As if it were brought around on a milk float!

"But our sommelier suggests this—"

A Mosel! He opened his mouth to object to this lunatic substitution, when she said— *whispered* as if it were the best-kept secret in Rye—"It's a very good year."

Melrose looked at the label. "It's a 1975. The musk is still wet behind the ears. It's a Riesling—white."

That hardly put her off. "It's from grapes that was grown in the Mosel district."

"Seeing it's a Mosel, that doesn't surprise me."

"On the *south* slope. Above the river."

"What river?"

"Why, the Moselle, of course."

Henry blew a smoke ring. His fingers crept toward the money.

"Germany doesn't have slopes." Of course it did, but she didn't know that.

She laughed. "Oh, you are a caution, sir."

"Actually, I'd love a word with your sommelier."

This earned Melrose a disappointed look from Henry. *Below the belt, dear fellow.*

"I'm sorry, sir. He's just this minute gone."

Henry snickered, Melrose sighed. "Just pour."

Henry pulled back his money—with Melrose's own two fivers on top of it.

She popped out the cork with great élan, tilted a little into his glass, and waited.

"Oh, no need to bother with tasting; I'm sure it's as fine as can be."

She actually looked disappointed.

So did Henry.

Melrose said to him: *Do you expect me to keep playing along with this?*

*Of course. What do you think life is if not this?*

Grudgingly, Melrose swirled the wine around, sniffed it, tasted it. The waitress was actually looking on expectantly as if she were really concerned.

"Excellent!" said Melrose, who had never liked Mosel.

"Thank you, sir. We thought you'd approve. Anyhow, it'll go much better with the *poisson*." She sailed off.

Henry blew smoke rings.

Following this entertaining interlude, after the unremarkable wine and grilled fish, Melrose was prepared to return to Lamb House.

He wondered, upon entering the house and seeing his suitcase still sitting resolutely by the stairs like an abandoned and still obedient dog, if he had left it packed because he would rather go than stay.

He tossed his coat over the banister again and went into the library, where he ran a finger over the spines of the Henry James *œuvre*. He pulled out one of the short story collections, read through the contents, looking for one of James's ghost stories. James was rather big on ghosts and

Melrose wondered why, as he turned to the window and stood looking out on darkness.

It seemed an anomaly, James and ghost stories. Hadn't there been some incident about the elder James, his father, having had an experience with an apparition? And his brother William was more than a little bit interested in ghostly phenomena.

Back to the book. He found "The Jolly Corner," which he could read in bed. It was one of the best known; Melrose had read it years ago. This volume in hand he walked back to the entryway, picked up his suitcase, and walked upstairs.

# TWENTY-FOUR

With his book still splayed beneath his hand, Melrose awoke to a morning that looked as fresh as a '75 Beaujolais Nouveau. An inept metaphor, but he would probably never recover from the previous night's wine list.

He heard sounds below that seemed to come from the kitchen. Cooking sounds, he hoped. He was aware that he was famished. Last night's meal had not hung about him for long, probably because he had expended so much energy that any supplied by the food and drink had been used up before he'd even left the restaurant. Ah! But that had been an excellent bit of

cabaret, hadn't it? He relived it as he finished dressing.

He was just on his way downstairs when
the door knocker sounded. Was he supposed to answer? Or was Mrs. Jessup?
What was the protocol—*Oh, who cares?
Just go to the door!*

The man on the step was tall, light-haired,
and with bones chiseled into handsome-
ness. *Very Germanic,* Melrose said to himself, aware that he did so only because he
knew this man's origins.

The man reached out his hand. "Kurt
Brunner. Superintendent Jury suggested I
might be of some help to you in Rye. You're
interested in the history of the area, he
said."

*Far from it,* thought Melrose. The last
thing he wanted to do was to go hacking
back through 1066 and its attendant mis-
eries, no matter how he'd sworn last night
to do precisely this. He'd wait for the miniseries. "Ah, yes! Yes, he did mention you,
Mr. Brunner. I'll be happy for your help. Shall
we sit down?" Melrose motioned toward
one of the armchairs in the sitting room, and
took the other himself.

"I'm especially interested in the history of

Lamb House. I'm writing a monograph on Henry James." Now why in hell did he have to add *that* bit of information? It would undoubtedly get him in hot water later on.

Brunner wasn't interested in monographs, fortunately. "I know Lamb House well. I was, I guess you'd say, assistant to Billy Maples." He paused. "I don't know if you know about—"

"His being shot to death? Yes. The superintendent told me about it; it was in all the papers. A terrible thing."

Mrs. Jessup appeared in the doorway at that point. "Lord Ardry hasn't even had his morning tea, Mr. Brunner," she said in a scolding voice, as if Melrose's oversleeping were Brunner's fault. She was all solicitation, that is, except for the look she shot Brunner's way. What was in that sharp glance?

"I'm sorry," Brunner started up.

Melrose waved him back down. "Thank you, Mrs. Jessup. Perhaps we could have it now. You'll have tea, Mr. Brunner?"

"Yes, I'd like a cup."

"I'll just fetch it, then." She went back to the kitchen.

"Have police made any headway?"

Brunner smiled slightly. "You might know more than I, considering."

Had that smile been shifty? "Oh, you mean from Mr. Jury." Melrose laughed artificially. "He doesn't take me into his confidence."

"As far as I know, no one's been arrested."

"No." Melrose paused to consider the best way to proceed. "You said you were Billy's—Billy Maples's—assistant? I'm not sure—exactly what did that involve?"

Brunner nodded. "It wasn't taking down letters, no. A bit of everything. Keeping track of his affairs."

"You mean engagements? Money things? Bills? All that?"

"Yes, but I don't think that was of as much importance as—" He looked strained, as if formulating an answer required concentration. "Say, adviser."

On the heels of that rather inscrutable statement, Mrs. Jessup came in with the tea tray, which she set on the table between them. Rather abruptly, Melrose thought. She left.

Brunner took over. "I'm not her favorite person," he said, raising the milk jug. "Milk?

Sugar?" He was, apparently, used to playing host.

"Both. One sugar. Why is that? I mean, her feelings about you."

Brunner shrugged. "I'm not sure. Jealousy, perhaps. She might consider Lamb House her own little fiefdom. I was in the way. And I'm German, of course, which doesn't help matters." He stirred his cup.

Melrose pondered that. "You mean, she's still a holdout over the war?"

"Most definitely. Some people have never gotten over the war. Wars, I should say."

"Still, she strikes me as the motherly sort. And your employer was young and"—he tried it out—"unattached."

Here Kurt Brunner gave Melrose a look, probably wondering if he should divulge confidences, even though the confidant was dead. Or maybe even *because* he was dead.

Melrose wanted to pursue this line, but Brunner should have by now pondered why the talk was rather distant from Rye and Lamb House. Melrose merely said, "He sounds a decent sort."

"He was, very."

"Interesting that he settled here in Rye."

"I don't think he meant to stay more than a year. He was a great fan of Henry James, I know that. I am, too."

"Ah! As for myself, I'm doing research. I'm writing a book on James. The middle years." God, but how stupid of him. He didn't know the middle years from the early years from the final years from the afterlife. All he knew was that James had written his three most involved novels later in life.

"Oh? I thought it was a monograph."

Look at that. He'd already blundered just fifteen minutes into the conversation. "Oh, that's an extract from the whole manuscript."

"The middle years." Kurt Brunner seemed to be casting around for an observation. He asked, "What marks that period for you? It wouldn't have been the three great novels. Those came later."

"You're right." Melrose steepled his fingers and cursed himself and tried to dredge up some memory of James's work in that period.

Then Brunner helped out by exclaiming, "*Guy Domville!* That's it, isn't it? That awful debacle?"

Melrose thanked him silently for providing

the work. Everyone knew about that play. "Yes. The play where James was laughed off the stage. Awful. The man took an awful beating for that."

Kurt began to laugh. "There's a caricature or a cartoon of James in which he's shown in Buñol, the site of the tomatina. We went there, Billy and I—"

"Oh, you're talking about that tomato-throwing thing? What in God's name is the attraction?"

"I have no idea. You get covered with tomato pulp. Billy said he'd never touch another tomato again in any way, shape, or form. In any event, this cartoon thing of James, clearly a victim of the tomatina. The caption read, another successful run of GUY DOMVILLE."

Melrose laughed. "Poor man."

"But he took that blasting and came out the better for it, didn't he?"

Melrose was ready to stomp all over that cliché. "No, he didn't."

"No?"

"Well, one doesn't, does one? One is lucky if one comes out *alive,* never mind better." He wondered if he could crowd one more "one" into his observation. "One becomes a little embittered, a little aggrieved." God! Did he have to bring in his horse? How stuffy he sounded! Yet it might be a good pose; no one as smug and self-satisfied as Melrose would appear in Rye to investigate a murder.

"You're probably right." Brunner set down his cup and asked, "Would you like to go out and walk around Rye?"

"Excellent idea!" Not really; the only walk Melrose wanted to take was a destination walk. From Ardry End to the Jack and Hammer, or across the street to the Wrenn's Nest, to annoy Theo Wrenn Browne. Or to the library, which was generally on his way to the pub, anyway, so that was two destinations for the price of one. He had heard London was a marvelous city for walking, people were always exclaiming over green expanses such as Kew, but he wouldn't know. Once he established himself in Boring's, that was London enough for him. The Boring's clientele was as frozen in place as the planets, as fixed as plumbing.

But this morning, he shrugged on his coat and he and Kurt Brunner set off.

It sounded absolutely Victorian.

"How much do you know about Rye?"

*Nothing.* "Oh, quite a bit, I mean I'm familiar with its history and all. You know, the Battle of Hastings—well, that's not Rye, exactly; it's one of the Cinque Ports. I've a friend who insists it's not five, but seven." Melrose laughed. "In spite of its being *cinque,* correct? She claims there are two towns thrown in. Extra."

"She's right."

Melrose stopped dead. "Right?"

Kurt smiled. "I believe it's formally called Cinque Ports and Two Ancient Towns. The towns I think are Winchelsea and Rye. They were, in medieval times, a maritime corporation. Very important because the confederation was responsible for naval defense."

"I'll be damned."

They started walking again.

They had set their walk toward the High Street and had turned off onto a cliff road. There was a sort of terrace with a telescope, a pleasant stop for tourists, who with the aid of the telescope could see—Kurt told him—to Dungeness and the cliffs of Dover. They looked out over the Town Salts toward the river. The area appeared to be a multiuse place where children could play, cars could park. Within it were pools of water, one or two the size of small lakes. It must have been bird heaven. There were fishing boats in the distance; beyond was the Rother.

"The Salts: it's hard to believe all that was covered by the sea a hundred years ago. There's a footpath down there. Billy walked there often. There are several bird hides, if you're a bird-watcher."

Melrose shook his head. "If they fly into the Lamb House garden, I'll be happy to watch them. But I've never understood the pleasure of standing around at dawn in wet grass or in a drafty box waiting for a glimpse of the copper-throated plover."

"I don't know that bird. Farther away over there is the nature preserve. That stretch of water is called Castle Water. It's beside Camber Castle." The sun made the water blaze.

"All of this was created by the sea's pulling back?" said Melrose. "It seems strange, doesn't it? The sea is usually what moves in and claims a place." Thinking of the best way to proceed about Billy Maples, Melrose drew out his cigarette case. He didn't want to appear too curious. "Your little description of Billy is surprising. I got the impression from Mrs. Jessup there never was much on Billy's mind. Rather, he was a bit of a playboy. If that arcane expression fits. She thinks him—thought him—rather spoiled."

"By what, I wonder? By whom? His parents? I seriously doubt it. Billy's problem was that he was scattered. His focus didn't last long. But when it was there, it was there. He was quite intense."

"Do you think he focused on the wrong thing and it got him killed?"

"What do you mean?"

"Why, I've no idea. I know as much about Billy Maples as about the copper-throated plover."

Kurt laughed again.

"Billy was fascinated, perhaps morbidly so, by the war. I mean World War Two. He liked to go over to Lambeth to the Imperial War Museum. And since I had been a child in Berlin during the war, he asked me endless questions about it. I was a little kid, I was three or four and told him I just didn't recall much. He wanted to know—ah, we were Jews, you see; my parents both died in Auschwitz. Billy thought I must have come out of the war terribly angry and bitter and wanting revenge."

Melrose was taken aback by Kurt Brunner's carelessly offering a motive for murder. "Revenge? You mean for your real or imagined mistreatment?"

"It wouldn't have to be that personal, would it?"

He turned from the shingle and the blazing water and stood looking at the street and the little buildings snugly fitted against one another. The street was filled with shadows.

"It would probably be part of the reason Mrs. Jessup is not very fond of me. Her family had a hard time of it during the war."

"She wasn't alone in that regard."

"No, but two of her sisters died in some evacuation attempt."

Melrose wanted to steer the conversation away from the cook and back to Billy.

They were walking again along East Cliff Street.

"Why would such a young man want to sequester himself in the world of Henry James?"

"Oh, I don't think it was that world. Though he did have a strong liking for

James's books. I think it was a bit of a lark, for one thing. Billy usually had a hundred reasons for things he did. It just so happened that the National Trust was looking for a stopgap, someone to take on Lamb House for a year. Until they could get things sorted. Well, Billy heard about it and thought it would be interesting. That, and a dare." Kurt smiled.

"A dare?"

"His fiancée told him he wouldn't last twenty-four hours in Rye. I think Billy was offended to be thought so city-bound, to be thought, well, shallow in that he couldn't manage this solitude because he had no inner resources."

Melrose flung out his arm as they passed the well-lit and well-attended Mermaid Tavern. "This is scarcely solitude!"

"No, not if you're inside it. I've walked this street time and again. Every time I've felt the quiet seep into my bones. The silence seems palpable. In winter when the fog rolls in or the mist covers the ground and you can't see your feet—it's all very isolating. Rye is like one of those places we wander into in dreams."

"I wonder how much of his work he composed walking these streets. Henry James, I mean."

"Very little, is my guess. I see James as an indoor man when it came to writing."

"Did Billy want to write himself?"

"No, or at least I don't think so."

"I'm assuming you knew him well."

"As much as anybody did. Perhaps better."

"That implies that he was unknowable, eh? A bit of a mystery."

Kurt stopped on the pavement and so Melrose did, too, and he became aware that their footsteps had been all there was to hear.

"Oh, everyone's *that*," said Brunner.

"That sounds . . . you sound like one of James's characters. You know, his characters sound to me as if they're always pausing to catch breath."

Kurt Brunner laughed. "I'll have to watch it. Perhaps anyone who lives in that house for a while begins to sound like a page out of James. Even Mrs. Jessup might come off sounding like the malevolent Miss Jessel one of these days."

"Good lord, I hope not!"

They had reached Lion Street and were

soon to come to St. Mary's Church. "Was
Billy—"

Melrose stopped.

"What?"

"I never knew him and yet I call him Billy."

"Everyone did," Brunner said, sadly.

Melrose smiled. "Everyone did, but why?"

"I never thought about it. But what had
you been about to ask?"

"I don't remember."

They walked on.

# TWENTY-FIVE

Malcolm Mott was standing in the front garden with his dog, Waldo, when the car came up the long drive.

*Who's this lot, then?* he wondered.

The car pulled up. The men, driver and passenger, got out. The driver, thinner and shorter than the other one, called over. "Afternoon, young man."

*Young man.* How smarmy. Malcolm didn't respond. The passenger, the taller and smarter-looking one, didn't address Malcolm at all. He merely looked at him. This annoyed Malcolm as it made placing him in the scheme of failed adults difficult. The tall man folded his arms and leaned against the car as if he could stop there all day.

The driver had come up to him now, smiling and showing Malcolm some sort of identification. "We're from New Scotland Yard CID. I'm Detective Sergeant Wiggins and that gentleman"—he turned to the other one—"is Superintendent Richard Jury."

*Blimey!*

To keep the excitement out of his face, he reached down and picked up Waldo, who clearly didn't want to be carried. Malcolm chewed his gum more ferociously. He was having a really hard time holding himself in check. Not only because this was Scotland Yard come to visit, but because they must be here about Billy.

Malcolm clutched Waldo tighter. He was holding off thoughts about Billy. When that other policeman had come, Malcolm had just gone out to the back garden and started scaling the wall, tying his dog to the end of the rope for a kind of balance.

Now the taller one was standing in front of him.

"You're Malcolm."

And was a mind reader. This was bad.

This person could be dangerous. Malcolm mustered his most ferocious look. He clapped his eyebrows together and gave the both of them a thunderous stare. Rain clouds gathering, ice shards spitting, lightning bolting—*lightning bolting?* Malcolm frowned, but at himself this time; that didn't sound right. Lightning ripping, lightning stabbing, lightning . . . Malcolm was writing a book, and he meant it to be terrifying. A lot of weather was in it.

"Are your mum and dad here, young Malcolm?" asked the thin one.

Malcolm wanted to just haul off and hit him. *Young Malcolm.* He stared at them. He hoped Waldo was staring, too.

"Malcolm," said the one who claimed to be a Sergeant Wiggins, "we're here about Billy Maples. Your cousin?"

As if he'd forgotten. Malcolm grew rigid with a kind of cold rage. No one talked to him about Billy.

"I expect a good friend." The tall one smiled.

*Fucking mind reader!* Malcolm turned and stomped away.

Jury watched him disappear around the corner of the house.

"You'd think," said Wiggins, "he'd be interested in Scotland Yard, wouldn't you?"

"He is."


The door was opened by a maid in black. She was thin, young, and unhappy looking.

When Jury identified himself and Wiggins and said he was expected, she whispered for them to step inside and went off on softly soled shoes to inform her employers.

There was the sort of hush that hangs over a place when everyone who'd lived there had gone. The silence of abandonment. The paintings, the bronze statue of the child bent over her cat, the statues in niches along the wall: all of these gave the impression of a sadness that might disperse if they could just find themselves somewhere else. If they could just go.

While Wiggins examined the bronze statue, Jury looked at a large painting—nearly four by six feet it had to be—by an artist he knew but whose name escaped him, a name by virtue of being nearly all consonants, hard to remember and hard to say:

Klp, Klt, no—Klimt, that was it. Jury frowned. But a Klimt would be worth a small fortune, wouldn't it? He looked at the frame. Perhaps that was why it was bolted to the wall; it would certainly discourage theft. The background was all gold, a membrane of gold against which the gown of the figure fidgeted in arithmetical shapes: triangles, squares, rectangles, bars, and circles. They were like bits of paper that flash around in a cage ready for the winning ticket to be drawn. Gold and copper squares, bars of black, slivers of gray and green tossed helter-skelter at the canvas. They formed, when the eye brought them under control, a bright gown on the figure of the black-haired woman before dissolving into the thin layer of gold one finds occasionally on an elaborate Indian dessert, edible and strange.

The maid came out of the room she had stepped into and motioned for them to come along.

Roderick Maples was the only other occupant of the room. He stood before a dying fire, poker in hand, with which he apparently

had been rousting the flames. He bore as little resemblance to Sir Oswald Maples as a
son could to a father—but why was Jury
looking for resemblance? Jury remembered
that Oswald was not the man's actual father.
His rangy body, his flint gray eyes, his de-
meanor—unsmiling and unwelcoming.

"I fail to see, Mr., ah, Jury is it?"

Roderick Maples knew of course it was
Mr. Jury and also knew Mr. Jury was a CID
superintendent. Jury didn't really begrudge
the man his defenses. He said, "It is. With
Detective Sergeant Wiggins."

"I fail to see why it's necessary to send
yet more police here about my son's death."

He said this stonily and looked as if he
had all the malleable warmth of the poker
that he had returned to the fireplace tools
suspended from an antique brass holder.

Jury said, "May we sit down?"

"What? Oh, yes. Yes of course. Sit anywhere," he said.

Jury wanted to laugh. The man made the
room sound like a restaurant in its slack
period. They sat down, Jury in a gray
watered silk chair, facing Roderick and the
fireplace. Beside the marble mantel hung
another small painting by an artist Jury

wasn't familiar with, though it reminded him of a van Gogh. Something about the brush work.

Wiggins had taken a seat on an acid green chair. Roderick Maples remained standing before the marble fireplace in the manner of one who meant to make an early exit.

Roderick said, "I can tell you only what I told the other one—"

Annoyed, Wiggins interjected, "We assume you mean Detective Sergeant Chilten?"

Maples gave a frigid little nod. "I can tell you only that."

"Then tell us," said Jury.

"The last time I saw my son was over a week ago when I went up to London to visit him at his Sloane Street flat."

"What was that about?"

"I beg your pardon?"

"What did you want to see him about?" Jury said.

Roderick clasped his hands behind his back as if warming them before the fire, which had all but gone out. "That has nothing at all to do with his death."

"Perhaps it does, though. If it was important enough to pay him a visit."

Roderick flinched and his expression grew stonier. "You officers—"

"Detectives, actually. CID."

"—appear to think that one's life must be an open book set before you."

Jury smiled at the accurate description. "That's about right, Mr. Maples. So, again, what did you go up to London to see your son about?"

"The matter of his trust fund. Billy was utterly profligate with money. I wanted to know why."

"What was the trust fund? I mean, who left it to him?"

"His mother, my first wife. Actually, there were two. The other came from his grandfather."

"Sir Oswald Maples?"

"No, not my father, his other grandfather. His name was Ames. James Ames. His wife is still alive, lives in Fulham, is it? Chelsea, perhaps."

"So you confronted your son. How did he react?"

"To say that it was his money and he'd

spend it as he liked. The young have no sense of responsibility."

Wiggins said, "Your son was in his thirties. Not really one of 'the young' as you put it."

Roderick tented his fingers and looked at them from the posture of the long-suffering.

Jury said, "I understand your son gave large amounts of money to help artists. His friends, the art gallery he supported. He was, according to others, very generous."

"He was mercurial, I know that." Roderick crossed to the silver tray that held the soda siphon and splashed more soda into his glass.

"In what way, sir?" asked Wiggins.

"Well, very moody. He spent little time here. To tell the truth, we didn't get on so well together. But I already said that, didn't I? But he did appear to like his grandfather. He lives in Chelsea."

Jury said, "I know him, Sir Oswald Maples."

Roderick looked at Jury in surprise. "My father? You mean you've already talked to him?"

"I have, but what I meant is that I knew him before all this. He was very helpful in a case I worked on last year. He was at Bletchley Park, as you know, of course. He must have a first-rate mind to have been involved in all of that code breaking."

"Yes. Yes, Dad's quite brilliant, really."

This seemed to be said in an affectionate way, which surprised Jury. "It was he who asked me to investigate your son's murder. The other detectives who were here were from Islington police."

"Yes. The one in charge was a woman. Rather aggressive, I thought, but extremely perceptive. I believe she could read my mind."

You don't know the half of it. Jury cleared his throat.

Roderick laughed a little, then abruptly stopped. "Not the most comfortable state of affairs, I mean, if you're talking to the police." He laughed again.

Jury warmed to him a little.

Roderick had been standing with his back to the fireplace during this exchange. "I think Dad knew Billy better than I did."

In this Jury detected a hint of regret, sadness even. "He said Billy came to see him often."

"Yes. More than I did, certainly. I've been

very derelict on that score. I would imagine that if anyone knew anything it would be my father."

"I don't believe he knows any more than you do, Mr. Maples." Jury wasn't altogether sure why he said this. It was some attempt at solace, maybe, as a parent rather hates to think he's the last to know what's going on in his child's life. "We hoped to speak with Mrs. Maples. Is she about?"

"Upstairs. It's all been hard for her to take."

As he made no move to get her, Jury said, "Could we see her? It's important."

Distractedly, Roderick looked at Jury, said, "Oh. Oh, yes. I'll tell her to come down."


The woman who entered the room was a good dozen years younger than her husband, which didn't make her young—say, early to midforties. Her dress was a green so dark it was almost black. Black for mourning is what Jury had first thought it was. The neckline of the dress was a sort of drape fastened at the shoulder with an amethyst brooch. Her good looks were authoritative.

"Mrs. Maples." Jury had risen. "I'm terribly sorry but we've come about your stepson."

She nodded and took the mate of the chair Jury sat on. "My stepson, but he was like a son."

Roderick's expression suggested otherwise, but what other?

She sounded, Jury thought, sincere when she said this. "Would you say you knew Billy well?"

"Better than Roddy, I think." She offered her husband a fleeting smile, but whether it was by way of apology or needling, it was hard to say. And Jury didn't believe her for a minute.

Roderick sat down. Apparently, he preferred to take her answers that way.

Jury wondered if the money that had furnished this handsome room was his or hers or even the first wife's, Billy's real mother's. Perhaps Roderick had been lucky in marrying two wealthy women.

"And how well is that, madame?" asked Wiggins with some acerbity. His patience didn't cover people being clever.

Her glance slid off Wiggins; her answer was for Jury. "I knew Billy quite well."

"If that's so, have you some insight into what happened?"

She sat back. "No. There I'm as much in the dark as the rest of you." The way her look traveled around the small circle of people in the room suggested that even her ignorance could compete favorably with theirs. "I doubt anyone knows what happened."

"The murderer does." Wiggins, again, a smile tilting on his face.

Jury said, "Then you don't know if Billy had enemies?"

She did not immediately dismiss this. "Well, there were one or two."

Roderick stepped in. "What are you saying, Olivia? The boy never made enemies."

"Don't be silly, Roddy. *Everyone* has an enemy. I'm thinking of the woman in London, whom he'd been seeing for some time. He broke up with her. Dumped her, you could say."

"Ridiculous," said Roderick. "She'd hardly have gone to a Clerkenwell hotel and *shot* him."

Jury smiled inwardly. The Ritz, perhaps;

Brown's or the Connaught. Mayfair, but not Clerkenwell. He said, "The thing is, Mrs. Maples, the scene itself is strange. He checked into this trendy Clerkenwell hotel, the Zetter. Then after his visit to the Melville Gallery, he stopped in at a club called Dust. He then went back to the Zetter and ordered a meal be sent up. Coffee for two to be delivered later. He was expecting someone to join him."

She asked, "Couldn't he have met someone at the gallery who joined him later, or at this club?"

Roderick said, "But then why didn't this person simply go back with him to the hotel?"

"A good question. Who," Jury said to Olivia Maples, "was the second person. You said one or two possible enemies."

She plucked at the brooch on her shoulder, straightening it. "I was thinking of Kurt Brunner."

"Brunner? His assistant?"

"Or whatever he is. Was. I have never trusted him."

Wiggins asked, "Why is that, Mrs. Maples?"

"I'm not sure he always had Billy's best interests at heart."

"Oh, for God's sakes, Olivia. Kurt's perfectly okay."

Anger sparked in her eyes. "Why would a man as worldly as Kurt find it rewarding to be at the beck and call of a rich young man who never worked a day in his life?"

"That's not true."

Olivia shook her head, ostensibly at Roderick's thickheadedness—or at his perennial blind spot, his son. She turned back to Jury. "Would you like something? Whiskey? Tea?"

Jury knew the mention of tea would bring Wiggins to full alert, so he said, "Tea would be welcome, thanks."

Wiggins, who'd been looking gloomy, beamed. "It would, yes."

Olivia rose. "I'll just tell Margaret to fetch it." She left the room.

Roderick watched her go.

Jury said, "I've been looking at that painting by the mantel. Whose is it?"

"That? That's a Soutine. That and the Klimt in the entry—did you see it?"

"Absolutely. It's remarkable. But very valuable, isn't it?"

Roderick smiled a little purse-lipped smile. "I wish it were. It's not the original.

Nor is this one. But they're remarkably good reproductions." They both studied the Soutine. It looked stormy with its thick-branched bending trees in the foreground. Behind them was a sturdy, crenellated house. "*Schloss Moser.* Austria, I think."

Roderick sat forward and brought the subject back. "Superintendent, my wife's suspicions of Brunner are completely unfounded. I think Billy was better for his association with Kurt Brunner."

"Better than what?"

Roderick grimaced and shrugged, as if he could shrug it away: "Billy could be a holy terror."

Olivia was back on the heels of that comment. "Billy a holy *terror?* Stop exaggerating, Roderick." To Wiggins, she said, "Tea will be just a moment." Then picking up the comment about her stepson, said, "He could be moody at times, that's all. Usually Billy was a lamb."

They were probably both right. Jury would come back to that.

"You said you questioned Brunner's influence. What exactly was his field before he came to work for Billy?"

Olivia shrugged, finished with the matter.

Roderick said, "He was a teacher. Taught at a public school in Berlin? Or at least the German equivalent of public school."

Wiggins, who'd been glancing at the door through which the tea would make its entrance, was rewarded. There was the rattle of a tea tray carried by Margaret. She set it down. Olivia thanked her and set about pouring.

Jury accepted the cup from Olivia together with whatever combination of sugar and milk she'd added.

"He taught European history, he said," Roderick went on. "What he seemed really interested in was the Russian dynasties. Czar Nicholas, that period. He was fascinated by Rasputin."

Wiggins said, "Wasn't Rasputin the one that got shot, poisoned, stabbed, and still didn't die?"

Roderick laughed. "And one or two others, Sergeant, if I remember rightly."

Jury thought about Rasputin's hold over Czarina Alexandra. "He taught in a public school?"

"One of the international schools that are everywhere, it seems. He'd dropped the teaching even before he started working for Billy. I think he has very little life of his own."

*Not a social life,* thought Jury. *But there was an interior life that could make up for it.*

Jury said, "You're suspicious of Kurt Brunner, Mrs. Maples. What would have been his motive for killing Billy?"

"Billy's fortune. It was considerable."

"But they met by accident."

"For heaven's sakes! One can meet by accident and carry on by design."

"True." Jury smiled. "But why would your stepson leave the fortune to Brunner?"

"Well, there really aren't many candidates," said Roderick. "Anyway, this is all beside the point since Billy left no will."

"He dies intestate, then."

Roderick nodded. "A shame really."

"The boy outside, is he your nephew?"

"Olivia's, actually." He seemed happy to wipe Malcolm off his own slate. "He's the son of Olivia's sister, Julia Mott, who dumped him on us and went on to pursue her own interests: drugs, sex, and gambling. We've not seen her since."

Jury said, "Not terribly happy, is he? He doesn't bother to make himself liked."

Olivia laughed. "He's wretched. But Billy got on with him. I think Billy was Malcolm's hero, if the child had one. Billy had him up to London several times. Took him places."

"But," said Jury, "that was very kind of your son."

"It was that other side of Billy. He could be a very caring boy." Roderick quickly rose and went to the window overlooking the front of the house.

"I'm very sorry for your loss."

Roderick brushed his handkerchief across his face, returned it to his pocket, turned around. "Yes. Thank you."

"Sergeant Chilten and I went to your son's flat in Chelsea. We were looking for some clue as to what was going on in his life. There was nothing definitive. But I wonder, did he have a religious bent?"

They both looked surprised. "Heavens, no. We could never manage to get him to church with us," said Olivia.

"Not that we go that often," said Roderick.

"Did he ever bring his girlfriend—or fiancée—here?"

Olivia laughed. "Fiancée? Well, that's

probably wishful thinking on the poor girl's part. Billy enjoyed playing the field."

"But when it came to it," said Roderick, "he didn't stick, no, he managed to get himself out of it. Too damned satisfied with his bachelor ways."

Jury thought about this. He thought about Kurt Brunner, about Angela Riffley, about the supposed assignation at the Zetter, which was hardly two minutes' walk from Dust. Dust, with its glowing lights, its reckless music, its old brick walls and dark corners. Dust would have encouraged an assignation.

"If you don't mind, I think I'll have a word with Malcolm."

"Oh? Well, if you want. He'll be outside somewhere, probably the back garden," said Olivia.

As he rose to go, still thinking of that supposed meeting at the Zetter, he asked, "Was Billy gay?"

Both of them froze. Could people still look out in horror at the suggestion? Olivia and Roderick both did.

Then Olivia laughed, uncertainly. "Superintendent, we've just been talking about his girlfriends. You should have seen the trail of broken hearts Billy left in his wake! Gay?"

"That'll do it," Jury said.

# TWENTY-SIX

"Who wants to know?" Malcolm Mott said when Jury asked him if he and Billy were friends.

"Same person who wanted to know before. Me." They were standing near the brick wall at the rear of the gardens, which were quite extensive.

"Well." Malcolm's tone was uncertain.

"Why are you tying your dog up that way?"

By Malcolm's feet, the little terrier sat, looking less than pleased. Jury could only have called it a scowl.

"His name's Waldo. We're going rappelling."

"Waldo doesn't look much like he wants to rappel."

"He's done it before."

"He probably didn't want to before, either."

Malcolm stopped pulling the rope around the dog and looked up at Jury. "You'd do better to mind your own business."

"It is my business." Jury gave Malcolm another look at his ID. "Everything's my business."

With as much sarcasm as he could muster, Malcolm said, "Who're you, then, God?"

"The next best thing. Scotland Yard."

Malcolm stopped tying the rope around Waldo's midsection. "If you came to ask questions about Billy, well, don't."

"Why?"

"*Because.* That's why not."

"I wonder why, though."

"Wonder away. Us, we're going over that wall." He picked up Waldo, who barked, but seemed to be doing it more at Jury than the wall.

"I've got a better idea."

Malcolm made a derisive sound, but he turned to hear it. "What?"

"I'll take Waldo's place."

That stopped Malcolm right in his tracks. "*You?* Don't make me laugh!"

"Of course, I can understand you wouldn't want to, as I'd get over it quicker than you. I mean if there was to be a contest, I'd win. Hands down."

Frowning deeply, Malcolm set Waldo down. The dog went round in circles, involving himself even more in the rope. Hands on hips, Malcolm looked at Jury. "You must be daft. You'd never beat me. You'd never even get over it. You're too big. Me, I'm light as a feather."

Jury shrugged. "That's what you say."

Malcolm started fake laughing.

"I guess," said Jury. "You're not used to competing for things." Jury actually guessed just the opposite.

Malcolm stopped the laughing and glared. "That's stupid. Not even Billy could—" He clamped his mouth shut, clearly upset over relaying this smidgen of information.

"Billy climbed with you, did he?"

"Yeah, if you have to know."

Waldo, unused to all of this talk and dangling his rope, looked interested.

"I want to." Jury reached down to rub the

dog's head. "You mean Billy never beat you? He must not've been as good as me, then."

*That* reeled him in. "Oh, yes he was! He was better'n you! Better'n you'll ever be!"

"Now just how would you know that? You've never seen me rappel."

Malcolm's face was a cloud of uncertainty. He sputtered, "Okay, okay, we'll just see. Hold on, Waldo." He started untwining the length of rope Waldo hadn't managed to get free of. When he'd freed the dog, he said to it, "Don't you go off anyplace, Waldo."

Waldo quickly went off someplace.

"You gotta put this round your waist and under your arms." He held out the rope.

Jury doffed his coat and ran the rope around himself in poor imitation of what an experienced climber would do. "Isn't it supposed to go over your shoulder?"

Malcolm heaved a sigh. "You're already trying to change the rules."

"No, I just think the rope's supposed to go under and over." Jury slid it beneath his thigh and over his shoulder. "That's how a real mountain climber would do it."

"Look—" Malcolm had a really hard time

staring Jury down, as he had to look up so far. "It's not mountain climbing anyway. It's rappelling."

"That's coming down, rappelling."

"No, it is *not*. But go ahead, put the rope anywhere. I won't care when you fall down and break your head."

"Okay. Which part of the wall?"

Malcolm pointed. "There."

An old garden wall, red brick perhaps fifteen feet high. The faded brick seemed almost soft to the touch. There were possible finger- or toeholds, places where the stone had crumbled away.

"Okay, let's go," said Jury.

Malcolm began squirming up the wall. He was moving fast. As Jury was so much taller, he gave the boy a head start. It took only two or three lurches and Jury was at the top.

Malcolm, of course, won. He sat on the wall beaming. Light gathered in his face.

"You win, I guess," said Jury, hitching himself around to sit down.

"Sure," said Malcolm.

The view from the top of the wall was pretty impressive. They could see beyond the front of the house north to what might have been Kent; there was a line of oast-houses along the horizon. Behind them was the weal and Romney Marsh. In the late afternoon sun, the marsh almost glowed.

"Some view," Jury said.

"Yeah. I sit up here a lot. With Waldo."

"Does Waldo know where the toeholds are?"

That got him a look. "Don't be daft. I pull him up. You saw."

Jury wished he had a cigarette, which was also daft.

"You can see to London," said Malcolm.

You couldn't, but Jury squinted as if he could and agreed that the tiny spire in the distance might be Westminster or the Houses of Parliament.

"I'm going there to live." Malcolm stopped and dropped his head. "I mean I *was* going there."

There are times you prompt and times you don't.

"Billy said I could when I got out of school, that I could live with him. But now, I can't."

Jury considered. "You still can go and live in his flat. It would be something like having him around, with all of his things there. I was there before. It's a nice flat. A lot of books and things."

Malcolm showed he was interested in this possible development. But he concluded, "Nah. They'd never let me."

"Well, maybe they won't have a say in it. If you were good friends—"

"We were! We were best friends! He didn't much like coming here. He never got on with Aunt Olivia. She's his stepmother, not his real one."

"Why didn't he like her?"

"She's always nattering on about something. He said she made it hard to breathe."

Jury thought this over. "Did you visit Billy in London?"

"A lot of times."

"Did you go round to see stuff? The Tower and Madame Tussaud's?"

A wind had come up and Malcolm scraped his straight brown hair back from his forehead. "We went to museums. We went to the Natural History and the Victoria and Albert. And the War Museum."

"The Imperial War Museum in Lambeth?"

"Uh-huh. Billy was really interested in the war. I mean the World War when his grand-dad did all of that secret stuff. That was cool. Codes and stuff. Anyway, Billy was fascinated by it. He really liked his grand-dad. He said he was about the only person worth talking to. I mean, besides me."

Jury smiled and made a mental note to tell Sir Oswald what Malcolm said.

"We went to art galleries sometimes. Mostly to that Tate one."

"The Tate Modern?"

"No the other one, the real one."

"The Tate Britain." The real one; Jury liked that.

"Yeah. Billy liked looking at certain paint-ings there."

"Which ones?"

"That painter with a lot of initials in his name that liked a lot of light in his stuff."

Jury thought about this. "J.M.W. Turner?"

"Yeah." Malcolm looked at him with a new respect. "Then others like the paintings in the house—" He stopped and continued again. "Billy told me stuff that I wasn't to tell anyone." He paused and gave Jury an assessing look.

"Did he? You know, there are times when I think I'd rather not know a secret. Secrets can be a burden."

"Yeah. Only now, he's dead. It makes me wonder."

"About what?"

Malcolm was running his hand over the brick, which must have felt comfortingly abrasive, as if he were trying to shed something. Dead skin, secrets. "What I wonder is if what he knew had to do with it—you know, him getting shot. If maybe I should have told somebody—" He looked away.

Jury put a hand on his shoulder, which Malcolm predictably tried to shrug off, but Jury kept it there. "You did exactly the right thing, kept a secret. There was no way of knowing what would happen. Anyway, what he told you probably had nothing to do with his death."

"Maybe not, but you don't know what he told me." Malcolm gave Jury another look, up and down, as if measuring him for a suit. "It's about those paintings, the big one in the entryway and the little one by the fireplace. Ones that weren't there when I came. Over a year ago. I mean they're probably not family heirlooms, or anything."

"I saw those, yes. They're quite astonishing reproductions."

"But see, this is what Billy told me: they're

not copies. That's what they tell people, but it's a lie. They're the actual paintings."

Jury looked at him, truly amazed. "But why?"

Malcolm seemed happy with this one-up on a Scotland Yard detective. "That's what *I* said. Billy said he wasn't sure; he was tracking their provence."

"Provenence. Their history, their ownership."

"Well, *I* said maybe it's because if people knew they were real, somebody'd try to steal them."

"That's a good guess, Malcolm. What did Billy say to that?"

"That there was another reason. But he wasn't sure about it."

"How did Billy know the paintings were originals?"

"Well, one day he came here with this lady. She knew a lot about art. She knows the difference between a real painting and a copy. She told him. I heard them talking about her later, saying she was his girlfriend, but I don't see how she could be because she was old. Like forty or more. Billy was only thirty-two, so I don't think so."

"When was this, Malcolm, when the lady came with Billy?"

"Last year. Maybe this time last year."

"Are we quite ready to go, sir?"

Wiggins's voice, down below, was accusatory. Jury looked across the garden. Wiggins must have come from the kitchen. He stood, hands on hips, looking much like Malcolm had looked before.

Jury said to Malcolm, "My sergeant. I expect we'd better rappel down."

# Twenty-seven

They were stuffed into a smallish booth at a Happy Eater, whose bright carrot colors were enough to make the blind see. Wiggins had complained that they had not had lunch, and that tea had not really forti-fied him for the rest of the afternoon.

"You," said Wiggins, shoveling down his beans on toast, "were out there for a good-ish half an hour."

"And you were in the kitchen for the same amount of time. I hope you used it wisely." Jury ate his eggs.

"I did. The cook was quite nice, gave me more tea and a slice of her apple cake."

This would be, for Wiggins, using the time wisely.

He went on: "Apparently, Roderick is pleasant enough, but the lady of the house is a right harridan. Margaret—that's the maid—got a real dressing-down the other day for using her duster on the frames of the paintings."

Jury frowned. "Why would that merit a dressing-down?"

" 'They's to be touched by no one but me and my husband.' " Wiggins fluted, mimicking the little maid.

Jury thought about this. "Billy was very much interested in art, to the tune of subsidizing it. There are two paintings in that house Malcolm says weren't always there, that were acquired perhaps a year ago. That strikes me as strange."

"Why?" Wiggins sipped what was probably his hundredth cup for the day. "You could go out and buy two paintings at the same time if you wanted."

"It's not exactly like bed linen, sets of sheets. You wouldn't be trying to match up two walls, now, would you? They might have come from the same source."

Wiggins shrugged again.

"Billy was tracing their provenance, so something struck him as strange, too. Find out about them and where they were acquired, if possible."

"Yes, boss." He sounded doubtful. "But if they're reproductions, well, there wouldn't really be anything, would there?"

"That's the point. Malcolm says Billy told him they weren't; they're the genuine article."

"A *Klimt*? But that's worth pots of money, isn't it?"

"Yes."

Then Wiggins returned to bemoaning the fate of the Happy Eater chain, which was to be shut down and turned into Burger Kings and more Little Chefs. He had nothing against Little Chefs as such, but nothing could drag him into a Burger King.

Jury had been forced to follow the Happy Eaters' demise because Wiggins talked about it whenever they got on the road. "Well, they're all owned, these motorway rest stops and A-road cafés, by Trust House Forte, aren't they?"

"Probably, but can you imagine a Burger King in place of this?" Wiggins swept his arm outward and very nearly knocked over the young waitress with her tray who'd come with fresh coffee. Wiggins apologized; she only smiled and poured.

As she padded away on rubber-soled trainers, Wiggins continued: "They're closing them down because, they say, Happy Eaters attract the gray-haired lot. They're after a different demographic."

"Please don't talk like a television presenter. 'Gray-haired lot'? That surprises me because I thought there was never anyone over six in Happy Eaters except for you and me." He looked at the children's play area, which was quite crowded even at this off-hour of three. The kiddies were having a marvelous time.

"Well, it's nice for the kiddies. Parents, too."

"Grandparents. The gray-haired lot."

Wiggins regarded him glumly. "So I guess you'd be just as happy at a Burger King."

"Wiggins, I'd be just as happy under the table. I know the demise of the Happy Eater is a historical event no less important than the Battle of Hastings, but would you stop going on about it for a minute and tell me what you found out after I left the living room."

Gloomily, Wiggins drank his coffee. "Roderick talked about his father. Sir Oswald. You know him."

"I do. He's the only reason we're here. What did Roderick say?"

"A lot about Sir Oswald's time at Bletchley Park. He said as a boy—he'd have been eight or nine then—that he loved knowing his dad was working on breaking codes, all very hush-hush. And this gave him a great boost in prestige around his mates. You know, the war was a giant playground for kids. Sounds weird, but there it is. They loved poking around in bombed-out buildings before they got chased off by wardens. Roderick described it as a wizard adventure. Hope and glory. All of that."

"That from Roderick? I'm surprised. He didn't sound as if he had a lot of play in him. I can see how kids might take the devastation that way. But what rather surprises me is that Roderick seems proud of his father. That doesn't fit with the picture Sir Oswald painted. There was a rift between the two. Roderick seldom goes to see him."

"Ah, *that,* I bet, would have coincided

with Olivia coming on the scene. Olivia clearly doesn't like Oswald. Nor he her. She pretty much puts the damper on the father-son relationship." Wiggins pushed back his plate and crossed his arms on the table. "I think Olivia's one of those people who doesn't like other people having relationships she's not a part of or doesn't control. She couldn't control Billy Maples. He and young Malcolm were apparently close. And she dislikes Malcolm intensely. Probably as much for that reason as for him being a pain in the arse."

"Money doesn't seem to be a motive, for which we might be grateful. According to their solicitor, he never made a will, which means he died intestate. It's too bad. It means it will go to his father, who surely doesn't need it. Maybe some to Sir Oswald. But Malcolm's too distant a relation to get anything. And Karl Brunner gets nothing because he isn't related."

"There's another part of Olivia Maples that sets my teeth on edge."

"What is it?"

"I think she uses people," Wiggins said. "I'm sure she used Billy, or tried to."

"Maybe he wouldn't let her. And that infuriated her."

"Enough to kill him?"

"I don't know. I can't work it out." Jury studied his coffee. "It's that Klimt."

# TWENTY-EIGHT

*"The Sacred Fount!"* exclaimed Melrose Plant, dropping the book he'd gone upstairs to get into Jury's lap, displacing the book Jury had been looking through.

Wiggins was in the kitchen, talking with Mrs. Jessup, though the talk might have revolved more around afternoon tea than it did her former employer.

Jury looked at the book. "That again."

"But you're the one who told me about it."

"I didn't plan on its dogging my footsteps forever. Actually, it was Kurt Brunner who told me."

"I'm fascinated, really. Olivia Maples and the vampire theme."

"Frankly, I can't imagine it in Olivia Maples or useful to Henry James." Jury looked at the bookshelves for a moment. "This is the writer who could peel the poses of social convention like an onion? The writer who could pack an entire moral universe into a look exchanged over dinner? The writer who could make rising from a chair the dead giveaway of an intimate relationship? The writer—"

"I'm impressed!"

"Don't be."

"I didn't know you were so conversant with the work of Henry James," said Melrose.

"I'm not. I was just reading this book while you were upstairs rooting around for this one." He held up *The Sacred Fount*. He turned it over in his hands. "But do you think that's the case here? I never knew Billy; I have to depend on what people say about him. Malcolm certainly was terrifically fond of Billy."

"Malcolm? Who's Malcolm?"

"Malcolm Mott, Billy's cousin, by marriage. Says they were best friends. Dislikes Olivia intensely. Olivia seems to be the trouble in that family. She's not that much older than Billy Maples, ten years perhaps."

"There they are again! The Brissendens."

Jury's smile was more ironic than good-natured. "You know, this 'sacred fount' stuff is drivel."

Melrose caught his breath, looking around the room as if the ghosts of every well-known Jamesian biographer and critic had heard and were now crowding in. "Drivel? Henry James—dear God—is drivel?" Melrose cushioned his forehead with his hand as if a migraine was on the horizon.

"Don't be so dramatic, for God's sakes. I didn't mean James; I meant this exchanging of youth and age. James didn't mean that—"

"Oh, you bet he did!" Melrose slapped his hands against his chair arms, rising and going to the window where he stood and wished he had a pocket watch to snap shut or pince-nez to twirl. "You'd be surprised at what James got up to in his stories."

Jury sighed, looking at Melrose in his velvet smoking jacket, and wondering if he was going to be sod-all use in this case.

"For instance," Melrose went on, "have

you ever read 'The Jolly Corner'?" He returned to his chair.

"No. The only things I've read are *Portrait of a Lady, The Turn of the Screw,* twenty-five pages of *The Ambassadors,* and several short stories, which were pretty good. Sinister, even."

Melrose said, "You're right. In 'The Jolly Corner' the narrator meets his own ghost— or rather, the ghost of a past he hadn't chosen. Brydon, he's the narrator—"

"Why are you telling me all this?"

Melrose paused. He'd forgotten. He searched the preceding conversation and remembered: "You said James couldn't possibly have meant that youth and age could be exchanged, one for the other, Grace Brissenden's age for her husband's youth."

"That's right. He didn't mean vampirism any more than Kafka meant a great big bug. It's only a metaphor."

"No, no, no, no. Unless you look at metaphor in a very special way. Neither was Kafka's bug a metaphor. Gregor really *was* that. Look"—Melrose shoved a little chocolate dish and a pen around—"Let's put you here, and the bug next to you."

"No, we'll put *you* here and the bug next to you."

"It's impossible to have a literary conversation with you."

"Don't I know it. And on a different note, why are you wearing that smoking jacket and fiddling with that cigarette holder?" Beyond the blank window the light was changing.

"What's the matter with it?" Melrose spread his hands on the smoking jacket, looking down.

"Nothing. It's a handsome ensemble. Listen: I think you should pop round to the Maples' place tomorrow and see what you can find out."

"Pop round? One doesn't just drop in."

"Well then, get yourself invited. I have a feeling the lady of the house has a real passion for a title. There's one thing I specifically want you to do: there are two paintings in that house, a Klimt and a Soutine. How much do you know about art?"

"A little more than how ants colonize. In other words, nothing."

"You couldn't tell an original from a reproduction?"

"Of course not, if it's a halfway decent

one. That's the point, isn't it? Who's going to hang a reproduction that looks fake?"

"Okay. When you go there, look at the Klimt in the entry hall and the Soutine in the living room. The Klimt is bolted to the wall—"

"I shouldn't wonder! My God, there's a fortune there; can you imagine?"

"That's the whole little mystery. They're reproductions, Roderick Maples told me. But according to Malcolm—"

"Malcolm again."

"Billy told him they were originals."

"Then why—"

"I don't know. The Soutine, which is much smaller, is hanging beside the fireplace mantel. I want you to look at the back and see if there's any identifying mark."

"Oh, that's brilliant! I just walk over to the wall and say, 'I think I'll have this'? And yank it off. That should get me invited back. What do you think I'll find?"

"I don't know. But I believe there's some connection between those paintings and the generosity Billy Maples showed to artists and that gallery."

"I'll try." Melrose got up. "Let's creak

along to dinner, shall we? I'm feeling rather
burdened by all of this."

Jury rose. "So was Malcolm."

"What?" Melrose was getting the coats.

"Go to see them."

# TWENTY-NINE

What did he expect if he was going to pub hop with Plant but a sizable headache in the morning?

Jury tossed down a couple of aspirin with his orange juice, followed by tea so strong the cup could have walked to the telephone by itself.

Jury held the cup and went to answer it.

"We need to talk," said DI Aguilar.

"Good morning. You always say that and we always wind up not talking."

She sighed. "I don't always, and we do."

Jury smiled. It sounded like Carole-anne: the tone, the injured pride, the syntax.

"Can you meet me?"

"Sure. In Piccadilly Circus."

A brief silence her end. "Is it my fault if you can't be alone in the same room with me?"

"Yes."

"Oh, for God's sakes. Come down to headquarters. Tolpuddle Street."

"I know where—"

But she had already hung up.


She led him into one of the interrogation rooms, which made him think he knew what suspects felt, and she closed the door behind them. Noncommitally, she looked at him and opened up a file.

"This is your doctor's report—"

"Technically, Dr. Nancy isn't my doctor."

She looked at him as one might at a deliberately obdurate child. "Please. Ballistics says the shot was fired from three to four feet away. There's very little tattooing. The path of the bullet and the angle of the gun suggest the shooter was probably about the victim's height."

" 'Probably' is the important word there."

"I was just thinking. . . . You talked to Kurt Brunner?"

"I did. Two days ago, in Rye."

"What conclusions did you draw? I mean, do you still think he's the one who did it?"

"I don't know. I have to talk to him again. But there is the fact that Kurt would hardly have made an appointment to see Billy."

"You said that before. But it could just have been that Brunner said, 'I'll see you at the Zetter later.' That's not what you'd call an appointment."

"Maybe not. Going back to the jacket, though. Billy wouldn't have kept it on to eat, probably. But if he removed it and then put it back on to meet whoever was coming, it wouldn't have been Brunner, would it? Billy wouldn't have made that formal gesture for Brunner."

"The thing is, Brunner would probably be too tall to hold the gun at the angle described here."

"Again, the 'probably' is important. I'll talk to Phyllis."

Lu looked down at the pages again. "She's very thorough. I expect she's quite a good pathologist."

"She is."

Keeping her eyes on the papers she was gathering back up, Lu said, "Have you known her a long time?"

"Yes." Jury waited.

"She's very attractive." Still not looking at Jury, she tapped the papers on the table, evening them up.

"Yes, she is."

"Is she a very good friend—oh, it's none of my business, anyway."

"Why isn't it?"

"What?" Her eyes widened. Clearly not the response she'd expected.

"Why isn't it your business?"

"Well . . . it just isn't. I mean, am I her business?"

"I don't know; I'll ask her."

"No! I mean, I don't care. I just thought if she's my business, I might be her business, if you know what I mean."

Jury was biting the inside of his cheek to keep his face straight. "No, I don't know what you mean. Do you even know what you mean?"

Her look was fierce. "Oh, don't get *smart*." Face flushed, she picked up the folder and sailed out of the room, dark hair flying, leaving him stranded.

When she was out of earshot, he nearly choked with laughter.

# THIRTY

As Melrose came to the end of the long drive to the Maples estate, he noticed a boy standing by the riotous bed of tulips just breaking free from the hold winter had on them. A terrierlike dog stood at the boy's feet. Melrose braked and got out of the car. The boy and dog stood and watched.

How old was he? Eleven? Nine? Three? One could no longer tell about children, childhood seeming to bypass many of them as they wore the same designer clothes as their mums and dads, went to the same chic places, smoked the same pot, leaving them, the children, by the time they were into their twenties and thirties, with nowhere new to go, nothing new to do.

These two stood still as statues, and Melrose, upon getting out of his car, called out a cheery hello. Neither replied by word or bark. Could they be mute? There had been a lot happening after the death of Billy Maples. First that detective, Chilten; then Jury; and now himself. Least of all himself. He turned away from the silent two and went up the steps to the door.

The maid let him in and asked him to wait as she went to fetch Mrs. Maples who, she was sure, would be down in half a minute. If it was only going to take her half a minute, why wasn't she present when he arrived? For he was spot-on time.

But the time here would not be wasted, as it would give him an opportunity to look closely at the painting that had caught his eye the moment he'd stepped inside. It was dazzling and it was, in all of its shower of golden glory, unmistakenly a Klimt. There was the dark-haired beauty at its center wrapped in a garment that was difficult to separate from its background—all of those bright, spangly colors. The painting was big and was indeed bolted to the wall. He looked at it from a distance and up close. But who was he to judge whether or not it was the original or a reproduction? That portrait of James in Lamb House. Were someone to tell him yes, that's the original John Singer Sargent, how would he know it wasn't?

Well, there was nothing to be gained by merely observing it.

Olivia Maples was a good-looking brunette in her forties with skin that looked untouched by anything but dew. She was wearing a dark blue cashmere dress the color of her eyes. He bet she had a closet full of things the color of her eyes.

"I'm so sorry, Lord Ardry, to keep you waiting," she said as she came into the living room to which the maid had finally led him as part of his house tour.

*No, you're not.* He smiled, took the outstretched hand. "Perfectly all right."

"My husband will be down in a minute. Shall we have tea? Or something stronger?"

"Oh, stronger, by all means."

She smiled and moved to a table between two long windows. The table held quite an array of bottles and decanters. These people took their drinking seriously. "Whiskey? Vodka? Perhaps a martini. I make quite good ones."

*I'll bet you do.* Melrose was stumped by her manner, which revealed nothing of her feelings about the murder of her stepson. "Whiskey is fine."

For a few moments she poured and measured and Melrose heard the gentle clink of bottles and glasses.

She brought him his drink and then took a seat at the other end of the sofa, turned so that she could see him. She sipped her drink—vodka or gin; one of the famous martinis, perhaps—and regarded him over its bowl. Slightly flirty? He couldn't assess it. She said, "We do appreciate your taking up Billy's lease. It will save us so much trouble. The National Trust was very understanding, but it does need someone in the place until the new tenants are ready."

"My pleasure. Anyway, I've always meant to visit Lamb House, never got around to it; one doesn't." Whatever that meant. "I'm very sorry about your son. You have enough to contend with without having to manage a piece of property."

"Billy was my stepson, actually. I don't mean I didn't feel—" She let that hang. "We both were of course shattered by it." She sipped her drink.

Olivia was clearly not shattered. That did not mean she felt nothing, naturally. He just wondered what constituted the something she did feel. She was hard to see into. Her flawless face, dressed down, no doubt because of what had happened, was opaque.

He said, "It's very pleasant, Lamb House." Now a completely natural question: "Why did your stepson want to live there?"

She leaned back against the arm of the sofa. "Billy was never one to confide in others."

Yet he had, to that priest Jury mentioned. And why would a simple explanation of his move be a confidence? Billy had hardly undertaken some hush-hush mission. Everyone knew where he was.

Melrose wondered about the boy's life and wondered why he had thought of Billy just now as "the boy." He felt a weight of sadness in it, in Billy's story. "Perhaps your stepson was a great admirer of Henry James."

"I expect so. Kurt Brunner is an admirer, I know that."

It was then the door opened to admit Roderick Maples. Melrose got up and took the man's outstretched hand as Olivia made the unnecessary introduction.

"I was just telling Lord Ardry," she said, "that he's taken a load off our shoulders."

"Indeed." Roderick gave him a curt nod, not at all uncivil, but as if the man could not animate his face enough for a sign of welcome. "Thank you." Roderick was not given to the hyperbole of his wife. He went to the drinks table, poured himself some whiskey, drank it down, then poured another.

Olivia watched and made no comment.

Melrose used the few moments by looking around for the Soutine painting. Ah, there it was, just to the right of the fireplace.

Roderick sank into a chair. He was tall and despite his age rather handsome in a worn-satchel way.

"Lord Ardry asked me if Billy was a Henry James devotee—"

There was no hitch in the voice at the mention of Billy.

"—and wonders why he took up the tenancy of Lamb House."

One would think she wanted to make sure that her husband knew what had been said out of his presence, so that he wouldn't fumble and let something slip.

Roderick thought about Billy's tenancy. "Well, I know he liked books, *loved* books. He said he found them a comfort." Roderick paused to reflect on that. "Are you a James scholar yourself?" Roderick seemed to have forgotten what had brought Melrose among them.

"Not at all." Drat, wasn't he supposed to be writing a book on Henry? "A scholar, I mean. Nothing so grand. I'm doing research with an eye to writing a book, but that's all."

Olivia laughed. "I should say that's quite enough!"

"Kurt Brunner, on the other hand, is a true aficionado of James. You've met him, haven't you?"

Melrose nodded as Roderick sat contemplating the ceiling, the cherubs overflowing each of its corners. "That might be the reason Billy took on Lamb House. He's an interesting chap, Brunner," said Roderick, frowning as if he'd not thought of that before. "German. From Munich, or is it Berlin? I think. Freshen that?"

He had risen from his chair and reached for Melrose's glass. He took Olivia's and went to the drinks table.

"Do you know Rye at all?" she asked.

"Only what I've picked up since being there." He hoped the conversation wasn't going to deteriorate into talk about the surrounding country. "Kurt Brunner showed me around. He's an interesting person, as you said. What will he be doing now?"

"I don't know," said Olivia. "Perhaps he'll go back to Germany."

Think him back to Berlin: a peremptory disposal of a man who'd been their son's employee and friend for five years. Anyway, one might think Roderick, if not Olivia, would be having Kurt Brunner around here every day in order to find out every last bit of information about Billy.

Melrose felt stricken for Billy Maples's sake. He seemed not to have made a very deep inroad into the affections of these two. A story of James's he'd been reading came back to him. "The Bench of Desolation."

Nobody here was sitting on it. Why?

Well, for God's sakes, it wasn't the mystery of the week: many grown-up children were simply estranged from their parents.

He was turned in such a way on the couch that he could see through the long windows on either side of the drinks table. They—Roderick and Olivia—were more or less facing him and could not. What he saw was the face of the lad he'd seen outside. The boy was standing there.

As Olivia and Roderick kept the talk up of the countryside, the quaintness of Rye, the history of Hastings, Melrose looked at the boy. The boy's gaze was adamant, not unfriendly but determined. Melrose quite enjoyed a good stare now and then, but he couldn't get the boy to drop his gaze and go off.

"Something wrong, Mr. Plant?"

"Wrong? Not a bit, no."

Olivia turned to see what was going on but before she could complete the turn, the face disappeared from the window. She looked a question at Melrose.

"There was . . . someone out there, I thought." Now, why had he not simply told her what he saw? He didn't know. Except that whenever he got around children, as hard as he tried not to get sucked into that vortex of childhood, he failed. There was something about him that brought out a child's patronizing ways. He liked to think of himself as an adult they could spar with. Actually, he was more like a seal they tried to train. They became their most condescending little selves around him. This was more or less encapsulated in the face at the window at that moment: with Melrose they stared. With other adults, they vanished.

Roderick turned to look. "Probably only Malcolm."

Jury's voice: *"You should talk to Malcolm."*

He had neglected to tell Melrose that Malcolm was a child. From Roderick's tone, it was fairly clear Malcolm wasn't theirs.

"Who is Malcolm?"

"Our nephew," said Olivia. "My sister's boy. She's hit, you know, a bad patch. Malcolm's been with us for two years now."

Roderick laughed. "I'd hardly call two years a patch, Olivia. It's more like the entire canvas, isn't it?"

What a break! "Speaking of canvas, I couldn't help but notice the magnificent Klimt in the foyer."

Roderick smiled wanly. "It's very good, isn't it. A reproduction, of course. Were it the real thing, it'd fetch millions—many,

many millions." He turned his gaze to the area of the fireplace. "Same goes for that Soutine. Not such a splash as the Klimt, but still good."

Melrose said, "Oh. I'm surprised. I assumed the Klimt was the original, seeing that's it's bolted to the wall."

Roderick laughed. "That's not for it's value, man; that's because it kept falling down. It's rather heavy."

"Would you mind my having a closer look at the Soutine?" Whether they'd mind or not, Melrose was already up and over to the fireplace.

"Not at all, not at all," said Roderick.

Whether the original or not, it was a landscape of tortured trees and a collapsing house—a storm, perhaps. It made Melrose think of van Gogh; the bold brushstrokes, the intense colors, the *feeling* that nothing was going well here. "I wonder, would you mind if I took it over to the light to have a look?"

Roderick's pause was notable. But it was a small painting and there was no reason— was there?—to refuse. "Why, no . . . I expect that won't hurt anything."

Melrose took it down, carefully, and

walked it to the window. He studied the painting for a moment or two, then ran his finger over the frame, and then, as if accidentally, turned it over for no more than two seconds before he looked again at the picture and took it back to its resting place.

Something, some mark, had been inked over on the back. He couldn't tell what.

Roderick, lit up by liquor, was talking about Malcolm. At least, Melrose assumed they were not talking about him.

"—nothing but! He's surly, unresponsive, destructive, and terrible to that little dog of his," Roderick said.

*Sounds a right treat,* thought Melrose.

"—ties the animal up and pulls him up that garden wall."

"He's only ten, Roddy."

"Won't be eleven if your sister doesn't get back here and see to him."

Melrose smiled. As mum hadn't been keeping up with Malcolm for two years now, the boy was probably in no danger of not celebrating his next birthday. "Perhaps he misses his parents." That mite of sympathy from himself surprised him.

"Surprisingly," said Roderick, "he did

appear to be talking to your detective friend."

"The superintendent," added Olivia.

"Ah, yes, Superintendent Jury does have a way with children."

Roderick barely let him finish before he said, "Can't imagine what the boy could have told him that's in any way helpful." The crease of Roderick's brow grew deeper, as if this were worrying him.

"Well, Roddy, you know Malcolm did get on very well with Billy. He quite liked Billy. He might have been the only person Malcolm did like." As if looking for the departed, her eyes searched the room.

"I expect my son had a way with children, too. I never understood it, as he hadn't much of a way with grown-ups." Roderick's hand slipped across his eyes, perhaps wiping at incipient tears.

Melrose set down his glass. "You know, I'd rather like a turn around your gardens. One of the things I most enjoy about Lamb House is its garden. I'm quite a gardener myself. *Oh, do shut up before you stick your foot in it again!* "Would you mind?"

They both shook their heads. How could they mind? This eccentric titled gentleman comes to visit and takes the painting off the wall and then invites himself out of your company? What's to mind?

"By all means, Lord Ardry," Olivia said. "Best be careful if Malcolm is out there."


"Oh, all right," said Malcolm from the top of the brick wall, as he heaved a great sigh and started lowering himself and Waldo down to the ground.

All right to what? Melrose hadn't ordered him to go into his tea. It was apparently an all right to just one more demand on him that he took like a curtain call. Melrose was fascinated in spite of himself by the descent. The terrier was tied around the waist with a red and blue bandanna over which were several windings of rope, much like the harnesses in pictures Melrose had seen somewhere of cattle being transferred from dock to ship.

The dog, unable to paw around at the wall for fingerholds, had to swing to and fro, sometimes hitting the brick, sometimes not. The boy had the rope tied about his waist and running over his shoulder in what he imagined to be mountain climber style. The other end of the rope had been slung over a sturdy branch of an oak. The dog was the first to plop to the ground and then the boy.

Under the riveting gaze of Malcolm Mott, Melrose introduced himself. "I'm Lord Ardry. How do you do?"

"And I'm Gene Autry. I've been better."

Melrose took a step backward. "Gene Autry? You're not old enough to remember him. That singer cowboy? Why that was decades ago!"

"Billy has records. We listened to them."

It was somehow poignant that Malcolm seemed to assume the whole world must know who Billy was.

"And do you sing?"

Malcolm scraped his poorly cut brown hair off his forehead and said nothing.

Melrose thought it might give him a leg up if he mentioned Jury. "You met a friend of mine the other day—a detective?"

Now Malcolm looked less hostile, but still suspicious. "You mean the one from Scotland Yard?"

"The very chap, yes. I'm sorry about Billy Maples. That was terrible. I'm living in his house in Rye at the moment—"

"You *are*?"

"I am. It's just until the next tenant's ready to take over. Have you been there to visit your cousin?"

Malcolm nodded. "A couple times, I did." He looked off. "There was a writer lived there once."

For some reason this struck Melrose as inexpressibly sad. It was as if something in his experience—and in Malcolm's—were summed up and sealed. But he didn't know what. "What did you do there?"

Malcolm shrugged.

Melrose waited but Malcolm said nothing more.

"I really like the garden. It has that high wall all around."

Malcolm was silent.

"Aren't you going to untie that dog?"

"No. Maybe we'll have another go at it."

"But doesn't he mind?" Waldo didn't look as if he minded anything. Melrose had never seen such a stolid dog before.

"Nah. He kind of likes it."

"Just how do you get that idea?"

"Well, you don't hear him barking or growling or anything, do you?"

"Perhaps he doesn't think it'll do any good."

Malcolm looked at Waldo, frowning. "Why'd he think that?"

"Because you're so determined." Melrose rather liked that morsel of analysis, but it didn't get him anywhere. "Did you climb the wall at Lamb House, you and Waldo? And perhaps your cousin liked to climb."

Malcolm gave him a pained look. "He did. And he used to like to walk on the nature preserve. Billy liked all the different birds and stuff. You can't see them anywhere else. Plovers and little grebes and that."

They stood in silence for a moment, and then Malcolm asked, "What's it mean if you die intes—what's the word?"

"Intestate, you mean? Ordinarily, it means your estate either goes to the Crown or perhaps to your nearest relation. Or both."

"*What?* Nah. You're making it up."

"Why on earth would I do that? I'm not getting your cousin's money."

"What about his flat in Chelsea?"

"I'm not getting that, either."

Malcolm was about to reply when their names were called.

———

Melrose thanked the maid, who had brought his coat.

Roderick was standing with him at the door. There was no sign of Olivia.

"Talking to young Malcolm were you?" asked Roderick. "That's an uphill battle. Malcolm is not very forthcoming."

"Neither am I," Melrose replied, holding out his hand, taking leave.

Roderick laughed and shook his hand.

# THIRTY-ONE

Jury had always liked this part of Chelsea between the Fulham and King's roads. Deep pink clematis spilled more profusely over gates; dogwoods were more abundant in their show of blossoms; willows lacier in their weeping branches. Perpetual spring had taken root here and flourished.

Rose Ames's house of ruddy brick was a patch of real estate on Bury Walk worth, he'd guess, a million quid, with its front and back gardens and old stone wall offering as complete a privacy as one could hope to get in London.

The stone walk from pavement to front door already gleamed in the afternoon sun;

still, a boy was sweeping it. Nearby, a gardener was hard at work on a bed of primulas. Jury wondered how large Rose Ames's staff was.

So when she appeared at the door dressed in black, he supposed she must be an elderly servant, very neat, not a hair out of place, a housekeeper, perhaps, and he automatically asked to speak to Mrs. Rose Ames, surprised to find that he was already doing it, then later thinking it wasn't surprising, Rose Ames not being the sort to bother with middlemen or protocol or image. She was direct, conceding a point or two to polite society in offering Jury tea, which he turned down.

"Thanks, but I'm tea'd up for the day."

A slight smile from Rose Ames. "I've always thought there could never be enough tea, though certainly enough day."

*Oh, Wiggins, where art thou?*

Jury grinned. "My sergeant would love you, Mrs. Ames."

She appeared to understand the allusion, but said nothing. Enough banter.

Jury had taken a seat in a crisp, glazed cotton chair in a riotous pattern of violets, hydrangeas, roses, and bright green intertwining vines. The material was so silky he nearly slid off its edge, where he was resting his elbows on his knees, hands folded before him.

"It's about your grandson, Billy, Mrs. Ames." He did not know why he chose to speak of Billy Maples by his given name only, as if he knew him, as if he knew *her*. Perhaps she was one of those people who suggest to strangers someone they know or once knew, but couldn't quite put their finger on. Jury wondered who it was Rose Ames brought to mind, this person he couldn't put his finger on. There was the old woman in that awful retirement hotel in— South Shields was it? Some place in Tyne and Wear; or the elderly Emily Croft who had cautioned him that "Death was always with us." Yes, these women did come along in his life, not quite stamped from the same stamp, but identical enough that he noted it now. He thought of Lady Cray and smiled.

Rose Ames waited with an uncanny calmness, a measured look, a repression of feeling that perhaps broke free in the carousing slipcovers.

He smiled again, before he remembered the woman was in mourning.

"Billy," she seemed to be reminding him. She cocked her head.

"I'm sorry."

"You're from Scotland Yard." Reminding him again of all the things he had forgotten. "Another policeman—or detective—was here." She thought a bit. "A man named Chilten? And a female." She pondered. "Aligar?"

"Aguilar."

"They were from the Islington station. She seemed to be in charge. She's awfully, oh, intense, isn't she? Rather ferocious. I'd hate to have her after me."

"So would I."

"Why now is Scotland Yard interested?"

"In this case, they asked me to help. You see, I was called in first because the person who found the—who found Billy was a friend of mine. So he called me."

Again she cocked her head. Running it all together like a string of beads. "But the one who found Billy was a child. A twelve- or thirteen-year-old boy, I understood."

Jury nodded.

"A friend of yours?"

He looked around the room, wishing he'd left out that detail.

But she had sat back in the sofa among the violets and roses smiling rather cheerfully. Apparently, she liked the idea. As if any Scotland Yard detective—a *superintendent,* no less!—who was that off the wall should be, if not exactly trusted, at least acceded to. She looked around the room, too, keeping him company. Even in the midst of what Jury felt must be real grief—her clothes, her strained eyes, her own lack of color spoke to that—in the midst of all this she could connect.

"I really am sorry, Mrs. Ames, but I need to ask you a few questions."

"All right." Her long narrow fingers plucked at the black sleeve at her wrist.

"You and Billy got on well, did you?"

"Yes, very well, but not always." She considered. "He was much too impetuous sometimes, and I took him to task for it. He thought I was too hard on him."

"Impetuous how?"

"One thing was that he'd give rather large sums of money away, I believe to artists, who of course could use large sums of money as they don't work."

Jury wanted to laugh. Or perhaps she

was being ironic. "Probably an artist thinks he does work."

She puffed out a breath through pursed lips. "Not from what I could see. This particular gallery that he favored appears to go in for paintings of pleased-looking cows, and there's one revisionist Mark Rothko by a color-blind painter. Have you been to that gallery?"

"I have, yes. The Melville. I don't know how I missed the Rothko imitation. I saw the cows; if those were the painters Billy wanted to support, I don't blame you for thinking he threw the money away. But I don't think those painters were the ones."

"Nevertheless, I told him he was crazy to be giving money to some artistic illiterate who could best paint by numbers. His answer was that it was his money and he'd do what he liked with it."

"That was true, though."

"Yes, it was true. But a good deal of that money he inherited not just from his mother, but from his grandfather. My husband, James. And it just irritated me to death to see Billy throw it away." She leaned forward, out of her glazed cotton garden. "If this artist had been the next Manet or even David

Hockney he was supporting, fine. Indeed I would applaud that."

"So would anyone. Manets and Hockneys are hardly thick on the ground."

She considered that. "Yes, you do have a point. I was expecting too much."

Jury wondered. "Do you think it was one painter in particular, then?"

"It would make more sense, wouldn't it? I mean artistic merit aside, he'd, the painter I mean, have had some value for Billy."

Jury looked into her gray eyes, the skin beneath them smudged from a recent bout of either allergies or tears. She looked away. "Do you think this artist was a particular friend, then?"

"Oh *please,* Superintendent. You mean was he just a little Nellie? I interpreted all of this breast-beating for the sake of art to be precisely that. Perhaps Billy fancied him, I don't know."

"You didn't object to that?"

"Well, really, what difference would it have made if I had? You're wondering if I find it, generally speaking, rather louche behavior? Yes, I guess I do. But after all, one's sexual orientation is a given, isn't it? Being an idiot about money isn't. It's learned behavior, and that can change."

"Did you meet any of Billy's friends at all?"

"Once, yes. He brought an extremely attractive woman here once. Her name was Anjelica, no, Angela something."

"And you still think he might have been gay?"

"Perhaps she was a screen. Or she might have been some unconscious choice. Or, more simply, perhaps Billy was one of those who liked it both ways." Daintily, she smoothed the arm of the chair.

Jury cornered a laugh and shoved it back in. "Why do you suppose he broke it off with her?"

Rose's eyes widened. She sat back among the flowers. "I have no idea. I'm surprised he was taken with her, though, because she was at least ten or fifteen years older." She pulled herself up. "Mr. Jury, if I don't have a cup of tea, I'll start baying. Would you come along to the kitchen with me? We can continue our talk whilst I put the kettle on."

"Happy to." Oh, how he wished Wiggins were here! For Wiggins, a trip to the kitchen was as rejuvenating as one to Lourdes. He followed Rose Ames out of the living room.

The kitchen was quite handsome. From one of those hanging racks, copper pots and pans glinted and gleamed. She filled a copper kettle, rather old and battered, and set it on a great Viking stove.

"I'm surprised you don't have staff—or a cook, at least."

"Oh, I have them; just God knows where they are. They're like mice. They skitter away at the most inconvenient times. I keep meaning to fire the lot, but I'm lazy. It would mean getting replacements and you know how difficult *that* is. Billy was lucky to have a quite decent cook, though she's not as good as she thinks she is." She whispered this last, as if in confidence.

"Mrs. Jessup?"

"Is that her name? I keep wanting to call her Miss Jessel, of course. Well, one does get awfully caught up in Henry James with one's grandson in his old house."

Jury leaned against the door frame as he watched her open the tea canister and spoon some out into a stoneware teapot.

"Well, the woman dislikes me with an intensity." She shrugged as she said this.

"Probably because I criticized her cooking. I went around to Lamb House for Sunday lunch a month ago. She served up a very handsome leg of lamb, rare. Now, I know rare is the going thing these days, I mean, restaurants seem to have cultivated a taste for raw everything"—she was collecting sugar and cups and saucers on a tray—"but you shouldn't eat rare lamb. It has to be cooked through to avoid that disease—BSE, I think—no, that's mad cow disease, isn't it? At any rate, there's one that sheep carry."

"I didn't know that."

"Well, you do now, so take heed. Or rather, tell your cook to."

"Oh, I shall definitely do that."

The kettle clattered over the burner and she whisked it off and filled the pot. "So Mrs. Jessup took umbrage and told me no one had ever criticized her cooking and I told her it was no criticism of her culinary expertise, only that lamb, no matter who cooks it, must be well done. She wasn't mollified. To add to that, on another occasion, she had served rabbit, which I refused to eat because of the danger of tularaemia."

"What's that?"

"A bacteria rabbits carry and it can be fatal. Again we went the route of her cooking ability, which, I told her, was beside the point. Can you carry the tray?"

"Glad to." Jury took it from her hands and followed her back into the living room.

Over her shoulder, Rose said, "There's also myxomatosis."

"Never heard of it." Jury set the tray on the coffee table.

"You don't recall that awful time when the government wiped out just about the entire rabbit population because of myxomatosis? I thought that was criminal; there was no need to go to that extent." She poured the tea. "Philip Larkin wrote a poem about it. Do you like Philip Larkin?"

"One of my favorites."

She handed Jury his tea, saying, "It's called 'Myxomatosis,' but poetry never is about what it appears to be, is it? In any event, the narrator is speaking to the rabbit trapped in a field. He calls it a 'soundless' field. I wonder if this is because rabbits were rounded up and slaughtered and now this one is the only one left. He's imagining what the rabbit must have been thinking just before he killed it. He addresses the rabbit: You must have thought everything would be all right *'If you could only keep quite still and wait.'* It's terribly poignant."

" 'If you could only keep quite still and wait.' Yes. We do that ourselves don't we? Hope if we don't make a lot of noise, the danger might pass us? Anyway, Mrs. Jessup didn't take too well to your commenting on the possible toxic effect of her cooking, or its possible fatal outcome." Jury laughed. "Can't say I blame her. What was the name of that disease?"

"Myxomatosis."

The small clock chimed the hour. Jury was surprised he'd been here for well over an hour. He was to be at Sir Oswald's by three.

But this question was important: "Mrs. Ames, did you wonder what was causing Billy's mood swings? It must have been the reason he impressed different people in different ways. Some found him easygoing, sweet, even; others found him explosive, 'on a short fuse' was how one put it."

"No, I didn't wonder what caused it. I *knew* what caused it. Billy was a manic-depressive." She poured more tea.

Jury was astonished that she would assert this so baldly.

She went on. "I tried to get Roderick and Olivia to take it seriously; I know my Mary would have—"

"Your daughter?"

She nodded. "But Roderick is simply too proud to admit there was a mental disorder."

"Did you say anything to Billy himself?"

"Oh, yes. But it's like talking to an alcoholic, isn't it? He's the last one to admit to a problem. I asked Billy to at least try and get medication. There are psychiatrists who are into pharmaceuticals who would prescribe something without demanding you see them two or three times a week. But he wouldn't do it, which was to be expected, since he wouldn't admit anything was wrong in the first place. I told him this condition runs in the family. But that had little effect."

Jury frowned. He recalled something Roderick had said about his first wife, that she was temperamental and moody. "You mean Mary?"

"Mary? Oh, no, I mean me."

His mouth literally fell open. *"You?"*

She laughed. It was a sweet and silvery sound. "I'm so glad you're astonished. Yes, I'm the villain of the piece. My own mother was in and out of institutions when they were even worse places than they are now. And I, I was luckier; my father found an excellent doctor who knew about manic-depressive behavior and its treatment long before we started calling it a bipolar disorder."

"When did you get this treatment? How old were you?"

"Twenty or so. But up until that time, I'd be ashamed to admit to some of the things I did. During the war, I . . . I was a hellion. I had no care nor conscience for other people. Much worse than Billy, I'll have to say."

He just looked at her, trying to imagine her hellion days, and couldn't. "Then could Billy have aroused somebody's wrath?"

"If he was as I was in the depressive state, he certainly could. So if you asked me if he had enemies, all I can say is I wouldn't be surprised. I hate to think it, but there it is."

Jury drank his tea and looked at her.

# THIRTY-TWO

Jury sat in the mellow light of a late afternoon sun in the little mews house off Cadogan Square. Sir Oswald Maples had answered the door himself. It was, he had said, one of his better days.

Jury was talking about his visit with Rose Ames.

Oswald laughed. "Rose is quite something. Billy, gay? That's what she told you?"

"I asked her."

Oswald looked puzzled. "But why would you think that? I'm sure you're wrong. Or she is."

"She thought it was possible, that's all.

That Angela Riffley was a screen, or could be, possibly an unconscious choice—"

"I never knew a person to analyze every detail the way Rose does."

Jury smiled. "No? What about your old workplace, GC and CS? What about you code breakers? Don't tell me that wasn't analyses right down to the ground."

Oswald laughed a little. "Yes, I get your point. I should admire the tendency. But I still think Rose is wrong."

Jury didn't comment on that. He said, "I asked her what, if anything, she thought about Billy's mood swings. Whether it was possible Billy had what they call bipolar disorder."

Oswald thought about this. "He was certainly moody, yes . . ."

"She hardly hesitated in telling me it was a long-standing trait in her family. She said she herself had suffered from it."

"I had no idea. When was she diagnosed?"

"When she was in her twenties. Apparently she found a very good doctor. But she said up until then she'd been a hellion."

Oswald smiled. "I can imagine."

"She tried to get Billy to do something, to

see a psychiatrist, something—but he wouldn't."

"No. He found Kurt Brunner. Billy needed somebody to prop him up at times."

"What were his parents doing about him?"

"Roderick didn't know what to do, and Olivia of course wasn't aware anything should be done, advocating, as always, freedom to choose."

"Addicts aren't free to choose." He thought about Aguilar; he wondered how free he was to choose.

"How true." Oswald leaned forward, plucked up his cane. "I have something here that's quite interesting. It might throw some light on things, certainly will upon Roderick." Oswald managed to get to his feet with the help of the cane and move to the bookshelves along one wall. The bottom shelf of one stored papers, notebooks, and folders. From a pile of folders, he drew out one, moved to the sofa, and handed it to Jury.

"Are you familiar with the Kinder-transport?"

"No. What's this?" Jury held up the folder.

"In a moment. Let me freshen these drinks."

As his hand went toward his glass, Jury rose and said, "Allow me." He picked Oswald's glass from the coffee table. "It's not often I get the chance to pour an eighteen-year-old Glenlivet."

"Just be sure we each get the same measure."

Jury did and handed Oswald his drink. Then he went back to his sofa and got comfortable. A sip of the whiskey was enough to ensure that.

"The Kindertransport was what one might call an underground railway, organized to get children out of Germany and Poland and Czechoslovakia. These trains went by way of Holland to England. This was in thirty-nine, right after the pogroms. What was needed was a country to take the children to. The US—I think to its shame—refused, as did many others. But we didn't. The trains eventually got ten thousand children out who would certainly otherwise have gone to the camps with their parents. And for the most part, these children never saw their families again. Can you imagine what that parting was like at the stations?"

"I'd rather not."

"No. Well, it was reported that occasionally a desperate parent would actually reach up to the window of the train and pull his child through it."

"How sad. I suppose the ones who allowed their children to go, probably knowing they'd never see them again, they were courageous."

"Yes. I try to put myself in their place. I imagine Billy's being taken away on one of the trains." He stopped and slowly shook his head.

But he *was* taken away. Jury could feel himself staring down miles of empty track, and he wondered what had been the use of it. The bombs, the burning buildings. He thought of his mother dying in one of them. Everything turns to rubble and dust in the end. He wondered how those parents stood it. Or how Oswald Maples stood it, his only grandson murdered.

Oswald took out a big white handkerchief, passed it over his eyes and under his nose.

Jury said, "I'm sorry."

Maples put the handkerchief back in his pocket. "Anyway, this document," he said, pointing to the file. "I found it in one of the huts when we were clearing out in forty-three. I don't know, nor did anyone, just how it got there. I don't attach any particular mystery to its having gotten there other than the mystery of carelessness in failing to log it; however, the content is quite interesting. It pertains to the Kindertransport."

He handed the file to Jury, who opened it and looked at the several pages inside. Jury looked up. "I don't read German." He smiled.

"Oh, dear. But isn't the translation there? There *was*—I had one of the secretaries type it out in English—well, sorry. I got so used to the language in the ordinary way of things. Here, let me read it to you."

Jury passed the file across the table.

Sir Oswald adjusted his glasses, saying, "I've read this so many times I very nearly have it memorized." Delicately, he cleared his throat.

Jury found him to be delicate in all of his movements, a thrifty person in that respect. But then if he, Jury, were hounded by pain with every movement, he'd be economical with those movements, too.

"It begins," said Oswald, "rather in

medias res; I have no idea what happened to the first page or pages. I supposed it could have been much longer, but who knows?"

"You're talking about Bletchley Park? Codes and ciphers?"

"Enigma, yes. But this wasn't coded. It begins:

. . . why being transported to freedom? Why being saved? Hans was not saved. He was not borne off to a better, brighter life. I walked that platform to the end and back again. I studied their faces, some of them no older than two or three, others fifteen or sixteen, and many Hans's age.

And then I stood quite still and looked at the children pressed up against the open windows of one car. There were forty or fifty of them crowded there, a few weeping for their parents, but most of them with a sort of astonished interest in this event, many laughing, many pleased. It was, after all, a trip, an adventure. One of them, a boy of eight or nine, was especially excited, as if he were about to get his first taste of freedom.

Freedom: I thought this ironic. I wanted to tell him there is no freedom. We are bound, each of us, if by nothing else, by our attachments.

Of course, the Jew had not meant to kill him. (He kept claiming he had not meant to shoot the boy and perhaps not, but even there I wonder.) He was insane to fire at the group of SS where a little band of schoolchildren was so close by. In my mind's eye I watch them, have watched them again and again.

The train rested there for some minutes while I regarded this car full of children and that particular nine-year-old boy, whose face turned pale at the trouble visited on his mother and father's having to watch him go. Just as the train began to move, I reached up and from that little crowd of children pulled him down. He was startled into silence and looked around, baffled as a blind boy seeking some exit. The others called and screamed after him, and waved and hung out the window as the train left the station.

I walked the boy back to the line of parents gathered behind a barrier, all straining toward their children as the train pulled away, weeping and calling out, and this still goes on endlessly in my mind, as if all of life were this weeping and calling out.

It was not hard to find his parents. They were astounded, seeing him there and not on the train and clearly torn between relief and anxiety. His name was Josef. That was the name they called him. I watched their faces, their pale, drawn faces and watched the light and color drain from the day. What was happening? They did not understand—how could they?—when I took my Luger from its holster and shot him in the head. I watched him fall like a star and crumple at my feet.

Strange to say, but I did not hear the shot. Inside my head was nothing but a drum roll.

The guards rushed over, but stopped short when they saw me. "The boy did not have clearance to be on the train."

I snapped this out at them and at the parents, who were too horrified to object. Anyway, what would be the point of objecting now? He was dead, and I . . .

"There it ends." Oswald Maples shut the folder.

"My God. Who was this person?"

"His name was Röhm. Obergruppen-führer Werner Röhm, a lieutenant general in the SS."

"A high-ranking SS officer. So the other men, the guards, the police—no one was about to dispute what he did," said Jury.

"Exactly. The SS had carte blanche. They could do damned near whatever they chose to do."

Jury thought for a moment. "Would that have appeared as news?"

Maples laughed. "In the media? The shooting of a Jewish child? Probably not. It must have been happening on a daily basis. Not, of course, with that particular intent, yet many children were shot down while their parents watched. No, it wouldn't be newsworthy. We looked; we couldn't find anything."

"But the first incident, the boy named Hans—?"

"The general's son. One of them; he had two boys. That I did discover. Yes, that happened. A Jew named Aaron Stein leveled a shot-gun at a group of German soldiers across the street from his apartment building. He killed one of the soldiers, but in doing it, shot a little boy by accident. Hans Röhm. The general's son."

"And what happened to the shooter?"

"That shouldn't be hard to guess: he was shot and killed. When the SS moved to round up the man's family, they discovered they were all dead. Murdered, naturally, in the course of things. So Herr Stein knew he wasn't putting them at risk."

"But the other people who lived in the building?"

"Ah. Yes. Herr Stein should have thought of that. Everyone in the building was gathered up. There was a pretense of demanding a confession from whichever of them had fired the shots, but naturally, no confession was forthcoming. The man was dead. The officers knew the shooter was dead on the floor of number 21 Lindenstrasse. Since obviously no one confessed, they shot them

all. Shot them where they stood. It was a
mercy, I suppose, to Herr Stein that he
didn't witness that. He should have thought
of that, but with his entire family slaughtered, he wouldn't be thinking too clearly."

"Such massive retribution. People not
only innocent but unconnected to this
Stein."

"There was one connection: they were
Jews."

Jury finished off his whiskey and sat
thinking. He said, "That bit about Röhm
wondering if it was an accident." He jabbed
his finger toward the file. Maples opened it
again and read:

" 'He claimed that he had not meant to
shoot the boy . . .' "

They were silent for a moment. Jury said,
"But what if he did? This Stein actually
meant to shoot Hans Röhm. That would
mean that General Röhm must have done
something prior to this. He speaks somewhere in there of revenge. Vengeance
against himself, I mean."

Maples gave an uncertain laugh. "Dear
God, it goes on and on, doesn't it? Röhm
commits some crime against Stein; Stein

shoots Röhm's son; Röhm shoots the child in the station."

"Yes, it goes on and on. There's never an end to revenge. It's all connected. Who was Aaron Stein and why did he shoot the general's son? Assuming that was really his target."

Maples shook his head. "We don't know. There was no more said beyond the report that such a shooting did take place. But not with Hans Röhm as the target. Just the SS troops."

"That nightmare part of the army."

"Yes. The Schutzstaffel. Himmler's boys. Death's heads on their hats, runes on their collars, murder in their hearts. It was an SS officer who murdered Stein's family. I'd say that might be a motivator."

"Röhm himself?"

"I shouldn't think so. He was too high-ranking to perform such a routine task." Maples picked up, set down his glass. "I've found that people who seek revenge can wait; they can wait a long, long time. They have no hesitancy about taking down the innocent along with the guilty. None at all."

Jury asked, "Why did you bring this up?"

Maples didn't answer immediately and Jury took the silence to mean he was questioning whether he should answer at all. But then he said, "Kurt Brunner is, as you know, German."

Jury waited.

"I've been thinking about this Kindertransport and Kurt Brunner."

Because of Sir Oswald's obvious discomfort, Jury tried to help the story along: "You think Kurt Brunner has something to do with this incident involving General Röhm?"

Curtly, Maples nodded. "I do, yes." He shifted his weight on the chair and went on. "Kurt is in his midfifties, I believe. That would have made him somewhere around three or four at the time the Kindertransport started. It was nineteen thirty-nine."

Jury frowned. "Yes. What?"

"The little Jewish boy shot by Röhm. His name was Josef Brunner. He had a younger brother." Maples paused, looked across at Jury.

"Are you telling me Kurt Brunner is that brother?"

Maples nodded. "It's possible."

"And you think he killed Billy?"

Sir Oswald opened his mouth, but seemed unable to form words.

"But *why*? Billy Maples wasn't involved in these back-and-forth acts of revenge."

"No, but neither was his brother, Josef, involved in the shooting of the Röhms' son. As you said, they are back-and-forth; the innocent so often have taken the blame for the guilty, have taken, in a way, the *place* of the guilty." Maples rubbed at his forehead with his thumb.

"The guilty meaning who in this case?"

Maples didn't answer directly. "I find it too coincidental that Billy was murdered while Brunner was working for him."

Jury frowned. "Coincidental? I don't see any connection, though."

"The connection, I fear, is Roderick."

"*Roderick?* What's his connection to Kurt Brunner?"

"You remember I told you he was adopted. That was after the war. He was one of the children sent here for safekeeping, and my wife—she had a lot of sympathy for these children—she wanted to take one in."

Jury sat forward. "What are you saying?"

"His father was German. I can understand, I suppose, the lure of vengeance in this case. It's rather horrible."

Jury leaned forward, elbows on knees. "Oswald, you're not telling me that Roderick's father was—"

As if he hadn't been dropping bombs all evening, Maples said in a perfectly calm and composed voice, rubbing his thumb across his brow, "Yes, I expect I am saying that— General Röhm. Which would make Röhm Billy's grandfather. Remember, I told you we adopted Roderick. I'm not the grandfather by blood. If you were the brother of Josef Brunner, the child Röhm shot, wouldn't *you* want to murder Röhm? And since the general wasn't available, having died of natural causes . . . Kurt Brunner could, of course, have murdered Roderick. But if you wanted to inflict as much pain as possible, the grandson would be your target, wouldn't he? It would cause pain to more people—" He shrugged. "I don't know; I just don't know."

Neither did Jury. He could hardly take it in.

# THIRTY-THREE

In Berkeley Square, the trees were just coming into leaf. It had been a cold spring.

A dwarflike maid with a face Jury did not want to compare with the objects on the wall opened Angela Riffley's door this time. She was a strange-looking little creature. Jury wondered if her misshapen face and small stature were a genetic thing or if Riffley had had a go at her at some point. He had the impression Riffley was not one of the chief supporters of PETA. Jury thought about Riffley while he cooled his heels in the hall and took in this time what he'd missed on his previous visit: at least a dozen niches in the plaster, no bigger than eight or nine inches high and each less than a foot wide, in which were housed various gargoylelike carvings that he had no desire to inspect.

Those were the Riffleys: he with his sadistic trophy-hunting streak, she with her only hinted-at illustrious career and genuine talent for mystification. Had Jury been a police profiler he would have come up blank as far as Angela was concerned.

"Mr. Jury!"

He smiled. Was this an attempt to demote him, or merely a sardonic comment on London's finest? He bet she would be happy to use the same lingo the denizens under Waterloo Bridge used to refer to the police, if she knew it.

"Mrs. Riffley." He allowed himself a sardonic little bow.

Today she was dressed in a tight white skirt with a graceful sort of ruffle at the hem, a white silk shirt, and a lemony cashmere cardigan tied jauntily around her shoulders. She looked ambrosial. "Come on into the library."

"How about some tea?" she asked.

He wanted to say, *No, and don't leave me alone in here,* but he put on a brave face.

Malcolm Mott would have done this better. "I think I'd like a whiskey."

That seemed to please her to death. "Absolutely!" She threw up her hands as if she'd been waiting all day for someone to ask for it. She went to the drinks table.

It was, he supposed, a compliment that she valued him more than his purpose in coming. "Soda? I know you don't want ice, you purist."

"Soda, yes. A lot."

She splashed around at the table with such abandon, she might have been swimming through it. She brought him his drink. "I don't see why diluting a drink one way is any better than diluting it in another." She returned to the table and made her own drink: whiskey and ice.

"It's the tradition you're toying with, that's all."

"Sorry." She eased herself down on the zebra love seat, a mate to the one on which he sat, and raised her glass to him.

He raised his glass and avoided looking at the wall.

He heard a slight rasp as she crossed her stockinged legs. The sound was not unpleasant. Nor were the legs. "Mrs. Riffley—"

"Can't you call me Angela? Or is that against code?"

He leaned forward, put his drink on the table beside the strange cigarette lighter. "It's about the time Billy took you to his parents' estate."

"Oh, that." She put her head back and gave a short laugh. "Isn't the father just too provincial? But the stepmother's worse."

"Billy wanted you to look at a couple of paintings—"

She nodded, sipped her drink. "He did, yes. A Klimt and a Soutine. That was a few months ago. That Klimt was a marvel. Just wonderful. It couldn't have been one of the two well-known portraits of Adele Bloch-Bauer's since we know where those are. What I think is that it's a preliminary sort of study. Billy wanted to know if they were reproductions. That he'd think so rather surprised me. And I wondered why he didn't ask his father; after all, they were his paintings. But Billy just said no and that he wanted my opinion. They're authentic, of course they are. Definitely originals. So what you want to know is why the father was fobbing them off as reproductions?"

"That's one thing. Another is how you can be so sure."

She took a cigarette from the inlaid box. Jury refused to pick up the lighter, so she lit her own cigarette and sat back. *Was she buying time,* he wondered? *In order to organize her past careers?*

"I know because I've a good deal of experience along that line. I was curator for a small gallery in Luxembourg."

Now there was a place the imagination probably didn't hover for long. Not that there was anything wrong with Luxembourg, it's just one didn't often think about it. Excellent choice! "Luxembourg? What gallery was that?"

"The Kersten. It's not there anymore. I have no idea what happened to it."

Jury sat back, wondering where it had gone and where it had been. "But in order really to know, wouldn't the canvas have to be subjected to tests?"

"Oh, my, yes, without question. One wouldn't want to depend on somebody's eye, no matter how well trained. But of course one couldn't tear the Klimt off the wall, could one? And the smaller work, the Soutine, not quite so valuable but it would still cost someone dear to own it—Roderick wouldn't see any reason to test it. He insisted it was a reproduction. Why are you interested in this?"

"Because I think it's important. Billy apparently did. Did he give you some idea as to what he was looking for?"

She shook her head. "Not a clue, no."

"Have you done that kind of work—I mean, as a curator—anywhere else?"

"Not as curator. However, I've served as consultant for a few collectors. Lucky for one I did, as he would have been stuck with a not-very-distinguished Raphael. He was laboring under the impression it was the Raphael that's still missing after it was taken to Germany."

"Who was this collector?"

Angela just looked at Jury and stubbed out her cigarette. With a smile she asked, "Why do you want to know, for heaven's sakes? One would think you were a detective."

"I do give that impression, unfortunately." He smiled. "I'm just curious."

"No, you're not. You're vetting me."

Jury ignored that. "There must be data-bases—"

"Of course. There's a central registry in just about any country involved in World War Two. And museums and auction houses—Christie's for instance—do provenance investigations. Museums have provenance lists. There's a great deal of information floating about. In the case of the Klimt and the Soutine, as I knew where the paintings are now, and to whom they belong, it wasn't hard." She drank off her whiskey.

"Wait a moment." Jury sat forward suddenly. "You mean you did investigate?"

"Well, of course I did. I assumed you knew that."

"No, I didn't. Why didn't you mention it before?"

Angela Riffley looked over at the half-alive wall of mounted heads and other things, and said, "It could be because I'm not a mind reader, Superintendent. What do you think?"

Jury gave a brief laugh. "Okay, sorry. What did you come up with?"

She set her drink down. "I'll just fetch the paper. Wait here."

Jury spent the five minutes it took her to

go and come back in practicing lighting the cigarette lighter buried in the awkward piece of wood.

"Here we are." She was back and reseating herself and holding a sheet of paper. "Both paintings were acquisitions of a Dresden museum pretty much demolished during the war; if I remember correctly, it was Dresden that was flattened, wasn't it? But some of the paintings were removed before this. Both the Klimt, unnamed, or, rather, name unknown. I like to call her The Golden Girl. And the Soutine, called *Schloss Moser,* turned up on a Nazi confiscation list. A number of the paintings were taken over by Göring, who considered himself an art critic when he was actually an idiot. The two we're interested in went to an SS officer named Werner Röhm. From there, there's no record of a sale. The two paintings fall off the radar until two years later when they turn up in the home of a couple named Burkhoff in Munich. My guess is that they were family or friends or colleagues of this General Röhm, and that he gave them to the Burkhoffs for safekeeping.

"Somehow or other, Billy's father, Roderick, was in touch with them and they packed the two paintings and sent them to him." She gave Jury a long look. "Roderick Maples was apparently the general's son."

"How did Billy react to this?"

Angela set down her drink and looked at the fireplace and seemed to study the cold grate. Then she sat back and said, "I couldn't tell. You'd have to have known Billy. He was the most unreadable person I've ever seen. If he wanted to be, that is. Other times, he was quite transparent."

"He didn't try to take it any further?"

"Oh, I'm quite sure he did."

"You mean, as far as this General Röhm is concerned."

"Yes. But he didn't tell me if he'd discovered anything." Her shrug was a little sad, a little helpless.

Jury got up. "I really appreciate this, Angela. You've been a lot of help; I understand more than I did about Billy." He handed her a card jotting down his home phone number in addition to Aguilar's. He'd like to hear a conversation between the two of them. "If you recall something later, just call one of us."

She took the card and sat looking at it.

Then she recovered some of her old insouciance. He wondered how much it cost her to keep it going.

She picked up her glass. "Would you like another drink before you go?"

"No, thanks."

"Would you like to take me to dinner tonight?"

He laughed. "I'd like it, yes, very much. But could I have a rain check?"

Angela Riffley was looking at one of the long windows where sun, the color of apricots, cast rhomboids of light on the floor. "Why? It isn't raining."

# THIRTY-FOUR

"It's a bit like that ship, isn't it?" said Wiggins, stirring his tea. He was thoughtful.

Jury looked across his desk—squinted, actually—thinking that might bring the question into focus as he had no idea what Wiggins meant. "What ship? What are you talking about?"

That morning he had been relating to his sergeant the story he had heard yesterday afternoon from Sir Oswald Maples about the Kindertransport and the shooting. Wiggins had been transfixed, stirring and stirring his tea. Why then was he dragging in irrelevancies?

"The seavacs."

"The *what*? What's a seavac?"

"It's a term they came up with during the war to mean evacuation by sea. Mrs. Jessup was telling me about it, you know, when you and Mr. Plant were lazying out in the garden. You don't recall that ship *Benares*? Its actual name was *City of Benares*."

Jury felt at this point so far from the shore of his Kindertransport, he would have to swim to it. He knew he'd never make it. "No, I don't, and we weren't 'lazying,' if that's a word, and I doubt it. What's this ship got to do with anything?"

"It was an ocean liner, usually plied the India route, you know the Indian Ocean. When the Blitz happened, it was billeted to transport children to Canada."

In spite of the conversation with Maples, Jury stayed as far away from the events of World War Two as possible. Maples's Berlin story, happening as it did in Germany, had not been mined with memories. Jury's father also had died in the war, his plane shot down.

Wiggins went on. "There was this evacuation of children to Canada. The *City of Benares* carried some six hundred kiddies across the Atlantic. This wasn't the safest route by sea, certainly, considering the German U-boats. The children were having a marvelous time—at least this is what I read—with all of that luxury, all of that *food,* sixty flavors of ice cream, the waiters in Indian dress apparently treating them like princes. Well, a German U-boat fired at the ship and it sank. All of these poor children tossed into the sea, including Mrs. Jessup's sisters. Awful, isn't it? Only a handful survived.

"That's very sad, but what's this got to do with—"

Wiggins wasn't listening to his superior, he was carrying on with his own story. "And there were quite awful stories, too, about kids being pushed from lifeboats by others—there were adults, too, with their children, who'd paid for the passage. But the bodies of these children floating in the ocean. God, it's a terrible story."

"Yes it is, Wiggins; it's terrible. And I don't mean to sound hard-hearted about it, but aren't you missing the point?"

Wiggins looked surprised. "Am I?"

"Yes. The point being not the evacuation of children itself, but that the brother of this boy who was shot in cold blood in front of him and his parents could be Kurt Brunner? And that Kurt Brunner could in turn have murdered Billy Maples in revenge? It's like a bloody Greek tragedy."

Wiggins sat back. "It doesn't seem likely, though. I mean, what's the connection? We've got"—Wiggins began ticking points off on his fingers—"that confession, or report, or whatever it was from this German officer—"

"General Röhm."

"—and you don't know really what that is. Its source is questionable."

Jury leaned forward. "You're suggesting Röhm didn't write it?"

"Mostly whether it was what it appeared to be. He could have been writing a book, for all you know." Wiggins gave a snuffling little laugh and drank his tea.

Jury ignored the laugh. "Let's assume for the moment it was what Oswald Maples took it to be."

But Wiggins, caught up in his own little schema, folded down another finger. "Ah, but it could even not have said what Sir Oswald Maples said it said. You don't know German."

"Oh, please. Maples is trying to trap me or lure me into doing something?"

Wiggins's smile was razor thin. "Let's not forget Harry Johnson, sir."

Harry Johnson. Jury wondered if Harry Johnson had channeled his cleverness to Wiggins by way of Jury, the empty vessel. "I haven't forgotten Harry Johnson. I'm still on his case. But you're not really suggesting Oswald Maples is concocting this story?"

Wiggins, quite full of his own interpretation of these events, events he had not witnessed, leaned back and studied the ceiling, although there was nothing up there to look at. Up came his hand again, third finger folded down. "What if it was Sir Oswald himself?"

"What?"

"Who's to say he didn't shoot Billy Maples himself?" Wiggins held both hands palms out to stave off Jury's objections. "Just another point to consider. We should explore all avenues."

"Don't be a horse's arse. Your avenue is about as likely as a moonbeam to Mars. Come down to Earth."

Wiggins sighed. "If I may say so, sir,

you've only one fault in this job: you empathize too much with witnesses—"

"I do? *I* do? And I hear this coming from *you*? Anytime a suspect so much as sneezes, you bring out your roots and herbs and black biscuits. You practically go to *bed* for them."

Unoffended, seeing he was sitting in the catbird seat above Jury, the emotional moron, Wiggins continued: "The thing is, why would Brunner go to such elaborate lengths to murder the Maples lad?"

Billy wasn't a lad, though; he was thirty-two. And it occurred to Jury that he struck everybody as being a youngster. "I don't know."

Sucking thoughtfully on his teeth, Wiggins said, "Still, the connection seems awfully weak. The SS officer shoots a boy right in front of his family." Wiggins came down from the ceiling and looked at Jury. "You said Brunner said he and Billy went to that church near Lamb House."

"They did a couple of times."

"But he's a Jew, isn't he?"

"There are any number of reasons one might jettison the faith of one's family or simply go with a friend to a different church. Still . . . it's a point, Wiggins." He thought for a moment, then rose, unhooked his coat from the ancient rack, and said, "Let's ask him."

Wiggins's eyebrows raised in question.

"Brunner. I want to talk to him again. And perhaps you could have another heart-to-heart with the cook. She might have some insight into Brunner and Billy's relationship. Don't spell it out for her, though."

On the way out of the building, down the hall, in the elevator, and through the front doors of New Scotland Yard, Wiggins kept on about the desperate accounts of the *City of Benares,* of incidents of adults and children pushing children out of a lifeboat back into the water.

"You'd think, wouldn't you, sir, it would always be women and children first? And the good old British sense of fair play?"

"No, Wiggins, I'd think it would be every man for himself and the hell with fair play."

# THIRTY-FIVE

They found an illegal parking spot just below Market Road and Jury told Wiggins to take it. He didn't feel like searching for a place where parking was at a premium, or negotiating the narrow and hilly streets of Rye with Wiggins at the wheel. They left the car and hiked up the hill of Market Road.

"Very nice. Very quaint," said Wiggins, swiveling his head back and forth until Jury expected it to go all the way round.

"You've got an amazing range of motion. Maybe I should call an exorcist."

"Funny. But it might be you who needs one, sir. Spooked, you are."

Jury stopped. "What in hell are you talking about?"

Wiggins looked enigmatic and walked on.


"He's not here at the moment, Superintendent; he's gone for a walk with Mr. Brunner. But please, do come in." Mrs. Jessup stepped back from the door.

He thanked her as she took their coats and then ushered them into the little room on the right, a modest repository of Jamesian memorabilia. It was scarcely large enough to serve as a waiting room. There were but two chairs.

"Lord Ardry's keeping you on then, Mrs. Jessup?" said Jury, rather stating the obvious.

"He is, which is very kind of him, indeed."

"Oh, I doubt kindness has much to do with it. He wants a good cook is my guess."

"Well, I hope he's satisfied."

Wiggins was checking out the framed pictures, one of which was a caricature of the great man himself.

"Lord Ardry likes to have his guests shown in here; it gives them something to look at."

They were interrupted by the opening of the front door.

"That'll be him now." She went into the hall, spoke a few words, and then took herself off to her kitchen.

He heard Plant's voice and then he himself stood in the doorway. "Well! This is a pleasant surprise!"

Although spoken for the benefit of Mrs. Jessup, who retreated to the back of the house, it still sounded too banal a comment to be coming from Melrose Plant.

"Kurt Brunner isn't with you?"

"No. He's gone back to the Lodge—that's over on the cliff road—where he's staying at the moment. I expect he'll be back in London in a day or two." Melrose still stood, clasping the book he'd been carrying to his chest. His other hand grasped his tweed jacket at a point between buttons one and two. What did this pose remind Jury of? Oh, yes: the portrait of Henry James, the famous one done by John Singer Sargent where James seemed to have a thumb hooked into his waistcoat pocket. A reproduction of the painting hung out there in the entryway.

"What are you reading?"

"James. A volume of his short stories."

"Why don't you sit down?"

"Right-o."

"Right-o?" Jury cocked his head and looked at his friend, about to become his former friend if he didn't cut it out. He was still holding on to his jacket. Jury was positive Plant would've been wearing a striped waistcoat if he'd had one.

Wiggins was still floating about the room, looking at the stuff on the walls.

"A wonderful room, eh, Sergeant Wiggins? I come in here often just to sit."

"Oh?" said Jury. "I thought perhaps you'd given up sitting, seeing as how you're still standing there."

"Droll, very droll." Melrose lowered himself onto a stool. "Do you know what I'm wondering?"

"I've no idea. Whether to invite your publisher down for the day?"

"What I'm wondering is whether the National Trust would be willing to sell this place. I've really become quite attached to it."

"You've been here how long now?"

"Four days."

"Four days, and you think you're him, don't you?"

Wiggins gave one of his snuffle laughs and said, or read from the notebook on a small desk, " 'Why use one word when five will do?' "

Melrose laughed and then returned to his topic. "I'd think the Trust would be happy to get the property off its hands."

"That rather subverts the whole idea of the National Trust, doesn't it?"

Melrose's brow clouded over again. "What do you mean?"

"Well, in your former life as a fairly intelligent grown man, I think you would have known what I meant. Think about it: trust is the key word here."

"Anyway, James paid two thousand pounds for the house. Can you believe it?"

"That's probably what you spend for a stay at Boring's."

Melrose had taken the other chair by now, and sat forward and tapped the book he'd been holding. "Have you read 'The Real Thing'?"

"No, I don't have much time for reading what with the mystery of who shot Billy Maples on my hands. Supposed to be on your hands, too, but I expect I can kiss that idea good-bye."

Melrose went on, inching forward in his seat. "In this story, a smart, prosperous-looking couple—who are actually desti-tute—prevail upon the artist to have them sit for him. For pay, of course. They're impoverished gentility. Quite smart, or did I say that? He draws them again and again, the woman and then her husband. And he finds they're impossible as sitters because they are what they are. The artist says of the woman, 'She was the real thing, but she was always the same thing.' I think that's a corker!"

"I don't get it," said Wiggins, turning from one of the pictures on the wall.

"There's nothing really to get."

"Well, not for you and Henry James, maybe, but Wiggins here and I are just a couple of mugs."

"An artist has no scope if what he's look-ing at is exactly what he's attempting to paint. For instance if I were to paint a cook, I wouldn't have Mrs. Jessup sit for me because she's too much of a cook. My mind would have no place to go beyond 'cook.' "

"But that's what you'd be painting," said

Wiggins. "A cook." He went back to the pictures.

"When you come back from Henry James land," said Jury to Melrose, who had crossed his legs and returned his hand to dragging down his lapel, "perhaps you could help me with this investigation."

"Watch for signs."

"I beg your pardon?"

"James said, 'Try to be one of the people on whom nothing is lost!' "

"I've been trying to be one of them most of my working life."

As if Jury hadn't spoken, Melrose went on: "Small things, what a gambler would call 'tells.' You see, people can give themselves away in the tiniest gesture."

"Like you're giving away you're the poor man's Henry James? Wait a tick; I've got it! If I were an artist and I wanted to do a book illustration of Henry, I would not want him, I'd want you! Henry is too much the real bloody thing!"

Melrose sighed hugely, as if every separate sigh in the town of Rye had collected here and Melrose were heaving it. "Don't be ridiculous. You know, for a detective, you can be pretty silly."

Wiggins snickered.

Jury smiled and crossed his arms across his chest. "At least I'm not morphing into Sherlock Holmes."

"What I mean by small signs is this: remember in *Portrait of a Lady,* Osmond and Madame Merle are in the living room of Osmond's house? When Isabel walks into the room where Osmond is seated and Madame Merle is standing, she knows immediately that something is going on between them. She knows they've been intimate."

"You mean Osmond's been fucking the lady in question."

"Very funny. Do you know why James didn't use language like that? Do you? Not because it's vulgar, not because he was prissy, but because it doesn't mean any-thing."

"You could have fooled me."

"How dense can you be?"

"Try me."

"I'm just making a point: that the whole show is given away in nothing more than Osmond's remaining seated. That's what I mean by watching for signs."

"You seem to forget, my friend, I get paid

to watch for signs. What I'd like to know is if you, who are not being paid, and no wonder, if *you've* discovered anything related to this case."

"I've only been here four days."

"Oh, now your brief tenure is being used to excuse you. It's been time enough to turn into Henry James."

"Don't be ridiculous. I've done no such thing. Although I will admit this house is somewhat overwhelming. There's a pronounced aura of habitation."

Jury made a sound through his nose.

"So it wouldn't surprise you," said Wiggins, come around again from his tour of the pictures, "if you stumbled on his ghost whilst you were going upstairs?"

"You know, there's another story where the narrator—in this one it's probably James himself—does exactly that: he meets his own ghost on the stair. Or the ghost of what he might have been had he chosen a direction other than the one he did—"

" 'The Jolly Corner,' " said Jury.

"You've a good memory!"

"That's another thing I get paid to do: remember things. Could we set aside the haunting of Lamb House and talk about Brunner? The one I really came to see."

"I thought I told you—"

"You've told me sod-all. You've been too busy reimagining yourself."

Melrose gave him a dismissive wave. "All right, but let's get out of here; I'm feeling claustrophobic."

"Yes, with all four of us in this small room, I can see why."

Wiggins was quick to remind everyone that he suffered from claustrophobia occasionally, but he'd found a good remedy for it, which he'd share with Mr. Plant if he desired.

Melrose thanked him and suggested they go into the garden, at which point Mrs. Jessup appeared and asked them if they would like coffee or tea.

Wiggins stayed in the kitchen with Mrs. Jessup and some fresh scones.


They sat themselves on a Victorian iron bench in the garden. It was a large and well-kept area surrounded by a high stone wall. It put Jury in mind of the wall he'd climbed with Malcolm. "How did you get on with Malcolm?" he asked.

"You could have told me he was ten."

"Oh, didn't I?"

" 'Oh, didn't I?' " Melrose fluted. "You know how anyone under twenty usually relates to me. They always take that lofty tone, as if they'd got so much better sense than I." He kicked a pebble onto the lawn.

Jury tried to hold back a smile. Then he asked, "What about Billy's parents?"

"Roderick is certainly taking it harder than Olivia. But Billy wasn't her son, so that's to be expected. Except, no, wait a moment—it really isn't to be expected. Billy was murdered, for heaven's sakes, and murdered in very mysterious circumstances. That should give anyone who knew him, and certainly family, a terrible jolt. She strikes me as being awfully casual. She isn't there—I mean, with the event."

Jury said, "She's easily distracted by any new man, is what I'd say. She's a strange woman, hot for sex but cold at heart. I've wondered about her and Billy. More than the Maples family, though, what about Kurt Brunner? Give me your impression and I'll tell you a story. He is, indeed, the reason we came."

"He's an extremely accommodating chap. Knows a lot about Rye. He's my historian. And he's a huge Henry James fan. I think he's read everything, including *The Sacred Fount,* which, as a matter of fact he finds overwrought. I argued that James might be a lot of things, but overwrought isn't one of them." Melrose slid down a little on the bench, hands now clasped behind his head. It was a cool, bright day. "Yes, we've had some jolly arguments about James."

"I'm glad they've been jolly. But leaving aside the jolliness of the talk, I'm especially interested in him—Brunner—because I think there's a good chance he's the shooter."

Melrose sat up with a jerk. "You can't be serious!"

"I am."

"Oh, Richard, come on! No, you're wrong, that's all. Brunner couldn't have done it. Wasn't he in Berlin?"

"Not on the day, or rather the night, of Billy's shooting. He was back that evening." Jury looked at Melrose and shook his head.

"You're not even asking me how I came to this conclusion."

"All right. How did you?"

Jury told him the story of the Kindertransport and of the little boy shot dead at the station in front of his parents. "Lieutenant-General Werner Röhm."

"My God! But the parents—and clearly the boy—had done nothing at all. They were innocent."

Jury looked at the high wall of the garden and thought of the Polish ghetto. He said, "Multiply that child's shooting by around six million of those others who had done nothing wrong. You're right. Now, mum and dad and little brother. They could only get space on the train for one of the children and thought the three-year-old was just too young to be sent away all alone."

"When was this?"

"Nineteen thirty-nine, I believe."

"So they suspected what was in store for them, this family?"

"Yes, but I imagine denial was pretty strong then." Into a thoughtful silence, Jury dropped the unwelcome news: "Their name was Brunner."

"Brunner?"

"The point is that there is a reason to suspect this little brother, the other child who had to witness the shooting."

"Wait a minute . . ." The obvious objection to Jury's ending came to him: "What has it to do with Billy Maples?"

"Roderick. Billy's father is the connection. Roderick is not by blood Oswald Maples's son. Roderick was one of those evacuated children on the Kindertransport. He's German."

Melrose looked as if Jury had thrown a basin of ice water in his face. He could say nothing.

"Oswald Maples adopted him when he was eight or nine. The exact age wasn't certain. Roderick's father had plenty of influence, enough to get the child out of the country. This was in forty-two and they saw what was coming."

"Then, well, what were they worried about? The war in general? Afraid they'd be bombed?"

"Roderick's father was a war criminal."

"What? You mean he was in with Himmler and Goebbels and the rest of them?"

"That's right."

Melrose was silent for a moment. "Surely

you're not saying the father was this General Röhm?" Melrose waved the rest away.

"Roderick is Röhm's son, that's right. This is what Oswald Maples is quite sure of. Given what Maples himself was involved with."

"What?"

"Don't you remember Colonel Neame's recommending Sir Oswald in the Croft case last year? Maples was at Bletchley Park, working in codes and ciphers. The Enigma code business. So he was accustomed to working with intense detail, to ferreting things out, to teasing out answers. The real identity of the boy was suspect, and following the adoption, Maples naturally wanted to know who the child really was. It was difficult because so much had been lost; many of the kids had no documents at all. But Maples kept up the hunt. This was probably why he was so good with code. He was relentless. Finally when Roderick was around fifteen, Maples comes to the end of the dreadful journey and discovers SS General Röhm . . . a mob man if there ever was one. The story of the little Brunner boy's murder was an item in a long list of crimes against humanity."

"Why wouldn't his trial then have satisfied Brunner's need for revenge?"

"There was no record of his having been tried. Maybe he got away—Brazil, Argentina—who knows?"

"Does Roderick know about his past, then?"

"Sir Oswald can't be sure; he doesn't know how much Roderick remembers. He might recall his father as a virtuous man who took him to the beach and told him stories and played the zither. Does he know his father wore the death's head uniform? None of us can say. He didn't speak about the family he'd left in Germany. I, on the other hand, am pretty sure Roderick knows about his past. The two paintings—"

Melrose interrupted. "Yes, you were right. I managed to get a look at the back of the Soutine. There was something inked over."

"I wouldn't be surprised to find it's a swastika. They put that on their confiscated art. I'm not sure why Roderick wouldn't simply have replaced the backing—"

"But why would he? There'd be no reason for anyone to suspect the painting was original, and even if someone did, that it was part of the Nazi loot. But I see what you mean. If Roderick knew about the paintings, then he probably knew about Röhm."

There was a brief silence, which Jury broke by saying, "You're not convinced, are you, about Brunner?"

"That he murdered Billy Maples? No. He didn't do it."

"Do you believe Brunner is the brother of the little boy Röhm shot?"

"That, of course, is quite possible, given that Oswald Maples traced this boy's history. Only there's plenty of room for doubt. I would imagine there must be at least one point in the chain of events that's weak. What about that boy, Hans? The one who might have been shot intentionally."

"Possibly—"

"Or by accident. What about that?"

"I don't know. He doesn't know."

"But that sounds like retribution. For what?"

"It was assumed the shots were aimed at the SS-Waffen across the street. Later, after the boy in the group of boys was killed, it was thought that perhaps that was meant to happen. The shot wasn't necessarily aimed at Röhm's boy. The shooter would have known the little band of boys there weren't Jews, but children of the Reich. Their school uniforms would have told him that."

"How do you know Sir Oswald Maples isn't simply wrong?"

"I don't. But I see no reason to doubt him."

"There's every reason. The story is too— it's too fevered. The work of a fevered brain." Melrose frowned deeply.

Jury burst out laughing. "I'll be sure to tell him that. Look: would you say the tales about all of the German officers that Elie Wiesel ran to ground were the work of a fevered brain?"

"No. Of course not."

"Do you think perhaps working out code is a fevered occupation—that sort of training is posited on one's ability to see what's there and not what's not there."

"Nevertheless—"

"You're not operating on the basis of any evidence at all except for your feelings about the man himself—Kurt Brunner."

"That doesn't strike you as evidence? The man himself?" said Melrose.

"No. It hasn't ever since I read *Hamlet* and joined the police force."

"You never feel you know whether a witness is guilty or not?"

"Of course I do. But that's only the beginning. That's not what lands them in the nick."

Melrose got up and thrust his hands into his pockets. "The thing is this: we're not talking about Brunner's shooting Billy Maples for, say, personal gain, or because Billy's got his sister preggers, or in a sudden fit of temper. We're talking about revenge on an innocent person for a crime that happened half a century ago."

"Right. Yet you seem to have no trouble believing General Röhm was the author of that crime: he shot a perfectly innocent boy, a member of a perfectly innocent family."

"Yes. Yes. But it's not just that. Billy Maples was the innocent person for whom Kurt Brunner had worked for five years. Who had treated him well. Hell, they never even quarreled."

"I'm not sure I see what this is in aid of."

"Simply that Kurt Brunner surely wouldn't have murdered Billy Maples if the original crime had nothing to do with Billy. Why didn't he murder Roderick? Why not Billy's father, since he was closer to the incident than Billy himself."

"But that, I believe, is the psychology of the whole thing. Where he'd do the most damage or cause the most suffering would be to kill Billy."

"And it was Kurt Brunner's brother who'd been randomly murdered by Röhm. That boy had absolutely nothing to do with any crime against Röhm. As far as I'm concerned, that was almost total madness."

They turned at a call. Wiggins was standing in the doorway. "Mrs. Jessup would like to know if you'd care for tea."

Jury feigned surprise. "You mean there's some left? You've been in the kitchen for a goodish hour."

"It was you who wanted me to talk to her."

"Right. I feel the reproof."

Wiggins sighed. "No, you don't."

Jury smiled. "I'm going to have a talk with Kurt Brunner. You say he's staying at the Lodge? Where's that?"

"On the East Cliff. Hilder's Cliff Road. Ten-minute walk. But you look pretty hardy for your age." Melrose got up from the bench and stretched. "I wouldn't mind a cup of tea myself. Are there any more of those home-made biscuits?"

"No," said Wiggins, with a purposeful look at Jury. "I ate them all."

# THIRTY-SIX

The Lodge was a well-positioned white stone building across from the wall and the lookout place over the town salts. Jury stopped for a few moments on the opposite side of the road where he could peer over the salts and river and the marsh beyond. When Rye had been one of the working ports along this southeast coastline, the waves had curled in almost to the point where he now stood.

He met Kurt Brunner in the lobby and they were sitting now in the shadow of the fire and under a painting of flying black-headed gulls, another of a bittern almost lost in reeds and sea aster, and a muted painting of a mallard drifting in a pond. The camouflages of nature never ceased to amaze him.

Kurt Brunner sat in a wing chair, his face in part shadow. "I'd be glad to tell you more about Billy, but that's all I know. As I said before, he was a very private person."

Jury had to credit Brunner with a good deal of patience; he had been asked the same question a half dozen times among Aguilar, Chilten, and Jury. He did not mind repeating an answer to a question he thought Jury had asked before.

"No, I don't mean Billy. I'm interested in your own life in Germany. Munich, wasn't it? Where you were over a week ago when Billy was murdered."

"Yes, I believe I told you that. And it was Berlin, not Munich."

"Could you expand upon it, though? Your parents died during the war, I know that. What about siblings?"

"One brother, older than I. He was shot when he was nine years old."

"That's terrible. Do you recall the circumstances?"

Brunner shook his head. "No, I don't. My parents wouldn't talk about it. They were devastated by his death. And I was so young—three or four, maybe—I can't really remember him."

"This shooting then, you don't know where it happened?"

"No. I mean, except it was in Berlin. At first, I asked a lot of questions about Josef—that was his name, Josef—but I soon gave up."

"It didn't occur to you, later, I mean, to trace him? To find out about the whole thing?"

"Of course it occurred to me. But I got nowhere. The trouble was, as you might guess, so much paper was lost, so many documents. I tried his school. He was six years older than I. The school had been bombed, demolished during the war. The same for official documents, birth and death certificates—all that."

This lack of records was always such a neat way of disowning the past or knowledge of anything inconvenient or incriminating. You could plead ignorance, and no one would call you a liar.

Except for someone like Sir Oswald Maples.

"Why all this interest in my brother,

Superintendent? Have you found out something I don't know about?"

Jury smiled slightly. "I'd say so, especially since you don't appear to know anything at all."

Brunner's expression changed. Two cou-
ples walked by, heading for the dining room
and an early dinner. He leaned forward.
"Why the sarcasm, Superintendent? I've
answered the same questions several times
over. I've tried to cooperate."

Jury chewed the inside of his lip, watching Brunner. "I don't believe so."

"I beg your pardon?"

"I think there's a lot you're not telling us.
For example, the school might have been
nothing but rubble, but there were records
that were saved."

"How did you come by this knowledge?"

"A rather thorough search by parties with
a lot of experience doing it."

Brunner frowned. "And what did this
reveal about Josef?"

Jury didn't answer. Instead he said,
"Where will you stay in London?"

"At the flat. In Chelsea."

"You shared that with Maples."

"Yes. It's a large flat. Billy had it put in both our names."

"That was decent of him."

"He was like that." Brunner smiled rather wearily. "You're not going to suggest I killed him for a piece of real estate?"

It did sound absurd the way he said it.

"You're thinking we were partners? Gay?"

"No, I wasn't . . ."

"Others seemed to."

"I've seen the flat It's spacious."

Kurt gave him a questioning look. "You had a warrant?"

Jury smiled. "You sound like my boss. We had one."

Brunner ran the toe of his shoe around a figure in the Turkish carpet. "I hope you were careful."

"Police are pretty careful."

Kurt Brunner said nothing.

Jury said, "You told us you were in Germany when—"

"Berlin." Brunner looked aggrieved. "I came back on that day, or rather that afternoon. Perhaps if I hadn't left . . . well, I won't get over that very easily."

"No, I expect not. That's one of the hardest things to accept, that we weren't there, that we might have been able to prevent it. Though you couldn't have."

They sat in silence for a few moments.

Jury said, "You were in Berlin for how long?"

"Five or six days. Six."

Jury had his notebook out. He made a note. "Would you have your passport with you?"

Kurt Brunner gave Jury a queer look. "Why?"

"I'd like to see it."

Brunner frowned. "That's not much of an answer."

"I know."

"It isn't here; it's in Sloane Street. I went there first, dropped off a few things."

"Why didn't you come directly here? I mean, the Chunnel's much closer to Rye than it is to London . . . ?" He left the question hanging.

Sitting forward and leaning his forearms on his knees, Brunner locked his hands as if they were playing the old nursery rhyme of "This is the steeple."

Jury sat looking at him. Then he said, "I

think, Mr. Brunner, you know more about your past than you're saying."

"What does my past have to do with this?"

"Perhaps a great deal."

"What do I know that I'm not telling you?"

"Well, I believe you remember what happened to your brother. I mean exactly what happened, not some vague report of its being a World War Two shooting."

"What are you saying?"

Jury watched Brunner's eyes change from dark amber to the color of weak tea.

"My God! You think I shot Josef? You think I did it?"

Jury was completely surprised by this response. "No, no. Not at all. You were only a child. Why would I think that?"

"Because you seem to be implying there's something so dreadful in the killing of Josef I must recall it."

"Other circumstances might do the same thing."

"What?"

"Like seeing him shot right in front of you."

Kurt Brunner fell back in his chair as if he

himself had been shot. "That couldn't have happened."

"Yes."

"I don't remember it."

Jury thought for a moment, looking at him. "I'll admit it is possible that you were so traumatized you shut it out of consciousness. That's possible. And, of course, you were very young."

"It's what happened. If those were the circumstances. I just find it hard to believe. And, anyway, what has this to do with Billy's murder?"

"A lot." Jury checked his watch. "I'm starving. Shall we get a bite to eat? There must be a decent pub around."

"There's always a decent pub." Brunner smiled and rose, and they left.

# Thirty-seven

They stood first at the bar, got tired of that, picked up their drinks, and settled at a table where, now, the remains of two cheese and pickle sandwiches sat before them.

"I met Billy in Munich six years ago," said Kurt. "I was teaching at one of the international schools, history, my specialty, Russian. I'd been there for a decade and was growing more and more dissatisfied." He moved his hand and brushed condensation from the table. "I met Billy sitting at a bar in Alexanderplatz. We exchanged a few words about the city, Billy saying he had just visited the most boring show in history at a fashionable gallery. Some artist named Rio

Bravura. I really liked the name, I told him. Wasn't that the name of an American Western with Dean Martin or John Wayne? No, he told me, that was *Rio Bravo,* and probably the artist Bravura had seen it several times. He didn't look much like Dean Martin, but he drank like him, that was certain.

"Billy went on about the paintings and the painter who was, not surprisingly, insufferable. It was a hell of a rant, but I found him superb company, really. We talked about Greek drama and so forth, and all in all, we shut the place down. That done, we went in search of something still open. I swear to God, Billy never stopped talking. He was extremely intelligent. He was manic." Kurt gave a short laugh.

"We got together several times after that over the next year. I'd told him I was going to jettison the teaching and he asked me to work for him. And here I am. He said he needed somebody to run things."

Jury watched the cigarette in the tin ashtray smolder and slowly burn down to ash; he almost reached over to pick it up. It had been nearly three years since he'd smoked and he was still like this. He heard Brunner, of course, but his eye was on that line of ash. What was it, he wondered, that was hidden in those ashes?

"So that's my role: running things." Kurt noticed the ash end of the cigarette and tipped it into the tray. He looked at Jury. "You were a smoker."

Jury leaned back. "I was. Stopped two years ago and I still lust after them."

Kurt shrugged, said matter-of-factly, "Maybe it's not cigarettes you really lust after. There are things you never get over. People who've never been addicts couldn't understand this. At first, it's like feeling saved, and then you find that you aren't. You're still lost. Wouldn't it be better not to have felt it in the first place? I think the trouble is we don't know what it meant in the first place. Cigarettes, booze, love . . . ?"

Kurt lit another cigarette and again turned the lighter in slow arcs.

Jury said, "You lived in the flat in Sloane Street together?"

Brunner picked up his pint and took a drink and set it down. "You've already asked that. I've already answered." Brunner added, "Why would you think Billy was gay, anyway? He had a woman, after all. I'm sure you've talked to her."

Jury nodded. "You mean Angela Riffley."

Brunner studied the coal end of his cigarette. "Yes. She's really something."

Jury nodded, smiling. "It's hard to know what's really going on with her. How much is she hiding, or is she hiding anything? Am I too stupid to see through her, or is there anything to see?"

Kurt laughed. "That's Angela. Her talent is to obfuscate."

"Has she really done all of the things she says she's done?"

"I doubt it, but there again, how can you know?"

"She's extremely attractive, but somehow I can't imagine taking her seriously. You know, in the long run, I mean."

"That's because you've got good sense."

Jury wanted to laugh.

"Billy hadn't; Billy wanted someone with a mind to spar with, to trade theories with. Billy had about as much understanding of what marriage is all about as a radish."

Kurt turned the lighter over and over, edge tapping the table at each revolution. Nervous.

At least that's what Jury thought. "How long had they been together?"

"Something over a year, I think."

"And did he propose marriage?"

Kurt stopped turning the lighter over. "I honestly don't know. I doubt it. Does she say he did?"

"Not . . . exactly."

They both laughed at that.

Jury said, "I can't imagine Angela Riffley telling one anything directly."

Kurt nodded. "And yet, I think one might also underestimate her. She's pretty sharp." Looking into his nearly empty glass, he said, "Billy needed someone to shake some sense into him occasionally." He smiled. "I'm good at that." He paused, then said, "Billy lived his life at fever pitch: crisis was always just around the corner. Armageddon, that was up the road." Kurt drank off his beer.

Jury asked, "What did running things entail?"

"For Billy? Oh, records, engagements, money, charities, upkeep. There's an astonishing amount of record keeping, even in the simplest lives, and Billy's wasn't simple." He picked up his pint glass, empty long enough that traces of foam had dried along the ridges. "We need another." Brunner stood.

Jury went to stop him. "Wait. My turn."

Kurt was up and holding both glasses. "Do we really care?" He walked off toward the bar.

Jury sat there wondering. Did he? Did he care about the simple ritual of getting the drinks. Maybe. Maybe rituals like buying drinks were worth caring about.

The fresh pint appeared before him, and Kurt sat down with his own.

Jury said, "Did you like this arrangement with Billy?"

Kurt took a drink, set down his pint before he answered. "Absolutely. I don't mind that sort of paperwork; I'm used to it, to keeping records, sorting things, you know. And the rest of it—well, that was hardly work."

In his voice was a note that made Jury want to pursue it, but he didn't. "Billy didn't leave a will."

"Apparently." Kurt drank his beer.

"That doesn't make any difference to you?"

"He's dead. That's the only difference."

"He apparently had quite a fortune. You don't care?"

"You've tried in six different ways to get an answer from me that would satisfy you." He smiled. "The answer's still no. Sorry, you'll just have to stand it." He scraped some coins off the table into his hand.

"I've got to collect my sergeant and get back to London." Jury glanced at his watch. "My God. It's nearly eight—" Desperate, he pulled out his mobile phone to call Phyllis Nancy, then found that it had run out of power. "Do you have a mobile?"

"Here." Kurt handed his over.

Jury called Phyllis, who didn't answer, and left a message of apology and excuse: the case he was working on had kept him in Rye. He would call her, or better, see her in the morning. He clapped the phone shut and handed it back to Kurt.

"Missed date?" Kurt held the door and they passed through it to the street.

"I don't know how I could have forgotten. Damn it."

"Perhaps the thought of slapping the cuffs on me."

"That would do it."

"Or simply the devilishly fascinating conversation."

Jury smiled. He realized he seemed to have moved off from the position of regarding Kurt Brunner as prime suspect.

Either Brunner was a talented actor, or Jury was dead wrong.

# THE LESSON OF THE MASTER

# THIRTY-EIGHT

"It wouldn't be the first time," said Harry Johnson, raising his glass.

It was half-eleven in the Old Wine Shades.

"Very funny, Harry. You always were a card. But when it comes to you I'm not wrong." He didn't raise his glass.

He hadn't been able to get hold of Phyllis. His mobile phone was now charged and on. As soon as he clapped it shut it rang. It must be her.

Harry raised an eyebrow. " 'Three Blind Mice'?"

"That's right. All we need is one more." He pressed the phone to his ear. "Jury."

There was a silence. He hoped it wasn't an angry one. "Phyllis?"

"It's not Phyllis," said Lu Aguilar. "I don't know where she is, sorry. But I'm at Dust." The phone died before Jury could say anything.

Not that that would have made any difference. He snapped the phone shut. His head began to throb. He rubbed his temple.

"Something wrong?"

He shook his head. He felt the stare. It wasn't Harry; Harry had turned away and was looking at the row of wine bottles, smoking happily away.

Jury looked down. Mungo was out from under the bar chair. Mungo's eyes were boring into Jury.

"Well? If you've something to say, say it. Not you," Jury said when Harry turned.

Harry looked down at Mungo and snorted. "He's giving you his double-down stare. That's how he looks at me when I'm at the blackjack table." Studying Jury's expression, he added, "He's usually right, too."

"Thanks."

"You don't waste words, if that call is any proof."

*Words,* thought Jury, between Lu Aguilar and him, *what good would they do?*

"I'll guess from your response it was the kidnapper with his ransom demand."

Jury half smiled. "No, Harry. I'd say that's more up your street, kidnapping. And murder, of course, let's not forget that."

"Let's do. You always work your way around to that tired subject." He swapped his cigarette for a small cigar and lit it.

Everyone in the bloody world smoked except him, chain-smoked, even. He wouldn't be surprised to see Mungo light up.

"It must be frustrating as hell not having a lick of evidence." Harry held up his hand and gestured to Trevor, who slapped his bar towel over his shoulder and came down the bar. "I'd like a Chevalier-Montrachet, Trev. I don't much care for this stuff." He held up his glass. "Not corky, is it?"

Trevor fixed Harry with such a dire stare, Jury laughed. As if he, Trevor, could possibly serve a wine in less than perfect condition. "I'll just ignore that, Mr. Johnson."

"But you won't forget it, will you?" said Jury.

"Oh, no. It's my reputation's at stake."

Harry smiled. Trevor tried not to and went in search of Harry's wine.

Jury said, "You see, it's just that sort of thing that'll sink you in the end, Harry. You shouldn't be taking chances with Trevor; you'll wind up with cyanide in your Chevalier-Montrachet."

"Don't sound so hopeful."

"Oh, I'm very hopeful. All I need is a search warrant."

"That's what you needed over two weeks ago and you didn't get one." Harry smiled. "So I see no reason you would now. Indeed, you were directed not to get within a hundred yards of my house, weren't you?"

"That's right."

"Well, watch your step, or I'll tell. I knew you'd been nosing around there the moment I got home that night. That's the reason you wanted your pal to distract me. Very clever, I have to say."

Jury snickered. "What pal?"

"You know, the Niels Bohr chap."

"Oh, him. Just some nutcase. Why? Do you want to have another chat with him?"

Jury checked his watch. "Got to go." He

slid out of the bar chair. "You know the villains that get caught first? The clever ones."

*Actually, those were the ones who got caught last.*

# THIRTY-NINE

He told himself not to do this, that he could still walk away, knowing he would and he couldn't.

Jury parked where he had parked before, in St. James's Green. He got out and locked the car. Then he unlocked it and tossed his mobile phone on the seat and locked the car again.

She was sitting alone at the bar, not chatting up the barman this time. The barman at the moment was nowhere in evidence. A glass holding a finger of whiskey sat before her. She was smoking a cigarette and looking straight ahead, at the bottles on the glass shelves or the mirror, as Harry had been doing at the wine bar twenty minutes earlier. She didn't see him until he was there pulling out the stool beside her.

She smiled what for Lu was a bounteous smile, since she seldom smiled at all. He would like to know why she took things so seriously. She stubbed out her cigarette and fanned away whatever smoke was hanging between them.

"You went to Rye."

It wasn't conjecture; it was Lu getting down to business, although business was not the reason she'd called. "You talked to the Maples family." Nor was this a question. She assumed he was doing his job.

"Yes. I was redrawing the parameters of what's yours and what's mine."

She turned on the stool, and he could get her full face. "It's all both of ours." Her look was level. "We're not competing. I told you that."

"We aren't? Where's Ty or anyone who has ten minutes to devote to the customers in here?"

Lu pushed her glass toward him. "Here." Jury didn't pick it up. "Did you call me here to compare notes about Roderick and Olivia Maples?"

"No." She made a sound in her throat—annoyance, or just clearing it. "You know why I called you. But in the meantime, we can talk."

"In the meantime before what time?"

Lu rolled her eyes. "Has anyone ever told you you can be awfully childish?"

"Yes. What were you saying?" He reached over and moved a strand of fly-away hair from her cheek, pushed it back with his finger.

"Maples. I thought little of Olivia except that she's grasping, and I find it hard to believe Billy Maples would find her very lovable."

"Who said he did?"

"She did. To hear her tell it, he had a hard time keeping his hands off her," said Lu.

"I doubt that. You went to see Rose Ames, but you haven't talked to Billy's grandfather, have you?"

She shook her head and drank the remaining whiskey. There wasn't much. "You knew him before. I wanted you to do it." She put her fingers on Jury's wrist, his hand lying on the bar. "Is it important, what he told you?"

"Absolutely. The most important of all."

"Tell me." She leaned toward him.

"Sir Oswald Maples was a significant figure at Bletchley Park during the war."

"Codes."

Jury nodded. "Roderick's not his son by birth. He's the son of a high-ranking Nazi SS officer—"

"What?" She was half off her stool, eyes wide.

He told her.

"Jesus. But are you sure it was Brunner's brother?"

"Sir Oswald is quite sure and he's extremely thorough when it comes to gathering evidence."

Her dark eyes seemed to swim with the knowledge of this. He tried turning away from the eyes, as he told her the rest of it, but he was soon back in their dark depths.

They did not seem to be exchanging information anymore; they were exchanging something else. Jury stopped in the middle of this recitation and said, "What are we doing?"

"Going." Lu was sliding the strap of her

bag over her shoulder. She started to get up, but Jury put his hand on her shoulder to stop her.

"Lu—"

"Look, Richard, we can, if you like, sit here until the club closes and then go. It doesn't matter; we'd end up in the same place either way." She rose again. "You're scared, and it's not about the job, the case, the professionalism or lack of it, or our working together. Come on." She took a step and, seeing he still sat there, stopped and put a hand on his shoulder. "Richard, I know all that because it's the way I feel. There's nothing I can do about it. There was nothing I could do about it from the moment I walked into that room at the Zetter. There's nothing you can do about it, either. If I believed in fate, I'd say that's what it is."

"But you don't believe it's fate."

"I believe there's nothing we can do. Choice has sod-all to do with it."

He got up, threw some money on the bar, still with no one around to collect it, and walked out with her.

They walked from Dust to St. James's Green in silence. When they reached the car, Lu put her arms around him and gave him a huge hug. "That's better."

"Uh-huh. Only this time, can we keep the noise down? My neighbor downstairs told me it sounded as if the furniture removal men kept dropping things."

Her face pressed against his shoulder, she said, "You're the one knocked over the coffee table and the lamp."

"Like hell I did." He kissed her for a long time.

The living room furniture remained intact and untouched, except for the initial impact when they first came into the room, with Jury pressing her against the back of the sofa, almost tipping the two of them over.

After that it was strictly the bedroom and the broken nightstand, the broken lamp, the torn blind, the spilled wastebasket, the car keys, change, and comb sliding from the bureau, to say nothing of the bunched bed clothes, the sheets twisted and rising up in the middle of the bed as if they'd been shot from a geyser. The storm.

When they finally fell down on the bed again, they were exhausted.

Jury fell asleep.

Again, he did not hear her leave. Again, the trail of her clothes had been collected, item by item.

He felt, sadly, without that trail, he might never track her down.

# Forty

The long sad face of Father Martin regarded Jury ruefully the following morning as they stood near the altar. "I'm glad to see you again, Superintendent, but nothing's changed."

The priest stood in his vestments, just having completed the baptism of an infant girl. From the shadows at the rear of the church, Jury had watched as the baby wailed at the touch of the water sluiced over her head. The mother had quickly received the infant back into her arms and bounced it up and down. The father had looked on, neutral and uninvolved.

"I'm still curious, Father, about that night when you bumped into my friend and me."

"I thought we'd settled about that."

"Settled? I don't think so. Had you been coming not from Dust but from the Zetter? They're very near each other." Jury could tell Martin was trying to assemble his answers, one after another, like shards of a splintered mirror. He knew he couldn't fix it. The best he could do with this one was, "I expect that's right."

"You're not sure?"

Irritated, Father Martin said, "No, of course I'm sure. I imagine I'd just got times mixed up. I was having dinner at the Zetter. It's quite well known for its food."

"By yourself?"

"Yes. It's rather pricey. I don't eat there often."

"This was just before we passed in Jerusalem Passage?"

The priest nodded.

"But that would have been almost eleven. The dining room was still open?"

"Not for people to be seated, no. But there were a few diners sitting having coffee and after-dinner drinks."

"And you rushed out."

"Not right then. I'd already left the restaurant when I remembered I was supposed to be back at the house for a telephone call. And before you ask, I'm sorry I cannot tell you who the call was from or the nature of the call. It's information given me in confidence."

"Which means of course that I can't check up on it?" He smiled. "Meaning, it's like the confessional, isn't it? I don't think that'll fly, Father. We can subpoena telephone records. Too bad we can't do the same with confessions."

"You don't believe me."

"No, I don't."

Father Martin rose, and Jury after him. "I can say no more about it, Superintendent. But perhaps you can share with me what I was doing, since you don't think I was having dinner." He drew off the stole and the cassock.

"I don't know. I only know what I'm pretty sure you weren't doing and that was moving that fast in order to take a phone call. You were running from something, and as there'd just been a murder in the Zetter, I'd guess you were running from that.

"Whether you were supposed to meet Billy Maples there or whether you went there of your own accord, I don't know. You walked in, didn't see the body. The room service waiter didn't either because it was out on the terrace. You went out there and that's when you saw him. Dead at your feet. I can imagine your fright. You got out fast. But there's another account of your actions that is less attractive: you shot him yourself. Billy had been waiting for someone to join him. Was it you?"

Father Martin smiled. It was an unnerving smile that appeared to say Jury was so dead wrong it was just short of laughter. "You really think I could have murdered Billy?"

"Not necessarily. I think you were there; I'd like to know why. Were you lovers?"

The priest did laugh now. "No. I'm not gay. Neither was Billy, as far as I know."

"But that's the point. How far would that be? You were obviously connected to him in some way other than just priest and penitent."

Father Martin sighed deeply. "Very well. I was there and, no, I didn't shoot Billy. I'd talked to him earlier, on the phone, and he sounded very down. I thought I'd just stop in and see him, see how he was. Yes, I did see him. Blood had pooled under him. My reaction—I can't describe—" He stopped and ran his hand across his forehead and breathed deeply.

"I checked to make sure there was no sign of life—listened for a heartbeat, checked his pulse, even—well, this sounds ridiculous . . ."

"I can't imagine anything relating to this that would."

"There was a small mirror on a shelf there. I held it to his lips. You know, like Lear did with Cordelia. I *knew* he was dead the moment I saw him, yet I still did these things."

Jury thought he sounded immensely sad. "So he was expecting you?"

"What? No, he wasn't."

"He was expecting someone at ten."

"Well, I wasn't the one. I'd just gone there on impulse. I left the room and went down in the elevator. I didn't rush out. I didn't even leave. Instead, I went to the desk and asked if the restaurant was still open. The young woman there nodded, said they'd be closing in a bit. I was shown to a table and ordered and that was all, until I did leave and ran into you. But I wasn't literally running, Superintendent. I was walking pretty fast, I grant you."

Jury was looking at him and shaking his head. "And you didn't call the management, the police, *someone*."

"No. I'm not proud of my behavior."

"I would think not. Yet you stick fast to principle when it comes to the confessional. How bloody strange. Well, since you won't tell me what was going on with Billy that made him want to confess, I'll tell you."

Father Martin smiled. "That would be a relief." He indicated a pew. "Care to sit down?"

"Not really. What really irritates me is that it wasn't really 'confession,' was it? I mean, not in the strict sense of the term?"

"It did take place in the confessional."

"So either Billy or you suggested that. I don't care which. Billy told you about his grandfather, the real one, the one by blood, the Nazi officer. He told you about the paintings, didn't he?" The priest hesitated. Then he nodded. "He did, yes. Billy apparently had the sort of conscience that few people have: guilt over what someone else has done."

"I agree with you; that sort of thing is quite rare."

"For Billy, it was close to obsession. Would you agree with that?"

"I would. I might say 'consumed' by it. I worried about him, you see. That's why I went to the Zetter. He called earlier and was talking about all of this."

"I thought you said he wasn't expecting you at ten."

"He wasn't, no. I offered to come, but he said, no, he was going to bed early, he needed to sleep."

"So you weren't the one."

"No."

Jury sighed. "I don't know if something like Billy's state of mind can be caused by depression. He appears to have been manic-depressive. Or if it's by way being— strange to say—a kind of spiritual gift."

Father Martin looked at him. "Nor do I, Mr. Jury."

Jury looked up at the statue of Mary, looked up at the Brunelleschi-like ceiling. "I wish I'd known him."

"What makes you think you don't?"

"Don't give me another conundrum, Father. I'm sick of mystery."

Father Martin laughed.

# FORTY-ONE

What Melrose couldn't understand about the Ververs was, one: how much they knew, and, two: whether Henry James meant us to see that Maggie Verver was guilty in the worst of ways of being a manipulator.

He was reading *The Golden Bowl,* among others. There were five books lying splayed on the arms of sofas and chairs in this sitting room and one on the dining room table. He would pick up one, read a few pages, then another. No wonder he was confused.

Nevertheless, it was difficult maneuvering around James's territory; one could so easily lose one's moorings and find oneself in a small boat in choppy waters, unsure as to

where land absolutely lay. (Was he beginning to sound even in his thoughts like a
Jamesian character?)

But that was it, wasn't it? That's how
Charlotte and Amerigo must have felt, trying
to steer their little boat in the wake of
Maggie and Adam Verver's colossal yacht.

He rose and walked into the dining room.
He peered out of the window at the beautiful garden and the fine day. He picked up a
collection of short stories that lay on the
buffet and continued reading "The Jolly
Corner." It was a little irritating that Jury
remembered it so well.

"Mrs. Jessup!" He called this toward the
kitchen.

Smiling, Mrs. Jessup came through the
swing door, looking very cooklike in an
apron so white it sparkled. "Sir?"

"Could I have a cup of coffee? Just that,
thanks. You needn't bring all the paraphernalia."

"Why, yes, sir." She turned and pushed
back through the door.

Melrose went back to "The Jolly Corner,"
reading it standing, on the spot, as he did
much of the time. He stood this way for ten
minutes and until Mrs. Jessup was back

with the cup and all the paraphernalia: coffeepot, jug of hot milk, sugar, biscuits.

He wondered if the word "biscuit" had been drummed into the mind of every man, woman, and child in Britain at birth. It seemed so entrenched that it was simply impossible to serve a cup of tea or coffee without biscuits.

"Thank you, Mrs. Jessup . . . No, I'll pour. Remember, there are people coming to see the house at four, so afternoon tea will be a little late." Melrose *loved* his afternoon tea now that Agatha wasn't there to share it.

The visit had been set up by a National Trust representative, who apologized profusely for the inconvenience. "This is what is usually done by our tenants—showing visitors through the downstairs rooms—but as you're just filling in as a favor to the Trust, well, we can't expect you to do the whole dog and pony show." She laughed.

Melrose took the receiver from his ear and stared at it. Dog and pony show? At Lamb House? Really!

"I do appreciate your letting them come, Lord Ardry, as they're great supporters of the Trust and have to go back to King's Lynn this evening and this is their only chance—" On she went, ending with, "You needn't feel obliged to say a word. They can just look."

Again, Melrose glared at the receiver. Not *say* anything? *Was* the woman *mad*? Here he was with Lamb House on his watch, as they say, with Henry James himself under his stewardship, with many of the Master's goods and chattels to protect.

Not say anything? Just thinking on this had him making that dismissive blubbery sound with his lips. Of course, he'd *say*!

Here they were now on the Lamb House doorstep. Melrose had been told by the Trust person there would be three in the party, a couple and their daughter. The couple appeared in the doorway on time, with their daughter, unfortunately, of a sullen aspect and, worse, the aspect of a child of only seven, possibly eight. Why had the couple brought the girl to see Lamb House? Obviously because they had no place to park her, so here she was.

There were few children in James's books except for the famous duo of *The Turn of the Screw,* and even there they struck the reader as so preternaturally smart they seemed like stunted versions of the adults. Henry apparently did not find children useful, and no wonder. This one, with her bobbed brown hair cut straight as a razor all round was licking a lollipop of swirling, neon-bright colors. The child seemed to regard this mission—investigating strange people's houses—as a means to torture her into being good on the way back to King's Lynn. It was clear from the way she regarded Melrose over the top of her psychedelic lolly that it wouldn't work.

He smiled thinly. "I'm so awfully sorry, but I don't think lollipops are a good idea for going round the many books and portraits and so forth in the rooms."

The mother was quite adamant. "Don't worry about Minnie. Minnie's a careful girl. We explained everything to her."

The father, Mr. Babcock, looked on darkly, as if unconvinced anything good could come of this visit.

Mrs. Babcock looked round the entrance hall and claimed it to be quite tasteful, quite pleasant. Melrose held out his arm to herd them into the little parlor on the right and began explaining to them the various photos, illustrations, caricatures hanging on the walls. He did this while keeping an eye on Minnie, who had slipped the noose and was inspecting on her own. She hung, as did the lolly, over the open notebook on the desk, turning over a page, then peering closer, turning over another, all the while the lollipop missing the pages by a hair.

"Child!" said Melrose, in his best Victorian manner. "I'm afraid I must ask you not to handle the notebook. It's of great value."

"Oh, Minnie won't hurt it; she's always so careful; isn't that right, Minnie?"

That was so far from being right, even Minnie knew it. The look she turned on Melrose was not so much triumphant as coercive. *You best stick with me, poor sod.* She turned back to the book.

Said Mr. Babcock: "What's all this then?" He was looking at the caricature of Henry James done by Cruikshank.

"It's rather good isn't it?" Mr. Babcock sounded much more Tyne and Wear than King's Lynn. He was leaning toward the glass, close enough to fog it. "Tell me," said Melrose, "what is your particular interest in Henry James?"

Mr. Babcock leaned back. "Me? Oh, not me; it's the wife here wanted to come. Mildred's got some idea she has to see all the stately homes, all the famous people's homes; all the monuments; all the portraits; all the statues, bronze, wax, or wood; all the flowers in the Chelsea Flower Show; and is keeping a record. Well, you get the idea."

Did Melrose ever get the idea! "I'm exhausted just listening to that agenda," he said.

Mr. Babcock's laugh was a roar, truncated, fortunately.

"Really, Bob," said Mrs. Babcock. She had a tight little ferret face and used wretchedly precise diction, mouth and words meeting like a row of snaps on a taut bodice. "And did Mr. James live out his final days here?"

"No," said Melrose, rather taken aback to begin with the author's death. "No. He died in London, at his house in Cheyne Walk."

"Was he as popular as Mr. Dickens?"

Not only his death, but his competition. "Oh, no. Charles Dickens was the most popular writer of his day. The most popular writer in the *world,* actually."

"That explains why he's been on the telly."

"Oh," said Melrose with a generous gesture of his arm, taking in the room, "so has Mr. James!"

Again, the narrowed look was fixed on him. "What was it, which book was on the telly? A miniseries, was it?"

"Why"—it had to be so—"*The Turn of the Screw.*" When she gave him an uncomprehending look, he said, "Surely, you recall that, featuring the two *awful children.*" He would make that clear, but in the course of it he realized Minnie wasn't there to hear it. "Where's your daughter?"

Minnie had vanished. How long had she been gone?

But Mrs. Babcock didn't care, apparently; she was ruminating over television.

Mr. Babcock looked a little alarmed. "Now where's that girl got to."

The answer came as if from God in a thunderclap. The sound of an avalanche of pots and pans and plates clattering away.

"The kitchen!" exclaimed Melrose, who led the way, Minnie's father on his heels.

Mrs. Jessup's face was so suffused with blood and rage Melrose was afraid she'd have a stroke. What had been overturned was a pastry table that had held cake pans, cookie sheets, bowls, and plates, all once full and all on the floor. Minnie's mouth was covered with cake crumbs and chocolate frosting.

"Why I never saw anything like it! Wasn't I only trying to take her off your hands with tea and cake, and she turns round and does this?" The sweep of her arm took in the wreckage. "All my nice cakes and tarts on the floor! Shoved them straight off the table, she did, and then upset the table itself!"

"Oh, lud," said Minnie's father.

But Minnie herself did not seem in the least disturbed.

Mr. Babcock went to her, yanked her arm, and quick stepped her out of the kitchen, making profuse apologies to the cook for his daughter's execrable behavior.

Melrose upended the table while Mrs. Jessup shook and shook her head. "She's a devil, Lord Ardry, that's all there is to it."

"I'll be right back," said Melrose and left the kitchen for the front of the house. There he heard from Mrs. Babcock: ". . . oughtn't to've been feeding the child cake, not with her blood sugar crazy as it is . . . well, it's no wonder, is it?"

Melrose came up behind her. "Blood sugar?"

Mrs. Babcock swerved and regarded him with steely eyes. "Her system's just short of being diabetic!"

"Oh? Is that why you're buying her lollipops?"

Mrs. Babcock stiffened and bristled even more. Melrose could have buffed his boots with her. "Every child's got to have a treat now and then."

"Well, don't worry about her blood sugar. I'm sure Dracula would be delighted to give her another transfusion." He smiled a death's head smile.

Her mouth dropped open. She sputtered a little and then brought out, "Well, I never! Don't think I won't report this to the Trust! You'll see!"

"Madam, I am under no obligation to the National Trust. I'm doing them a favor by being here. Now, I suggest you do them an equal favor and get out." He strode to the or and flung it—he made sure it flung—open dramatically.

Mr. Babcock muttered an apology as they went through it.

Minnie treated Melrose to a sticky, stuck-out tongue.

# FORTY-TWO

Mrs. Jessup was trying to salvage her day's baking as best she could, picking up her tarts and cakes, when Melrose returned to the kitchen.

"Well, that's the last of the Babcocks," he said. "Let me help you." He knelt to shovel some cookies back onto a cookie sheet.

"You'd just as well throw those out." She was collecting cutlery and talking at fever-pitch about the way children were being raised these days. "Why, if any of us when we was kids would've acted like that, we'd not be able to sit down for a week! We'd've got a proper thrashing. Well, I can't really imagine it because it'd never have happened. You'll pardon me, sir, but I just can't get over the sight of her pushing my tarts and cakes onto the floor!"

From his kneeling position, Melrose looked up at her. "Why don't you just sit down for a while, Mrs. Jessup?"

She paid no attention to this, but started busying herself at the big kitchen sink, while Melrose salvaged a lemon tart and tried to steer the subject away from Minnie. "So you had a large family, did you?"

"Did have, yes, sir, fairly big. There were three of us girls, Dora, the eldest, and a brother, Bertie."

"That's quite a nice number of siblings." He inspected a ruined seed cake, not for the first time wishing he hadn't been an only child. "Do they live near you?"

"Two of them's dead, two sisters. Drowned, both of them."

"How awful. That must have been a black day for your parents as well as yourself." Melrose seemed to recall Wiggins's saying something about this. "Were you at the beach?"

"No, sir. Happened during the war. A ship was evacuating us kids—I mean a lot of us—to Canada and it went down. The doomed voyage is what they called it."

"I'm so sorry." He frowned.

She shrugged. "It was a long long time ago. I only thought of all that because of that dreadful child." She plunked a pot into the sink. "They'll be sorry, her mum and dad, when the girl grows up to be a selfish, cold-blooded, joy-riding specimen."

Mrs. Jessup was on a rant, a woman of a much more fiery aspect than Melrose had seen before. "Look, why don't you rest for a while? Put your feet up. Go home if you like. The cakes and tarts can wait until tomorrow."

Hardly before the first of this was spoken, Mrs. Jessup was shaking her head and kept on shaking it. "No, sir, thank you anyway. Today's my baking day, and I do want it done." Her small-muscled arms were busy with a flour sack, some of which she was measuring out into a basin. "I expect I'm a creature of habit, but I'll tell you this, sir"— she was returning the flour to the nether regions of a big old wardrobe—"habit, force o' habit is what saves us in the end. If you always do what you promised yourself you'd do, well, you'll be all right."

Melrose couldn't imagine anything less likely. He preferred to train others up in the art of habit, at least when it came to attending to him. His cook, Martha, for example, was to make a habit of putting only store-bought fairy cakes on the tea tray for his aunt. His hermit, Mr. Blodgett, was to make a habit of appearing at the drawing room windows when Agatha was there. Melrose's goat, Aghast, and his horse, Aggrieved, were to make a habit of awaiting his appearance with carrots.

And his little circle of friends—ah, yes, they were to gather, habitually, at 11:00 and 6:00 in the Jack and Hammer.

Theo Wrenn Browne was to make a habit of being an idiot.

The list went on and on. He hadn't realized until the good Mrs. Jessup had made a point of it, how habit played so large a part in his life. Yes, habitualness was a virtue, as long as it wasn't his virtue. "You're quite right, Mrs. Jessup, never a truer word, et cetera."

She smiled for the first time since the onerous child had sent her Banbury tarts and Eccles cakes and Maids of Honor flying.

He picked up a currant bun and moved

over to the window facing the wide lawn. The rain had ceased and the gray afternoon rendered the garden beautiful and disconsolate. The bugle-shaped, rich red Campsis; the roses and jasmine all climbing the high old brick wall; the flower beds of bulbs, lilies, and lavender bordering the lawn; the trees, shrubs, and high hedges: no wonder Henry James had loved living here, what consummate tranquillity for a writer.

He said, still looking out, "I think Billy Maples must have loved this place."

"He seemed to, and that's the truth."

"It's very odd but no one can fathom why he took up the lease. A citified young man such as he, buried away in this village?"

"It's because he was so fond of Henry James."

Surprised, Melrose turned to see that she had rolled out the pie dough and was now covering up the apple mixture she'd assembled.

"He did?"

"That's what he read. He was always reading one of those books. Whenever I took in breakfast or afternoon tea, there he'd be with a Henry James book. He told me Henry James wrote his three greatest books here. I don't remember . . . was one *The Golden Bough*?"

Mrs. Jessup seemed to be sharing the volume with Diane Demorney. "*The Golden Bowl,*" said Melrose.

"Yes, that's it. And then there were two others. What were they called?"

"*The Wings of the Dove* and *The Ambassadors.*"

She was crimping the edges of the piecrust. "He said once, that's what they're like, families. Manipulating and vicious."

"My goodness. That's rather strong language. Do you suppose he was referring to his own family?"

She gave an abrupt laugh. "Wink's as good as a nod, there!"

"Did you ever meet any of them?"

"Oh, yes. You know the type: never wanted for nothing, spoiled, rich, opinionated—" She was off on another rant. "Billy, I have to say, was awful spoiled. There's things he'd eat and more things he wouldn't; those he'd see, and those he wouldn't. I couldn't understand the lad, he was that moody." She chuckled.

Well, she was back in good humor,

Melrose was glad to see. "They, him and Mr. Brunner, went to that tomato-throwing place—such nonsense, don't you think?—in that little town in Spain. You know, where they keep throwing tomatoes for hours and everybody's covered in them." She chuckled again. "Never wanted to see another tomato as long as he lived. I couldn't even make spaghetti—me, I love spaghetti, though I can't say I do most Italian food." She shook her head and chuckled again. "Tomato throwing. Can you imagine grown-ups spending their time doing something so silly?"

"Oh, I don't know—"

But she cut off his tomato reflection. "The worst of them was that grandmother. Would have thought she was the queen. She acted like she owned him—well, his mother was dead—that was Mr. Roderick's first wife. At any rate, the grandmother was always talking to him about her, that'd be her own daughter, Mary. Talking on and on and naturally putting him off his stepmother. Still, I guess that stepmother isn't much to write home about. Mrs. Ames—the gran—gave him money hand over fist, which he turned around and spent the same way." She shook her head. "You oughtn't to do that with a lad."

Considering Melrose had been pretty much in the same hand-over-fist boat, he didn't comment. Well, but he'd turned out all right, hadn't he?

"What about his father?"

"Mr. Roderick? Oh, I expect he's all right. Would be if he wasn't married to that dreadful woman. I'm surprised you came back in one piece."

Melrose was astonished. He'd never imagined Mrs. Jessup capable of such a louche judgment.

She went on, "Well, you were there. Don't tell me she didn't put herself round. Vamps, that's what we used to call them." She was knifing the extra dough from around the edge of a second pie.

Without confirming this verdict, Melrose said, "Then did she make a play for Billy?"

"I'd certainly think so. Billy was so attractive. Ten, fifteen years younger, but that makes no odds to the Olivias of this world."

Melrose smiled. "What happened to his mother?"

"Boat accident. She drowned when she

was not much over thirty. Well, what goes around comes around, is what I say."

Melrose thought that a strange pronouncement. "Were you fond of Billy Maples?"

She didn't answer immediately and Melrose wondered what she had to think about.

"I expect I was, yes. We were never about much at the same time, except meals and tea. It was Mr. Brunner who saw to the running of things, mostly."

"He seems a nice enough chap."

"Except he's German." With one smooth sweep of the hand holding the knife, she carved the excess dough away from the pie.

Melrose laughed. "You're still fighting the war, are you, Mrs. Jessup?"

When she didn't answer, he assumed this was a very sore spot and he should stop. And he didn't want her to be suspicious of Lord Ardry's hanging about the kitchen picking up broken tarts. He sighed. "It's been a long day. I think I shall enjoy letting the National Trust know how the Babcocks' visit turned out."

Something then occurred to him. "The beastly child was licking a lollipop when they came in. I imagined she brought it into the kitchen, but I don't see it. Did you?"

She put down the pie and looked about. "No, sir, I don't recall seeing it."

"I know she didn't have it when they left." He looked around the room, saw nothing resembling the hellish lolly. He wondered what Minnie had done with it.

"I suppose I'll have to search for it. I'm surprised it's not in my hair."

Mrs. Jessup laughed. "Beastly child's too good a name for that one. That one'll go through life drowning kittens."


He was searching the library bookshelves when the phone rang. It was Jury.

Melrose said, "I'm going to London tomorrow. I need a little peace and quiet. Living in a famous writer's house has its drawbacks." He related the afternoon's festivities, wanting sympathy.

And getting none. "Kids have always been your bête noire. You want to argue with them, or reason with them. Neither's going to work."

"Argue? I don't argue with a child." He

was at the dining room sideboard, opening drawers, looking inside.

"Well, then, you do seem to enjoy a confrontation with them."

"You would have confronted this one; you'd have slapped her in the nick. Mrs. Jessup was beside herself." He told Jury the whole thing in vivid detail.

Jury laughed.

"Henry James rarely had children in his stories, and no wonder." Carefully, Melrose thumbed through the James notebook on the dining room table; the lolly might be stuck in between its pages. He wouldn't put it past the wretched girl. "Did you know James wrote journal entries in this astonishingly good prose."

"Yes. I looked at his notebook. Why are you surprised?"

"Well, just because his novels were beautifully written doesn't mean everything was."

Jury said, "I doubt the man was capable of slipshod writing."

Melrose thought about this. "Maybe not. If you're calling to ask whether I've found anything, the answer is no. Oh, but wait a bit—"

"What?"

"The reason Billy took Lamb House. According to Mrs. Jessup it's because he loved James's books. Always reading one, she said."

"That's interesting. I'm surprised. From what I've heard about Billy, he doesn't strike me as having had that much patience."

"You mean to read Henry James? That sounds like the kiss of death for any writer. If a book isn't immediately engrossing, it's doomed, don't you think?"

"Like Proust? How many people are immediately engrossed there? I've only read the opening of *Swann's Way.* That's the only thing most people have read. They read up to the madeleine dipped in tea and then give up."

"Anyway, according to Mrs. Jessup, that's why he wanted to live here. She hasn't much use for his family. The one she really hates is the grandmother."

"Rose Ames?" Jury laughed. "Mrs. Ames criticized her cooking. Mrs. Jessup takes such criticism very seriously. Mrs. Ames's daughter was Roderick's first wife. She died in some boating accident."

"Like Mrs. Jessup's sister. Or sisters. Dora and somebody. An evacuation attempt to get children to Canada? Thwarted by a German sub."

"Seavacs."

"Who are they?"

"Not *they.* Evacuation by sea. Get it?"

There was a silence during which Melrose looked under the cushions of the parlor sofa.

"Are you still there?"

"I'm looking for the lollipop."

"Oh, of course. Did I call at a bad time—?"

"No—There it is! There it is!" Melrose dropped the receiver.

Stuck to the bottom of James's waistcoat in—or on—the portrait was the ghastly girl's lollipop. What he surmised she had done was to step up on the stool and, unable to reach the hand or the mouth of the subject, had planted the lollipop there at the bottom.

Oh, where were the ghosts of Miss Jessel and Peter Quint when one needed them?

Behind him, the telephone squawked.

# FORTY-THREE

This time it was the housekeeper who came to the door. She nodded and smiled when Jury told her who he was. He followed her into the cozy sitting room where Sir Oswald Maples was putting aside a book, his two canes balanced against the arm of his easy chair.

The housekeeper left and Jury could see Maples was about to hoist himself up. Jury dropped into the chair he had used before and sighed. "Hope you don't mind my falling down in a heap. I'm knackered."

"Not at all, Superintendent, but don't you want to take off your coat?"

Jury looked at his coat as if he were reacquainting himself with it. He stood and removed it.

"Drop it anywhere."

"I like your housekeeper."

"I've had her for nearly ten years. She's a nice woman. She doesn't fuss. I hate fuss."

"I wanted to talk to you about Roderick and Billy. Did Roderick know who his father was? And did he remember that day at the station?"

Oswald hesitated, as if he was not going to answer, then said, "He knows his father was an SS officer. He's never asked me anything, though. The SS, well, that's probably why he doesn't want to talk about it. Whether he knows what General Röhm did that day in the station, I don't know. He remembers the Kindertransport, of course, and his coming here to England.

"Did Billy know?"

"Billy?" There was an element of shock in the word. "No. I can't imagine his father would have told him."

"I think Billy might well have known."

Oswald looked astonished. "Why would you think that?"

"You haven't been to your son's house in some time, have you?"

"Years. Only when Mary was alive. That's a long time ago."

"You haven't seen the paintings Roderick acquired about a year ago?"

"No. Paintings?"

"Your son says they're reproductions. One a Klimt, another a Soutine. Billy was suspicious; he took his friend Angela Riffley along to see what she thought. She'd been a curator, among other things, but whether or not she was qualified isn't really relevant. Anyway, she assured Billy the paintings were originals. To confirm this, she tracked their history, did a provenance check. Those two paintings were on a list of Nazi-confiscated art. You know the way they looted; you know the way they stripped museums and private collections."

"Yes, the Rothschild collection, that was one."

"Angela Riffley found the history of ownership, how it left one hand and came into another. It's not the paintings, you see, that are important here; it's who had them."

"Röhm. He must have left them with someone for safekeeping if Roderick has them now. And you think—"

"That Billy took this information and carried on with it. He found out who General Röhm was. I mean, if Roderick was heir to Röhm's paintings, that would be reason to wonder just what his connection was. And he *did* find out."

There was silence for a moment.

Then Jury said, "I think that confiscated art, the symbol of what Röhm and the *Schutz*—what's the German?"

"You mean the SS. *Schutzstaffel.* Sounds almost harmless doesn't it? Like some Bavarian pastry."

"The thing is, it might explain some of Billy's actions with reference to art, the generous outpouring of money to the gallery he liked and to certain artists. Trying to make up for the atrocity of the past, trying in some small way to wipe out what his grandfather might have done. Billy had a conscience, a real conscience; he felt guilty, even though he'd done nothing himself."

"Yes. I can see that. If, of course, your theory is right. It's rather clever, but—"

Jury shook his head. "It's not a theory. I know it's right."

"How?"

"My source was impeccable. A priest."

Oswald blinked as if dazzled by light. "My

word." He shook his head. "But you're right, it would explain his behavior."

Jury got up. "I've got to go—no, don't get up. There's one question, though, that I couldn't find an answer to, I mean until now. In all of this tracking down of the past—his father, the paintings, his grandfather—why didn't he ask you? If anyone had answers, it would be you."

"Yes. I wonder that myself. Either he thought I didn't know anything or he didn't trust me."

Jury shook his head. "I'd say no to both of those possibilities. I finally worked it out."

Despite Jury's telling him not to get up, Sir Oswald did. "Then what?"

"He was protecting you." Jury smiled. "He didn't want you to share in his suspicions and later in his knowledge. He assumed you didn't know. And you were protecting him for the same reason. I don't know what that does for you, but it does a hell of a lot for me. Good-bye, Sir Oswald."

Jury gave him a small salute and walked out.

# FORTY-FOUR

Trevor, wine expert, was holding out a bottle for Harry Johnson's inspection.

Jury sat down on the bar chair beside Harry and said, "Stick it to him, Trevor. Find one that costs at least a hundred quid."

"I did." Trevor applied the corkscrew.

"Hello, Mungo," said Jury. The dog slid out from under Harry's chair. Jury reached down and scratched his head.

It was a warm afternoon in the Old Wine Shades, insulated, really. Trevor took another glass from the shelf behind him and poured wine into both.

"The utter relentlessness of London's finest astonishes me," said Harry. His smile was touched by a sort of genial defiance. "That's fine with me, only I'd think you'd have more interesting cases to be going on with." He sipped his wine and made an appreciative sound.

"Golly, Harry, what could be more interesting than a highly cultivated psychopath with a lot of money?"

"Golly, Richard, let me know when you find one. But I'd think even that would wear thin after a while."

"Don't you believe it. We're now seeing if the kids you kidnapped can identify your voice."

"Really? Where are they, then?" Harry made a show of looking behind the bar, around the room, and under the bar chairs.

Mungo woofed again.

"Nope. No one here but Mungo."

"It's a tape, Harry."

Harry raised his eyebrows. "Where did you manage to get me on tape?"

Jury wished the man would show some honest surprise. "Last time I was in here." A lie.

"No! You're saying you came in here *wired*?" Harry laughed. "I've always wanted to say that word."

"That's right."

Harry feigned indignation. "You're interfering with my civil liberties. Or is that only in the U.S.? Surely that's illegal."

"Afraid not, Harry."

"And what do these children say?"

"I don't know yet."

Harry lit a small cigar and, remembering Jury didn't smoke, waved the smoke away. That just killed Jury. The man was a murderer, a kidnapper, a fraud, a nutcase, but he waved the smoke away. "Well, they won't be able to do it."

"And why is that, Harry?" *Go on, say it, Because I didn't talk to them. Say it!*

"Because I wasn't there."

Hell. "Where?"

"Where? I assume there must have been a time and place where this scene unfolded, or are you back in the ten dimensions again?" Harry beckoned to Trevor. "This is great wine." Then to Jury: "You want to make a mystery out of everything. I expect you can't help it, though. What are you working on these days?"

Trevor refilled both glasses and went down the bar to the other end.

"That's police business."

"You know, it's all so cops and robbers with you, Superintendent. Would I bother asking if it *weren't* police business?"

"Just your garden-variety murder. Not nearly as interesting as yours."

Harry made a *tsk*ing sound through his teeth. "I keep telling you I didn't murder anyone."

"And I keep not believing you. DI Dryer doesn't believe you either. Don't think he's stopped working the case."

"Ah, yes. He struck me as extremely intelligent, probably more than you. But not nearly so *soigné.*"

"Thanks."

"So what is this one? Stabbing? Shooting? Garroting?"

Jury didn't answer; instead he asked, "Have you ever been in a club called Dust?"

"You mean that place in Clerkenwell? It's one of those trendy clubs with crazy live music where you can really get down. Barmen in torn T-shirts and so forth."

"A hotel across Clerkenwell Road—"

"The Zetter. The big Z. I've eaten in their restaurant. It's quite fabulous." He checked his watch. "Care to go?"

"No, thanks. I've got a mountain of

paperwork I'd much rather do. You're trying to pick up where we left off?"

Harry smiled. "Hardly. Where we left off was my being a psychopathic killer. Which I'm not. No, I was just thinking of a good spot for dinner."

Mungo slipped out from under the bar chair and looked up at Jury. Had he not known that dogs really couldn't roll their eyes, he'd have sworn Mungo just did. The dog slid back under the chair.

"That's where the murder took place, the Zetter."

"Shooting?"

"Right." Jury, in spite of himself, told him the story. It was as if he was compelled to. Harry was one of those people who enticed others into telling stories, though no one was as good a storyteller as Harry himself. Harry was *about* stories.

Harry watched the long mirror behind the bar and blew smoke rings throughout Jury's tale. Harry was also about smoke and mirrors.

Then he asked, "The grandfather, Maples, was in codes and ciphers, you said?"

"Bletchley Park."

"How can you be sure he's telling the truth?"

Jury laughed. "Because not everyone's like you, Harry."

"Seriously," as if Jury couldn't have been, not with that response, "how can you be sure this is a crime *en famille,* so to speak? Perhaps there's another agenda. It sounds as if there is."

"Harry, if there's anyone who can turn a sow's ear into a silk purse, it's you."

"I'm merely saying there might be broader ramifications."

"Such as?" He signed to Trevor.

Trevor came down the bar, picking up Harry's bottle on the way.

"The code and cipher branch is a function of MI, isn't it? There could be something going on—"

"There's always something going on, Harry." Jury watched Trevor pour the wine, the last of it to Harry. "And how in hell do you know about GC and CS?"

Harry didn't bother answering that. He said, "You should talk to him again, keeping that in mind."

Jury was getting irrationally angry. "With *what* in mind?"

This earned him a condescending look and a head shake. "Are you having trouble following? Bad for a copper." Harry lit another cigar. They were small and lasted not much longer than cigarettes. "Keeping in mind that you might have made up your mind too soon; that you're focusing on the wrong thing. There may be another agenda."

Jury set down his glass and stared at Harry. "That's more up *your* street, Harry. As it's exactly what you did. You got me focused on the wrong thing."

Harry smiled. "I don't know what you mean."

"Bollocks. You know exactly what I mean. Come on, it's just us."

"It's never *just* us."

"If you mean the wire—" Jury opened his jacket wide. "I told you I'm not fitted out with anything."

"I don't trust you, sport. I'd sooner trust Mungo."

"Hell, so would I."

Mungo eased himself out from under the chair and sat looking at Jury. Looking at Harry. Looking from one to the other.

"Let's get out of here and take a walk. Trev?" Harry held up a ten-pound note like a little flag. Trevor nodded. Harry dropped it on the bar.

Jury checked his watch. It would be an hour until he had to meet Phyllis at Ruiyi.

"Then come on." Harry was up and shrugging into his coat, the black cashmere. The ten pounds was clearly for Trevor's tip. The bottle would be added to his account. Jury imagined he must have one. He must spend thousands in this place, considering the price of the wine Trevor usually chose. The pub was apparently Harry's regular, even though it was a distance from his home in Belgravia.

Jury pulled his coat on, definitely not cashmere, just his old Burberry with a lining against the cold. It was still chilly for April.

Mungo followed them out.

They walked along Cannon Street, which seemed harshly modern and modish after the smoky ambience of the Old Wine Shades and the old-world character of Martin's Lane.

"So what are we doing, walking around out here?"

"Walking around out here."

"How illuminating. *Why* are we?"

"Walking is a good way to talk."

"I think sitting on a bar chair is a better way."

Harry shook his head, seemingly at Jury's own thickheadedness. "That depends on who's in the bar chair next to you."

"What? There was no one next to me."

"There was next to me."

"Who?"

"Oh, for God's sakes, I have no idea. That's the point."

Jury stopped. So did Harry, then. So did Mungo.

"Harry, you're the most paranoid person I've ever known."

Harry didn't bother denying the charge. He said, "You wondered how it was I was familiar with codes and ciphers—GC and CS. It's because my father worked there."

They had come by now to St. Paul's churchyard and Jury stopped cold. "*What?* Your father was at Bletchley? Don't make me laugh!"

"Why is that so impossible? He was a friend of Alan Turing—"

Jury picked up the pace and was walking again. Harry and Mungo followed. "Harry, is there *anything* you don't connect up with?

Is my life in your company to be spent in a vast sea of coincidence? When it isn't a pack of lies."

"Don't you get bored," said Harry, "with people always telling you the truth?"

"I'm CID. *Nobody* tells me the truth." They were walking up Ludgate Hill. "Least of all, you."

This earned a belabored sigh. "You're such a cynic. That's not good in a detective. It's true, though, my father was at Bletchley Park. You know what the Poles said about the Enigma?"

"I have no idea."

"To defeat the Enigma code, you need a counter-Enigma."

"Your point being?"

"I'd say you need me."

Again, Jury stopped dead. Near Ludgate Circus, he did a 180-degree turn, as if inviting someone, anyone, some *thing* to explain such double-dyed duplicity as was vested in that suggestion.

"Oh, come on," said Harry. "You know I'm exceedingly smart."

"Yes, Harry, believe me I know you're smart. Now if you were only *sane* I'd say you have a bright future." They were the same height, more than six feet, and Jury got right up in Harry's face. "You know that I know that you know that whole story was a pack of lies. It was all diabolically clever."

Harry yawned. "You have a rich fantasy life, Richard, and you're making the same mistake you made before."

Jury started walking again. How in hell had they gotten to Farringdon Road? "What mistake?"

"You've forgotten your Gödel."

"I never *remembered* Gödel. I couldn't understand him."

"Of course you did. You're one of the quickest studies I've ever known. Gödel's incompleteness theorem: you can't formally prove the consistency of a system of arithmetic within the system."

"What in hell are you talking about? This isn't arithmetic."

Another deep sigh from Harry. "Yes, it is. Look: you've got the victim, the villain, for once not me, at least not yet, the suspects, the innocent, you, me, your sergeant, and so forth, you know, people on the fringe, such as Trevor back there—*and* whichever suspects prove to be innocent." Harry smiled.

"Which is the problem, isn't it? Remember Schrödinger's cat."

That set Mungo to pacing back and forth along the pavement as if he were trying to work something out.

Jury looked up at a tilting moon. Was this how the world would end for him? Him, listening to Harry Johnson? Yet knowing he was allowing himself to be sucked in, he couldn't resist asking, "How does Schrödinger's cat come into it?"

"Obviously: the cat's dead, the cat's alive. Simultaneously. Your man is guilty, your man is innocent. Simultaneously. And you—the detective—wander in on this conundrum—"

"Do me a favor and shut up, Harry."

"—and you change things. The players are not what they were before."

"All you're saying is I'm not objective."

Harry mashed his hand against his forehead. "No, no, no, no! That's *not* what I'm saying. You impose yourself upon the scene. Say, the crime scene. And you change it. It isn't what it was before. The incompleteness theorem."

"Harry, this is the most arrant nonsense

I've heard. Gödel would kick you all the way to Clerk—" Jury stood looking around. "How in hell did we get to *Clerkenwell Road*?"

Harry pointed. "There's the big Z. Dinner?"

Jury stepped out into the Clerkenwell Road. "And here's a cab. Good night."

# FORTY-FIVE

Late again.

Ruiyi was crowded, as usual. He could see Phyllis sitting at a table in the back of the room, not looking at all as if she were waiting for someone. She was reading a book and eating. Jury had wedged himself through the door, where a number of people in the closely packed and highly concentrated line gave him killing looks.

"Phyllis, I'm so sorry. How long have you been here?"

"Hours!" She looked at her watch. "Actually, twenty minutes." She laughed and pointed her fork at her plate. "Delicious. I was starved, so I ordered. I hope you don't mind."

He did and wondered why in the hell he had the *right* to mind. Absurdly, he felt as if he himself were an afterthought. He'd rather she'd been cooling her heels and tapping her fingers on the tabletop. How ridiculous.

"Of course not," he said as he draped his coat over the back of his chair.

"Then why do you look so gloomy?"

"I do? Well, I don't feel gloomy." His smile did not light up his eyes. Nor hers. He gave a cursory look at the menu, knowing he'd order the Peking duck. He was almost as bad as Wiggins, who studied the Ruiyi menu every time they came and then always ordered the crispy fish.

"At least you're smiling now."

"Oh. I was just thinking of Wiggins. This is his favorite restaurant."

"By the look of it, Sergeant Wiggins is not alone." She inclined her head toward the line. "It's always like that, isn't it? You'd think that after a couple of times, they'd wise up."

"And make reservations? Danny doesn't take them. Or get here earlier? Not unless they came at eight a.m. It's like a U2 concert."

"No. I was thinking more along the lines of joining the Metropolitan Police." She rooted her ID out of a carryall. "I elbowed my way straight to a table. It's really thrilling to be able to do that."

The little waitress, as big as a thimble, bowed slightly to Jury and his menu. "Suh?"

Either sir? Or so? Jury smiled at her and ordered the Peking duck and another pot of tea.

"Here," said Phyllis. "Have some of mine." There was a second little stoneware cup; Phyllis had asked for two. Now she poured out tea for Jury, and now he wasn't an afterthought.

He watched her do this and felt the tea already warming his insides, and hers, too. "Thank you."

Phyllis was one of those attentive persons who seemed to know you needed something before you were aware of it, from a tissue for an incipient sneeze to the path of a bullet. To a cup for your tea. He smiled. It was a better smile.

"What's going on with Billy Maples?"

"I talked to Oswald Maples today. I think understand at least Billy's contributions to art and artists." He told her about the paintings.

"Who is this Riffley woman? There seem to be so many women tied up in this case." Her eyebrows did a little dance.

And Jury noted that she didn't mention one particular woman. "Melrose Plant calls her the talented Mrs. Ripley."

Phyllis burst out in laughter.

"None of this helps much with relation to Billy's killer, though." He looked at Phyllis's fortune cookie sitting on a tiny plate and decided not to break it. "I'm almost certain this killing was for revenge."

"Revenge? What could he have done?"

"Not Billy. Billy was the surrogate. Revenge against Sir Oswald Maples is a strong possibility."

"Why?"

"That's where I'm not sure. It's just that this crime seems to stretch so far back. The motive isn't money, that's pretty clear."

"How about love? How about a *crime passionnel*?"

Jury would rather not go into that. He

cleared his throat, shook his head. "I don't see it that way."

"What about Kurt Brunner?"

"He wasn't involved in the Kinder-transport; I mean other than being in the station on that day. He was too little. No, he met Billy when he was in Berlin. Says they hit it off so well that Billy offered him this job. Kurt said he hated teaching, and was going to retire anyway. I don't know. I don't know how much of what he told me I believe."

"But if you're going to accept one history—that is, what Sir Oswald told you about Roderick's history—wouldn't you have to accept Brunner's?"

"Why?"

"Because it's more logical; they reinforce each other."

The little waitress was at his elbow, having crept up without his noticing. She placed his duck before him. He thanked her. "You're saying that because Roderick was the SS general's son and Kurt was the Brunners' son, they must be connected by the shooting in the train station. I don't think one follows from the other. There's a logical flaw, isn't there? It's like saying 'all women are beautiful; Phyllis is beautiful; therefore Phyllis is a woman.' "

"Sounds perfectly logical to me."

He laughed.

"Still, it's quite a coincidence."

"Yes, it would be."

"So these paintings," said Phyllis, "were part of the Nazi plunder and General Röhm got them and stashed them someplace and Roderick only recently got possession of them again."

"I'm going to tell Lu to get a warrant to inspect them."

"Lu?"

"Aguilar. Islington police? You met her."

"Oh. Yes. The beautiful woman. I mean, if your syllogism holds up, she *would* be a woman."

Jury felt her gaze and concentrated on inspecting the old familiar duck.

"What do you want most, Richard?"

Quickly, he looked up. Was this some pointed time-to-choose remark? "What do you mean?"

"Just—what most do you want in life?"

He smiled a little and reached over and took her fortune cookie. He broke it open. "Solace."

She frowned. "It doesn't say that."

"No. Remember that great film with Bette Davis, *All About Eve*? There's a scene after the scheming Eve steals Margo's role through trickery and then gets this magnificent review. Margo of course is effing and blinding all over the place. And crying. Her director rushes into her house, puts his arms around her, and says, 'I ran all the way.' " Jury smiled. "That's what I want."

She sat there just looking at him and saying nothing.

He said, "Life is just too bloody hard. You lose too many things. 'I ran all the way.' " Jury smiled bleakly. "Solace."

# FORTY-SIX

"Ah! Superintendent Jury," said Colonel Joss Neame, looking up from his Telegraph and repositioning his whiskey glass. He was always made buoyant by the presence of Jury. "Come for your friend, have you?"

"That's right." Jury looked around. "Where's Major Champs?" They were ordinarily in tandem, like an old vaudeville act. Jury smiled, contemplating this.

"Said he felt a bit queasy." Colonel Neame shielded his mouth with his hand. "Don't have the fish pie for luncheon if you're planning on eating here."

"What else is on offer?" asked Jury. His eyes were heavy and the soft leather chair in which he sank nestled around him, held him in its dark bloodred embrace. He tried not to think of Lu, and thought of Lu.

"The portobello mushroom is quite good."

"But not the fish, right?"

"No, and it's a stargazey pie, too, always been one of my favorites."

"What's that?"

"Oh, it's a cleverly made pie: several of the little fishes' heads are fixed to poke up through the top crust, looking at the stars, I assume. It's quite the thing in Cornwall."

"Most things are. Listen: I had another meeting with your friend, Sir Oswald Maples, just a few days ago. You remember, you told me about him."

"Maples, yes, brilliant man, brilliant. Got an OBE, didn't he?"

"Apparently. Did you know his family?"

"No, can't say I did. What are you—wait, wait just a tick." Colonel Neame rescued his paper from in front of the fireplace. "I was just reading . . . here, on the inside. A Billy Maples was shot in a hotel in Clerkenwell. You don't mean to tell me—"

"Yes. Billy Maples was his grandson."

"Dear God." The colonel looked from the

item in the paper up to Jury's face as if trying to reconcile the two pieces of information. "Dear God," he said again. Then, shunning sympathy for curiosity, he asked, "But is this a case you're working on, Superintendent?"

"Yes. Did you know any of Sir Oswald's family?"

Colonel Neame shook his head. "No. You pretty much parked your private life at the door. Private lives and Station X didn't mix."

"Station X?"

"Bletchley Park. That's what we called it."

"Tell me, since it must have been a very stressful, very competitive, and highly charged environment, could he—Sir Oswald—have made any enemies there?"

"Could he have? I expect so." Colonel Neame frowned and hunched over in his chair.

"What did you know about Oswald Maples?"

Joss Neame frowned. "Well, he was regarded as quite brilliant."

"You said you left your personal lives at the door. Was that true of all of you?"

Neame's laugh was short, abrupt. "We

didn't have them, if that's what you're wondering. Short rations in that department."

"Most of you would have had families. Did you have leave to visit your wives and children?"

"I myself hadn't married yet. Good thing, too, as there was no shortage of good-looking women there. As to wives and so forth visiting, not in a blue moon." He cocked his head and gave Jury a slightly disbelieving look. "Are you suspecting Maples was a skirt chaser, or something?"

Jury laughed at the antiquated term. "That's the furthest thing from my mind. No, I'm only wondering how much freedom there was to give to personal affairs."

"Very little. And for Maples, even less. He was too valuable. I don't mean the man was under guard, only that he was indispensable."

Jury thought for a moment. "Do you recall the evacuation of German children on what was called the Kindertransport? These children were transported, most of them to Britain, to keep them safe."

"Hmm. When was this?"

"Nineteen thirty-nine. There were several trips made."

Colonel Neame shook his head. "Sounds familiar, but . . . Memory's not what it used to be. But what's that got to do with BP?"

"Nothing, directly. The children were taken in over here. All that was required was a fifty-pound note to defray expenses. I wondered how Bletchley Park would welcome its people taking these children in?"

"A German child? Hmm. I rather doubt it, but anything's possible, isn't it. Yet why in heaven's name would Maples *want* to saddle himself with a child."

"I think it was his wife who wanted this. And most of the country was extremely sympathetic to these kids."

"Right. Understood. But most of the country wasn't engaged in cracking the Enigma code."

"Here you are," said Melrose Plant, coming up behind Jury's chair. "I see you're checking what's on the menu." He sat down and said to Colonel Neame, "He's been cheating all along, finding out from you what's on the menu and then betting on the information you give him. He always wins, and no wonder."

Colonel Neame laughed. "I like to bet occasionally myself. Roulette, that's the ticket. You know we've a largish room back there"—he dipped his head—"that's going to waste; no one uses it anymore. I've been trying to work up interest in a casinolike venue. We could have a few tables—blackjack, poker, and definitely roulette. Hire a croupier. And none of those hellish machines"—here he raised his arm and pulled his hand down on the arm of an imaginary slot machine—"they're too noisy and cheap. I'm telling you, there's a lot of interest around here in a casino."

"There's a lot of interest in it over in Vice, too."

"Come on, come on," said Melrose. "Let's go to our portobello mushrooms."

"Mushroom."


They let the portobello mushrooms alone and ordered the Boring's club sandwich.

Young Higgins appeared with their wine, poured a smidgen into their glasses, and stood there.

Melrose took a sip. "It's woody, isn't it, Higgins?" He set the glass down.

Higgins took a step back. Then he held

the glass to his nose and whisked the bottle away.

Jury held on to the small drink in his glass. "Woody? What in hell's that?"

"I just made it up. You can say anything about wine and it gets results." Melrose set his glass down. "Quite good, actually. What were you talking to Colonel Neame about?"

"The Hitler Youth."

"How unpleasant."

"I was thinking about Kurt Brunner. He seems to have been a true friend. The way he talked about Billy. I mean, the way he remembered conversations from eight years ago. And in detail. Hell, I'd be hard put to remember details of a conversation I had with you eight minutes ago."

"Thank you."

"According to Malcolm, Billy especially liked the Imperial War Museum. You know, in Lambeth. There's a huge display of World War Two memorabilia and weaponry."

"And Billy was interested in this because?"

"Because of his grandfather, I imagine. It's so hard to connect the dots in this case that I indulge myself in intuitive leaps. Those paintings: the Klimt and the Soutine. Angela

Riffley's tracking down the history of those paintings."

"And what about Mrs. Ripley? She was in love with Billy Maples. The motive could have been love lost."

"Yes. Another motive might be revenge."

Melrose was taken aback. "For what? Against whom?"

"Possibly Oswald Maples. The murder of his grandson has been a terrible blow. He really loved Billy Maples."

"So Billy could have been murdered by default—well, that's a rather cold interpretation. You mean the worst punishment to mete out to Sir Oswald is not his *own* death, but his grandson's. The trouble is none of these people has been eliminated as suspects. They don't have alibis."

"Oh, I think Sir Oswald has one. Not because he can prove where he was at the time of the murder, but because he's plagued with arthritis; he needs two canes to make it to the door sometimes. No, I'd say he's straight out of it."

"What about the talented Mrs. Ripley?"

Jury laughed. "What about her?"

"I think I might just go and see her, present her with this conundrum, and see what she says. She's done everything; she knows everything; she's quite inventive."

"Her inventiveness stops at her own doorsill."

"I could go tomorrow morning."

"I can't deputize you."

"Who's asking you to? I'll just be myself."

Jury laughed briefly. "See how far that gets you."

"Thanks. But if Billy threw her over, she'd certainly have motive."

"Perhaps. Though I simply can't imagine Angela Riffley's being that passionate about anyone. It would take a lot of passion to walk in and shoot the man you love."

Melrose sighed. "True. And what do we know about passion?"

"What do we know, right." Jury smiled and drank his wine.

# FORTY-SEVEN

When he got back to Islington, she was sitting on the steps, twirling her keys around her finger.

Jury had called the station, but she wasn't there. He was about to ring her mobile when he saw her sitting there.

He got out of the car, locked it, walked over. "I was going to the station. This will save time."

"I doubt it." She got to her feet and brushed off her skirt.

On their way up to Jury's door, she said, "An extremely pretty girl—no, more than pretty—passed me on the steps. Does she live here?"

Jury put his key in the door. "Upstairs. Top floor."

He opened the door and she went in and whatever else she had to say about Jury's pretty girl and whatever he had to tell her got lost in a kiss. Their lips touched, not just touched, not just kissed, but clung, as if, in the act of drowning, they were buoying each other up. Her arms locked around his neck. He marveled at the way clothes could fall away, as if they were blown off by the wind coming through the window.

Then they were on the bed, and whatever had seemed so urgent was forgotten.

"Why are you so solemn?" he said and brushed the dark strands of hair from her face.

"Am I?"

"You usually are, even in the midst of this—"

She smiled. "This what?"

He propped his head on his arm and looked down at her. "You never seem to be happy."

"Is this the sort of thing that makes a person happy?" She rolled over on top of him. "It's so hopeless to control. Like a fire that will burn us up. I hate to think of that."

Jury was angry. He pushed her off, got up. "Okay, if this isn't making us happy, then why in the hell do it? If it's nothing but some malignant force?" He'd yanked on his shorts, was looking for his pants—*how had they landed in the bathroom?* "The hell with it. It's dangerous. We'd be booted off the force in an eyeblink; it's interfering with what we're supposed to be doing—"

He stopped. She looked stricken. He sat on the bed, she inched over and lay her head on his back, snaked her arms around him, said she was sorry, sorry, she had thought he felt the same way.

Which he did; that's what made him angry.

He put his hand on hers, knotted around his waist. "No, I'm the one who should be sorry. Listen: get dressed. I've something to tell you."

He went into the kitchen, pulled two beers from the fridge, and opened them. When he took them into the living room she was just stepping into her skirt. He told her about the paintings and said, "I don't think it necessarily gets us any closer to our killer. What do you think?" Jury stuffed his shirt into his pants, took a pull on the beer. She didn't answer; she seemed to be concentrating hard. "Lu?"

"She's a sexy-looking woman, isn't she?"

Jury frowned so he wouldn't smile. "Who?"

He assumed the tapping at his door was Mrs. Wasserman, come again to make another worried report about an intruder.

He pasted a smile on his face and opened the door.

"I understand," said Carole-anne, poking her head in and giving the room a quick canvas, "there's been a lot of noise coming from here and Mrs. Wasserman is scared to death."

The head was followed by the rest of herself, a self no one could quarrel with, clad as it was in lemon and what looked like meringue frothing at her neckline. Her hot ginger hair brightened in the lamplight beside her when she sat down—flounced down, more like—on his sofa, her usual seat for discussing Jury's life as it revolved around his Islington digs. Meaning around her, or, throwing the net wider (but not much), around Mrs. Wasserman, Stan Keeler, Stone. His life was all of their businesses, especially Carole-anne's.

"What noise? Oh, you mean that table falling over?" He pointed out the guilty party beneath the window on which sat magazines, papers, and an old green shaded pharmacy lamp.

"Then it must've kept on falling as the noise was repeated many times." She regarded her nails, as if she were about to get out the polish and give herself a manicure. She liked to do that sort of thing around Jury.

Jury had by now sat down across from her and crossed one leg over the other, cradling a knee. "Carole-anne, your being so great at interrogation, maybe you could solve my recent case for me?"

Right now she had dropped off her sandals and was looking at her toes. Pedicure? "I'd be happy to, after I find out what was making all that noise." She leaned forward, planted an elbow on her knee, clamped her chin in her hand, and regarded him.

Jury threw up his arms. "All right, all right, I had a small party and we all got drunk as lords."

"You having a party?" She hooted. "Tell me another! Anyway, if it *was* a party, I'd have been invited." Her look at him was uncertain.

His at her was annoyed. In another moment he'd bloody well tell her. No, he wouldn't. He didn't think he could bear Carole-anne's looking like she'd taken a hit by a lorry.

He frowned. "Look, you didn't hear anything yourself. You're getting all of this from Mrs. Wasserman and she always exaggerates, you know she does. She's paranoid." Jury tied a shoelace, having wedged his foot into the shoe.

"What's paranoid got to do with it? If a piece of my ceiling fell on me, would you say I was being paranoid for saying so?"

"That question is completely illogical."

"Well, don't tell her that I told you she told me because you told her you didn't want her to."

Jury sat back, one foot over his knee, plucking at his shoelace. "In the time it would take me to work out what you just said, I could have my case locked and loaded."

"What?"

"Let's see: 'don't tell her I told you she told me,' etcetera—"

"Well don't. She's upset enough without you complaining."

"Complaining how? I'm not complaining."

"In case you would complain about her complaining."

Jury rose and widened his arms. "Am I caught in a swinging door with you?"

She got off and did a bored-to-tears stretch. "Don't you wish."

# FORTY-EIGHT

There was a different desk clerk this time being treated to a look at Jury's and Wiggins's warrant cards.

She frowned. "There's already another officer up there." As if one detective at a time was the Zetter's limit.

Jury smiled. "We're from different worlds."

They headed for the elevator.

"Another officer" turned out to be DI Aguilar, whom he'd just seen or not seen leaving his flat.

Jury wasn't surprised. She was the sort of

detective who believed that if you look often enough and long enough, something will give itself up. And she also believed that the more people looking often and long enough would double the chances of seeing it.

She was alone.

Jury wasn't.

Thank God.

The crime scene tape was still in place, so they had to dodge beneath it. When they walked through the door, Lu Aguilar walked in from the patio. "What I don't understand," she began, as if they'd been having a conversation, "is the second tray, the coffee." She looked down at the long ledge where the two trays had been sitting. "Why didn't this person turn up?"

Wiggins, as if he, too, had been a part of the ongoing conversation, said, "He didn't come. I mean, whoever it was didn't show. Happens all the time." He shrugged and rolled his latest miracle pill or sliver of digestive gum around in his mouth.

DI Aguilar looked at him. "Billy Maples shot himself?"

Jury wished she'd keep the vinegar out of her tone.

But Wiggins was unflappable. "Someone

else. Someone Maples didn't have an appointment with." He chewed.

DI Aguilar actually looked abashed.

"We're talking about a third person?" She thought about this. "Right now I'm assuming he was interrupted when he was eating, that he was shot and placed on the patio or perhaps they even went out there together."

She walked slowly round the room as she had that night, fingers passing over surfaces like water.

"Occam's razor." Jury smiled. "That's what your sergeant would say. The simplest explanation is probably the right one."

She nodded. "Maybe. I'm going back to the station."

"It's late, Lu. Go to bed."

She smiled. "I don't have time."

Very funny.

They'd parked the car in Farringdon Road, a couple of blocks away. They crossed over Clerkenwell Road, managing to stay clear of the four buses all arriving at the same time and belching to a stop. London Transport had conveniently deployed the buses so as to make everyone wait a goodish half hour, unless you were one of the lucky ones who'd just joined the queue. No, he recalled that Wiggins had a theory about this pileup of buses all together, but Jury didn't want to know what it was.

In Cowcross Street, he saw a McDonald's. "You peckish, Wiggins? I am."

Jury was aware that stopping in a McDonald's would prompt Wiggins to continue his harangue about the American scourge now spreading its tentacles along the A roads to squeeze out the Happy Eater chain. He was not disappointed: as they took their place in one of the four lines, Wiggins started in on Burger King.

"Yes, Wiggins, you apprised me of that dastardly plan on the way to Rye. But chin up, Burger King will serve up a British menu. Beans on toast and grilled tomato."

They were next at the counter and Jury ordered a Big Mac, a small order of fries, and coffee. Wiggins studied the big menu signs behind the counter as if there might be a surprise in store. The girl at her station looked unbelievably bored.

"I'll have . . ."

The girl brought her fingers to hover over the computer list of dishes and Jury felt like warning her: *No, no, don't ready yourself yet, he's a way from the actual decision.*

Silently, Wiggins scoured the menu again while the couple behind them, both in black leather and heavily studded, shifted from one foot to the other, waiting, one would have thought, with surprising patience, until Jury decided they were completely stoned, so not there.

". . . Big Mac and a large chipped potatoes—"

(Refusing to give in to the American term "fries.")

". . . and a Diet Coke."

Jury shook his head and went in search of a table. Wiggins, he knew, would stop at the counter with its array of condiments and sugar and milk.

Wiggins slid into the seat, and Jury said, "You got the same thing I did. But I only made one pass at the menu." He reached over to Wiggins's tray and picked up a couple of slippery little packets of mustard and ketchup.

Wiggins had unzipped two ketchup packets and was spurting them on his potatoes. "I never could stand the idea of tomato sauce on chips until I started eating these."

Jury had just bitten into his Big Mac when Wiggins said this. He nearly choked and had to grab Wiggins's Diet Coke to get the bite of his sandwich down.

Wiggins had stopped dead in ministering to his hamburger. "Sir, are you all right?"

"He didn't eat it." Jury stared at Wiggins.

"Pardon? Who?"

"Billy Maples didn't eat that burger or those potatoes. The ketchup—tomato sauce as you call it—was on both. Billy would never have put that on the food. He hated tomatoes in any form, according to Mrs. Jessup. Somebody else was messing with that food."

Wiggins frowned. "But why?"

"To make it *look* as if Billy had been eating."

Wiggins's frown deepened. "But why *that*? Is it a time thing? Something to do with an alibi?"

Jury fell back against the back of the booth. "To make it appear that someone had come and interrupted him."

"But the order for coffee—we know that was for two people, we know that he expected someone."

"That's much weaker. It was never

served." Jury leaned his forehead into the palm of his hand, as if he might, in this way, force some memory.

*"Don't try private detective work when you retire,"* said Harry Johnson.

*"You think I'm that dumb, do you?"*

*"Yes. You're, let's say, 'detective dumb'; whereas, the rest of you is quite bright."*

Jury held up two fingers, appealing to Trevor down the bar, either for a quick saving or another glass of wine, this evening's being a Première Côtes de Bordeaux, no, a St.-Emilion Figeac—no, a Médoc—but which one? There were so many.

*"Let's say,"* Harry embellished upon an earlier point, *"you have a photo and negative. Two separate things and yet the same. You, my friendly detective, can't get them to match up. You're always a tiny fraction off, which is as good as a mile. Though it's the same picture, same subject, same everything—"*

*"Wait, wait, wait a minute. I have a feeling Schrödinger's cat is coming into this."*

*"No, for God's sakes. The cat's dead, the*

*cat's alive—those are polar opposites— those two states are different. Your two states are the same. You've got the victim, the dinner, the waiter, the coffee, and the second waiter. But you've also got this other player—rather like a chess piece; which one is it? Rook? Knight, which can move freely about the board? Then there's the supper not eaten by the victim. Someone else ate it. That's certain. The someone else is pretty obviously, the killer . . ."*

The voices grew fainter and fainter, something like the dazzling bright spot on the telly fading when you turn it off.

Jury switched it on again: *"And you know who it is."*

Harry Johnson looked at him. *"Only an idiot wouldn't at this point."*

"Fuck off, Harry."

Jury switched his brain off, rolled over in bed, and tried to sleep.

# FORTY-NINE

*I'll just be myself. Well, not exactly myself,* thought Melrose as he pushed the button on the white pillar of the house in Mayfair. He didn't have to wait long.

Angela Riffley answered the door wearing spangled green and sunny yellow and, upon seeing Melrose, looked back quickly over her shoulder as if someone were following her.

*Danger lurking?* Melrose wanted to laugh. "Mrs. Riffley? Angela Riffley?"

Her eyebrows went up a fraction in surprise that anyone she hadn't given it to would know her name.

"It's about a friend of yours, Billy Maples."

She went from surprise to suspicion, a deep sensuality underlying all reactions. The artist in James's "The Real Thing" could make a fortune off her face; he could really go to town. Not only was she not the real thing, she was, he bet, never the same thing.

"My name is Digby Plant. I'm a private investigator and I understand you knew Billy Maples better than anybody."

She liked that (as he knew she would), and stepped back and waved him in.

What he saw in the entryway was an eclectic mix of what appeared, at first glance, to be junk. He supposed it would appear at second and third glances still junk to the uninitiated—and given the dark icons in the wall niches, he imagined initiation had a lot to do with Mrs. Riffley. At the very least one would imagine the person who put everything together to be well traveled and worldly, and would not question (for example) the purpose of the owl, flightless in a stunted tree, or the cheetah skin rug hanging on the wall next to a poster for the old film *The Blue Angel.* He did not think Marlene Dietrich had owned a cheetah in that film.

He followed her into an interesting study or library or den, where two zebra-striped love seats faced off. Between them was a coffee table of some kind of gnarled wood, glass-topped, and on which rested another small piece of gnarled wood whose purpose he couldn't discern.

Beneath the glass were several pages of what looked like an ancient, flaking manuscript written in Arabic or Hindi or Sanskrit—who knew? He thought the squiggles were extremely dense and black for a document several thousand years old—as she would no doubt claim. The visitor here would certainly not lack for ways to start a conversation.

"Care for one?" She was drinking something green, ground grass, no doubt, and offering the same to him. *No thanks.* "I would absoluteiy love a glass of water." The talented Mrs. Ripley, he thought, would be able to garner something from that modest request that would make her appear waterworldly.

"Tap? Well? Spring? I've some excellent Zandinski I get from Saint Petersburg. Of course, it's improved by a shot of vodka."

He returned her smile. "If you have any San Pellegrino, that would be fine."

"Of course I have it."

Anyone who wouldn't could hardly hold her head up, could she?

She set her green concoction on the table and rose. Then she fluttered away. She was wearing harem trousers. They were yellow and the fancy sequined top was the color of her drink.

While she was gone Melrose looked around the room. Particularly intriguing were the small black objects hanging on the wall between various animal heads. He debated what they might be without going any closer to them. There were photo-graphs studding the walls, of course. One was a shot of mountains, or a mountain, in front of which stood a small group of people who were either setting out to climb it, or had returned, or were just considering it. Where was it? The Swiss Alps? Annapurna? Kilimanjaro? The hill behind the roundabout just coming into Northampton?

Then she was back with his Pellegrino, which she set on the table. "It's almost impossible to get staff anymore, especially if one wants a maid without an accent.

Really, every little shop is managed by foreigners. Thank God for Fortnum's! I confess to getting many of my meals from their food section."

"I rather like Harrods Food Hall" (into which he had never ventured), he said, wanting to show that he too was in the habit of pick-up meals.

"Oh, absolutely. My cook of twenty years got married and moved to Haworth, poor thing."

"Ah, Haworth. I was there just a few years ago." What he remembered of Haworth was not the Brontë house, which he had neglected, but the visitors' information center and that beastly boy.

"Billy was very lucky in that cook of his."

"Mrs. Jessup?" It was out before he could call it back. How could he know Mrs. Jessup?

She *was* surprised. "You're acquainted with Mrs. Jessup? How extraordinary. Well, in your line of work, I expect you talk to everyone."

He silently blessed her for supplying the reason, even if she did make detective work out to be only a step above shopkeeping. "In the line of investigating, I naturally question everyone in the house. I've found that one's servants often know more about one than the wife or husband knows."

Laughing, she said, "Yes. It's one of the reasons I was against marrying Billy."

Melrose frowned. "Mrs. Jessup? His cook?"

"No, no. The man who worked for him. Kurt Brunner. One would think he was a bodyguard. I wondered, really, just *what* he was! Billy would say only that he kept things in order."

"What did you think?" Melrose's smile was sly.

Angela Riffley's was slyer. "I naturally tried to shut it out, but it was all so ambiguous."

Melrose waited for something to make sense.

"Kurt had too much influence." She lit a cigarette with the brown stump on the table.

"Influence in what way?"

She exhaled a plume of smoke that looked as fancy as her clothes. "Over what Billy did."

"Did Billy Maples need direction?"

"Of course not. He was perfectly capable—" She pulled a handkerchief from her sleeve.

Lord knew what else she had up it. Apparently she had suddenly remembered how close she and Billy had been, and now he was dead and she deeply felt the loss. "It's awful, just awful. He should have stayed—"

Again, Melrose waited, but she stopped. "Should have stayed?"

The handkerchief waved that away, but Melrose persisted: "You mean stayed in London? Or in Rye? Have you been there, then?"

She shook her head. "No. He wanted me to come, but—"

Again, she didn't finish. Melrose inclined his head toward the photograph beside the fireplace mantel. "Would that be you there with that group?"

"Oh, lord, yes. Monte Bianco. Yes, there's always been a dispute as to which country its summit falls in. Hell to climb, isn't it? It was nearly the finish of me."

"Indeed?" Melrose blinked and blinked and thought of no reply at all to this.

"It was one of my first attempts, and I was quite unseasoned. I very nearly fell into a crevasse." She shuddered pleasantly. "Well, one with little experience shouldn't attempt to climb Mont Blanc, obviously."

Giving it back to the French for the moment. Melrose sighed. "Now," she said, "you say you'd heard I knew Billy well? Who might have told you that?"

"I can't really tell you; you know, protecting one's sources and all that."

"Ah. I think I know who it might have been." She smiled. "Yes, I probably knew Billy better than anybody."

"And why was that?" Melrose sipped his Pellegrino.

"I think because when he was around me he could be himself."

Melrose could imagine a lot of things happening around Mrs. Ripley, but selfhood wasn't one of them.

She said, "I don't think many people knew how introspective Billy was. How very serious. I think it's why he was so moody."

"Was he?"

"Yes. I could tell you in confidence—"

The offer apparently included her moving from her side of the coffee table to his. "—But I expect I shouldn't."

"That's too bad. Have you talked to police about all this?"

"Yes, certainly. But there are a few things I've held back—"

"Don't," he said, leaning into her space, "hold back on my account." He smiled suggestively.

She laughed suggestively. "I think perhaps you're a dangerous man, Mr. Plant."

"Not a bit, not a bit." Something she'd said had snagged on a mental rock. Oh, yes. The cook, Mrs. Jessup. "I thought you said you'd never been to Lamb House. How did you come to see Mrs. Jessup?"

"Billy's cook? When she was here. I mean in the Sloane Street flat. She'd do that, you know—come to cook for him. Them."

Melrose wondered. "All the way from Rye? She must have been quite devoted to him."

"Actually, I didn't get the impression she liked Billy very much. Well, *approved* of him, I should say. How is it we get off approving or disapproving? She came up to London occasionally. I believe her family lives in Lambeth. Horrors."

"Yes, horrors." Sharing a joke. "When was this?"

"I'm not sure, really." She cocked her

head. "For a private investigator, you don't seem to know much—if you'll pardon me."

"And for one who isn't, you seem to know a great deal."

"I? Oh, *I* know nothing."

He pretended to reflect. "Still, you must have an opinion as to what happened?"

"It won't, I expect, be the same as yours."

"I'm only collecting information. Details."

"Have you spoken to Rose Ames?"

Rose Ames. "His grandmother?"

"He was fond of her. Of both his grand-parents, the two still living."

"Mrs. Ames. I believe she was the cook's bête noire."

"Ah. She's an odd little woman."

"Mrs. Ames?"

"No. Mrs. Jessup. I can't quite make her out."

"Is there any reason to? Her dislike of Mrs. Ames does seem excessive."

"So you *do* know a lot. I don't imagine she'd look kindly at a Lambeth back-ground."

Melrose frowned. "Mrs. Jessup?"

"*No.* Mrs. Ames. Rose would hardly be from Lambeth, would she? You have talked to her?"

Melrose got a wicked little smile for his troubles.

"Of course. We do seem to be talking at cross-purposes a bit."

"That, or you're confused. The cook lives, or lived, in Lambeth with her brother." She rose and collected the two glasses.

Here he was on firm ground: "Ah, yes. Bertie."

He had outmaneuvered her in the details department.

"Bertie? Oh, yes. Gilbert."

Her parting shot.

Too bad she didn't know it was a bull's-eye.

He stared. *"Wait!"*

She turned, tilted her head, looked at him with her wide blue eyes. "What? Did I say something?" She smiled and added, "At last?"

*That was a good one,* he thought, as she returned to the sofa and sat down, empty glasses on the table now.

"Gilbert. Is his name by any chance Gilbert Snow? Her brother?"

She had no idea why this was a point, but she'd take whatever points she could get. "Yes, that's right."

Since she had been moving in his direction ever since he'd walked in, she wouldn't mind. He reached behind her, clamped his hand on her neck, and pulled her over. After a long and appreciative kiss, Melrose whispered in her ear: "The talented Mrs. Ripley."

She sat and stared, for once unable to recover speech.

He said good-bye, walked out of the study and to the front door and through it.

He pressed the mobile, as good as a kiss, against his ear.

# FIFTY

"Where's DI Aguilar?" Jury asked, receiver crushed between shoulder and chin, one hand around a mug of tea and the other stuffing his shirt into his pants. It was after nine and he'd overslept. He was in a hurry. "I've been trying her mobile, but there's no answer."

"I don't know," said Chilten. "She was at the station all night."

"No, she wasn't. I tried to call her."

"Does she have a life? I don't know if she has a life."

Jury said nothing except "Meet me at the Zetter." He paused. "No, wait. Just bring in

Gilbert Snow for questioning. Take him to the station and I'll meet you there.

Chilten was silent, then said doubtfully, "You said Gilbert Snow. The waiter?"

"That's right. He shot Billy Maples." Jury drank some tea and listened to the silence. "Ron? You there?"

Ron Chilten cleared his throat. "*Snow* shot him? For Christ's sakes, why?"

"Well, if I knew that, and if I had some hard evidence, I'd say arrest him." He thought some more. "DI Aguilar had that dinner bagged, right?" She's brilliant. He smiled.

"Ye-ah." Ron brought it out in two syllables, as if the prospect were lethal.

"Then get it to the lab for DNA testing."

"Billy Maples—"

"I'm not talking about Billy. I'm talking about who ate it."

Jury took the silence to mean understanding, repeated his request for Ron to go to the Zetter, and hung up.

He gulped his tea and thought of Lu's having that dinner bagged.

"*Why?*"

"*Why not? You never know.*"

Indeed you don't.

Jury had his coat on and was out the door.

They put Gilbert Snow in a bleak little room at the Islington station. It was the smallest of them. Jury preferred it for its claustrophobic ambiance. They sat across from Snow at a scratched-up table.

"Don't know what you're talking about," said Gilbert in a perfectly equable tone, as if shooting Billy Maples were not only beyond his ken but should have been beyond anybody's. He even gave a little harrumphing laugh.

"Yes, you do, Gil," Jury said. "Let's go through it. Who took Maples's so-called dinner order? Who said he ordered coffee for two? Who made a point of telling us Maples was very particular about that? You did; you said so yourself. There was no one to verify that there really had been an order, either for the food or for the coffee. What you needed was a reason to go to his room *and* make it appear that he was expecting a visitor. That he was expecting someone was important. We would certainly be trying to track down Billy's guest for he would, presumably, be Billy's killer."

Jury was up and walking slowly about. "Then the murder weapon turns up at the Sloane Street flat. Throwing yet more suspicion upon Kurt Brunner. How did you manage that? What's your relationship with Brunner?"

Gilbert Snow sat quite still, following Jury's circuit of the room with a blank look. The question regarding Brunner brought a cold smile to his now expressionless face.

Jury leaned against the wall. "What's your connection with Brunner?" he asked again.

Sullenly, Gilbert Snow looked at him. "I haven't one. I never met the man. I want my brief." He folded his arms across his chest. "I've not got to answer any questions without a solicitor."

"Why's that, Gil?" asked Ron Chilten. "Are you in trouble here?"

Gilbert gave another guttural laugh, dismissing Chilten's question, and leaned back in his chair and looked at them with hooded eyes.

He reminded Jury of a tortoise: slow, plodding, but certain of where he was going.

No one spoke.

Into this silence stepped Detective Inspector Aguilar.

As if he'd been found smoking weed in the toilet by his third-form teacher, Jury pulled away from the wall.

Lu Aguilar stood in the doorway, pointing her chin at Jury and tilting her head back: *out here.*

Jury left the room, after telling the tape he was doing so.

Aguilar snapped out a question: "What in the fuck are you doing, Superintendent?"

Back to dirty words and titles.

"You arrested this man Snow without any evidence. No murder weapon, no motive."

"You'll certainly grant me it screams *opportunity.*"

She took this in. "Yes, all right, that's true. But the murder weapon was found in Brunner's desk, and Brunner has a *motive.* This man"—she hooked her thumb around toward the door behind which sat Gilbert Snow—"has neither. What happened to Occam's razor? Are you going to bring in Benny Keegan tomorrow? It'd make about as much sense."

"This isn't over territory, is it, Lu? You

were the one who wanted me to stay on this case."

"Territory? For God's sakes, did you just hear what I said?"

"Do you want to know? Or do you simply want to throw dagger looks at me?"

The dagger disappeared back into its sheath somewhere. But she held the look. So did he. Would either of them have looked away if Ron hadn't come out into the hall?

"It's lawyer time. He's raising hell." Ron went back in.

Lu opened her mouth to say something when her mobile rang. She listened, frowning, said her gloomy thanks, flipped the phone shut. "That was the lab. The DNA will take a week. At least." She sighed heavily and leaned against the wall.

"It was Snow who ate that sandwich," said Jury. "Nobody else could have done it. Nobody else *would* have done it. It explains the jacket. Billy didn't take it off because he didn't eat. Beat a confession out of Snow; that's all we need."

"That's all?" She smiled wanly and pushed away from the wall. "I've gotten in trouble once or twice with the way I treat suspects, you know, breaking plates over their heads, that kind of thing—" She shrugged. "Of course, it's still a long way from eating a meal to shooting a man." She chewed around the end of her thumb.

"What possible reason could Snow have for eating the food except for making it look as if Billy ate it?"

"But we don't have the proof yet."

"He doesn't know that, does he?"

A WPC poked her head in the door this time. "Call for you, Superintendent."

Jury picked up the receiver. "Jury."

"God!" complained Melrose Plant.

"Not really, but go ahead."

"I've been through fifteen of your cronies this morning. Why does it take fifteen connections—?"

"That's the life of a private eye, Digby. Any luck?"

"Yes. But what I don't understand is why you don't know this. Don't you do background checks on suspects and so forth?"

"Know what?"

"What is it?"

"Gilbert Snow is the brother of Billy's cook."

Jury's mouth opened, but didn't say anything for two seconds. Then, *"What? Jessup is his sister?"*

"That's the way it works. If he's her brother, then she's his sister. Without fail."

Lu Aguilar was mouthing *what?*

"How in hell does Angela Riffley know this?"

"Oh, come on: she's the talented Mrs. Ripley."

"Thanks." Jury hung up, said to Lu, "I think we've got our connection between Snow and the victim." He told her.

She stared at him, was still standing stiffly as he started out of the room.

"Oh come on, Inspector. Let's break a few plates."


Snow's expression, when Aguilar sat down opposite him, was hugely condescending. *The lady detective. Pfffft.* He looked her up and down and pursed his lips.

Jury, leaning against the wall again, felt his hand twitch, wanting to curl into a fist. He wondered how much of Lu's time was spent putting up with this sort of reaction.

She reached over, shut off the tape,

leaned across the table, pulled his shirt collar tight with those long fingers, and got into his face. "Listen: we don't *think* you're the shooter, Gilbert, we *know* you are."

He looked as if he were choking and grabbed her hand.

With a sour smile, she let go and turned the tape back on.

Rubbing his neck, he said, "Even if the gun's not mine? Even if it's goddamned Brunner's?"

"You know, the funny thing about this gun is its lack of prints."

Gilbert Snow hawked up a laugh. "I guess not. Wouldn't Brunner have wiped them off?"

"And then tossed the gun in a *desk drawer*?"

Snow looked away. "People do funny things." He was inspecting his nails as if she'd just given him a manicure.

"No. They do stupid things. In your hurry to get rid of your own prints, you wiped all of the prints off. You have any siblings, Gilbert?"

She had changed course and he looked up, surprised. Also confused. "What'd'you mean?"

"Siblings. Brothers? Sisters?"

Snow was calculating, Jury knew, how far they'd come. He could hardly deny a fact so easily checked by police.

"Yeah, I do, a sister. Why?"

Slowly, Lu smiled. "Just curious." She opened the folder before her, and seemed to read, and let him sweat. "Back to the gun." She looked up from the folder, leaned toward him again, but this time as if they shared a secret. "Gilbert, it was stupid in another way, leaving that gun in Brunner's desk. If it weren't for that, we might never have connected you with this murder. And if we hadn't, we might never have found out about your sister. Annie Jessup. Billy Maples's cook. So why don't you just tell us what *her* little part in this is?"

Blood had suffused Gilbert Snow's face. "I told you, I want a solicitor. I know my rights."

"Absolutely. We'll get you one. God knows you need one. But think of it this way: Annie Jessup *might* have nothing to do with this. Annie might be innocent, or if she was acting for you, might have done so in ignorance. So if you can tell us about her, save us some trouble, it might pay off for you. We might work out a deal with your lawyer." She smiled. "When you get one."

He sat there, his face rigid and red. "I know my rights."

"Right." She told the tape the interview was terminated and shut it off.

Then she stood up and looked down at him. "Wrong choice, *Gil.*"

They walked out.

"Do we have enough to pick her up?" Jury asked, knowing the answer.

"Richard, it's going to be hard enough holding Snow. I've got seventy-two hours, and then I need something real. Like DNA."

"In seventy-two hours you could get blood from a turnip."

"I'm wondering who's the turnip, him or me."

They paced, Jury and Aguilar, walked around the empty room, circled around each other.

She stopped and said, "Are we absolutely certain it isn't Kurt Brunner?"

"Yes. Snow's whole attitude, his failure to

mention Jessup's being in Lamb House, the half-eaten dinner—of course we do. We can certainly question her." Jury paused. "But wait a minute. If police go marching into Lamb House . . ." Jury lifted her mobile from the table, looked at his watch, and dialed Boring's.

He knew it was the young ginger-haired porter who answered because he spoke in a whelping voice. " 'Allo! Borin's!"

"Mr. Plant, please."

There arose a mild commotion at the other end, as if any request for Mr. Plant would find them not knowing how to deal with it.

Finally, Mr. Plant pulled up and answered. He sounded enormously pleased with himself," Jury said. "You're not through yet. You're going back to Lamb House."

"What?"

"Work your way into Mrs. Jessup's good graces; see what you can find out."

"You mean where she stands vis-à-vis her brother? What if she doesn't know anything? What if she had nothing to do with it?"

"That's possible, but I'm betting she did.

He'll get in touch with her. He wants a solicitor, so he'll certainly want a phone."

"She'll know we suspect her of something, won't she?"

"Yes, but it won't really frighten her
because Gilbert Snow will be out of cus-
tody."

Jury watched Lu Aguilar try to assimilate
that bit of information. He told Melrose to
get back to Rye as soon as possible and
flipped the phone shut. "You're going to
have to let him go."

"What?"

Was that everyone's word for him these
days? "We've got to make the Jessup
woman feel safe; we've got to convince her
nothing's happened to her brother. That
we're still plugged in to Kurt Brunner."

"Who is this Plant person? Why are you
letting some friend of yours take charge of
Annie Jessup?"

"Because we can't. That's what I've been
talking about."

She started walking again, her arms
folded across her chest. "I don't like this."

"Neither do I, Lu, but what've we got? If
one of us walks in there, or one of the local
police, she'll know immediately what's

wrong. Look, this will solve your problem of the seventy-two-hour hold, won't it?"

She had to agree to that.

"This friend of mine is the one who discovered Mrs. Jessup was Snow's sister."

"He did?"

Jury nodded. "So he's not some crazy who's running around London thinking he's Sherlock Holmes."

Actually, he was, but Jury saw no reason to share that with DI Aguilar.

# FIFTY-ONE

"I can't imagine," said Melrose, sitting in the Lamb House kitchen, "Kurt Brunner's doing such a thing. I was truly shocked." He was watching Mrs. Jessup slice through a roast lamb, carving it for that evening's dinner. Her face was pink with the effort, an effort more than was called for, surely. It was only a leg of lamb. On the other end of the pastry table, little lemon tarts and custard tarts and airy little cakes rested. There were two large pans in the oven. He found the smell of the mince pies tantalizing. But he wondered what on earth she did with all of this baking, as he himself ate only a mite's portion of it.

"I've never come right out and said, but I never much cared for Mr. Brunner. I always found him a bit of a mystery, and kind of too secretive."

"Really?" Melrose munched on a biscuit that had come, as usual, with his tea. "I found him to be quiet, but never secretive."

She regarded him with a smile that Melrose found unpleasant. Or was this merely his reaction to Jury's insistence that she was part of the plot to murder Billy Maples?

*"Gilbert Snow hasn't the wit to have done this on his own,"* Jury had said.

The cook put down her knife and went to the oven to peek at the little mince pies and slide them out. "I might be prejudiced, but I don't have much liking for the Germans." She set the cookie sheet on the table.

"Yes, you did mention that before." He set down his teacup. "You mean because of the war?"

"I certainly do."

"That's a rather old battle to be fighting, isn't it?" He laughed, quite deliberately, hoping the laugh would set her off.

She took a brief break from the meat

carving. "You think that us that lived it should forget?"

Obviously, Mrs. Jessup hadn't. So he trotted out an old shibboleth to further annoy her. "No. But it's best to let bygones be bygones, wouldn't you say?"

"No, I most certainly would *not.*"

The doorbell rang.

"Who can that be? It's not Wednesday."

Cheerily, Melrose said, "Who indeed? I'll see!" and left the kitchen.


He had come back last night from London and sat for a long time in the study, thinking. Every once in a while he'd pick up the book splayed over the chair arm and read.

It was *The Turn of the Screw.* He was looking to Henry James for inspiration. The housekeeper, Mrs. Grose, was aptly named—a pleasant, ordinary woman, her thinking opaque, without an ounce of imagination, and a poor companion and confidante for the unnamed governess, who had entirely too *much* imagination. Or at least that's how Melrose read it. He could be wrong; those two children, Miles and Flora, perhaps really *were* trying to drive her away.

Melrose walked back and forth, back and forth. *Oh, come on man, give me an idea!* This "little problem" would surely have interested the Master. *Come on, it's right down your street!*

There were no children like these, like Flora and Miles. So why was the reader prepared to believe in them? Because of the ambiguity? Because all of the events that transpired could be accounted for in at least two different ways?

Ha! Melrose tried to imagine Henry James dealing with the dreadful Minnie Babcock, dealing with her in fiction, if not in fact. He couldn't imagine James dealing with any children in fact. In his mind's eye, Melrose watched Henry James exiting the kitchen from which falling crockery, breaking glass, and screams issued.

Melrose rewound the tape in his mind. The glass breaking as if it had been inadvertently swept from the table, glass tumbling, shards of it sent flying. Henry James would have registered every single shard.

*Try to be one of those people on whom nothing is lost!*

Suddenly he had it.

Melrose sat forward so fast he might have been shot in the back.

He walked some more. He just didn't know who the original perpetrator was.

His mind was full of the beastly Minnie Babcock, the effect she'd produced in Mrs. Jessup. Yes, he was pretty sure he had it, or at least the part that sent the cook into a frenzy.

Right then, last night, he had smiled a Peter Quint smile and picked up the phone.

Today, the doorbell rang.

*Who can that be? It's not Wednesday.*

*Who indeed? I'll see!*

Melrose all but ran to the front door.

He opened the door and looked down. "Hello, Malcolm." Farther down. "And Waldo. Do come in."

Malcolm did, but Waldo paused to raise his leg and pee on the step.

Melrose saw this as an auspicious beginning.

He took them into the study. He said, "Malcolm, I'm releasing you from the confines of childhood, from all moral and civic obligations to your fellow man."

Malcolm chewed his gum a little slower, as if the gum itself didn't want to miss any of this intriguing harangue. He swept the unruly hair from his forehead and said, "You ought to be up on a box in Hyde Park, you."

"I know. Anyway. This freedom of movement is limited to *only* the kitchen and the garden, for I imagine you might have some overweening need to rappel. There's quite a good stone wall out there."

Waldo gave out a murmurous growl. They both looked at Melrose with a frown.

Malcolm asked, "So what's all this in aid of?"

"I'll tell you if you agree not to tell anyone else."

"Who'd I tell around here? There's only us."

Waldo walked away and began sniffing the furniture.

"Please remember: this is a very famous house and that makes everything in it valuable."

"Except in the kitchen?"

Melrose was reassured. Malcolm was a quick study.

"Right. Now I leave it to you to decide what is the most annoying behavior in the circumstances."

"Okay, but what's these circumstances?"

"Good question. I want you to rattle the cook, you know, a really good rattle—drive her crazy. No, let me rephrase that: I want you to make her really angry."

Malcolm's forehead pleated into little folds as he smiled slyly. "No problem," he said, pleased. "Why?"

"I want her to incriminate herself."

Malcolm's eyes widened and he blew out his cheeks. He looked as if this might be the opportunity of a lifetime. "I bet that Scotland Yard detective's behind all this."

"You're absolutely right."

"Is this to do with Billy's murder?"

"It most certainly is. If you can wring something out of her—I mean, Miss Jes—Mrs. Jessup, you would be instrumental in solving the case."

Malcolm fairly glowed with righteous purpose. "Prob'ly she won't want Waldo in her kitchen." He gave one of his snorting little laughs.

"Depend upon it. But first—" Melrose reached into the sitting room and plucked a coil of rope from the desk where it had been waiting by the James journal. "There's an excellent old brick wall round back, as you know. Come on."

Melrose returned to the kitchen, where the leg of lamb, looking succulent and pink, rested on the table, nicely sliced. Here would be an unwelcome remark! "You know, Mrs. Jessup, it's not really safe to serve rare lamb. There's some bacteria that might get into it, can't remember the name of it, but it can be fatal."

Oh, *that* was a hit with the blood pressure!

"Begging your pardon, sir, but I've heard that criticism before and I don't much care for it. You think I'm out to poison you, do you?"

He held his hands, palms out, to ward off her words. "Sorry, I wasn't criticizing your cooking, I—"

"Who's that child and what's he doing out there? Look!"

The lamb forgotten now, she was looking out of the window. Melrose came to stand beside her. "Oh, that's just Malcolm. Don't you recognize him? He's a cousin of Billy Maples. His uncle is Roderick. He lives with them. He's to be my dinner guest. But I don't see how he'll make it up the wall, do you? Not with that dog."

Mrs. Jessup stared at Melrose. She was momentarily speechless, hearing that Melrose not only countenanced this affair but that he was largely responsible for it. "Now, sir, you go out there and get that boy out of the garden!"

Ah! A promising sign; she had forgotten her place enough to start ordering Lord Ardry around. "If you insist," said Melrose, sighing.

"It's just priming the pump," he said to Malcolm, as the boy unhitched his end of the rope.

Waldo got free on his own. "You know, I don't think Waldo would even get halfway up, the way you tie that rope."

"It's just for show," Malcolm answered obscurely.

Malcolm and Waldo, both looking surly, followed Melrose into the kitchen.

"Here they are!" said Melrose, as if Mrs. Jessup had only wanted boy and dog in for tea and tarts. He made introductions all around, met by Mrs. Jessup with her hands on her hips, glaring.

"Might I ask what you're doing here, young man?"

Malcolm had immediately sussed out that day's baking and headed for the pastry table. "Come by train," said Malcolm, reaching for a mince pie.

Waldo was sniffing up a storm, not neglecting Mrs. Jessup's ankles.

She gave him quite a nasty kick. "I won't have a dog in my kitchen!"

"Why?" said Malcolm. "He ain't done nuffin'."

Ah! That paean to the excellent British public school!

Melrose watched as Malcolm handily picked up a little cake square waiting to be iced. Malcolm stuck his finger in the bowl and iced it himself.

Bravo! Bravo! Melrose wanted to applaud.

Mrs. Jessup was revving from zero to eighty in fifteen seconds, her face growing mottled as a house in flames.

Malcolm saw this and smiled. Then he looked at the pastry table, stood back, cake in hand, and in a carefully calibrated move led Minnie one better: in a little jump and with his foot striking its edge, upturned the whole table, everything, including the too pink leg of lamb, and sent it clattering to the floor.

It made the most godawful noise!

In the seconds it took her to scream out, "No! *No! Dora! Janie! You old devil!*" she had picked up the knife and would have been on Malcolm in a flash had the table not been between them, and had not both Melrose and Waldo launched themselves at her (Waldo beating out Melrose by a nose).

What struck Melrose as most dramatic in all of this was not the action, but the voice yelling *"Dora! Janie! You old devil!"* For what he heard was another voice, the voice of the governess, yelling *"Peter Quint, you devil!"*

Henry James still lived in the Lamb House kitchen.

The National Trust would make a meal of it, if they were smart.

# FIFTY-TWO

Local police took Annie Jessup to the station where they waited for London to come and collect her, London in this case being Richard Jury and Ron Chilten. A Sussex WPC had accompanied Mrs. Jessup to her home to pick up a few things she would need while she was in London. They didn't know how long that would be. It was all very easy, Mrs. Jessup making no demur, saying nothing.

It was much the same nothing her brother had said that morning in Islington. They appeared to share some belief, almost superstitious, that there was safety in silence.

Sitting now across the table in one of the

rooms of the station in Cinque Port Street, Jury assured her that safety did not lie in silence; indeed silence could sink her.

"Because if you don't help us out here, Annie, you'll be certainly looking at a charge of accessory to murder, even if you didn't pull the trigger." Jury said this while leaning over the table. "We know what happened. Your being silent as the grave is only going to make it harder."

She sat there with her big imitation leather purse pushed like a breastplate against herself, arms folded across it, looking as stern as if she'd just taken on the three of them as staff and was regretting it. She looked at them as if they were raw country people whom she'd have to whip into shape.

Jury leaned back, as incensed by this woman as he had been by Gilbert Snow. They truly seemed to think they were exempt from the ordinary rules of behavior.

"Wiggins." Jury nodded for him to tell it.

"It was that 'doomed voyage.' Remember you were telling me about it and that you had two sisters who drowned. There were instances of bigger children pushing the younger, littler ones away from the lifeboats, pushing them into the sea and even pushing out children who'd already managed to climb in. That's what happened to Janie and Dora, isn't it? They got pushed out of the raft. Horrible, it must've been, completely ruthless. But these were children, after all, and you shouldn't, in the circumstances, have held them to such exacting standards."

Jury could see the steam rising in Annie Jessup. She had to fight with herself to hold her tongue. Wiggins couldn't have taken a better tack than to minimize the children's behavior in this dreadful voyage.

"You'll be accessory to murder, you realize that," said Jury. "Gilbert was the shooter, but you're the one who stashed the gun in Kurt Brunner's desk. Not a smart move, really. For you, it was easy to get into the Sloane Street flat; you'd been there several times before, probably had your own key."

She simply stared at him. He'd never felt in such a witchy presence before. He rose. So did Wiggins. "Sergeant Chilten will take you to London," said Jury.

They left.

———

"They're both going to do themselves in with this not talking," he said to Ron. "Tell your boss she might have more success in getting something out of the woman, given she's a woman, too."

"My boss," said Chilten, "isn't really going to like that reasoning, but I'll tell her."

Jury smiled. "I have to call her anyway. Got your mobile on you?"

"You're worse than a guy who's always filching cigarettes." Ron handed Jury his phone. He said, "Look, I'm not getting all this. Who's the guilty party here?"

Jury was pushing numbers with his thumb. "There's only one person it could've been. *You've got a photo and a negative . . . You can't get them to match up.* Jury had imagined Harry Johnson saying this. He'd been right. The two things that were off by a fraction were two different attempts to evacuate children: the Kindertransport and the ship *City of Benares*. Children from Germany, children from England.

Jury walked away. When she finally came on the phone, he told her what had happened and told her what he wanted her to do.

Without argument or exclamation, she said she'd get right on it and hung up.

Jury handed the phone back to Ron Chilten, who was talking to Sergeant Wiggins.

He folded a stick of gum into his mouth. "You going to take the kid home?" Ron looked over at the two—Melrose and Malcolm—waiting on a bench.

"Which one do you mean?"

Wiggins snorted. "Considering they just took care of half this case for you, you could show more appreciation." Wiggins loving it that Jury was giving someone else a hard time.

"You're right, Wiggins. Let's go."

"Maybe I'm just thick, but who was it?" asked Melrose as they stood beside the car.

Jury was holding Waldo, whose attempt to pee on the leg of the woman police constable was quickly squelched. "Who was what?"

Wiggins had unlocked the car and Jury tossed Waldo in.

"Hey, watchit!" said Malcolm. "Waldo's delicate."

Waldo? Delicate? "It's all that rappelling you make him do."

"You know," said Melrose, climbing in the backseat with Malcolm, "perfectly damned well *who*! The one in the raft, the child who shoved out the others."

Jury, in the passenger seat beside Wiggins, turned to look into the back. "Think about it—"

"No, I don't want to *think* about it, I want you to tell me."

Jury was shaking his head. "No, no. Think about it. There's only one person who fills the bill. Only one." He turned around again, and to Wiggins said, "Don't tell him, Wiggins."

Wiggins hadn't planned on it, since Wiggins was trying to work it out for himself.


It was Malcolm who pointed out the Happy Eater ahead, drowning in its own light. He'd missed the promised dinner at Lamb House, but accepted Melrose's apology as he could understand getting Billy's killer took precedence.

However, he had limits. He had not had

dinner and the Happy Eater was approaching.

Jury told him he was in luck because Sergeant Wiggins was driving and he'd never passed up a Happy Eater in his life.

They parked and piled out of the car and into the cheerful environs of the same Happy Eater Jury and Wiggins had stopped at just a few days ago on their way to Rye.

To Jury it seemed like an eternity.

They sat with coffees and teas before them, Malcolm insisting on coffee.

"God bless Minnie Babcock," said Melrose. "I just don't want to be around when He does. It was the table going over—"

"Who's Minnie Babcock? I'm the one who did that," said Malcolm, handing down a piece of a roll to Waldo underneath the table.

Patiently, Melrose said, "Yes, you did; you also did it better."

"Right," said Malcolm.

"Don't be modest."

Wiggins said, "It made her think of the life

raft her sisters got shoved off by *some-body*." Pointedly, he looked at Jury. Jury did not respond. "I was telling you about that doomed voyage thing, but you were only interested in the Kindertransport and paid no attention."

Lord, how sanctimonious Wiggins could sound! "Again, I feel the reproof, Wiggins."

Wiggins was mining that reply for sarcasm.

"Seriously," Jury added. He meant it.

The same waitress brought them their food: eggs and chips, eggs and sausage and chips, beans on toast, a mountain of toasted tea cakes, and one enormous hamburger. Malcolm was having the hamburger.

Jury said, "I don't think I ever want to see another hamburger."

"Well, when the Happy Eaters close," said Wiggins, "and the Burger Kings take over, you'll be seeing a lot more of them."

Malcolm stared. "What'd'ya mean they're closing?" He put down his hamburger.

Wiggins told him the story of the planned takeover. Malcolm was scandalized. "They can't do that!"

For the remainder of the meal these two

hearts that beat as one paid no attention to their late-night companions.

Roderick Maples was waiting by a window and came immediately when their car pulled up. He seemed genuinely glad to see Malcolm, who had, in all of this, acquired a kind of luster.

However, he would not take all the credit. "Waldo did his part, too! He rushed her! Splaaat!"

Waldo took this as a direction and ran around the pillars and raised his leg to one.

"If I could have a word, Mr. Maples," said Jury.

"Of course."

They went into the living room.

Yes, the Klimt and the Soutine paintings had been kept by friends of his father's. He had remained in touch with the family. The son, who had been Roderick's age then, upon finding out who they really belonged to now, crated them up, and sent them to Sussex.

"And you know how your father came by them?"

Roderick didn't answer this question;

instead he asked, "How do you come to know all of this?"

"Billy knew." Perhaps he shouldn't have said that; there was nothing to be gained except to see Roderick's stricken look.

"I'm sorry, Mr. Maples. We'll be going. Malcolm really helped us."

"I'm glad of that." Roderick stood and shook hands. "We should pay more attention to the boy."

"Yes, you should."

Jury put out his hand to Malcolm. "Thanks, Malcolm. You were brilliant."

Malcolm took Jury's hand. He looked as if he'd just been released from a black hole or a mine shaft into the bright air, despite the darkness of the night.

"Thanks to you, too," he said. He picked Waldo up and went inside.


At the same time, in London, DI Aguilar was knocking on a door. A light went on in the hallway and the door opened.

"Mrs. Ames? Rose Ames? You may remember me . . ."

# FIFTY-THREE

The call came as she was switching off the overhead lights. The fluorescent buzz stopped and they flickered out, sometimes together, sometimes separately. She liked this phenomenon, as if the lighting in the morgue was standing up for itself, somehow showing off its regenerative powers, showing it was not dead yet.

She was always the last to leave; she was the last to wipe down one of the stainless steel tables; she wanted the room left spotlessly clean, feeling it was the least they could do for the dead.

For her, the dead were fully dead only if forgotten. After she had collected coat, purse, scarf, extra shoes, she said good night to the bank of stainless steel enclosures. She always did this, said good night, sometimes reciting a little Dylan Thomas, or a little Shakespeare, only a line or two, sometimes singing a few bars of a song. And always the snatch of words or song had the phrase "good night" in it.

The call came as she went out the door, a little after midnight. She sighed. There was always something, something terrible. It amazed her that anyone lived past ten years old. She fished her mobile out of her purse, walked toward the car, alone in the lot.

"Dr. Nancy," she said, then listened and stopped in her tracks. "Oh my God, no. I'll be there in five minutes." Five minutes didn't allow much time to get from St. James's to Islington.

She ran to her car and peeled out of the area. She went through three red lights, didn't give way to traffic in roundabouts, flew past other cars, leaning on her horn.

When she got to Upper Street, it wasn't hard to find the site of the accident. Ambushed by lights—red, blue, and white— she stopped, left the engine running, nearly fell out of the car, and shoved her way through the layers of the curious, who were ogling the wreck. She joined the paramedics and the ambulance.

"Lateral impact," one of the officers told her. "He's dead." He nodded toward a Hillman. "She isn't. Yet. Over there."

It was, thought Phyllis, a miracle that Lu Aguilar was still breathing, given the massive trauma. Compound fractures in both legs, bits of bone showing through the lacerations. Her chest? A collapsed lung? Other things—hard to say. The paramedics had done everything necessary, everything they could do.

Lu's breathing was ragged but at least she was still doing it.

And she was conscious and disoriented and full of fright. Phyllis could tell from her eyes. Phyllis got down on her knees.

Carefully, she slipped her arm under Lu's neck, bent down, said in a low voice, "It's all right, love. It's going to be all right, you'll be fine. Listen: I'm the best doctor in London."

Amazingly, Lu managed a little smile, one corner of her mouth rising a fraction. And some of the fear seemed to drain away. Phyllis wiped her hand over Lu's forehead, pushing back the hair that wanted to veil her face. Phyllis looked up at the medics and nodded. She held Lu's hand as she was moved to a stretcher.

It had started to rain. She looked around for somebody she knew, saw no one. She pulled out her mobile, hit Richard Jury's number. It rang and rang. Damn him! Couldn't he keep charged? His flat wasn't far from Upper Street. She went to her car, saw someone had switched off the engine for her, shut the door. It would be harder maneuvering the car through all of this clotted traffic, these people. Now the rain was coming down hard.

Phyllis pulled her coat collar closer and simply ran.

Richard Jury had deposited Melrose Plant at Boring's, had a nightcap with him, and then driven to his house. It was after midnight and he'd been home less than fifteen minutes, just missed the heavy rain that was now pummeling his windows as if spoiling for a fight.

He heard a clatter on the stairs. Carole-anne probably, running from the rain. Carole-anne for certain when he heard the knock. She had a hard time passing his door without knocking. He opened the door.

"Phyllis!"

He had never seen anyone so wet, so ragged from rain, so breathless from moving through it.

"There's been an accident," she said. "Lu Aguilar—no, wait, she's not dead, but she's hurt. Tried to call but your mobile was off." She took a deep breath and propped herself up against the door frame.

"I ran all the way."